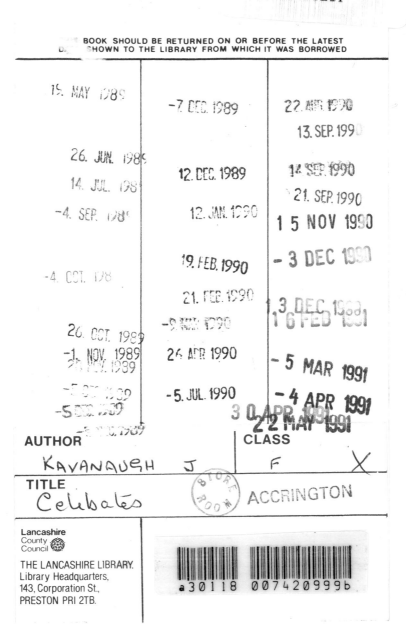

BOOK SHOULD BE RETURNED ON OR BEFORE THE LATEST
DATE SHOWN TO THE LIBRARY FROM WHICH IT WAS BORROWED

THE CELIBATES

THE CELIBATES

James Kavanaugh

Weidenfeld & Nicolson   London

To my brother Bob, who left the priesthood
but lived and died a priest.

To all the former priests and nuns who
lovingly labored among the people and would
labor still if law and history could submit
to reality and love!

To Gene Burke, John David Hamilton and Gerry.

THE CELIBATES

Chapter 1

In the late fall of 1967, the stuffy chapel at Chanute Air Force Base in Illinois was jammed. At the Friday evening Mass, Father Ted Santek surveyed the crowd of eager young cadets and smiled secretly at their naiveté. To them Vietnam was nothing but a distant movie set of mysterious green splendor or a childhood forest where they had played their heroic war games.

He glanced at Tom Shinners, tall, with a dark brush cut and innocent brown eyes that a week ago had flowed with a child's tears in Santek's office.

"They washed me out, Father. No guts. I was the best linebacker on our team at Saint Mel's. They called me the 'clothesline.' Now I'm nothing." The tears came again.

"Who the hell says you're nothing? You're one of the finest young men I know."

"I don't know what to do with all my dreams, Padre. Ever since I was a little kid I wanted to fly. I made Messerschmitts and Mustangs out of balsa wood without plans. I used to lie on my back and watch the planes come out of Midway Airport at night and dream of drifting off into space, discovering some lost planet. It probably sounds nuts, but it's like there's nothing left. My dad was a flier in World War Two and my uncle was killed over Germany. I don't know what to tell my folks. It's like I'm a chickenshit failure."

"Only if you think you are. You'll fly; you just won't get killed in this stupid war." A year ago he would not have admitted his feelings about 'Nam. "If you want to be a pilot, just learn everything you can while you're in service, and when you get out of here, you'll be a pilot and all those dreams will happen, baby."

Shinners's jaw came up, his eyes flashed and the priest knew he would be all right. Now, as Santek looked down at him from the altar, he saw the instinctive trust that a Catholic has in his priest. He glanced around at the wizened jet jockeys, grown cynical and old in their twenties, yet waiting for his words with rare respect. They were a strange breed to him, with a kind of courage that denied fear and bordered almost narcotically on danger.

Charlie Northrup had shared his chopper experiences with him after two terms in Vietnam. Over too many beers he had talked freely about the wife he had lost to a college professor in Syracuse, where she was taking some part-time classes to "keep occupied" while he was gone.

"My kids are calling that son-of-a-bitch 'Daddy.' I'd like to kill the motherfucker, Padre! All the while I'm fighting Charlie in that boiling, stinking, maddening goddamned jungle! Christ, they won't even let us win the damn war! We just fly around putting out fires and risking our ass. I hate the whole goddamned country!"

Santek just listened. Lately the inside talk had been that the United States had already lost the war and that the death toll approached that of Korea.

He looked down at Ed Carruthers, a leg donated to a land mine and his balls blown off. He had no illusions about war. Neither did Nellie Ventano, sitting next to her quadriplegic husband in his wheelchair, faced with three little kids to raise.

"I think I could take it, Father, if his mind weren't crazy. He just sits and stares all the time. It's like we aren't even there. Sometimes I just want to pack up the kids and run away. Then when he talks"— she started to sob—"he says he's going to kill himself. I do everything. I mean, I try to get him excited and play with him and all that. . . ." She blushed fiercely. "I don't know if it's a sin or not, but . . . he asks me all the time."

"Don't worry about sin, Nellie. If he can feel sex, it might save his life. You do whatever the hell you have to do."

She nodded appreciatively. "Does God want me to hang on, Father? It all seems so pointless. Like I'm all alone with the kids."

"I think God will tell you what to do. Just hang in there. I'm here whenever you need me. I'll be over Sunday to take the kids to the rodeo."

He was Christ among his people, suffered with them, especially

2

with young minds torn and tortured by memories they couldn't talk about, even to him. He looked at the array of stoic wives of the pilots, strong women, almost as silent and uncommunicative as their men. Wondering how long they could endure, wondering about divorce, trembling at every phone call that might sentence them to widowhood or life with a battered robot reassembled with baling wire.

As he began to read the day's Gospel, he felt the love of his flock as an almost tangible embrace. Yet he knew that Dave Leary, sitting soberly off to one side, had never forgiven him for refusing him permission to marry a divorced Catholic after all canonical resources were exhausted. Although Ted had seen her only once, he remembered her guileless blue eyes and perfect face and body every time he saw Dave glumly attending Mass out of some ancient loyalty or guilt. The anger and sadness of Dave's silent stare was a kind of physical attack.

In his late thirties and almost tall, the stocky, blond Major Ted Santek would have been handsome save for the too large, twice-broken nose which gave him a rugged, fearless look that matched his words and growing reputation. The gentle blue eyes and sensitive mouth completed the picture of a man strong enough to challenge any enemy and gentle enough to listen to the most homesick, frightened teenager. But it was his obvious passion, his freedom to say whatever came to his mind that endeared him to his people. He had bristled over the race riots in his native Detroit the previous July.

"Forty-three dead blacks and more than five thousand homeless! What the hell for? I grew up with those blacks, played ball with 'em, fought with 'em, lived next door to 'em, was as poor and deprived as they were. But they became my friends, damn good friends. And who was selling them dope and pimping their ladies? And who's beating the shit out of them now? Good Christians, God-fearing people who've been taught to be scared. Christ didn't hedge. 'Whatever you do to the least of my brethren, you do to me.' Christ is black and brown and yellow, and don't you forget it! Otherwise, don't talk about your sweet Christianity."

And they loved his wild and unpredictable sense of humor as well. When Thurgood Marshall had been named the previous week as the first black Supreme Court Justice, Santek had announced from the pulpit, "Now if they'd just put a couple of my Polack boys up there, mixing kielbasa and cabbage rolls with soul food, the garlic alone should teach those other arrogant bastards what life in the streets is like."

3

He finished reading the Gospel with a dramatic flourish, kissed the book according to the rubric, although perfunctorily, as if embarrassed, then turned to face the people again, his simple white chasuble hissing to keep up with his brisk, staccato movements. He repeated the words of Matthew's Gospel: "'You shall love the Lord your God with your whole heart, your whole soul, and with all your mind.' This is the greatest commandment. The second is like to it: 'You shall love your neighbor as yourself.'"

Santek paused to wipe the sweat from his face. The only sound was the baritone echo of his own words. The clear blue Polish eyes grew intense and reflective. He interlocked his fingers in a gesture that seasoned pilots imitated when they quoted his cryptic epigrams of spirituality, so totally unlike the parish priests back home. He had overheard them mimicking him at the ramshackle bar, Lady Jane's in Rantoul, where the older men liked to drink and gulp down greasy tacos. His chaplain's assistant, Mike Fitzgerald, was best at it. He got a Humphrey Bogart look on his face, lowered his voice, and locked his fingers. "If Christ had been a coward, he would have shacked up with Mary Magdalen until Calvary had blown over."

They had all roared for more, and Fitzgerald had continued. "You don't trade your immortal soul for a piece of ass"—a boyish grin—"but if you do, you'd better find me before the gooks find you."

Santek had roared too, then slugged Fitzgerald playfully on the arm and bought the next round of beers. But now, in the pulpit, he was all priest. He paused until the whine of a jet moved off into the distance, and wondered if the young pilot would come back alive. His friend Dave Harmon had crashed yesterday afternoon, and Santek had been up all night consoling Margie and the kids.

Someone in the congregation started to cough but thought better of it. Ted released his fingers gradually and spread his hands shoulder width. A congenial breeze filtered through his thick blond hair and ruffled his wilting white chasuble. He began, as he always did, softly, almost hesitantly, as if he didn't know what to say.

"Christ didn't complicate things. The Pharisees did a damn good job of that. They made religion as complicated as the Pentagon."

A few of the younger men smiled broadly, one laughed out loud, but Santek's expression announced it was not time for amusement, as he began to tell the story of the good Samaritan. "'Who is my neighbor?' the Pharisees asked. Christ never batted an eye. He told a simple story about a traveler who was viciously mugged, and about

4

those who passed him by. Finally a Samaritan came along. Don't miss the irony. To these Jews, the Samaritan was like a black in Detroit or Alabama. He stopped and took care of the man, got him to a hospital, and promised to return later. Christ silenced the critics with a sentence: 'Which man showed himself a neighbor?' In other words, who loved God?"

Santek paused dramatically, then spoke almost in a whisper.

"The service can be a lonely, miserable place, especially if no one gives a damn about anyone else. Does Washington care about you?" He laughed. "They want you to win the war, but do they *care* about you?" He paused to let his words sink in. A couple of generals squirmed and looked down at their hands.

"Christ knows your pain and so do I. Your fear, your loneliness, the terror of crashing and dying, of crawling through a sweating, stinking jungle wondering if the snakes will get you before Charlie does, or if some frightened buddy gone berserk will hear a sound in the brush and blow your head off from behind. Meanwhile, when your life is threatened, when your sanity is up for grabs, when someone is trying to sell you dope to forget it all, fifty thousand Americans descend on the Pentagon and say the whole war is ridiculous. And you try to believe they're wrong so somehow you can keep going.

"You were snatched from your hometowns, from jobs and school, from parents and wives and kids, torn from friends and dreams and tossed in with the kind of person you never knew existed. You've been marched until your feet bled, been insulted until you wanted to kill anyone in sight. But Christ understands. 'If you only love those who love you, what reward have you?' He's with you every moment. And with his help, you can emerge from service as a loving, heads-up man no matter what the odds, or you can become a confused misfit living on dope and self-pity. It all depends on love.

"Some of you think sex is the only sin." They were ready for another one of his classics. "I don't think a weekend of R and R in Bangkok or Saigon will send you to hell with your drawers in your hands. But I'll tell you what will. A life without love! Don't tell Christ you carry the Bible in your pocket, or you behaved in 'Nam because you feared V.D. Tell him you gave a damn about your neighbor who needed a friend! Hell is lined with pious frauds who confused virtue with a lack of opportunity to sin. Don't confess your petty sexual sins to me. Save those to tell your grandkids. I want to hear what Christ wanted to hear, that when someone was hungry or

5

thirsty for human understanding and compassion, you were there to take his place. In the name of the Father and the Son and the Holy Spirit. Amen."

They crossed themselves as he turned to finish the Mass in his whirlwind fashion. Fifteen minutes from sermon to the end. Santek distributed Communion like a man under fire, blessed the troops again, and it was over. He knelt briefly, prayed for an end to the war, for harmony among the blacks, for strength to do his work, prayed especially for God to forgive his carnal weakness. He tossed his vestments to his assistant.

"Will you be around this weekend, Padre?"

"No, Fitz, I've got a seminar in Chicago. I'll be back Monday. Try to get over and see Margie Harmon tonight and take Helen with you."

Then he went into a side office and waited for the wounded to come to Christ. And they came.

A young cadet's girlfriend had married someone else. He was crying. Santek stood up and put his arm around him like a son. "I know how much it hurts, Andy, but it'll pass. It just wasn't meant to be. There's a girl at the parish in Rantoul I want you to meet. She'll call you tomorrow. You've been grieving long enough. It's time to get involved. Besides, she's gorgeous. If I weren't a priest, I'd keep her for myself." He laughed his outrageous laugh and Andy had to smile. Things would be all right. Andy would heal. Santek would see to that.

A captain's wife had cancer. Six months of hell and no hope.

"What can I say, Mel? You've been in my prayers every day."

"I can't believe God could let her suffer like this."

"I know. I don't understand it either." Santek shook his head and embraced his friend, who let the tears come, tears he could show no one else. "I'll be over Monday."

The brigadier general's boy had ODed on heroin. He blamed himself and the service. "I never should have stayed in. Too damn lazy to get out! Grace says if we'd had any kind of normal home life . . ."

"Hey, Jud, it happens to bankers' kids. You did the best you could. Besides, these kids need you. You're one officer that treats them with respect."

Santek would write letters, console the desperate, laugh with the newlyweds, drink beer with the old-timers. The legend had grown until he was ten times larger than life. He had risked his life to give

6

last rites in a chopper crash, made Catholics out of the air force's toughest men.

Jud himself was an example. "I wouldn't be a Catholic if God himself appeared to me in rose bloomers!"

"He doesn't wear bloomers. But he does like Jack Daniel's." Santek had pulled a bottle out of his desk drawer and poured both of them a healthy shot. "No one's asking you to be a Catholic except your wife and kids. Did the pope send you a letter? Have I been knocking on your damn door? Hell, maybe you don't need God. But I'll make you a bet." He poured more bourbon. "You take instructions from me and you'll be a Catholic."

"You haven't got enough money."

"How does a case of Old Bushmill sound?"

"You got yourself a bet."

And Santek also got a case of Bushmill.

He had become a legend, not because he was so unusual but because Catholics asked so little of their priests. Even mediocre and self-centered priests earned their respect, and ill-tempered and neurotic ones somehow received more than tolerance. But a good priest, one who cared, who took the time to understand, would never be forgotten. It didn't matter if he drank or gambled, if he drove a Cadillac or took expensive vacations his flock could not afford. They would defend him to the death.

Santek reached the BOQ, the bachelor officers' quarters, slipped a few clothes and a letter from his friend and classmate in Michigan, Gerry Beauvais, into a leather bag, chatted and smiled on the way in and out, then jumped in his sporty red MG and headed south on Interstate 57 toward Urbana. The cooler fall weather made him homesick for the autumn beauty of Michigan. He remembered the football games at Catholic Central in Detroit, pheasant hunts, the sour smell of burning leaves, and the annual drive north to enjoy the incredible pageantry of color. He didn't like this area of Illinois; it seemed dull and barren. He missed the excitement of the old neighborhood. He had always hoped to live and die in Michigan. Detroit had everything he wanted: the warmth of the Polish community, the drinking buddies, the excitement of a football weekend when sports had been his whole life. It was the drug of the men on the auto assembly line, and when the Tigers or Lions had a good year the whole city seemed to come alive. To an outsider it was a dirty industrial city with massive racial problems and a horrendous crime rate. To Santek it was trees and hidden lakes, down-to-earth people, and a thousand memories.

Memories of bars and games and women. How he had liked the women!

He remembered talking to Father Al during his senior year at Catholic Central.

"I like them all, Father. I want them all. I think of sex all the time. It's like I want to screw almost every woman I see."

Father Al had laughed. "You only get one unless you turn Mormon. Maybe you'll have to be a priest. Or a pimp." They had both laughed heartily.

An hour later he was exploring the moist panties of a sexy young cheerleader on a favorite grassy spot, hidden by elms, at the edge of a tranquil lake. She was as helpless to resist as he was. Both Catholics, they stopped short of intercourse, but not until he had explored her full young breasts, brought her to orgasm with his fingers, and taught her to fondle and suck until he came. Then he held her for a long time until she was calm enough to talk.

"Do you think we committed a mortal sin?"

"Do you feel bad or something?"

"I feel great," she said, and began touching him again.

"Then don't worry about it. No one's perfect." He returned her caresses.

She was not a stray experience, an insignificant seduction. He liked her, cared about her, worried about her conscience and his own, and talked about his experience with no one—except the priest in confession, where he promised to reform but never really could. It wasn't only because of his sexual hunger, but because the neighborhood girls, raised in poverty and abrasive families, longed for his tenderness and soothing words of caress. He was an eloquent lover and a caring young man, but try as he might, he could not keep the sexual rules of the Church. The harder he tried, the more sex was on his mind.

He turned off the highway and raced toward a small apartment complex of perhaps twenty units. It was well hidden from the access road and the surrounding buildings. Santek parked his car in the visitors' section around the corner and slipped the chaplain's insignia from his uniform into a side pocket. He pulled his brown leather bag across the seat and looked cautiously around.

A middle-aged couple were on their way out for a gala Friday evening. They laughed loudly, then embraced while he stayed glued against the side of the car in the shadows. When they pulled away, he walked stealthily around the rear of the building and unlocked

8

the door. Briskly he strode up the back steps to the second floor and cautiously opened the door to the main corridor. He waited for three or four noisy people to board an elevator, then moved quickly to apartment 206 and knocked quietly. He heard the chain lock release and then the bolt. The door opened slowly and two eyes peered out. Instantly the door swung open and he entered the room swiftly, as a female figure stood aside in the semidarkness.

She moved back toward the door, closed it quietly, bolted it, and slipped the chain lock in place.

Chapter 2

In the summer of 1967, when Pope Paul VI published an encyclical firmly reinforcing the Church's traditional view of priestly celibacy, Ted Santek had gotten devoutly drunk. But the encyclical was only a faint foreshadowing of what was to come.

Word had already leaked out in the spring of 1968 that the pope was ignoring the strong dissenting opinion of the commission he had appointed to review the matter of birth control. He had decided to issue the fateful *Humanae Vitae* that again condemned contraception in clear, unmistakable terms and would lead to a massive exodus of both lay and religious members of the Church. Late in May of that year, Gerald Beauvais celebrated his mother's funeral Mass and was equally distressed by the misguided leadership of the vacillating pope. His mother's death seemed the end of an era, and Paul VI's fearful leadership felt like the termination of Catholicism's entrance into the modern world. Gerry's own emotions were at the breaking point.

Genny Beauvais, mother of twelve and grandmother of fifty-one—apparently no one had kept track of the great-grandchildren—was never really troubled by the problems of her Church. Although widowed for twenty-seven years, she had remained totally loyal and provided her children with all they needed to succeed. Everyone in the town had had some business dealings with a Beauvais, and all the children—save an errant son, Louis, who had moved to California—remained, at least externally, loyal to their faith.

The youngest son, Gerald, had become her priest, and he sang his mother's *requiem* in the traditional Latin she had requested.

Ironically, the soon to be published *Humanae Vitae* would have pleased her as much as it was to disappoint him. Her only embarrassment would have been the presence of Louis, who had divorced his wife, left his children, and escaped the judgment of Kentfield to become a character actor in Hollywood. He was occasionally seen in coffee commercials, and Genny and the whole Beauvais clan refused to purchase anything he advertised, even avoiding Nate's Café, which served one of his products. Yet, despite the presence of Louis, it was not a sad funeral, and any slight disgrace was more than compensated for by the priest son, who chanted the Latin Mass in a brilliant baritone.

Although shorter than his brothers and lacking the round face and bushy hair that characterized the family, he had the same thick build, dark brown eyes, and broad smile. He had lost weight in recent years and his hair was thinning, but unlike the other Beauvaises, who had surrendered to the novelty of TV, and read nothing, he had a brilliant mind and a great genius for music.

"No one else in the family can carry a tune," Genny had said. "I think God always had special plans for Father Gerry."

No one would have doubted her words as his voice filled every crevice of the ancient pseudo-gothic structure. As a teenager, Gerry had dreamed of becoming a famous opera star, encouraged by one of the nuns at St. Michael's High School. But his father, a stern hardworking plumber with thick hands and unsmiling dark eyes, had abruptly put an end to that notion. And Genny, forever praying for her husband's conversion, had feared to cross him, especially when he had been drinking—which was most of the time.

"Singing is for church and women. You can't make a living at it. It's bad enough that you're the first Beauvais who never made the football team. You're built like a truck driver and you waste your time singing like some damned queer."

Gerry had not known what he meant till he joined the navy near the end of World War II, a few years after his father's premature death in a local tavern and whorehouse. It was about seven thirty on a gray Sunday evening in September when he and his brother Dennis had gone to identify the body. Gerry was not prepared for the sight.

His father was sprawled naked across a cot in a storage room filled with beer cases, stacks of toilet paper, janitorial supplies, and an old urinal that was cracked and rusted. He had always imagined his father as a powerfully muscled man, but now his huge potbelly

11

was hanging over the edge of the dirty cot with only a motheaten army blanket as a bed covering. A young black woman in a tight silver-beaded dress that barely covered her thighs was still screaming nearby. Dennis and Gerry were paralyzed with fear as she told her story.

"I didn't do a damn thing. Nothing! He just took off his clothes and got down on me like he always done. Then he grunted and just laid there. Oh, my God, he didn't move. It took Barney and Al just to roll him offa me!"

The boys struggled to put clothes back on the stiffening, lifeless body and to drag him from the shameful room. Dennis managed to close his eyes, but they couldn't force his mouth shut. Finally they got him dressed and deposited him in an empty corridor just outside the bar to await the coroner. Gerry dreamed about the grotesque scene for months. Genny was told only that he had had a heart attack on the way to the toilet, and out of respect for the Beauvais family, word never really got around. Maurice Beauvais was honored at a High Mass with the bishop in attendance—and a weeping young black woman. Gerry had not been able to shed a tear.

Shortly after his father's death and an aimless year in junior college, he felt a strong urge to leave Kentfield and joined the navy. His interest in the priesthood had been almost an accident. While he was recovering from a foot infection in the infirmary at Great Lakes, time had dragged until he met the benign, saintly Father George Misch, a giant of a man with a booming laugh, curly gray hair, bouncing jowls, and a great love of life. He took to Gerry immediately and after they shared their enthusiasm for *The Glass Menagerie*, Bach, and the work of young Jackson Pollock, Misch invited him to listen to his classical records. Gerry had never talked so personally to anyone in his life. Since he had been an altar boy all through school, he was a natural candidate to serve as chaplain's assistant when the job opened up.

Chaplain's assistant was not Gerry's vision of the navy, but the charm of the priest overwhelmed him and somehow the work reminded him of a happy boyhood around the nuns and priests at home. He was especially impressed with the great love that the men had for their jovial chaplain.

"I don't really drink with them, but I'm here when they need me. I think they lose respect if they see me like any officer."

Gradually they spent more of their free time together. Gerry had never met a man with such broad interests and deep personal spir-

12

ituality, a man whose whole reason to exist was to serve his men and to enjoy life to the full.

"I think the greatest sin is to waste time," said Misch. "Or to ignore beauty. It's everywhere!"

And they found it—in Chicago and New York, in Bangkok and Manila—and gradually Gerry also found the paternal approval he needed. They were in Manila, exploring St. Augustine Church in the Intramuros, the walled city, which by some miracle had withstood destruction by the Japanese, when Gerry felt a strong yearning to be a priest. They had examined ancient missals, had sung like college boys from five-hundred-year-old psalters, and had marveled at the faith that had built the massive structure.

At dinner, Gerry was unusually reflective over a welcome steak.

"I guess I never realized what 'Catholic' meant. The Church has been around for a long time. The same music, the same beauty, the same effort to make people's lives mean something."

"People didn't have as many distractions when that old church was built. They weren't as apt to be confused by life. That's why I like my vocation. It keeps life simple and I don't wonder who I am."

Later that evening Gerry walked for several hours through the walled city, staring at the church as it stood like an unassailable giant amid the rubble of war, not unlike Father Misch. The priesthood, he felt, offered a total life of service and exploration and gave him a direction he had long been without. There would be time for music, to travel, but most of all to do something worthwhile with his life. And, perhaps, to be more than the son of Maurice Beauvais—another toothy, smiling Beauvais from Kentfield.

In the early years of his priesthood, his dreams had been realized, until he received a lonely appointment to a rural parish and the unfortunate papacy of Paul VI seemed to undermine Pope John XXIII's work and divide the Church. He began to experience a strange depression that prayer and hard work could not dissipate. A light had gone from his life.

Now, as he stood above his mother's last resting place, he had to resist a strange impulse to hurl himself on her grave. In his early forties, he felt as though life had passed him by, and the death of Genny, who had loved him beyond all measure, was a final blow. Stoically he concluded the service, the words emerging haltingly.

"May the angels lead you into paradise . . . may her soul and the souls of all the faithful departed, through the mercy of God, rest in peace."

A chorus of Beauvaises and their neighbors responded "Amen" and moved back from the grave to the parade of cars. Gerry, still fighting tears, stood motionless over the grave as Genny was lowered into the plot next to her late husband. Only the family outcast, Louis, approached him and, unlike a Beauvais, put his arms around him gently. In the distance, an attractive dark-haired woman, of Italian heritage, dressed in black, stared lovingly and painfully at Gerry. He did not notice her as he slowly walked with Louis to the waiting cortège.

The same woman watched from a safe distance as he entered the parish hall, then drifted back to her car and drove away. Inside the hall, Father Gerry took his place at the center of the head table while Louis sat in the rear, where he would not embarrass anyone. Life went on and Genevieve's journey to paradise was celebrated with ham and green beans, scalloped potatoes, and an assortment of homemade pies. And a hundred toothy Beauvaises laughed with sparkling brown eyes at all the jokes they had laughed at before.

"Hey, Gerry, when they gonna make you a bishop?" The voice was shrill.

"Wait till his hair grows back. They don't want bald bishops."

Everyone laughed too loud. Maurice would have been right at home.

"They're just waiting till his collections go up. Rome doesn't go for homemade jam and cow manure."

"Hell, those farmers got money! You just gotta find the right mattress."

"You should know, Dennis. The night your shed caught fire, the kids got out after the mattresses."

Everyone roared. It was another typical Beauvais party.

"Why would Gerry want to be a bishop? All that time for golf and the great food. 'For your penance, two pies and three sirloins.'"

"Hell, those farmers don't have nothing to confess!"

"Don't forget the sheep, Mike. Don't knock it if you ain't tried it."

The room again rocked with laughter. Then the old gray-haired pastor stood up, assured them that Genny was safely in heaven, no one doubted that, and joined in bliss with her hard-working husband of so many years. Gerry reflected briefly on the mercy of time, which had lifted Maurice from a whore's cot into the heavenly vision. And who the hell knew? Then the depression descended on him again as he remembered his efforts to pull his father's pants on

14

over stiff, swollen, scarred legs. There were scars and bruises all over his body from crawling under houses and into sewers. Gerry had only known his mother's sacrifices, for Maurice had never complained.

When the crowd was fed, the friends and neighbors extended thanks and condolences and slowly went back to work. The dark-haired woman watched from outside the hall as the immediate family got into their cars and made their way to the tree-lined street and the old Victorian house in which Genny had lived for sixty years.

A bar was set up, and the Beauvaises got down to some serious drinking and reminiscing in the French-Catholic tradition. Their voices were high-pitched and even more discordant when they drank.

"I remember the one Ma liked about the country kid who came home from the service—I think it was in Gerry's parish."

They all laughed too hard.

"Anyway, he was demonstrating a hand grenade to his dad and blew up the outhouse. Well, the shit flew and the father turned white. 'You hadn't oughta done that, son. Grandpa was in there!' Well, pretty soon a hat appeared and Grandpa crawled out of the hole. He shook himself as clean as he could, adjusted his hat, and said quietly, 'Sure glad I didn't let that one go in the house!'"

An older sister spat out her drink and two others had coughing spells. It didn't matter that they had heard the joke before. They had come to laugh and drink away death—their mother's and their own—until they were exhausted. Gerry sat off to the side, talking quietly with Louis, who was trying to convince him to come to Hollywood and record. Louis finally got up to leave, after having been ignored by everyone except Gerry from the time of his arrival.

"Why don't you spend some time in California? You seem depressed as hell. What the devil happened to you? You started out like a house afire. Now you're wasting away in the sticks."

"They're good people, Lou. . . ."

"I know, but any dolt could meet their needs. Why don't you sound off?"

"I'm in no position to sound off."

"For God's sake, why not?"

Gerry paused and looked directly into his brother's eyes. They were the same shade as Maurice's, small and dark, without the apparent anger but outlined in fear. He almost saw in them a gentle understanding beyond the stylish long hair, the tailored Hollywood

15

clothes, and the West Coast veneer, an understanding created by pain and rejection and a new life away from Kentfield.

"I wish I could tell you the whole story. It really . . . well, hurts."

Louis was suddenly frightened by his brother's admission. Gerry had always been the priest, strong, sure of himself, the only one who had kept in touch through the years. Louis slowly backed away.

"Well, anyhow, California's waiting. I'll get you a recording contract. That young Singing Nun did all right." He grinned. "I've got some connections." He laughed sardonically. "Everyone's leaving the Church anyway. No sense you being the last." It was his only hint of strength.

Then he was off, still Beauvais enough to joke his way around his brother's need. Gerry picked up his breviary from the coffee table as a sudden wave of depression engulfed him. The stories had begun to subside and the gloom of too much alcohol had settled over the once-jubilant mourners. Two brothers were quarreling loudly about a business deal. They were at the point of blows when their wives led them to their cars, knowing the family would fall apart without Genny, but not regretting an end to the ritual of Sunday Mass and breakfast at the old homestead, not to mention the endless arguments and too much booze. Two or three of the Beauvais sisters had fallen asleep with guttural snores. The wake was complete. Gerry drifted out into the backyard, still unable to shake his massive depression. It was beyond words, a kind of darkness that seemed unremitting and overwhelming. He had known it before, but never like this. Pope John XXIII was really dead and so was his mother. No one could help. He was all alone, without a family or a compassionate Church.

He saw the cherry tree in the moonlight and remembered Genny's admonition.

"Don't forget to cover it with old sheets. The robins and sparrows won't leave anything but pits."

His father had seen him enshrouding the cherry tree and heard him singing an aria from Puccini.

"Let the birds have the damn cherries. You'd be better off learning to hit a baseball like your brothers. I didn't work all these years to raise sissies. If you've got so damn much time to sing and do nothing, you might as well help me put in some sewers. You'll learn what work is." He laughed. "Then we'll see how much singing you do, Mrs. Chickadee!"

So, barely fifteen, when two of his older brothers had gone into the marines, he began helping his father and brother Dennis with the family plumbing business, hating every minute of it. He was not good with tools and the huge chain wrench consistently confused him.

"Not that way, stupid, bring the chain around like this and snap it here! My God, you're a nervous one. I think this boy is getting old enough for a little pussy, Denny. Maybe we oughta have old Mabel take him in hand."

Dennis laughed appropriately. He was a different person when he was with his father, loud and coarse and obscene, and their conversations from job to job, crowded together in the truck with Gerry between them, were consistently of sex. They drove through "nigger town" to survey "some black ass."

"Those bitches will fuck you till you can't stand up. I remember one night Barney and I got drunk in the Moon Bar and got us a couple of those black cunts to blow us under the table till we couldn't piss for a week."

They took Gerry down a dirty alley on a sweating summer afternoon, after installing a couple of toilets and sharing a six-pack. They stopped in front of a tarpaper shack with a sloping roof, three wrecked cars, and an array of garbage in the side yard. Two mangy dogs howled their stubborn protest, then went yipping off when Maurice threw a handful of bolts at them. Mabel, a stocky, smiling black woman of about forty, was sitting on the dilapidated front porch, fanning herself with a newspaper. Her faded cotton shift was open in front, revealing large, pendulous breasts; her legs were spread apart to display thick black thighs.

"We brought you a customer, Mabel." Maurice was flushed with beer and the excitement of a new adventure. Gerry blushed fiercely and hung his head. One of the dogs approached and licked his hand. Gerry petted him nervously.

"He looks a little young to me, honey," she drawled without moving. "I doubt he knows where to put it."

Dennis and his father laughed loudly, and Gerry continued to blush with fury and embarrassment. Maurice handed her five bucks.

"Why don't you show him? I don't want a goddamned sissy on my hands who can't make the football team and spends his time singing queer songs in the basement. I think he needs a little different music."

Mabel looked up lazily. "Can't show him much for five bucks."

17

Maurice tossed her another five and bounced back into the truck with Dennis. "We'll be back in half an hour to pick up a man."

Mabel led Gerry by the hand toward the door. The dogs began to whine as the truck sped away. She opened the door and took him inside. He was terrified and even now could not forget the smell of grease and sweat and stale perfume. Or his father's laugh.

It all seemed such a short time ago. Where had the years gone? What had they meant? All the dreams had disappeared. Life had been on him before he knew it. Now there was only darkness. He glanced around the yard in the dim light. The peach tree looked as old as his mother. Every tree and flower held a memory, the cistern and garbage cans, the basket on the garage he never mastered, the clothesline Genny used even in winter because "things smell better!" The blackness that had eroded his spirit would not lift. His family seemed like strangers. Even Genny's life seemed to mean nothing and Maurice would enter heaven on the time-payment plan. Gerry had finally begun to understand his father's pain. What would he himself have done with a dozen kids and a devoutly Catholic wife? And Genny was as much a victim. There were no judgments to make. Perhaps Louis did better than any of them.

He gazed at the sky which had been his ocean. The stars had lost their luster, maple trees that made him feel alive and poetic were empty shadows, the sky held no more mystery, and even the sounds of night which had thrilled him now seemed the monotones of some other life. The skinny moon was an intruder, the hoot of an owl in the elm an alien. Life had begun to leave him years ago, and he had barely hung on. Now he could no longer force smiles, bless marriages, bury gnarled old farmers or teenagers killed in the usual small-town crashes with the sympathy he wanted to give. He was wooden, a man with no reason to go on, no hope, no joy. Even his colloquy with God had grown repetitious. He felt separated and alone, as if he had never learned to love. Watching his family cling to their empty lives, he found no meaning in his own. His effort to become someone other than a Beauvais had failed. The youngest, who should have learned from the rest, had learned nothing, and the floundering Church had finally stripped him of all that was human and dear. Or he had stripped himself. He could not even judge the mottled Church.

Once he could spend whole nights before the tabernacle, finding solace for pain and isolation, pleading with God to make known his will. Finally, it had become impossible; even *La Traviata* and

18

Rigoletto could not release him from himself. He was finally all alone without escape. He continued to stare at the stars, remembering a teenager who had sung his lungs out in the same backyard, dreaming of Europe and the stage, when music gave him so much joy there was no vessel to contain it. It all seemed like a tragic opera he had seen in some distant past, not a part of his life. He tried to sing, but his whole body felt tired, his spirit dead.

He made his way to the garage. Inside were battered sleds, once-proud Flexible Flyers, a pair of skis, a stick of elm he had used for imaginary conducting. Along the side were a few old concrete weights he had used to prove to his father and brothers he was a man. A heavy wave of sadness engulfed him as he closed the door behind him.

Chapter 3

"You're not eating much."

Angela Fortier sat looking at Father Ted Santek, now in his T-shirt and green plaid bermuda shorts. He sipped his favorite Chateauneuf du Pape and toyed with the remains of a T-bone steak, a baked potato with all the extras, including sour cream he didn't need, a giant salad with Roquefort dressing with the whole chunks of cheese he liked.

"Christ, Angie, that steak must weigh three pounds. You'll leave me for some trim young executive when I'm old and fat." It was a persistent fear he only joked about, but he knew the long absences were hard on her.

"I'll be old and fat with you." Her laugh was a low, almost guttural chuckle. Despite her madonna face, she was plain-looking until she smiled, then was suddenly radiant. The tired, resigned look disappeared. She had the kind of inner beauty talked about frequently but rarely seen. Now Angie brushed her fine hair back from her right eye, a frequent gesture when she was nervous. Her voice and ripe, voluptuous body gave her a powerful sexuality that was not apparent on her face. Her voice, deep and resonant and a trifle off key with its Canadian accent, was a surprise in contrast to the subdued features. Her blue eyes were almost dull until they flashed with anger or joy, and then they lost their distant, dreamy look and gave immense character to her face. On closer scrutiny, her face revealed the secret pain and peasant wit that saved her from looking like a child. Yet, it was still hard to imagine that she was thirty-three. The sophisticated, almost haughty air she assumed around strangers seemed misplaced. It was a subtle betrayal of personal anxiety. She knew that Santek wanted a cultured woman, and she did her best to conform. She would have been far happier without shoes or makeup, raising five children in a small village in her native Canada.

Dressed in a beige silk blouse and tailored brown skirt, she assumed a self-conscious kind of elegance even at home, an elegance that was reinforced by her long aristocratic neck and proud upturned chin. Rarely did Santek see her in casual clothes even after they made afternoon love on the floor. She showered and dressed, too uncomfortable with her new status as a major's lady on display to lounge about in jeans. She seemed difficult to approach until she laughed, but despite the roles she assumed to hide her humble background, Angela Fortier was a woman of character and quality, and a deep inner grace. Most of all she lived to please Father Ted Santek. She was a contrast to Santek, who could be the Polish kid from Hamtramck, Michigan, the minute he walked in the door and a smooth car salesman the minute he reentered the world. Angie never questioned his behavior, what he wore, or how he felt about anything. He was still priest, father, usually gentle master.

"Do you want some Black Forest cake? It's just the way you like it."

"Maybe later," he mumbled. "My God, you went all out."

"It's our anniversary!"

He laughed as he always did when she grew sentimental.

She smiled softly, then grew serious and looked hurt.

"What's wrong?"

"You don't want to hear about it."

"I'd rather hear about it than see that look on your face. Are you still worried about a marriage ceremony?"

"I've got all the records."

"Damn it, Angie, we're married before God! What else matters?"

She looked like a frightened little girl. "I want to feel married."

He bristled. "I've told you a hundred times, we'll get married when I retire from the service. We'll get a nice private place on some little lake in Michigan without neighbors. By that time Pope Paul and his celibacy will be long dead and we'll have someone in charge who won't let the Church go down the tubes. Or else I won't give a damn. There'll be nothing left." He looked concerned. "I

heard from Beauvais. Helms and Fitz left the priesthood last month,
Zuidema and Grady the month before. The best guys! And Gerry
sounds depressed as hell." He studied her quizzically.

"What's really bothering you?"

She paused, brushed back her hair, and fought back tears. "My
dad called again. I just can't keep on lying. He said it's time for a
woman my age to have a child." Her eyes grew moist. "He said, 'A
beautiful woman like you.'"

"We'll have a child," he said softly. "I told you that. Three of
them if you want. Right now I'm worried about Margie Harmon and
three kids without a dad. There's nothing left of him to bury!"

Usually his priestly concerns would have distracted her, but now
she turned away angrily. "We've had this discussion a dozen times.
It's always someone else's kids. I want to worry about our own kids,
damn it!"

She rose and began clearing away the dishes. Santek could think
of nothing to say. He took his brandy and sprawled on the living
room couch. The suedes and gentle earth tones of the room reflected the tastes Angie had acquired in years of travel. Tasteful oils,
quaint curios, pottery and macramé, expensive cut glass. Nothing
was pretentious or out of place. Santek demanded it. He would
never be a poor, dumb Polack again. But her outburst had frightened him. He had never seen her really angry before and he interrupted her as she continued to clear the table. It was unusual,
because he could not tolerate any kind of mess, in the kitchen or
anywhere else.

"Come over here," he said gently, as if to a little girl.

She hesitated, then reluctantly obeyed, still flushed with anger.

He pulled her next to him on the couch and began stroking her
soft hair and sad face. She began to cry softly, even though she knew
he hated her tears. He kissed her gently, then gradually more passionately. She became helplessly excited as she always did. She
could not resist him even when she wanted to. She never tired of
him, longed for his body when he was gone, ached for his touch. He
continued stroking her as he gently undressed her. When his hands
slipped under her skirt she trembled, then shook almost violently
when he slipped off the brown silk panties and matching bra he had
bought for her birthday.

He entered her body only when she pleaded with him, when she
could no longer stand his exploring hands. He entered slowly,

22

gently, as she wriggled and tugged impatiently as she always did and came immediately, twisting and tearing in massive orgasm. He continued kneading her breasts, kissing her face all over, then thrust more vigorously, knowing infallibly everything she wanted. She screamed out her pleasure, her whole body shook with successive spasms, and she flowed in warm, passionate spurts again and again. He had never known a woman like her: in the beginning, stiff and almost frigid until she had crossed some cultural or religious barrier, then, almost overnight, carried away like no one in his experience. At first he had thought she was a kind of nympho, then realized that her late introduction to sex and the total abandonment of her native inhibitions made the experience almost hysterically exciting. Her wild response always carried him away, and now he was lost in her. His own breathing was as gasping and unbridled as hers. Her eyes rolled back in her head, she began to utter loud guttural cries and then low, animal screams. Finally he came in thrusts and groans that set her screaming again. Then they lay in each other's arms, silent and exhausted.

When they had first met in Florida, she was totally inhibited, terrified of sin and pregnancy, guarding her body like an Italian virgin. She had never known another man, while he had known dozens of women. Even after they began living together, he had been disappointed, but perhaps when she feared to lose him or had settled some Catholic account with her French God, she began to open up, and her sexual reservoir was as deep and mysterious as his own. No one woman had ever held him sexually before Angela Fortier. It was as if sex with her was forever totally new. Everything about her excited him: the soft texture of her skin, the shape of her almond breasts too large for her build, the long, ultrasensitive nipples that swelled like sea creatures to his kiss or touch, the very curve of her thighs and tilt of her butt, but most of all the total and almost naive commitment she made without calculation or restraint.

She lay motionless, still strangely troubled, and spoke in a whisper.

"It's more than my father," she said. "I need children; you do. We were meant to have them. I want more than vacations and waiting for you until you can sneak away from the base. I want my life— our lives—to mean more."

She had never been so assertive. He could always make her laugh and distract her with their outrageous sex, then take her on

23

another trip to Bermuda or Hawaii. In reality, he was as tired of the trips as she was. He tried to think of something funny to say, but nothing came out.

"Christ, Angie, you knew what you were getting in for. It's hard enough hiding like we do. With kids, I wouldn't know what the hell to do."

"We can move farther out and live more simply. We throw our money away trying to have fun. I'm tired of fun. I love you, I want your babies. The Church will change and have married priests, and when it does we'll be too old."

He could think of nothing to say. Suddenly there was a loud knock on the door. They both froze. Again, a loud knock. Then a concerned voice.

"Security. Are you all right, Miss Fortier?"

"Yes," she said softly, "I'm fine."

"I'd like to check. Some of the neighbors heard screams."

She ran to get her bathrobe and opened the chain. Ted fled into the bedroom and pulled up the covers like a scared child. She looked through the small opening in the door.

"I'm just fine . . . my boyfriend and I were laughing and teasing. . . ." She blushed totally.

The security guard grinned knowingly. "Sorry to trouble you. There's been a lot of craziness in the neighborhood with all these damn foreigners. Have a good evening."

He grinned his embarrassment and was gone. Ted moved in from the bedroom. "Let's get out of here. I feel like a damn teenager."

Angie beamed. "*A Man for All Seasons* is on at the Palace. Everyone at work says Paul Scofield is great. Let's go see it, then have pasta at Aldo's, then we can talk. I want to talk some more. I need to." She knew she could convince him to have a child and wanted to tell him she was off the pill.

"My God, Angie, I'd be spotted in a minute. The guys from the base are all over town this weekend. Let's get out of town." He laughed. "I've covered myself till Monday. There's a private place I heard of outside of Peoria, along the lake. It's a plush resort called Oak Grove. We can swim and dance and eat ourselves silly. I'll even take you shopping." He smiled. "I want you to wear something sexy while we're dancing."

Oak Grove was the perfect spot. They spent Saturday morning at

24

one of the pools, drinking margaritas, then made love outside in a secluded spot along one of the fairways.

"I love to make love outside," she said jubilantly. "It seems so sinful!"

"Where the hell don't you like making love?" He laughed. "We'll try it in the Jacuzzi tonight. I'll teach you a new trick."

She giggled, then shuddered, thinking about it. She forgot about having children, as she always did when they were happy together.

Later they drove to Peoria to shop. She modeled several dresses until he was satisfied with a low-cut peach-colored mini-sundress that exposed the top of her breasts and exaggerated the long legs that had always excited him.

"Not many husbands pay this much attention," said the thin, six-tyish saleslady. "You're lucky. My husband wouldn't notice me if I wore a bikini out to dinner."

"I'd notice you," Ted said. The woman beamed her appreciation.

"You're a wonderful couple. What sort of work do you do?"

"I have my own business in Detroit. Investments. We're just mixing business with pleasure."

Angie had grown to love their rare moments of sociability with strangers. It was exciting to talk to anyone, so much of their life was lived alone and in hiding. Yet today she was impatient to get away from the pointless conversation. Finally he stopped chatting with the clerk, and they made their way back to the isolation and serenity of the expensive honeymoon suite Ted had engaged for the weekend. It was complete with mirrors and canopy, a private patio and secluded view, and TV even in the exotic master bath with its free-form Jacuzzi tub for two. He sent down for margaritas while she changed into her new outfit. Watching her undress excited him again. His sexual appetite seemed insatiable, and she was as ready as he was. He massaged her gently for a long time, stroking and teasing her, apologizing playfully for exciting her.

"I can't stand it," she said. "I want you! Do something! Please!"

"What did you have in mind?" he asked playfully, stroking her butt and lower back with oil, then "accidentally" touching her breast or upper thigh.

"Ted, please, please!"

Abruptly, almost fiercely, he turned her over and began sucking her hungrily. She gasped and groaned with delight, then made the

25

jungle sounds that excited him. Again they made love until they were exhausted. But then Angie's mind returned to children.

"Lately I dream of children. We would be the best parents in the world."

"How do I explain to Teddy that his dad's a priest?"

"You won't have to until he's old enough to understand. By that time the Church will wake up. Hundreds of priests and nuns are leaving now. The Church will have to face facts, or there won't be enough priests left."

"Maybe if Pope John were alive. Hell, the Church won't give on anything except trivial liturgical changes. Pope Paul is as archaic as long underwear. He just wrote a whole encyclical on the 'great gift' of celibacy."

"He'll have to change. Otherwise there won't be a Church. You were never meant to be a celibate."

"Maybe I was never meant to be a priest."

"You know better than that. You're as good a priest as I've ever known."

He thought about the young widow whose husband had crashed two miles from home. He'd have to go over there again Sunday night. He always wondered what to say. What the hell could he say? Three little kids under ten, and her life was over. He never knew what to say. Nor did he understand God's ways.

Angie saw him grow reflective, almost sad. "Let's go downstairs and dance," she said.

They made their way to the darkened Madrone Room, where there was a little combo. They sat in a far corner where they could watch everyone coming and going and ordered more margaritas. The room had the kind of quiet elegance he liked, plush booths of maroon leather, a long bar of natural oak, and dim light even in the late afternoon. Two or three couples were dancing to the slow rhythm of music from the fifties. They got up to dance after he had surveyed the room, and Angie glowed like a new bride. Ted Santek could dance with the best, and several older couples turned to enjoy the attractive pair, obviously deeply in love, who moved like magic. Angie was beside herself with joy at such moments. All the hiding was worth it when she floated in the arms of the man she loved. The loneliness didn't matter, the lies to associates at work, the search for just the right secluded apartment, the guarding of all she said or did, the move and hunt for another job just as she had begun to enjoy the old one, the pain caused her father, the barren nights without Ted, the lack of friends she craved, and most of all the empty womb.

At this moment, everything made sense, when she was lost in the music and the arms of her man. She loved his body, his wit, the rugged face, and most of all his unswerving devotion to his priesthood. She knew that she was the special woman of a very special man, and she reveled in this rare freedom when there was no need to wonder if they were being watched. Children would make it all perfect. She was sure she could finally convince him. Each conversation about it seemed less threatening, and he seemed slightly more amenable.

Suddenly, in the midst of "Misty," she felt him stiffen and begin to sweat and she emerged from her reverie.

"I know that guy that just came in," he whispered anxiously. "He attended one of my retreats at Chanute."

He turned his back to the intruder and kept dancing. His face was pale and his hands trembled.

"Maybe he won't recognize you." She was pleading and felt the pain in her stomach.

"No chance, he followed me around like a puppy. He's one of those super Catholics who could ruin me." He paused to think and shuffled aimlessly to the music, stepping on her foot. "As soon as the music stops, you go out the side door and head for the car. I'll pack and check us out."

"Honey, there are three dining rooms in this place, or we can eat in our room and talk. I'll go up to the room. You buy him a drink and find out if he's here for the weekend."

"Nobody just pops in here. It's too out of the way." His voice was gruff and frightened, almost panicky. "Just do what I said!"

She resisted. She had too much to say this weekend and was tired of running. "Darling, it's almost dark. We can just walk around the grounds, find out where he is, and go somewhere else. It'll be kind of fun. If he sees us together, I'll pretend I'm here with my husband. We need the time." She wanted to scream or burst into tears.

"Angie, that bastard's a boy scout. He'd turn me in as his official religious duty. He thinks I'm too damn liberal as it is. I can't risk our whole life on one weekend."

*

They drove in silence directly back to their apartment in Champaign and went through the same cautious routine of reentry. Settled in the apartment, Angie took pot roast out of the refrigerator and began preparing dinner. She mixed him a drink and he sipped it slowly, crestfallen at the aborted weekend. She poured herself some chablis and sat close to him on the couch.

"Maybe it's just as well," she said. "I need to talk." She paused. "I want to get pregnant. Now! It's time."

He was startled at the firmness in her voice, then glared at her almost angrily. "There's no way right now! You're just worried about your dad."

"It's not my dad, it's us. I want our life to mean something."

He was hurt. "It does mean something. It means everything. I can't be a priest without you. I'd have to leave the priesthood."

"I don't want you to leave. The priesthood is your whole life. Too many are leaving! If priests like you leave, there'll be no Church. The Church needs you, the boys need you. They adore you." She paused. "I'll have to go away."

Now he was pouting. "If that's all I mean to you, then leave, damn it! I thought you loved me, I thought you loved our life together."

"You know I do," she said softly. But this time she would not be put off by his pouting and promises. "You mean everything to me, but I want to start a family. I know it's what we're meant to do."

He grew cold and silent. She had never really confronted him before. He picked at his dinner, watched TV, finally turned it off and went to bed. When she tried to cuddle with him, he moved away. In the morning he got up early and made his own coffee, ignored the paper, even the sports section, and refused breakfast. He sat out on the patio for a while, made himself a drink, then another, and still was silent. A little after noon, he put on his uniform. Normally she would have come to him by now, promised him anything, but she had not made a move. He was furious but also frightened. His silence and angry withdrawal hadn't worked. She had never been able to tolerate it before. He decided to leave, hoping she would restrain him.

"I've got to see that dead pilot's wife and kids this afternoon. I'll be back around midnight."

"Will you want to eat?"

"No," he said sullenly, deeply hurt that she made no move to delay him. He did not kiss her goodbye, nor did she complain as she had before.

"See you later," he said as he moved toward the door.

She just nodded, which hurt him even more. This was an Angie he didn't know. Then he was gone and Angie felt a greater emptiness than she had known since she first met him. She wanted to call him back, to laugh and make love and know that everything would be as it was. It had taken every bit of courage and strength not to give in to his deep, apparent hurt. Her eyes filled.

At about three in the afternoon he entered the home of the young widow, Margie Harmon, an attractive brunette in her early thirties, her eyes red with weeping. Another pilot and his wife were there, her parents, and the three young children crowding around their mother, touching her hands and face, kissing her and telling her not to cry. The oldest boy, thin and pale and about ten, reassured her.

"I'll take care of you, Mommy."

"I know you will, darling."

Margie cried even harder, and Santek put his arm around her. There was nothing to say. The kids crowded around at her outpouring of tears, and he hugged them as well. The other visitors drifted into the kitchen.

"Are you hungry, Father? There's plenty of food. Everyone's been so good to us. . . ."

He declined gently and sat on the couch with his arm around her. The kids were all over him. The five-year-old asked, "Is Daddy in heaven, Father?"

"Yes, Daddy's in heaven and he wants you to take care of Mommy and one another. Your daddy's with God. God wanted him. We don't know why, but you're all gonna be okay." He wished that Angie could be here with him. She would know what to say and could take care of the children.

Damn the Church! he thought. Righteous old cardinals and popes who wouldn't know a real person if they stepped on one. Now's the time I need a wife, right here!

He wondered about Angie. He should have talked to her, promised her to have children, promised her anything. He was as tired of their clandestine life as she was. Somehow it wasn't quite real. He continued to rub the heads of the children, keeping one arm around

29

their mother. Still, there was nothing to say, so he knelt and began the rosary. He knew that only faith could sustain the widow through this madness. Already she had stopped crying and her eyes said that she would keep going. There were the children to think of. Children made it all work, and the comforting monotony of the rosary would help. He would stay as long as she needed him, do whatever he could, stop by every day to make the kids laugh. Angie had finally strengthened his commitment to a life of service. Without her he would be like a dozen other chaplains he knew, drinking, chasing, sleeping around, doing their work perfunctorily, even well, but waiting for leave when they could drink away their loneliness or screw their brains out, usually with anyone who was available.

He remembered weekends in New York or Dallas with Al and Pete, his chaplain buddies, as bored and lonely as he was, and with a pocketful of money for the first time in their lives. He remembered the three English girls, fucking all night, drinking, getting stoned, then back to the base, confessing it all, and starting over. Then another weekend and it was the same thing. The faces of the women were a blur, their own priestly identity concealed behind a "classified" job. Usually they stopped confessing after a while and just went through the motions, loving their priesthood with some strange, honest attraction but, unable to live without women, settling for what was available. To know any sense of softness and synthetic love.

Some priests never strayed, content to do their work, to travel and enjoy new experiences, as if their celibacy was of no concern. Others hid behind booze or madness. But Santek's kind, the jocks and high-energy guys, finally went after the women.

Angie had changed all that. Without her nothing made any sense. He looked at the little children without a father. He drank in their beauty, their simplicity, their innocence, their nobility and determination to help their mother. Angie would have her family. He would see to that. He owed her everything, not only his priesthood but his life. Now was not quite right, but soon. Soon! Meanwhile, there was time.

But not for Angie. She lay on the couch, half watching afternoon TV, and thought about tomorrow. He would be gone for three or four more days while she went on with her secretarial work for a heavy equipment company, dodging the men who wanted to take her out, as they increasingly undressed her with their eyes. She told them any story.

"He's in Vietnam. He'll be home soon."

"Can't we just have dinner? Or a couple of drinks? What kind of guy is he if he expects you just to work and wait and knit?"

"He's the greatest man I've ever known."

"Well, I'll just make you appreciate him more."

At times, she was tempted. Just to have company and a few laughs. She was even afraid to make girlfriends lest she somehow betray Ted's work or not be immediately available when he wanted her. She had learned to use her time. She went to Mass frequently, usually at a local parish, occasionally at the base when she had to see Ted. She made most of her own clothes, bought gifts for her father while shopping during her lunch hour. She had read Manchester's *The Death of a President* and *Nicholas and Alexandra,* even *Rosemary's Baby*, which she hated. She had cried her way through the movie *A Man and A Woman* and saw *Doctor Zhivago* three times, only once with Ted. She had even read *Fanny Hill*, when Ted was gone for a whole week, and masturbated for the first time in her life—thinking of him. She also had been making clothes for a baby boy.

Now, too restless to sleep, she got off the couch, turned off the TV, began weeping softly, and fell down on her knees. She needed to talk to Ted. She needed to know that they would have children. She also knew that he was not ready.

"Please, God, help me! I don't want to interfere with his priesthood. You know that! But I can't live this way. Help me to know what to do. You know how much I love him. I know what the Church says, but it hasn't always been that way. Priests need wives and children too. Maybe they need them more than anyone else. Help me!"

She lay down on the couch again, and briefly drifted off to sleep. She dreamed she was in a hospital bed in Canada having Ted's baby. Ted came in wearing his priestly vestments, smiling that smile, kissed her, and then kissed the baby. She had never seen him so happy. Then the door opened and the French bishop from her childhood, a thin, saintly man with large red ears, walked in the door with her father. Ted stood aside, and the bishop bowed and took the baby from her arms, blessed it, and walked out the door with her aging father, who only stared at her sadly without a word.

Ted began to cry and hold his head in his hands. She got out of the bed and rushed to him—then she woke up sobbing. It was only five o'clock.

She got up and walked to the closet and pulled down from the shelf two designer suitcases Ted had bought her. "Nothing but the best for my girl," he had said. She would have to go away. There was no other way. She had to start a whole new life. But how, God, how? Ted was her whole life. She started packing as the tears flowed freely. And even God seemed silent.

Chapter 4

In the spring of 1948, Gerry Beauvais was honorably discharged from the navy after four years. He might have remained in the service if Father Misch had not retired the same year and returned to California. They spent a few final days together in New York, enjoying the movie version of *Hamlet* and *Miracle on 34th Street*, and especially delighting in *The Medium*, a two-act opera by Menotti at the Ethel Barrymore Theatre. They wandered around Broadway and 42nd Street, assessing the popularity of blatant pornography, commercial sex of every variety, and an assortment of dime-a-dance parlors. Father Misch grinned when a faded blond prostitute approached him for a "party."

"I'm afraid I'd be a party pooper at my age."

"How about your son here? He looks like he could use a good time. How about it, sailor boy?"

Gerry could only blush and stammer and walk away. Father Misch grew reflective. "Sex is big business. I suspect it always will be. Look at the people going into those movies, the nervous ones who glance around before they enter. They're typical successful Americans, not perverts or transients. I wonder if my celibacy hasn't been a kind of freedom."

"Sex can be confusing," Gerry said quietly.

"Unhappy, restless people seem to think it will cure that emptiness. I wonder how many people have really satisfying sexual lives. I also wonder if the Church has been a help or a deterrent. Our preoccupation with sex seems unhealthy."

Gerry loved their talks, although most of the time he listened. At their final dinner, after watching a splendid *Aida*, Beauvais talked about the priesthood over veal marsala and a bottle of good Pommard at Mama Leone's.

"It seems like what I want, but I don't feel any dramatic call."

Misch laughed. "I never did. It just seemed to happen. Like you, I met a priest I liked and somehow got interested. My dad wanted me to be a stockbroker—even after the crash." He paused reflectively. "You should take some time to make up your mind, date a bit, and do something about your musical talent. The priesthood can be a lonely life if it's not for you. There were times when I wondered. . . ."

"Do you regret it?"

"Not any more. When I was younger and celibacy was a problem, I used to think that my life was difficult. As I matured, I realized that marriage was the more difficult way to serve God. The priesthood is as hard or as easy as you want it to be. When you want to get away from it all, you just drift off. Marriage doesn't usually offer that opportunity, unless you're out of town. Then you go to porno movies." They laughed.

After promising faithfully to keep in touch, Gerry Beauvais was off to Kentfield and his mother's home. When he talked to her of the priesthood, she was ecstatic. It had been her most fervent prayer for years. He attended daily Mass, cringing at the inept organist's playing and singing, but enjoying the opportunity for silent reflection that his spirit required. And on Sundays, in the sober era of Pope Pius XII, he was forever reminded that the ravages of war had taken their savage toll, dragging morality to its lowest ebb. Materialism and communism were the new enemies, and Catholic sermons were consistently ready to meet the challenge. Although Beauvais had glimpsed a more positive view of life through Father Misch's gentle eyes, when he talked about opera and the stage, his local pastor, a silver-haired Monsignor LeBlanc, with thin lips and ascetic lines on his face, objected strenuously.

"Get your head out of the clouds, Gerry. Your father was a down-to-earth practical man. It's enough that your brother Louis has made a mess of his life. Music is a hobby, not a way of life."

LeBlanc's word was still a kind of law, so Gerry took a few courses at the local junior college in voice and musical composition and received enthusiastic encouragement from mentors who were no match for the opinions of his family and Church.

He began dating occasionally but not with any great enthusiasm,

34

usually on a basis of gentle friendship and a shared interest in music. He spent some time with an attractive flute player at the college, Marney Cornell, red-haired and chubby with thick glasses, who had great talent and a wry sense of humor. She misinterpreted Beauvais's innate kindness for love, and as she was ready to marry anyone who asked her, she managed to lure Beauvais to her room on a weekend class trip to attend a symphony in Cleveland. After too much wine and some heavy necking which Gerry enjoyed, she abruptly unbuttoned her blouse and loosened her bra. She frantically dragged his hand over her breasts and began stroking his groin. Before he really knew what had happened she was lying on the bed naked.

"I want you! I'm ready! Take me!"

It sounded like a scene from a mediocre Italian opera. In the midst of his rising passion, he suddenly felt giddy and embarrassed and his brief burst of excitement evaporated. Suddenly she was not a fun companion and purveyor of magnificent sounds on a flute but a plump, naked girl he barely knew. When the dramatic moment was ruined by his awkward withdrawal, she jumped up from the bed, dressed tearfully, and startled him with an angry barrage of words.

"You're just another queer like all the rest of those musicians. What the hell are you trying to do? You've been leading me on, you son-of-a-bitch. Get the hell out of here!"

It was as if he had never known her. But it was important to him that she not feel bad, so he wrote her a letter telling her how special and talented he thought she was. He got no direct reply but was content when she smiled at him as he walked across the campus. Later he confessed to a scolding Monsignor LeBlanc, who told him not to see her any more. Actually, his only concern was Marney's hurt feelings. The brief sex seemed inconsequential.

Curiously, he was not preoccupied with sex like most of his peers. Although his mother, Genny, was a devout Catholic, she had not smothered her children in guilt. Had he met the right girl and enjoyed a sensitive, loving relationship with her, chances are he would have had a normal sexual response. Marney had startled him, and he felt no strong physical affection for her. Although he was almost twenty-four, his greatest passions seemed not sex but a love for music and solitude and a growing desire to help other people.

Occasionally he wondered if his father's coarse approach to sex had scarred him and he would think of entering the tarpaper shack, with Mabel leading him by the hand. He remembered the two

35

mangy dogs and Mabel, fanning herself, in the faded cotton shift displaying her large, pendulous breasts and her thick black thighs. He could still see the unmade bed in one corner of the room. There was an old chipped oak table with mismatching chairs, a sofa with ratholes on the side, and a rug that had lost any pattern save a faded rose. The room smelled of stale grease. Two men were talking in a back room.

Mabel led Gerry to the couch and sat him down.

"Slip off your pants, honey. We gonna see what you got to work with."

"I . . . I can't. I'm a Catholic."

"Ain't no different for Catholics. We all the same when it comes to diddling. Pull those pants down, now. You'll be glad you did." She moved to help him, undoing his belt and sliding his pants and shorts over his hips. She pulled off her dress and sat naked next to him. The stale odor of sweat and cheap perfume sickened him. Her huge body seemed firm, and her breasts were even larger than he had imagined. He couldn't move but felt his penis swell in the strange setting. She reached under his shorts, slid them down, and began milking his penis.

"My, my, you got a nice big one. You gonna give Mabel a good time."

She leaned over and began sucking him with loud slurps. He pulled away but she persisted. He felt like crying.

"Now, now, just settle down and enjoy yourself. Your daddy paid me to give you a good time."

The talking continued in the back room. He saw a roach exploring the edge of the oak table and the remnants of a greasy meal. Mabel continued her ministrations.

"There now, honey babe, don't that feel nice and soft and good? My, my, you're just as hard as a rock."

She lay back on the couch and pulled Gerry on top of her. He could not look at her, but he was as excited and curious as he was confused and frightened. She directed his hard young penis between her legs. The stiff, dark hair scratched him. Suddenly he felt a strange warm moisture and a series of frightening but pleasurable spasms in his legs and groin and wondered if he had peed on her. He expected her to scold him.

"My, my, you a quick one, honey babe. Well, now you a man just like the rest of them." She wiped his penis with a dirty washcloth and slipped on her dress.

Gerry, suddenly over his fear and filled with anger and remorse, slipped on his clothes, fighting back the tears. He had never felt dirtier or more miserable in his life. He made his way to the front porch. Mabel sat back down in her chair as if nothing had happened and began fanning herself again with the newspaper. Gerry stood by the gray splintered railing and wondered about going to confession, fearing that he might die in mortal sin and go to hell.

Mabel continued chattering. "I don't know how long this hot spell gonna last. But then, I guess I'll be complainin' 'bout the snow before long. You a fine-lookin' boy. You come back anytime, and Mabel show you some more tricks so you be ready to give those young white girls a good time. They ain't no differ'nt. They likes it too. Feels good, don't it?"

Gerry couldn't look at her or open his mouth. He would have burst into tears. He saw the plumbing truck round the corner and screech to a stop. Maurice and Dennis had drunk more beer. Dennis jumped out to make room for Gerry.

Maurice gave him a lecherous grin. "Now you're a man, boy. We don't want no queers in this house."

He handed him a beer. Gerry shook his head, then could resist no longer; the tears came pouring out. Dennis put his arm around his shoulder. Maurice looked confused.

"What the hell's wrong with you, boy? That's what life's all about."

Gerry did not really feel at home on the community college campus, and although he smiled easily and chatted freely, he was very much a loner. He also spent long hours just sitting in church, not really praying but content to be in the presence of God in an almost mystical way. At other times, he wandered through a large woods of birch and pine trees, an assortment of wildflowers, and a dark, silent pond framed in lily pads. There, in competition with a variety of birds, he hummed his arias and rejoiced to be alive.

Marriage did not seem inviting to him, and a life on the stage seemed out of reach. The priesthood would make possible the contemplation and mysticism his spirit craved and would provide him with the chance both to help others and to use his musical talents. He was not really concerned about communism or materialism, nor was he even excited, as any decent Ohio male should be, when Cleveland won the American League pennant and destroyed the Boston Braves in the World Series. He lived in a world of his own, and the priesthood seemed an appropriate vocation for such a gentle misfit. Especially since it seemed to please his mother, Father Misch, and even his older brothers and sisters. They had him slated as the first American pope even before he enrolled. When word got around of his decision, Marney the flute player finally felt vindicated.

The major seminary proved a comfortable home for Gerry Beauvais because it reminded him of the discipline and regularity of navy life. Since his college education was spotty and the Ohio diocese he belonged to had an abundance of priests, it was suggested by Monsignor LeBlanc that he join a small diocese in Michigan that was badly in need of clergy. Actually, unbeknown to Gerry, the local bishop was concerned about the scandal surrounding his father's demise, and it seemed appropriate that he work in another area. The Bishop of Lansing, after meeting him and reading the letters of recommendation from his pastor and Father Misch, was overjoyed.

He enrolled him in St. Gregory's school of philosophy, a dull, fortresslike building that housed 150 students on Price Hill in Cincinnati. The majority of students were four or five years younger and considerably more sheltered, since they had been in the seminary since ninth grade and had seen little or nothing of the world. For the most part they were the typical seminarists of post-World War II: middle-class, ambitious, and hard-working, largely of German and Irish and Polish stock, considerate and friendly and singularly naive. To them, communism was an imminent threat and materialism was the beast of the Apocalypse that sought to destroy the world with sex and self-indulgence.

Beauvais was soon called "Pops," a designation he enjoyed, and despite an abundance of Latin makeup work to supplement his high school Caesar, he found the studies only moderately challenging and the ecclesiastical Latin quite simple in comparison to the classical Virgil or Cicero. He went once to a serious discussion club that traced the origin of communism and simplistically plotted its decline through the Christian strategies of the pope's encyclical.

A tall young philosophy student with a mound of blond curly hair, thick glasses, and a prominent overbite, dressed in a cassock like Beauvais and the other dozen students, looked up.

"The reports of the House Committee on Un-American Activities are must reading! Even though our arrogant President Truman chose to ignore their findings and only ninety-eight federal employees were dismissed, there's every reason to believe that the Commies are running our government! What are we going to do about it?"

There was a murmur among the disciples. "Do you think Truman is a Red?" This from a nervous boy whose left eye twitched when he spoke.

"At least a pinko," said the blond. "Don't forget the Displaced Persons Bill admitted two hundred thousand Europeans to our country. Truman supported that one. How many of those do you think are Commie plants?"

Gerry Beauvais didn't know and didn't really care. He slipped out quietly while the big blond was shaking the encyclical and the committee reports like a giant broom to sweep clean the universe. Causes made Beauvais restless.

Beauvais also found the dramatic skits that gently mocked the faculty, or the assortment of practical jokes on newcomers—frenching their sheets or hiding their underwear—too childish to be funny, although he always laughed with the others. He did enjoy the annual "lights-out-toilet" prank, which consisted of stuffing a dummy in pajama bottoms and depositing him in one of the toilet stalls. The neurotic priest disciplinarian, Father Miller, paced for an hour after lights out, not wanting to disturb this apparent case of severe constipation. By the time he discovered the hoax, the entire student body was one giant roar of laughter.

Actually, Beauvais spent more time with the younger professors than he did with the students, whose interest in pranks and sophomoric discussions belied their age. The well-traveled Father Duncan, the choir director, who enjoyed his beer and schnapps and all varieties of music from the Rodgers and Hammerstein hit *South Pacific* to Bach, Beethoven, and Leonard Bernstein's new Symphony Number 2 for Piano and Orchestra, became a friend. Father Duncan reinforced Beauvais's vocation, insisting that it was not necessary to be a fight and football fan and to see Commies in every rectory and convent to be a good parish priest.

Duncan smiled at Beauvais's report of the discussion group on communism. "I'd better be careful about wearing red vestments."

"And reading Faulkner."

"Actually, the New Testament is the first Commie Manifesto."

They shared more wine or good German beer and talked about navy life and travels to Thailand and Manila. Gerry talked about his vocation and Father Misch but never felt quite free enough to talk about his father. They shared their record collections and enjoyed their personal ruminations on the best in contemporary literature.

Even Tennessee Williams was not forbidden, nor was a toast to the last American troops evacuated from Japan in 1949.

There were also private music rooms where Gerry could indulge his deepest passion and find ample time to read the authors who would give him a broader view of Catholicism than textbook Thomistic philosophy. He managed to read Kant and Spinoza, John of the Cross and Teresa of Avila, Augustine and Nietzsche, Hume and Teilhard without jeopardizing his Catholic faith or blindly accepting the simplistic, insulated approach to great philosophical issues that was offered at St. Gregory's.

The gentle, scholarly, organized life agreed with him, even though he was assuredly not a typical seminarian. He had no illusions about bringing the world to God, and he was not greatly troubled by any of the classic theological questions which had been treated *ad nauseam* for centuries to no one's real satisfaction. Instead, he continued to create his own intellectual dilemmas outside the banalities of the classroom. He read Luther and Calvin privately and was startled at their good sense and spirituality. He enjoyed Sartre and Camus, H. L. Mencken, and wily old Bertrand Russell. He occasionally talked about his more complex readings with a retired philosophy professor in residence, Father "Spike" O'Brien, another atypical faculty member like Father Duncan, whose mind ranged far beyond the narrow parameters of mid-twentieth-century Roman Catholicism. They shared Arthur Miller's powerful new tragedy, *The Death of a Salesman*, and W. H. Auden's "Age of Anxiety." When Gerry talked about his brother Louis's recent divorce and the family reaction, O'Brien said that divorce would one day be accepted by the Catholic Church, and Beauvais knew he had found another important friend and teacher.

"The whole approach to sex is monolithic." The roly-poly O'Brien was wearing his usual grin and cigar ashes on his cassock front. "And it will get worse! People won't marry as young, they'll live together, they'll practice artificial birth control, and the Church will go right on singing its song of textbook chastity till only the ignorant and terrified listen. We're in for some bewildering times, Gerry, times in which you'll have to keep your wits about you. The Church can be a great institution in the next fifty years or it can become rapidly obsolete."

At the end of two years, Beauvais received his B.A. degree *summa cum laude*. He was advanced to the final four years of theology leading to the priesthood and assigned to St. John's Provincial

40

Seminary outside Detroit. Bishop Wieber was delighted with the accomplished candidate he had picked up, not unlike a coach finding a star athlete who wanders in without portfolio.

Gerry's spirituality had developed without the self-conscious intensity or scrupulosity that often characterized the devout young men who determined to be perfect in their priestly vocation. He accepted the Mass for what it had been since childhood, a joyous act of worship. He did not ponder it any more than he would have *Carmen* or *Rigoletto*. It was the same with his prayers and the prescribed daily meditations, which he accepted as congenial conversation with his hidden God and a chance to reflect on his future dreams. He had none of the self-loathing of Irish-Catholic guilt which was so prevalent in the American Catholic Church among all nationalities. His confessions were chats with the priest, and although he occasionally reminisced about a naked Marney and a nudie show he had enjoyed on Clark Street in Chicago, he felt no need to confess the fleeting remembrances. He could even admit to Father Duncan that he wished he had more sexual experience.

"I think I would have liked to have had intercourse a few times with someone I cared about. I remember a beautiful girl in Manila. . . ."

"I did," said Duncan. "It was wonderful. I thought I had invented sex." He laughed heartily. "I'm afraid if I had much more experience, it might have terminated my vocation. Maybe you're lucky the flute lady cut you off. She probably had great lips."

They laughed and were back into the music of Bartók or why the Filipinos never developed any really decent cuisine.

Beauvais missed Duncan and O'Brien when he entered the theological seminary in the fall of 1950, but he was glad to be on his final leg to the priesthood. Curiously, the theological seminary program, operated by the Sulpician Fathers, who specialized in seminary training, was far more rigorous than that at St. Gregory's. There was no Duncan or O'Brien, no casual treatment of the rule of silence, and very little free time. Beauvais's boot camp had been a tremendous preparation for the theological seminary.

Some loved the program, which gave them little time to decide anything for themselves. Others gave up and went home or turned griping into a consistent hobby. Gerry went along with the flow, not really from dedication but from an innate temperament that did not quarrel with life. He was not moved, as were many, by the frequent spiritual talks, which encouraged impossible ideals, but stood sufficiently apart so as not to be swallowed by the idealistic program. Of the ten young men who had started in the seminary at the age of fourteen, nine left before ordination. To Gerry, it was only another navy with nicer people around, and he accepted it as the road to the priesthood.

It was at St. John's, shortly after his arrival, that Gerry Beauvais met Ted Santek. That they became friends was probably due to Beauvais's loneliness in the new setting and a side-by-side seating assignment in the refectory.

The two apparently had little in common. Santek was the middle of five sons raised in the Polish ghetto of Hamtramck and the tough east side of Detroit. What Beauvais had learned in the navy, Santek had learned even more concretely on the streets. He had fought with enough blacks and whites by the time he was fourteen to earn respect as a fearless combatant, and he won a football scholarship to Detroit Catholic Central High, one of the real gridiron powers in the entire country. He thrived in the earthy milieu because of his outstanding street savvy and an almost unbelievable charm, especially for women.

And he loved sex. Craved it, from the time he was first introduced to it at thirteen by an eighteen-year-old black girl who traded her favors for a Clark bar and a chrome bicycle horn. This first foray deep in the bushes of Pilsudski Park lasted for two and a half hours until the black girl finally protested.

"You got me raw as a bucket of perch, honey."

"How about later tonight, baby?"

"How about a month from now? You is something. I'm lucky if I can walk home. You gonna need half a dozen ladies like me."

And he found them, wherever he went. Already fully grown at fourteen, he was an athletic five-eleven with thick, wavy blond hair and those innocent Polish blue eyes that looked as if they couldn't lie if life depended on it. His twice-broken nose curved slightly to the left and made his face not quite pretty. But it was his sense of humor, a bellowing laugh, and a gentle, caring spirit that were the real sources of his attractiveness. As his older brother Stan put it, "Ted could have three eyes and two left ears and he'd still make out like a bandit."

Yet he was as innately compassionate as he was charming. When the Jacksons' house burned down, he organized a neighborhood campaign for the uninsured black family to rebuild their home and find food and clothes for six young children. He talked the Superior Lumber Company out of enough boards and sheetrock, nails and doors to build a better house than before.

"We'll see that everybody in Ham Town and East Detroit trades here."

And he tried, getting newspaper coverage, conscripting buddies to go door-to-door announcing what Superior Lumber had done, and asking the local pastor of St. Adelbert's Polish Church to buy all his material for the new parish hall from Superior. His troops canvassed the neighborhood for clothes and food, promising free tickets to a Detroit Tigers baseball game, which he got through the Athletic Director, Father Al Kupinski, at Catholic Central. The Kroger food chain, after a hard sell, came through with enough damaged canned goods to keep the Jacksons in nourishment for six months. When anyone tried to praise Ted for what he'd done, he'd make a joke out of it.

"Shit, I set the damn fire to toast marshmallows. It's the least I could do."

Then he joined the gang at Kosminski's Café and told more jokes. There was the guy who stole lumber and went to confession. After admitting to stealing yards of pine and fir, he told the priest he was really sorry and would never do it again. The priest sighed and asked, "Can you make restitution?" "You get me the plans, Father, and I'll get the lumber."

They all roared and he was off.

"Did you hear the one about the golfer who went to hell and found out it was the most beautiful country club he'd ever seen? Gorgeous girl caddies, plush fairways, and brand-new McGregor clubs. He stepped up on the first tee, waggled his ass a few times, and turned to the sexy caddy.

"'Where's the ball?' he asked.

"'That's the hell of it.' She grinned."

Then he sneaked off with Betsy Dellums, talked a guy at the car lot where he worked part-time into buying a bottle of Mogen David, and was off to Orchard Lake in a borrowed '36 Chevy. He didn't embarrass her by walking out with her, but, concerned about her reputation, he met her in the lot behind Gradowski's Tire Store. When they settled on a blanket at the shore of Orchard Lake, he was suddenly a philosopher, wondering about life, questioning the future, pondering if war ever accomplished anything.

"Sometimes I think I'd like to live in a small country in Europe.

Maybe Austria, up in the mountains. We could ski and drink beer, laugh and raise kids, know everybody in town. You wouldn't have to be on your toes all the time or out hustling to make a buck at the car lot or the Rouge plant."

Betsy was enthralled. He told her about his dreams to have his own car agency, to have a house with a huge pool in Grosse Pointe, and to coach kids on the side.

"I'll make enough money to build a big recreation center so the kids have something to do on Saturday and Sunday. We'll have bowling alleys and tennis courts, the whole ball of wax."

Then he was a clown again, imitating a loon from across the lake, explaining the "hopping people" that lived on the moon, telling her about the hatchet murderer who wandered the shores of the lake on moonless nights. Then he was gently kissing her and reaching under her blouse, stroking her full young breasts, telling her that she was the most beautiful girl he knew and meaning it. Gently he un- dressed her, kissing and laughing and promising he would not get her pregnant, and then patiently taught her sexual moves she had only wondered about. He devoured her with lips and mouth, hands and arms, as if he could never get enough of her, all the while whis- pering everything she ever wanted to hear. Only when she was ex- hausted did he stop. Then he helped her dress, held her lovingly for a long time, and continued talking about how much he'd like to help the poor people all over the world.

"Do you still respect me?" she asked fearfully.

"Why shouldn't I? You're a beautiful, loving woman. Now we can really be friends. What we do is our secret."

It was almost the only reassurance she needed.

"Do you go to confession?" she asked, like a good Catholic girl.

"Of course. Usually about once a month."

"Do you tell about this?"

"If I think it's wrong."

"Is it?"

"What do you think?"

"It doesn't seem wrong, but Sister Rita said it is."

"I guess you have to make up your own mind. Sister Rita isn't God." He laughed. "I wonder if Sister Rita ever did it."

She began giggling. "I think that's sacrilegious."

"It's okay to do it with a nun if you don't get into the habit."

Then they were both laughing and rolling on the ground. Con- fession seemed part of another world. When he dropped her around the corner from her house, he kissed her hands lovingly, again told her how beautiful she was, and promised soon again.

Instinctively Ted never talked of his sexual exploits, but he did go to confession to Father Al at Catholic Central.

"Are you trying? I mean, really trying?"

"I think I am, Father, but I don't seem to have much resistance when it comes to sex. I think about it all the time. I just can't get enough. Maybe I should quit coming to confession."

"I want you to keep coming. Some people have a harder time than others. Do the best you can, but keep receiving the sacraments. God understands and loves you. He'll give you the grace."

A hundred other priests would have driven him away in the forties and fifties. Not from church, he was too Polish for that, but from the sacraments. Ted picked his priest the same way he picked his friends. And his God remained someone who understood. He knew that once he married he wouldn't have the sexual problem any more.

His vocation to the priesthood was as surprising as that of the fishermen from Galilee or Ignatius of Loyola, the tough Basque founder of the Jesuits. It is such men, who have tasted the world and its realities deeply, who usually make the best priests. And like Ignatius, who was wounded in battle, it was a serious accident that transformed Ted Santek.

It was the summer after he graduated from Catholic Central with letters in every sport, State honors in football and basketball, and straight C's on his report card. He had been working at the car lot on Livernois, determined not to submit to the assembly line like his father and two older brothers. He had great plans that extended far beyond Hamtramck and River Rouge. He wanted the world.

Chapter 5

The summer of 1946 was an exciting one for Ted Santek and Detroit, for America and the Catholic Church. Not only was the war
finally over, but the Detroit Tigers were the defending national
champions in baseball and Notre Dame was expected to win national
football honors under Frank Leahy. All this gave a certain vicarious
confidence to Wally Lehmke's leading used car salesman, Ted
Santek. Dressed in white bucks and a two-hundred-dollar white
suit, there wasn't a more debonair high school graduate in all of the
Motor City. And he could sell cars. Especially since the postwar car
market was booming and there was a flood of used cars in the excitement over the first new models in five years. Although in reality he
didn't know a carburetor from an air filter, most customers liked him
and he had that instinctive savvy to know when an individual was
hooked on a car.

When a tall, lean, well-dressed refrigeration salesman with
greased-back hair fell in love with a '40 Olds Ninety-eight with the
new Hydramatic, Santek edged his offer to a thousand dollars.

"I wouldn't dare go in to the boss with anything else. He'd throw
me out. It'll mean a big cut in my commission, but I like you and I
know it's the car for you."

Santek was gone for a full fifteen minutes, sipping coffee and
reading the sports page while the nervous buyer paced. Finally he
reappeared, all smiles.

"We've got it, baby."

The skinny salesman beamed, combed back his hair, and paid
the grand. He got his Olds and Santek got two hundred dollars. The

boss would have let it go for eight hundred. Ted gave the smiling salesman two free tickets to a Tiger-Cleveland game and made a friend.

"I'd like to do something for you."

"Send your friends around, baby! Tell 'em to mention your name!"

Married women without their husbands were a particular cinch. He matched their eyes to the upholstery, their hair to the paint color, and more often than not broke in the back seat with a love tryst at a favorite spot along the Detroit River after a couple of margaritas at the Marine Inn. If anyone had a vocation to sell cars, it was Theodore Aloysius Santek. He had more money than he could spend, and one of the delightful perks was the use of any car in the lot. It was not unusual for him to sell the car the same night he took it out.

He had never been happier in his life. Irving Berlin's most recent songs, "I Got the Sun in the Morning" and "Doin' What Comes Naturally," were a reflection of postwar relief and veritable theme songs for Ted Santek. He had a pocket full of hundred-dollar bills which he dispensed freely to anyone in trouble, more women than he could handle, the best car on the lot, and a bad knee from football that kept him out of the service. He was not concerned about the atomic bomb tests at Bikini Atoll in the Pacific or the Russian takeover in Germany. It was "shoofly pie" time, new cars were rolling off the line, and war and rationing were a million miles away. There was no stopping him.

Until one night in July. He had met Darlene Davis at a Tiger ball game and thought he was in love. A sophomore at Smith College, she had class and sophistication, a body bulging seductively out of a tight cotton dress, and a wild, impulsive strain that was ready for anything. She also had a sense of humor to match his own.

"Why don't we run away and get married tonight?" He laughed.

"My favorite bridesmaid is in Hong Kong."

"We'll fly to Hong Kong."

"My Chinese is atrocious."

"Shit, I know all that stuff. 'Chop suey, Louie, chow mein!'"

They passed on Hong Kong and, after dismissing her two girlfriends, took a ride out to Orchard Lake to one of his favorite trysting spots with a fifth of Southern Comfort. It was one of those magic chemical moments, and they tore at each other's clothes and made wild love under the trees, then went nakedly for a swim. Santek had finally found his woman, wealthy, bright, and as fast as he was.

Driving home, they cuddled and made plans for the next two weeks.

"Have you been to Mackinac Island?"

"No, but if that's an invitation, I'll go."

"I hope you can ride a bike. They don't allow cars."

"Seeing you on a bike would be worth the trip."

Those were the last words he heard her say. He reached over to slap her playfully on the head, missed a curve on the Orchard Lake road, and wrapped the cream-colored 1940 Chrysler around an oak tree. Darlene was crushed in the death seat and died instantly. Ted was unconscious for three days and in intensive care for two weeks. That he lived was a miracle his mother attributed to the intercession of Mother Cabrini.

When he finally regained consciousness, keeping his visitors down for the first few weeks was a full-time job for the head nurse on the second floor of Detroit Receiving. With casts on both legs and a collection of generally obscene graffiti in every available space, not to mention an assortment of "personal physical therapy" from his ladies, the first few days out of intensive care were a cross between a class reunion and a mild orgy. It kept him from realizing the horror of what had happened. Even one of the night nurses provided him with special favors when the crowds were gone.

"Not so loud," he whispered. "The orderly's too big to fight."

When she finally managed to mount him between casts, he laughed so hard he almost ruined her excitement. When she became convinced she was in love, he finally had to tell her he was engaged, to get any sleep. Even then he woke up more than once to find her hands under his covers.

After a month or so, however, his friends returned to the streets and their own struggles, the horny nurse found a boyfriend, and Ted Santek was frequently alone for the first time in his life. A deep depression set in. The thrill of money and cars and sex on demand was largely gone, and the thought of returning to the car lot and spending the rest of his life there lying and jiving to make a living was more than he could handle. When the accident haunted him, he began to talk to God and ask for some guidance and direction. He wanted to make something of his life, to be respected and loved, and to make his family proud of him. Intermittently, his resolve cooled when one of his stray lady friends stopped by for conversation and furtive sexual manipulation under the covers, but when she had left and Ted was alone with himself, the same haunting, almost idealistic yearning returned.

Nor could he dismiss the dead girl and his own brush with death. One minute he had been making wild love and a half hour later he had seen the battered, ghoulish face of a once-beautiful Darlene before he slipped into unconsciousness. He had destroyed a human life by his self-centered childishness, and although he felt terrible remorse and guilt, he felt more strongly a need to do something with his life.

In an almost superstitious sense, common among his people, he saw the hand of God in this tragic incident, and if he returned to the same way of life, he feared that his whole existence would be scarred with failure. Deep in the blood of this second-generation Pole was the courage that had lived with war and oppression for hundreds of years, and the Catholic faith that managed to surmount even the horror of Hitler. In the depth of his bones and historic subconscious, life had to mean more than pleasure and success. And beneath the playfulness and sexuality of Ted Santek was all the Polish passion for justice.

He knew the streets of Detroit and their poverty, their drugs and emptiness, the broken homes and the kids without a chance, and deep down in his heart he wanted to do something about it. He just didn't know how to begin. He had been in such a mood for days, despite interruptions, when Father Al, the athletic director from Detroit Catholic Central, showed up unannounced. The priest was startled and briefly embarrassed by the lurid graffiti, but even more by the attractive, clinging young busty brunette who had insisted on giving Ted a therapeutic massage while, more out of total boredom than passion, he roamed freely around under her loose blouse with his unbandaged hands. Father Al pretended to admire the assortment of candy and flowers until the "masseuse" regained her composure and scurried away with a hurried "God bless you, Father."

He walked over to the bed and rubbed the blond hair of his favorite fullback. "You've got hair again. For a few days I wondered if you'd have brains. Apparently you're doing much better."

Santek blushed furiously and stammered for several seconds. Father Al reassured him. "I didn't come to cramp your style. What are you up to?"

"Well, I'll be out of this place in a week or so, then on crutches for another month or two." He laughed. "It should be a great come-on at the lot—if those other bastards don't beat me out the door."

"You're going back to selling cars?"

"What the hell else, Padre, screw on fenders? Not this cookie!"

"Are you okay about the dead girl?"

He sobered quickly, losing his suave veneer. "I guess I'll never be okay about it. I wrote her folks a letter and I expect I'll get slapped with a probation, at least that's what Barney Oleksyk says. I think I'll visit her parents when I can get around." Suddenly, his eyes moistened.

"Jesus, Father, what the hell's wrong with me? If I'd died that night I'd have gone straight to hell. And now a girl's dead and I'm still screwing around. Life's bullshit!"

"It doesn't have to be. My life isn't."

"Yeah, but you're different. You got God on your side and you're not out drinking and chasing ladies half your life."

"I did my share of that. It just didn't cut it for me."

"Well, it doesn't cut it for me either, Padre, but I don't know what the hell to do."

"I always thought you'd make a great priest."

Santek almost fell out of bed. "A priest? For God's sake, Father, you know damn well I'm not the type."

"What the hell's the type? Was Peter, a tough, brawling fisherman? Or James and John? Even the Bible says they were hell raisers. You've got brains and a born leadership ability. More than that, you've got a good heart. That's really what it takes."

"I like the ladies too much, Father Al. I mean, I've told you, I think about sex all the time. It's in my damn blood. I could never give up women!"

"But ultimately, you only get one! You want every attractive woman you see! You can learn to handle your sex drive. I did. God gives you the help you need. So do the people; they love you like their own family."

Santek was moved briefly. "It doesn't make any sense."

"What the hell does? You'll get somebody pregnant, get married, have six kids and end up getting bullied on the line like your dad and brothers. The priesthood's an exciting way out! You've just got to learn how to keep your pecker in your pants."

"How the hell do you do that?"

"You find something that excites you more than that."

50

Santek finally laughed. "I'd like to have the franchise on that and sell it in big red boxes. I'd replace Rockefeller."

Finally the priest left, after depositing a biography of New York's Mother Cabrini, the slum nun, on his nightstand.

"Here's some good reading if the nurses ever let you alone."

Santek remained in silence for several minutes, profoundly moved. It was almost as if Father Al had offered him a solution to his dilemma, but it seemed a totally preposterous one. The priest was probably the coolest man he had ever known. He had once hit two home runs in Detroit's Briggs Stadium, had ignored a major league contract, and had the profound respect of the entire student body at Catholic Central. And he thought Ted Santek could be a priest. Ted toyed with the fantasy for several more minutes, then whispered "Bullshit" and fell protectively asleep.

Later that summer, when Ted had largely recovered from his wounds, Father Al came by the small frame house, badly in need of paint, to take him for a drive. Santek had finished the life of Mother Cabrini and admitted to being moved by it.

"That was one hell of a nun, Padre. That's the kind of work the Church should be doing more of. On the streets. Those people appreciate, and they've made up their minds that no one really gives a shit."

"That's what I had in mind for you."

They laughed and drove out west of Detroit and ended up at St. John's Provincial Seminary near Plymouth. Ted was still using a cane, but they managed to inspect the golf course briefly and were just in time to share a T-bone and baked potato dinner with a few members of the faculty. Then they repaired to the faculty room to enjoy a brandy and leisurely conversation. In a few minutes, Ted felt right at home despite his cane.

"This is what happens to old fullbacks," said Father Al.

"And this is what happens to old priests," said a kindly, gray-haired little scripture professor, who refilled his glass and toasted the laughing group.

"No," said a wiry moral theology professor, with dark hair and eyes, who was playing with a golf tee to cut down on smoking. "They're like old golfers, they just lose their balls."

Santek was pleased but startled. He had never really been in the company of a group of priests and had no idea they were just as with it as other men. He had seen Father Al as a total exception.

51

A lean canon lawyer with thick glasses and curly gray hair asked Ted if he had heard the one about the nun on the train. Ted shook his head.

"Well, it seems this nun was traveling from Philly to New York and was joined by a Catholic businessman, who promptly ordered a martini, then another one. Feeling a little guilty, he prevailed upon the nun to join him. After a couple of refusals, she finally agreed if he'd have it served in a teacup so as not to give scandal. So the businessman unobtrusively walked back to the bartender and requested a martini in a teacup. The bartender looked up and scowled. 'Is that damn nun on board again?'"

Santek was at home. A final tour of the building overwhelmed him. An imposing granite exterior with long bright halls of Spanish tile, private rooms with built-in bookcases, expensively tiled bathrooms and showers, a breathtaking chapel and refectory, an ultra-modern kitchen of aluminum and stainless steel—the poor boy from the streets of Ham Town was speechless. When he saw the bowling alleys, pool tables, regulation gym and baseball diamond, not to mention that lush golf course, he was ready to sign up. It was a world he never dreamed he could be a part of.

He was enrolled in the Polish preparatory seminary at Orchard Lake, and a Sunday afternoon party at his parents' home made him conscious of his new status. The pastor, Monsignor Pilarski, was there and four Felician nuns from the parish school. Mrs. Santek, a plump, motherly woman with straight hair and a thick accent, did her best to hide in the kitchen. Never before had the pastor or the nuns visited their humble frame house crowded with statues and worn, overstuffed furniture. Now there were balloons, red and white crepe paper, and an assortment of cabbage rolls, kielbasa, sauerkraut and dumplings, and cakes and pies from all over the parish. Mr. Santek, a muscular, balding man with a massive potbelly, drank too much beer and called his son "Monsignor." The nuns beamed as if their mission had been finally rewarded in the rugged vineyard, the neighbors insisted they "always knew," and even Santek's brothers were overwhelmed at the presence of the pastor, especially when he had too much whiskey, sang his lungs out, and insisted on dancing with a scarlet-faced Mrs. Santek. It was an unforgettable afternoon, and Ted knew the pride of the seminarian in a Catholic subculture. No presidential candidate could have been treated with more dignity by the Polish community, which danced and sang until everyone was suitably drunk. They finally put Mr. Santek to bed when he demanded that Ted say Mass for everyone. The next day at Orchard Lake Seminary, Ted was a burgeoning priest and his mother's favorite child.

He did reasonably well at his studies and, with a new determination, miraculously almost managed to avoid the ladies. Once during a summer vacation weekend at Lake Huron, after too much beer, he almost succumbed to a water skier who insisted on wrestling with him on the sand. Another time, a married woman whose house he was painting attempted to seduce him during a morning coffee break by sneaking up behind him and rubbing her ample chest and sinuous thighs against his sweating, naked back.

"Let's take a bedroom break, you big hunk."

"I belong to God," he said nervously.

"Can't he spare you for about fifteen minutes?"

Somehow he survived and was congratulated by Father Al in confession. He was also advised to paint someone else's house.

The four years at Orchard Lake passed quickly. It was no St. John's but the beautiful setting and refreshing camaraderie delighted him. The street kid from Hamtramck knew as much about Thomas Aquinas and Martin Luther as he needed to and was one of the sixty freshmen admitted to the prestige and luxury of St. John's in Plymouth, to complete the final four years before the priesthood. Fortunately, he had not lost the vitality and humor which were too often buried in the rigid demands of silence and prayers and classical studies imposed in the minor seminary routine.

And at St. John's, two days after he met Gerry Beauvais at dinner, he knew it was safe to be himself, even to tell his nonstop smutty jokes. The six others at the table, more typical, serious-minded seminarists, generally ignored them and left them laughing uproariously to themselves. Gerry, with his sparkling brown eyes and uncritical acceptance of the whole world, was the most receptive audience possible.

"Hey, Ger, did you hear the one about the two dogs chasing a lady dog in a snowstorm? The lead dog looked back at his buddy, almost blinded by the blizzard, and said, 'It's a bitch, ain't it?' The other dog kept right on running and said, 'It better be!'"

Santek howled as loudly as Beauvais and was off and running.

"What's the difference between a pound of butter and a pound of horseshit?"

Beauvais threw up his hands.

"I'd sure as hell hate to send you to the store for butter."

53

Despite the golf course and bowling alleys, the private rooms and plush surroundings, St. John's had little of the freedom Beauvais and Santek had experienced in their previous seminaries. The Sulpician Fathers were a reclusive bunch, for the most part, and the faculty dinner Santek had shared before entering was a closer contact with the professors than he ever felt again. Although the studies were not difficult for Beauvais, Santek was under constant pressure to survive scholastically. Beauvais tried to calm him, but Santek was not convinced. "There are so damn many laws. Riley said there are more than two thousand of them in the Code of Canon Law. And Caretti said that scripture is all different now. Shit, there weren't even three real wise men! And Christ never went to Egypt."

"The scriptures have opened up slightly. There's a new realization that God didn't dictate words to the sacred writers. They were just people and only knew as much about the world as the men of their own times. Each Gospel is written to convince a different audience, and as archaeology grew, so did the understanding of the Semitic mind."

"I thought evolution was taboo. Now they all talk like it's a fact."

"The 'seven days' of creation were just a literary device and not a week in our terms. We don't know how the world came to be. The same way with the star and the 'wise men' at Christ's birth. They were just a typical way of embellishing an important event."

"Does this mean the Church has changed and people don't know it?"

"Not really. The Church is still as infallible and as doctrinaire as it's always been. Divorce is impossible, artificial birth control is immoral, and premarital sex is as sinful for an engaged couple as it is for curious teenagers."

"It doesn't make sense."

"It will change. But there's no sense fighting the party line."

Beauvais and Santek got the first taste of Sulpician moral rigidity when they were caught smoking by the director of discipline in Beauvais's room with the door closed. Monsignor Ellis. A sallow, squinty man with a narrow bald head and a shrill voice, he opened the door abruptly without warning. Santek was sprawled across the bed in his shorts, dragging on a cigarette, while Beauvais, seated at his desk, was attempting to explain that Purgatory was invented to soften the idea of hell. Since it was a muggy day, he too was clad only in cut-off khakis.

54

"What's going on?" Ellis was convinced he was on the brink of breaking up a homosexual orgy.

Santek jumped a foot at the sudden intrusion and almost swallowed his cigarette. "We're just discussing Purgatory," he stammered.

"The way you're dressed, it looks like you're getting ready for it."

Beauvais smiled, never losing his composure. Santek burst out in a loud guffaw. Ellis covered his prominent upper teeth with a tight lip.

"This is no laughing matter!" he shouted. "You know the rules: no smoking, no one in another's room except in case of emergency, and the door must never be closed. And, I might add, the faculty thinks you two are segregating yourselves from the rest of the community! Particular friendships are forbidden!"

He made one final appraisal of the scene, his eyes brimming with anger and disgust. "Now get dressed, both of you. Mr. Santek, repair to your own room!"

He stalked out and Beauvais began to laugh. Finally Santek joined him.

"My God, he thinks we're a couple of fags," Santek said. He continued dressing and then paused at the door.

"Aren't you gonna kiss me goodbye, sweetie?"

Beauvais laughed. "No, but if you hang around I'll let you wash my back."

Three months later, Santek had more to worry about than smoking in his shorts in an alien room. The rector, a small, wiry, lantern-jawed man with close-cropped black hair and piercing dark eyes under thick eyebrows, called Ted into his office. Despite his appearance, he was a kind, fatherly man who admired jocks and thought they made the best priests.

"You're not making it scholastically, Ted. The Latin seems too tough for you. You're failing dogma and just getting by in canon law and moral theology. I'll have to put you on probation for three months. You're a fine public speaker, and you'll be a great influence on the youth, but a priest must be a man of learning."

Beauvais would say later, "Bullshit! Some of the dumbest men I know are priests!"

The rector continued. "It takes more than even a good heart and great compassion for saving the world. You've got three months."

Santek was crushed when he circled the scenic path around the

55

seminary grounds with Beauvais. "Christ, I learn to keep my pants zipped, work my ass off, and I still can't make it. That damn Latin's like Chinese to me." He paused and his voice grew soft. "I'll be back painting houses in three months. Christ, it'll kill my family."

Beauvais shrugged it off. "I can teach you Latin the simple way. We'll study together in the music room."

And they did, every spare moment, with Beethoven or Mozart softly in the background. Santek stopped telling jokes. His blue eyes lost their twinkle and gleamed with the intensity of a boy who once fought his way up from the streets of East Detroit. Beauvais broke down the roots of Latin words, selected the five hundred words most frequently used, simplified tenses and declensions, and ignored all the refinements of subjunctive moods. He outlined each doctrinal thesis in its most basic terms and constantly insisted that Latin was an incredibly simple language.

Santek studied while they lifted weights, took Latin lists to bed, posted them on his mirror, and hid them in his missal at Mass. If Ted was anything, he was a battler, and he called upon his immense Polish ferocity to wage the most important fight of his life. In three months he turned it around, not only because of Beauvais's talented tutelage but because he was actually a bright student despite a background horrendously lacking in fundamentals. At the end of the probation period, he could respond in decent Latin to Beauvais's test questions. His pronunciation and grammar might have turned Cicero in his grave, but he got the job done. The rector congratulated him on his semester exams, unaware that he had barely slept for the three prior nights, studying in his bathroom.

"I've never witnessed such a remarkable turnabout. You'll be the great priest that Father Al said you'd be!"

Santek beamed, stole two beers from the priests' refrigerator to celebrate with Beauvais, and later that night sneaked out alone to a small bar nearby called the Oasis. He checked the scene carefully to see if any of the professors might be having a nightcap, then seated himself at the far end of the bar, where he could watch all incoming customers. It was a dangerous ploy which, if detected, would have resulted in immediate expulsion, but he was tense and restless enough after the weeks of stress to take the chance.

After a few beers and loud discussions about the heroics of Bobby Layne and Gordie Howe, he passed himself off as a yacht salesman specializing in movie stars and Arab royalty—and had enough rhetoric and imagination to carry it off, even though he had

56

never even set foot in a rowboat. He danced a couple of times to the jukebox with a young factory worker with great legs and a hungry body that moved sinuously around his chest and biceps.

"You're a great dancer," she said. "I'll bet that's not all you do."

He laughed. "I won the hopscotch tournament in my neighborhood."

"Is that what you guys called it?"

"I think I won the same tournament in my grade school."

He liked her open face and chiseled features and earthy sense of life. She fit into his arms like she wanted to rent space. A few drinks later she invited him to her car for the "greatest hopscotch tournament since Adam and Eve," and although he was wildly excited and in one of the most triumphant moods of his life, he hardly knew how to turn her off.

"I got the clap," he said. It worked. Immediately.

He finished a beer and made his way back to the seminary. Refreshed. Invigorated. And proud of his resistance to the first smell of sex since the attentive night nurse in the hospital. It was also the first time he slept through morning prayers.

Chapter 6

As the weeks and months of the early fifties slipped by, regular tutoring kept Ted Santek on top of his studies, and his friendship with Gerry Beauvais held it all together. He had never met anyone like him.

Beauvais was spiritual by temperament and did not seem to have to struggle with the mechanical religious exercises provided by the seminary system. He rarely used a missal at Mass, ignored the morning meditation read aloud by the spiritual director, and drifted off into his own quiet colloquy with God without words or pressure. While most students were "working on" patience or humility, chastity or self-discipline, Beauvais appeared to be working on nothing but living his life. He was kind and humble by disposition, patient and understanding without effort, and esteemed, if not loved and admired, by everyone. If he had any doubts or private struggles, they were not apparent. He continued to read widely from current literature despite occasional chiding from one of his more staid classmates.

"I think *Forever Amber* is forbidden reading."

Beauvais smiled. "I hadn't heard." It had been scathingly attacked in the Catholic press.

"You've got to be kidding!" Then, dropping his voice, "Is it as filthy as they say?"

Beauvais laughed. "I have to agree with the Supreme Court Judge in Massachusetts. 'I found it more a soporific than an aphrodisiac.' You can read it when I'm finished."

Although he led the class in examinations, his private theological views instinctively questioned hell, original sin, the virgin birth, infallibility, and most of the Church's teaching on divorce, birth control, and premarital sex. Yet he had no need to argue with anyone. He somehow recognized the Church as a historic institution.

"It will change when people change," he told Santek. "The Church doesn't really force people. Ultimately they force it." He remembered his conversations with Father Misch.

In class he could challenge the most significant teachings, and his gentle, respectful manner prevented his professors from exploding. "I wonder if the Church wouldn't gain more by emphasizing that the Holy Spirit works in all people and truth seems to evolve throughout the world," he asked Dr. Lenz, his dogma professor. "Take divorce, for example. If thousands of sincere people are convinced that their marriages don't work, gradually there might be a new attitude toward divorce in the Church. I wonder if time and common sense don't eventually guide the Church. Maybe it's not really a total change, but a clearer understanding."

"There's truth in what you say, but the Church is not a democracy. The pope doesn't take a vote," answered Lenz.

The class laughed loudly. Santek led a mock ballot with two or three other students: "Let me hear it for divorce!" More laughter until Dr. Lenz intimated that the clowning should terminate. Beauvais continued.

"If enough good people come to the conclusion that divorce and birth control, even hell and sin, have distorted human psychology, perhaps as human understanding grows, so does the doctrine of the Church."

Lenz was not prepared for this vision, yet Beauvais's mild, respectful manner made it impossible for him to pontificate.

Santek had a much harder time, because he had no real sense of history and thought that the Church's charter and code were practically dictated by Christ to the apostles. In moral theology class, he quarreled about premarital sex.

"But Father, God can't expect an engaged couple to follow the same rules as a couple of horny teenagers."

The class erupted with laughter. Even Dr. O'Meara smiled.

"You don't presume to speak for God, Ted? Sex is sex is sex. You would probably tell your horny teenagers to break up, and work with your engaged couple to avoid occasions which lead to sex."

"It seems like just being together would lead to sex, and the more you forbade it the hornier they'd get. I think you've got to learn about sex like anything else. What if you married someone and found out that she didn't really start your motor? Or how about this Catholic girl I knew who could only get excited if her husband took her for a drive and seduced her in the back seat of the car? It was only exciting if it seemed sinful."

The class fell apart laughing. Few of them were really comfortable with sex, and practically none of them knew exactly where a vagina was. O'Meara laughed with the class as if Santek were joking. It was always that way. When he complained that rhythm was impossible for poor, ignorant people, O'Meara got impatient.

"Are they too ignorant to take their temperature?"

"Sex isn't like that, Father. If a woman starts refusing her husband, he starts going out. That's the way it is in my neighborhood. Guys are sleeping with whores because they can't sleep with their wives without another bun in the oven. A guy comes home with a heat on, he's not about to take his old lady's temperature."

O'Meara's face reddened as he waited for the class to stop laughing. "Sometimes your use of the vernacular leaves something to be desired, Mr. Santek. The Church can't base its whole moral code on your neighborhood." It was a signal that the discussion was over. After class, Beauvais encouraged him.

"You're right about what you said. Rhythm won't stand up. The Church doesn't change people, people change the Church."

"I wish you'd said something in class. I felt like a damn fool."

"O'Meara's trapped. He can only think so far, then he has to accept what is. I like him, but I don't want to take him on. It won't change anything."

Santek nodded, still puzzled. He lived in the present and couldn't wait for history. Nor did he realize that he was a very part of the history that would change the Church.

Santek's vocation remained a struggle. The summers at home were the most difficult, with sexual temptations and assorted memories leaping out from under every bush. Father Al was his savior, hiring Ted to run CYO programs, organizing baseball clinics for poor kids, creating a city-wide track meet, and making arrangements for Ted to serve his daily Mass and join him for breakfast. Somehow he made it, and at the end of his third year of theology he was ordained with Beauvais and the rest of his class to the subdiaconate, promising to recite daily in Latin the Roman breviary (an hour's reading of psalms and selections from scripture and the ancient fathers) and promising to be celibate for the remainder of his life.

The night before, Beauvais broke the sacred silence, invading his room at midnight with two stolen beers and a graphic picture of a nude woman he had saved for just this occasion.

"She called yesterday and wondered if you had any time tomorrow afternoon. I forgot to mention it."

"You son-of-a-bitch," Santek laughed. "Tell her I'm only allowed to have blow jobs in the confessional."

"You mean they leave us with our balls. But I thought—"

Then he finished his beer and went laughing out the door.

By nine o'clock the next morning they had taken the first of the major orders leading to the priesthood and vowed never to know the sexual love of a woman. Santek was frightened and depressed. Beauvais felt stronger, somehow, and dedicated to his secret God. He wrote to Father Misch of his joy.

> It all seems right now. The stage would have been just another life. I have the same feelings I used to have when we had dinner in Manila or Hong Kong, that to ignore beauty is the only real sin. I miss you all the time and hope you are over your bout with pneumonia. "Only the good die young," so you should live forever.

The final year in the seminary was the most interesting because their work was more practical and related directly to the priesthood. Twice a week Ted taught religion classes to adoring high school students who had never met a "priest" like him. Gerry transformed a parish choir into near-seminary caliber. On Sundays they often went to the Detroit House of Correction, a nearby prison, where Santek preached powerful, earthy sermons and Beauvais had a small group singing Latin like seminarians. The work made them feel like real priests, especially since the prisoners always addressed them as "Father." Santek's sermons won a standing-room-only crowd.

"God's got a plan for you, no matter how you screwed up. That's why Christ took time with thieves and harlots, publicans and sinners. The only people he had no time for were the proud and the arrogant. He knew that criminals had received enough punishment, that their mistakes were open and humiliating. He was put off by the 'whitened sepulchres,' the politicians and scheming businessmen, the pimps and hustlers, the respected citizens who looked great on the outside but inside were 'full of dead men's bones.' He wants you to start over because he knows there is someone he wants you to love: a child, a wife or husband. Or there's a job out there that only you can do. I don't mean blowing a safe." He paused and laughed with them. "I mean finding out what your own genius is, what your gift is, and giving it all you've got. Then life will start to mean something, and you'll know what real joy is. Don't let the system beat you! It's only a narrow line that separates you from us on the outside. That's the narrow line you gotta learn to walk!"

At the seminary they practiced baptizing or anointing dolls, spent hours learning the complex rubrics of the Mass, correcting each other's mistakes in performing the varied bows and confusing positions of hands and head and fingers governed by ecclesiastical law to ensure that all Masses were said exactly alike. There was to be no intrusion of personality in the sacred mystery of salvation. Most of all they enjoyed hearing each other's mock confessions to test their ability in moral theology and canon law. Santek's was outrageous.

"I stole a pound of cocaine and had a sex orgy with four nuns for a weekend—but I did see that they all got to Mass on Sunday. And I stole three cars, killed two cops and a fink pusher, and burned down a friend's house because he needed the insurance money to pay off his bookie. And, let's see, I don't know if this is a sin or not, but I killed three dogs in the neighborhood that kept me awake. I also killed at least four cats, maybe five, because I was bored on a Sunday afternoon. I think one of the cats may have been pregnant, so I don't know if I owe any restitution to the father.

"And I had intercourse with three different married women and paid for two abortions. Then I robbed a church safe, seduced an organist—but it was in a Methodist church, so I don't feel too bad about that. And, yeah, there are some other things that are *really* bothering me. I missed my prayers before meals a couple of times and I used foul language a half dozen times. I really wish I could get over that, it worried the hell out of me. I might have set a bad example for the nuns by using foul language during the orgy, but I tried to watch it. And I sassed my mother once. I think that's about it, Father."

When Beauvais could stop laughing, he asked, "How long has it been since your last confession?"

"A week, Father. I try to go every week unless the dogs are running."

Again Beauvais laughed aloud. "Have you ever thought of becoming a Baptist?"

"Oh, no, Father!" He was deeply hurt. "I've been a good Catholic all my life. It's the one true Church."

"Do you have a rosary?"

"I did, Father, but you advised me to say my rosary when I was tempted to masturbate at night and I broke both of them. It was a tough trick. Oh, by the way, I also masturbated about fifteen times."

"I'm surprised you had time." Then they both laughed.

Finally Beauvais absolved him and computed his restitution to the families of the murder victims at $285,762.31. Santek said he could come up with the money in a week, and Beauvais was afraid to ask him how. Finally it was time for Ted's penance.

"Are you in pretty good physical shape?" asked Beauvais.

"Yes, Father. God has blessed me with great health."

"Good, good. Then I want you to attend the pope's Mass in Rome."

"That's easy, Father. I could use a vacation. I'm beat!"

"And you've got the time."

"Nothing but time, Padre."

"Good. Then I want you to walk to New York, cross the Atlantic in a rubber raft, swim the English Channel, and walk on your knees the rest of the way."

Santek was not put off. "No Hail Marys?"

Beauvais fell on the floor laughing. "No Hail Marys," he gasped.

On June 6, 1954, Gerald Martin Beauvais and Theodore Aloysius Santek lay prostrate on the gray marble sanctuary floor of St. Mary's Cathedral in Lansing, Michigan. With five other classmates, they were vested in the long white linen albs and cinctures that symbolized their purity of body and spirit. They had just concluded a week-long silent retreat in which they were reminded of the awesome responsibilities of their work. The latest encyclical of the prolific Pius XII, "Sacra Virginitas," had been frequently quoted by the powerful Jesuit retreat master, Father Larimer. A fortyish former athlete with broad shoulders and booming baritone, flaming red hair, and a vivid imagination, he was an outstanding preacher and talked straight from the hip, much to Santek's delight.

He quoted St. Thomas: "The deepest natural instinct is the instinct of conversation; the sexual instinct comes second." He laughed. "So if you're tempted, talk like hell!"

Santek leaned over and whispered to Beauvais, "I think I'll promise silence instead of celibacy. Think they'd go for it?"

"You wouldn't get much sex without that Polish charm of yours. I don't think a smile would do the job."

Larimer ignored the disturbance. "As the pope tells us, 'Virginity fully deserves the name of the angelic virtue,' and St. Thomas states, 'To virginity is awarded the tribute of the highest beauty.' But such virginity is not for all, and as the pope warns us, 'perfect chastity demands . . . a free choice by Christians before they consecrate themselves to God.' It is not for everyone, only for those who choose it. So don't whine later on and say you didn't know what you were in for! Celibacy's for men, real men! Christ put it most simply of all: 'He that can take it, let him take it!'"

The words exploded in the seminary chapel. It was obvious that Father Larimer could take it. Santek paled noticeably and wondered if he should be selling cars on Livernois Street in Detroit. Beauvais seemed a hundred miles away, wondering why Larimer spent so much time on celibacy and so little on love.

The cathedral was packed with priests and nuns and several hundred lay people, at least a hundred of them smiling Beauvaises and beaming Santeks. Father Misch and Father Al knelt nearby, ready to assist their beloved protégés in the concelebration of their first Mass in union with a delighted Bishop Wieber. The altar was alive with candelabra and roses, the choir boomed out its joy, the organ roared delight, a trumpet bellowed the triumph of seven new priests in a world that desperately needed them.

Then Bishop Wieber's voice rang out in the solemn neo-Gothic setting of St. Mary's Cathedral. "If anyone has anything against those to be ordained, before God and for the sake of God, let him come forward confidently and speak."

Santek's heart stopped briefly as he imagined a procession of females protesting his ordination. There was only profound silence. An hour later, Ted and Gerry were priests forever, standing in full vestments with the bishop, blessing the congregation. They moved to the communion rail to bestow individual blessings on members of their families, lingering a little longer over the bowed heads of their proud, weeping mothers. Tears trickled down Santek's cheeks, and Beauvais beamed his proudest smile. Father Al and Father Misch looked through moist eyes, wondering where the years had gone and grateful to God that he had brought their "boys" to the

64

priesthood. There was no greater gift than to have "fathered" a priest.

An ex-navy man and a street kid from Hamtramck now had the power of Christ himself, to say Mass, to forgive sins, and to heal the sickness and despair of a troubled world. The organ pealed joyously, the choir shouted the mighty "Te Deum Laudamus," echoing through the vast cathedral and out onto the streets of Lansing, Michigan. And Beauvais and Santek, as weak and frightened as the rest of mankind, were finally prepared to do God's noble work.

Beauvais's appointment to the cathedral was no surprise. Bishop Wieber had a special affection for this talented, mature young priest who was five or six years older than his classmates. The bishop, a square short man in his late sixties, whose gentle face revealed suffering and whose soft blue eyes shone with kindness, had served as a chaplain in World War I and distinguished himself for courage and dedication. He loved to tell Beauvais of the terrors of the battles of Argonne Forest and Belleau Wood, or the brilliant encounter at San Mihiel where Billy Mitchell had directed the world's largest aerial assault of fifteen hundred Allied planes. Wieber's hand moved vigorously as he talked, and he occasionally coughed from too many cigars.

"It was the Americans who won the war, Father Gerry, seventy-eight hundred marines died in Belleau Wood, the 'Wood of the Marines' Brigade.' And it was our boys at Château-Thierry who kept the Germans from crossing the Marne to Paris. That was the beginning of the end. Of course, we weren't the only ones, the Canucks and Aussies were fierce fighters, but it was the American doughboy who really proved his metal. Even Foch admitted that!"

Beauvais hid his ignorance of the war with nods and smiles, but it was more than enough. Bishop Wieber had a comrade-in-arms who knew the hell of war and the sacrifices necessary for victory. And war was really no different from the priesthood. Wieber's affection meant that Beauvais was headed for ecclesiastical prominence and would undoubtedly be a monsignor in a few years. His brothers were certain he would be a bishop, and even Father Misch wrote, kidding him.

You'd better start picking out your episcopal ring, and it wouldn't hurt to brush up on your German and your World War I.

But in the first flush of his priesthood, the honeymoon stage, there was little time to learn German or anything else. At the request of his jovial, chubby, and warm-hearted pastor, Monsignor Grady, Beauvais began teaching high school religion classes, and with his easy manner he soon was a hero to the students. His navy experience, his stories of Munich and Hong Kong, Paris and Bangkok, made him a uniquely romantic figure. It was honor enough to be a priest, but to have entered after an exciting hitch in the navy was exceptional, and a fertile legend grew up around him. He enjoyed eavesdropping in the locker room.

"Hell, he couldn't have been in the navy without having women all over the place. With his class and looks, he got anything he wanted. My brother said he met him in Norfolk and he had a real doll on each arm."

"I heard he was commander of a PT boat and nobody gave him any crap."

"He's built like a brick shithouse. I wouldn't wanna tangle with him."

"Donovan said he was Shore Patrol and took on three marines in a bar in Pensacola."

It didn't matter that Beauvais had never been to Pensacola. Nothing mattered. He was their priest, and they loved him.

There were students to advise, marriages to repair, converts to make, the sick and the poor to attend, novenas, weddings and funerals, football games and confessions. He was unbelievable in confession, and his lines of waiting penitents extended to the rear of the church. Word traveled fast, and the weak and frightened came to make their way back to God.

"It's been six years since my last confession, Father. I guess I've done it all."

"It took a lot of courage for you to come. I'm glad. Why don't we make this as easy as we can. I'll ask the questions and you answer them as well as you can. God doesn't expect you to be an adding machine. Are you married?"

"Yes, Father."

"Kids?"

"Seven, Father."

"My God, how do you do it? It must be tough to support them."

"I work at the Olds plant, Father. It's tough, but it's worth it. Sometimes I get tired of the line. They really push you around. So I swear a lot and drink more than I should."

"Have there been other women?"

"A few times, Father, when I was drunk."

"I understand. Do the best you can. Do you and your wife get along okay?"

"Well, she's a good woman, but she don't want no more kids. And once in a while I jack off. She won't let me use anything."

Beauvais was always upset when he heard the same story. A man with seven kids living like a celibate and his wife scared to death to love her husband. "Don't worry about it. You're a man. God understands."

Six years of fear were brushed away in gentle, loving conversation. Beauvais could feel the tangible relief.

"For your penance, take your wife out for dinner."

The man couldn't believe it. "Is that all, Father?"

"No, the worst part is yet to come. I want you to go dancing after dinner. Can you handle that?"

He laughed like a boy. "I sure can, Father. Thank you. Thank you so very much!"

"Come back soon and let me know how the evening went."

He played cribbage with the arthritic Monsignor Grady, who was never known to complain about his affliction. Consistently Grady drubbed him.

"I thought you navy men could play cards."

"When you want to shoot craps, let me know. I'll own your car."

Grady laughed loudly, then looked gently serious. "I hope you're here for a long time, Gerry. You're giving a life to this parish it's needed for years."

He loved his work, and troubled people came out of the walls to see him. Marriage cases were resolved that had been put on hold for years.

"I hated to bother Monsignor, and Father Palmer said he would get back to me."

"It seems like a simple enough case, Mary. It's called a Pauline Privilege case. It will take a few weeks."

"How much will it cost, Father? I think Father Palmer said a hundred dollars or maybe more."

He looked at her frayed brown coat with its neat little patch on the sleeve and a worn spot on the elbow. "There's no charge. Just some time and forms to fill out. We'll have you receiving communion in no time."

When records were not available, he ignored them and made

67

liberal use of canon law to take matters in his own hands. "It's all cleared up!"

"But what about my first husband's statement? I don't know where he is. He left me and the children years ago. . . . I've written everywhere!"

"It's all taken care of. You and Jack can set the date for the wedding."

"Can't we do something for you, Father?"

"Yes, two things. You can come to bingo once in a while and save me a piece of the wedding cake."

"That's easy," she said, tears forming in her eyes. "You know we love the bingo games."

"And I love cake."

"It's been twelve years without communion, Father. You don't know what this means."

"It means God loves you, and welcome back!"

She burst into tears of joy and embraced him.

Convert classes grew, increasingly brides and grooms requested his presence for a more personal ceremony, and he was faithful in his hospital visits and bringing communion to invalids in rest homes. But beyond all this he turned the parish choir into a disciplined body of musicians worthy of the stage. The director, Ed Sanders, a music major from Michigan State who had sung in Europe and New York, had struggled for three years to produce mediocrity. Beauvais raised his meager salary and worked with him frequently without intruding. They became close friends, sharing a love for music and theater and determined to make the cathedral choir the best in the country. They had dinner every Wednesday evening at the Jack Tar Hotel, where the prime rib was outstanding.

Ed, balding and bespectacled at thirty-two, was a slight, wiry man, gentle and artistic, with a frail constitution that had crippled his singing career. Over a brandy, he was ecstatic. "I can't believe what's happened! We've had three more members apply this week. One's a hell of a tenor and the other two are above-average baritones. Word is getting out."

"I think it's your solo Ave Maria that's drawing them. Gounod would be proud."

"Like hell! You've got the choir inspired. I don't know how you do it. Old Fred Berrigan is reaching notes he only dreamed about. I thought Palestrina was out of reach. Now I wonder if anything is.

People are starting to nod at me on the street. They used to act like I was an assistant janitor."

Gerry laughed heartily, then drove to Ed's apartment for more brandy and listened to a new septet by Igor Stravinsky and selections from *Pajama Game*. They made plans to see *The Caine Mutiny Court Martial*, which was playing in Chicago.

"I should be able to get away next Friday around noon and get back Saturday in time for confessions."

"Don't you ever run down?"

"I thought that's what we were doing now."

He stopped in the darkened cathedral on his way to the rectory. It was his favorite time of silent prayer, reflecting on his day, thanking God for all the opportunities he had had to be of service. He finished compline, the last part of his daily breviary, and made his way into the back door of the rectory. There was a light in the kitchen, and Monsignor Kelley, the chancellor who lived at the cathedral, came out of the darkness with his glass of warm milk.

"It helps me sleep," he told Beauvais for the tenth time. "You're out a little late, aren't you, Father?"

"Just listening to music and unwinding."

"At one of the rectories?"

"No, over at Ed Sanders's apartment."

The sallow, sway-backed chancellor mumbled a noncommittal sigh. "You don't spend much time with the other priests, Father. There was a dinner at Resurrection tonight. You missed a good feed."

"There'll be others." He wanted to say he was tired of talking about the Notre Dame–Oklahoma game and the Detroit Lions. He didn't really care about the Tigers or the Red Wings or the Cleveland Browns, either. Nor did he like golf or poker or clerical gossip. Priests were nice men but they largely bored him, whereas an evening with Ed Sanders was exhilarating. Instead, he said nothing and made his way upstairs to listen to Bach until he fell asleep.

Kelley slipped away in the darkness soundlessly. He had admitted to Grady that he didn't like Beauvais. Actually, he didn't really like anyone who had talent and the affection of the bishop. Behind Kelley's skeletal exterior was a brilliant legal mind and a deep yearning to be a bishop too. Grady had reassured him.

"Beauvais's got a mind of his own. He's a damn good priest. If he doesn't like poker or football, that doesn't make him a bad priest."

"He's rarely around the other priests."

"Neither am I," said Grady. "I usually prefer Papa Hemingway and O'Neill. Priests can be a pretty boring, petty lot at times. He seems to like Santek. They've been friends for years."

Kelley said nothing. He didn't like Santek either. Much too cocky for a young priest, he thought.

The parishioners at Sacred Heart parish on Flint's tough north side would not have agreed with Kelley. Ted Santek was the most exciting and vibrant priest they had ever known. Even Skronski's Tavern was not out of bounds.

"Christ, half the parish is here!" he bellowed. "Who's buying?"

And after a beer or two he was all priest, questioning Mike Salatka on his last confession, urging Pete Sturgis to come back to church.

"They wouldn't bury my old man unless we came up with two hundred bucks. Shit, my mom didn't have two bucks, let alone two hundred. All you guys want is money!" He couldn't have said it without half a dozen beers.

"I don't want your money, Pete. I want your smiling face in the front seat at Mass. You don't go, soon the kids won't go. Then you got trouble!"

"The kids go. I'll kick their ass if they don't go."

"What about the day when you're not around to kick their ass?"

Two weeks later Pete Sturgis went to confession and communion. "You can't say no to that Polack son-of-a-bitch!"

Santek dropped in on Beauvais late on Saturday night after confessions. Beauvais, lost in Bartók, looked up delighted and uncorked a beer out of his mini-refrigerator.

"Where've you been? I hear there's not a backslider on the north side who's safe from the Polack. Even the prostitutes are giving rosaries instead of green stamps."

"Christ, I've been busier than hell. This priesthood is more damn fun than a crap shoot in Barney's back room. Sacred Heart, unknown to anybody, is now about two thirds black. The Slovaks who built the place are leaving and trying to get top dollar for their house. The damn blacks will pay anything."

He laughed.

"I'm taking a census of the parish, and the weird thing is that the blacks let me in without a word. That collar is magic. I've got a class of fifty blacks taking instructions, I'm going after the damn absentee

70

landlords, several of them good Catholic Slovaks, who are robbing these people blind. I've even got an employment service set up with Chevrolet and Buick. There's more discrimination than you ever dreamed. I feel like a damn missionary in Africa. They're great people!"

"God, you're something else. I couldn't do that in a hundred years."

"I grew up with 'em, baby. But we need facilities, a big gym and rec hall. Monsignor Slowinski died for all practical purposes five years ago. He's still waiting for the Poles and Slovaks to come back home. They're all in the suburbs and their kids are changing their names to sound like WASPS. I think I'll become Father Ted Cocksman. That oughta get some attention!"

Santek had not lost his fire or his sense of humor, and the people adored him. Even Monsignor Kelley smiled at his raw jokes. And Santek never missed a chance to haze his best friend.

A phone call late at night interrupted Gerry's sleep.

"Father?" The voice was inebriated.

"Yes?"

"Does you know Monsignor Sheridan?" Sheridan was the conservative and sophisticated pastor of a large, opulent parish, a man beyond all reproach both in conscience and in tailoring.

"Certainly, is anything wrong?" Beauvais was obviously upset, but he couldn't imagine Sheridan in any kind of trouble.

"Well, you see, Father, I runs a cat house—I mean, a good-time house—on Logan Street, and he's had three of our best girls, all Catholic. When I ask him to pay up, he tells me he wants a clergy discount. I don't want to call the police, and I thought—"

"Oh, no, God, no, don't call the police! Give me your address. I'll pay."

"Thanks a million, Father. I owe you one. Can I fix you up with a nice Catholic girl? I mean nice!"

"No, that won't be necessary. Just the address!"

Then the roar of Santek's laughter, and Gerry knew he had been had again.

"You crazy son-of-a-bitch." He heard the laughter in the background.

There were fake postcards commending his sermons, fake invitations for his choir to sing in Washington, fake calls from desperate women who wanted Father to come over and rub their backs with holy water to get to sleep. And one Saturday night there was an extraordinary confession.

"It's been about three years since my last confession, Father." The inflection sounded familiar.

"Why don't you tell me what you've done?"

"I've done it all, Father."

"Well, the Church requires you to be a bit more specific. I know it's hard to remember. Just do the best you can."

"Well, I became a Mormon, married several different women, and had intercourse with two of my nieces. And I've been stealing money at the bank where I work and covering up the records."

Beauvais was suspicious. "Anything else?"

"I took a mortgage on my mother's house by forging her signature, and I started a fire in the bank to wipe out some files."

Suddenly Beauvais began to laugh. "Damn you, Ted!"

He ripped off his stole, charged out, and pulled back the penitent's curtain. There, totally startled, knelt a handsome, middle-aged man Gerry had never seen before in his life.

Chapter 7

In January 1961, when John Fitzgerald Kennedy was inaugurated as President, Catholics had finally reached a milestone of acceptance in American life. It was a time of great prestige for the Catholic Church, with a charming, loving Pope John XXIII and an American President whose energy and popularity throughout the world somehow enhanced the glory of the Church.

Santek was delighted that "his boy," Kennedy, had made it. It was a real personal triumph for a kid from Ham Town. Furthermore, the leadership of John XXIII made the papal office appealing to Protestants and Jews and unbelievers who formerly had seen it only as a closed, historic dictatorship concerned with its own prosperity and power. Santek's goal of half a million dollars for his recreation center at Sacred Heart in Flint was suddenly realized by substantial gifts from Protestants and Jews, as well as Catholics, and he felt compelled to honor Kennedy and Pope John.

"You could call the center 'the Big Johns,'" Beauvais suggested.

Santek laughed. "Wieber has agreed to John XXIII, but no reference to Kennedy. He says politicians, even Catholics, have a way of screwing up."

"I'm sure he didn't say he's a Republican like all bishops."

Beauvais grinned. "Kennedy's no docile Catholic. That scares the bishops. They'd rather vote for a phony Quaker like Nixon. And in twenty years, John XXIII Recreation Center will sound like it was named after a Shakespeare play or a medieval English king."

Bishop Wieber, the mayor, and over a hundred priests and civic officials were present to celebrate the groundbreaking for the Pope

John XXIII Center. Beauvais's boys' choir, which had become the talk of the area, sang American folk music brilliantly. Santek's persistent dream of almost seven years was about to become a reality, and he enjoyed his moment on stage. The mayor, concerned about the black vote, told him to "drop in anytime," and the bishop, who had considered closing the dying Sacred Heart parish, was overjoyed at its new and intense spirit. When the crowd had finally thinned and even a renewed Father Slowinski had gone to bed, the aging bishop, looking frail and tired, quietly addressed Beauvais over a final brandy.

"The cathedral choir's magnificent, Father Gerry! Just magnificent! And I hear compliments everywhere on your work throughout the diocese."

Beauvais grinned. "I'm sure you've heard a few complaints, Bishop. Good musical directors cost money, and pastors tend to be a little—"

"They'll spend the money! I want good music, the best! And that boys' choir of yours sounds like one I heard at Koblenz when the armistice was signed. I'll never forget it. The sound still rings in my ears almost fifty years later, and your choir brings all that back." His eyes were moist.

"You've given me a lot of time and freedom from parochial duties, Bishop, to concentrate on music."

"I want you to have more time, Father Gerry. Come over for dinner tomorrow evening, and we'll talk about it."

The bishop finished his brandy, extended final congratulations to a delighted Santek, and was off. Finally, Santek and Beauvais were alone in the rectory. Beauvais beamed with pride.

"Well, you did it, Ted. Seven years a priest, and you've got the start of a monument."

"It's funny. I feel almost let down, like there's nothing more to do."

"Now that you've got money, you have to build the damn thing! But you probably need time off. I felt the same kind of emptiness the other day when I read about Hemingway shooting himself. You'd think he had everything to live for. Meanwhile I run around the diocese trying to create decent church music without upsetting the pastors, and Papa does himself in. What's it all mean?"

"Your boys' choir is great."

"I know, and I love the kids, but something's still missing. I feel so damn alone in my work. Your friendship is a big help, and Ed

Sanders and I get together once or twice a week." He laughed. "Maybe I need a family."

"And maybe I need a woman. It's been a lot harder lately. Whenever I give a talk or even a sermon, I find myself talking directly to some attractive woman who revs my engine. Usually the men's group bores me."

"That's no crime."

"I know. But it's fantasy bullshit that just makes me lonely." Santek seemed to have something on his mind, but Beauvais was too weary to pursue it. He got up to leave.

"God, we sound great on the night of your triumph! Like two despondent old men."

"It must be the brandy." Santek sounded distant and depressed.

The following night Beauvais entered the bishop's brick two-story Tudor home with its sprawling yard and neglected fountain, formerly the estate of a General Motors executive whose widow had left it to the diocese. After a prime rib dinner and a good Beaujolais, the bishop gathered in the formal living room with Beauvais and his other guests, Beauvais's pastor, Monsignor Grady, the chancellor, Monsignor Kelley, and his secretary, young Father Schneider, a shy and awkward country boy.

The bishop, glowing with wine and his delight in the presence of Beauvais, came quickly to the point. "Father Gerry, I want you to spend a year in Europe, to see what is happening in Paris and Munich, Salzburg and Monte Cassino. Spend some time with the Trappists and the monks of Solesmes. I'll make arrangements for you to sing with the Vatican choir and visit some of the cloistered convents of the Carmelites. I want you to bring the best of Europe to our diocese. We can have the greatest musical program in America!" It was an old man's final dream.

The rotund Grady beamed as if the bishop had rewarded him, only praying that Beauvais would return to the cathedral parish after Europe. Kelley, whose own ambitions for the episcopacy were dwindling with age, looked sallow and wounded as he tried to appear congenial. Privately he was angry and jealous, feeling justifiably that his own efforts in the diocese had been largely ignored. Young Schneider just smiled.

Beauvais was briefly speechless. He had not anticipated Europe. It was a dream come true. He was only sorry that Father Misch had been ailing and would be too ill to accompany him.

Still glowing with excitement, Beauvais had dinner with Santek the following evening at Santinelli's in Flint.

"I'll miss the hell out of you, Ger! But you deserve it. You're on your way! Don't forget to make some important friends in Rome; that's how it all happens."

Beauvais laughed. "I don't want anything to happen. I just want you to be here when I get back. Save some vacation time, and we'll go to Florida."

Santek nodded, almost sadly.

Beauvais looked at him. "Are you okay?"

"It's just the same old shit. I love the ladies, black ones, white ones, brown and yellow ones. After seven years it still gets lonely. I like the work, but the fire is gone." He paused and looked embarrassed. "And I want to go to confession."

Beauvais continued to devour his linguini, which was swimming in garlic and oil. "Go ahead. What's bothering you?"

Santek paused for a waiter to move away, buttered a slice of sourdough bread, and munched slowly. He sipped his chianti.

"I got involved with a graduate student, Monica, who's been keeping my books for the center. We had a drink in my office late at night to celebrate going over the top.

"After a couple of drinks, I kissed her and started rubbing her hair and touching her shoulder. I wasn't seducing her, it was just a real good feeling being with her. We'd been through some shaky times together when the whole center seemed an impossibility. I don't know what the hell really happened, whether I started it or she did, but we were both tired, excited about our success, and half bombed. Anyway, somehow we were kissing gently, long and soft and peaceful like. Then I guess I started stroking her breasts, almost without thinking, and we just kept kissing, but without any real passion. At some point while I was playing with her breasts, I slid my hands under her dress . . . and under her panties. Even when she came, it was all very gentle.

"When she kept saying she wanted to make love, I backed off a little, but God, I wanted her! It was different than ever before—like I couldn't help myself. She's really special, beautiful inside and out, and all the time I tried to resist her, I kept kissing and touching her and she kept coming to my touch. I couldn't seem to stop until she was exhausted. Somehow, I was afraid to make love to her, but later, after she left, I kept wanting her till I fell asleep. I'm really

76

sorry, Ger, because she's such a good friend and I was doing so damn well.

"Anyway, I called her the next day and told her how sorry I was. . . . . I promised her it wouldn't happen again. I really felt bad because she's getting married soon and had asked me to perform the ceremony."

"You've hung in for a long time, Ted. Don't focus on your failure. God understands. You care about this student and she cares about you. That's what makes it so damn difficult. I think you've grown a great deal. Just plain fucking doesn't do it any more."

"Maybe this is more dangerous."

"Maybe, but it's more human. Now you know you can have a friendship with a woman, maybe eventually even one that doesn't threaten your celibacy."

Santek almost laughed. "Christ, Gerry, I doubt that."

"Just hang in! God won't let us down. That's what I keep believing."

"That's what I'm beginning to doubt. I don't know if the loneliness makes any sense."

The waiter interrupted to fill their wineglasses, right after Beauvais had given an official absolution that no one could have noticed.

"To Europe," said Santek. But he was still lost in private thoughts and said it without his customary enthusiasm.

"To Europe," said Beauvais. "I can hardly wait." But he was still concerned about his confused friend. "And to Florida when I get back."

The trip to Europe was everything Gerry could have wanted. As exciting as were Rome and Monte Cassino, Austria was the most thrilling, especially Vienna. He attended the assortment of musical events at the Musikverein, the State Opera House, and the Volksoper, and on several Sundays he heard the Vienna Boys' Choir singing in the Hofburgkapelle. There were side trips to Salzburg, where the mountains startled him with their powerful presence and the Sunday-afternoon chamber music delighted him. It was the land of Brahms and Haydn, Mozart, Schubert, and Strauss, and all of Austria somehow became the home of Father Gerald Beauvais. The music of his favorite composers came alive in a new way, and as his German improved, he met a variety of exciting people—students, composers, musicians—who cared little about his priesthood but

77

were delighted with his perceptive love of music. It was as if he were no longer a priest.

This was especially true of his friendship with Dr. Karl Metzen, the choir director at St. Stephen's Cathedral, and Metzen's blond and attractive niece, Ursula, a twenty-five-year-old soprano, who had a hopeless crush on Father Beauvais. A quiet young woman, unaware of her exquisite beauty, she was a constant delight at dinner or the opera, on picnics in Prater Park along the Danube or on walks through the Vienna woods at the western edge of the city.

Once, when they were picnicking, Karl teased him about his niece.

"You should remain here, Beauvais. You have immense talent. Besides, you are a European, not an American. No American could have such love for music. And should you leave us, who will console my lonely niece? Her despair would inspire another opera."

Ursula blushed furiously, but Gerry only laughed with Metzen, unable to face her genuine affection as he sipped wine under the trees and munched the dark bread Ursula had made.

"It doesn't work like that, Karl. The bishop has great plans for me to bring music to the whole diocese. It's not Saint Stephen's, but we do the best we can."

Karl was pensive. "Life takes strange turns, Beauvais. You are still a young man, the future looks promising, but that can change. And Austrian women are the most beautiful and gentle and loyal in the world. Ursula will gladly introduce you to the warm social life of Vienna."

Ursula nodded shy assent, then boldly took his hand and kissed him warmly on the cheek. Beauvais blushed as broadly as she did. Karl shook his head, then nodded and was gone, and Gerry Beauvais was alone with Ursula.

For a time Ursula talked of growing up in Vienna, a skinny, self-conscious girl, of skiing and hiking, and of her dream to sing opera.

"Curiously, my father was opposed to it. Were it not for Uncle Karl, I would probably have four fat children by now. . . ."

Beauvais laughed, then talked of his own father and his yearning to sing, of his days in the service and his friendship with Father Misch. He even talked discreetly about the gross sexual experience that had been forced upon him. Ursula, sitting next to him on the picnic blanket, with the warm sun pouring through the tender leaves of spring, took his hand gently and kissed it. As he looked at her, Gerry thought his heart would explode in his chest. He had

78

never felt like this. Nor had she. They continued to hold hands and stare at each other as if they could not believe what was happening.

"I love you," she said quietly and kissed him gently on the mouth. He felt her breast against his arm and could not move away. Then, awkwardly, he took her in his arms and kissed her. They fell back on the blanket and he held her close as she buried her face against his neck and chest.

"I love you too, Ursula." The words sounded strange and incredible coming from his lips. He had never really wanted a woman before. It was not what he expected. A feeling of utmost tenderness combined with some deep desire to squeeze her with all his strength. His whole body trembled as he held her until the air grew chill and the sun began to disappear. He was almost afraid to move. Then, slowly, they walked back to her apartment, where she made coffee.

They sat at a small table munching strawberry tarts. Neither had said anything personal since they left the woods. Finally she spoke.

"Will you stay with me tonight?" She saw him pause and struggle with himself. "Just to hold me. To let me hold you. I respect your priesthood."

She was beyond description in the dim light: full, almost pouting lips, round, sky-blue eyes still moist with joy, skin glowing with some new radiance, long blond hair that smelled of earth and sunshine. He could still feel her breast against his arm.

"I don't think I can. I feel as if I'm going to explode."

She nodded in understanding. He took his coffee and sat on the living room couch. She sat at his feet and rested her head against his knee, then embraced his leg. "Do you leave soon, Beauvais?"

He loved the way she said "Beauvais" in her Austrian accent. "Yes," he said softly. "Next week."

"My God, the time has gone so fast! I want you to stay, Beauvais. I have never wanted anything so much in my life. Please do not go. If you must be a priest, be a priest here in Austria."

"I can't," he said. "It is not possible."

She stared at him for more than a minute. "I will be here, Beauvais—not forever, but I will be here if you come back."

He nodded, got up and kissed her gently, then held her until he began trembling again. She pulled away and smiled.

"If you must go, we will celebrate Vienna for the rest of your stay!" She looked suddenly like a teenager.

"I should go back to Rome."

"You have seen enough of Rome. This is where music lives!"

Then he was alone, walking back to his small residence hotel. He could not dismiss her presence. Nor could he remain in Vienna. The following day he left for home, promising a quietly weeping Ursula to write, holding her until he again began to tremble, then kissing her and inhaling her unforgettable fragrance. He was still breathing it when he landed in New York, yearning to be back in Vienna.

Santek was lonely without Beauvais. He had lost not only the most understanding confessor in the world but his very best friend. Even though they might go days or even weeks without contact, he always knew that Gerry was available, and that made all the difference. So, counting the days until Beauvais would return, he plunged into his work.

He never stopped, reaching in every direction like the energy of spring or a warm, cleansing rain, talking, listening, laughing, consoling, praising, loving, challenging, and giving with every ounce of his being. Because he spoke street language far better than Latin, no one was outside his parish. And whether he ate the hottest tacos in the city or bought a round of beer at a factory bar, he was all priest, giving courage to the weary auto workers, smiles to the defeated blacks, courage and understanding to frightened, abandoned mothers. He was at home in a jail or pool hall, in back alleys and on avenues, as friendly to the garbageman or junk dealer as to the mayor. Even the police began to appreciate his power on the tough north side of Flint as his recreation center emerged from the ground little by little. Donations continued to pour in, not large sums alone, but nickels and dimes and quarters from the poor as well.

Usually he ignored his day off because idleness or drifting only made him more conscious of his loneliness. He visited the jails and hospitals, talked to everyone, even accompanied mothers to the welfare office when they were given a bad time. He was humorous, not aggressive, in his approach. He gave the social workers names like "Mrs. Rockefeller" and "Florence Nightingale," and they all loved him.

"What have you got today, Father?" asked a graying supervisor. They knew he usually brought legitimate claims.

"You're not going to believe this, Miss Bedroom Eyes, but my friend here played Amos on the 'Amos 'n' Andy' show, before your time. But he lost his voice singing the national anthem in Madison Square Garden and has had a tough time ever since one of your young and zealous apostles questioned his veracity. He is now working part-time in a car wash until his back royalties come through on a couple of records he cut in Swahili."

By the time they had all stopped laughing, "Miss Bedroom Eyes" had solved the man's problem. The next day she received a dozen roses from Santek with a note that the roses were free, a gift from a friendly undertaker. Meanwhile, Father Ted was off wandering the streets like the Pied Piper, giving away bats and balls and gloves to those who answered catechism questions on the "Santek International Quiz Show." The gifts came from merchants who appreciated the decrease in petty crimes and break-ins in the neighborhood. Regardless of religion, anyone who knew the catechism could earn one. He announced laughingly from the pulpit one Sunday that Jewish and Baptist kids were getting sharper than the Catholics. The item appeared the next day in the Flint *Journal*, and more donations came in for the center.

But it was not all roses. He challenged Chevrolet and Buick officials when any of his black parishioners were victims of obvious bias and, with the support of Bishop Wieber, he appeared on picket lines, no matter what the Catholic executives thought. He was a priest for the people, and his flaws were only the extensions of his virtues. Even his yearning for love was but the flip side of his desire to give it. During the year that Beauvais was gone, he had only a brief involvement with a Mexican woman after several hours on a picket line on a cold, rainy evening. She had invited him over for coffee. Ultimately nothing happened, even though she was as lonely as he was. Santek's concern was that a devout parishioner had seen him coming from her apartment, but the parishioner was not suspicious. Nothing would justify such behavior. If discovered, he could be suspended from his priesthood in ten minutes. Celibacy was the real proof of Christlike sincerity and devotion.

He joked about it with Beauvais after picking him up at Metro Airport in Detroit on his return from Europe.

"You can be lazy as a pet raccoon, but by God be celibate!"

Beauvais was able to talk about his relationship with Ursula. "It's strange. I could have stayed right there, but when I get back here it all seems impossible. Europe was another world and I was another person, and if I had stayed a few more months, I think I would have ended up with Ursula. It was the first time in my life that I really wanted to spend time with a woman, a lot of time!"

"I probably would have jumped into bed with her and ended the friendship," said Santek.

"Or begun one," said Beauvais reflectively. "We all do what we have to do." Then he brightened. "Are you ready for Florida?"

"Hell, yes, we leave next week. I've got everything taken care of."

The night before their departure, Santek stayed at the cathedral and the bishop dropped by to toast their vacation with Grady and Kelley. He looked pale and had lost weight, but his eyes sparkled.

"Here are two of my finest priests, Monsignor Grady. Santek has his center almost completed, and Gerry is going to share his new musical knowledge with all the parishes of the diocese. I want you both to get a good rest."

Grady beamed, delighted to have Beauvais back. Monsignor Kelley smiled wanly without speaking, only wondering why Beauvais needed a vacation after a year in Europe. Kelley didn't take vacations any more. There was no place to go but his widowed sister's, and they had nothing in common.

Santek had made reservations at the Deauville in Miami Beach for two weeks, and after the first few days of sun and water, food and rest, they were ready for a month more. Ted had been too tired to play golf.

"Sometimes I don't feel much like a priest," said Beauvais, as he lay on a deserted beach applying suntan lotion. "I wonder if I wouldn't have been better off in Vienna, happier and more useful." A warm letter from Ursula had disturbed him.

"Hell, Bishop Wieber wouldn't let his boy go."

"I'm sure of that, but I don't really do a priest's work any more."

"Christ, Ger, the people need music and the liturgy. It's the heart of the whole thing!"

"But you're in the thick of things—with real people."

Santek laughed. "And after eight years that gets tiresome too. I finally understand what happens to a man like my pastor, Monsignor Slowinski. He probably did it all: people needing jobs, wives and kids deserted, people without enough food to eat and too proud to tell anyone. Now he just counts the collection, watches TV, pays the bills, and drinks his half a case of beer a day. I used to criticize. Now I look and see myself down the road: no kids, no wife, no reason to go on. Once in a while he hears confessions or says a funeral Mass for someone he's known all his life. He's sixty-three going on eighty. I guess it's a lonely life if you lose your way."

Beauvais nodded and rubbed on more lotion, then handed it to Santek, who continued talking.

"Sometimes I wonder if Slowinski believes any more. He just sits in that old chair, chain-smokes and drinks, glances at the paper or his breviary. It doesn't really matter what's on TV. Usually he won't answer the phone. My heart goes out to him. I think he worked so hard for a Slovak parish for thirty years that when the blacks moved in he was devastated. Now I work for the blacks and then what? Christ, it scares me. There are too damn many priests who quit after ten or twenty or thirty years. I think celibacy really sucks! It's not that hard for most of 'em, but it just doesn't make any sense."

Beauvais nodded. "I think if you love what you do, it can make sense. I mean, Ursula is a beautiful woman and a great friend, but somehow I felt I had some work to do and marriage might interfere."

"But what about twenty years from now, Ger?"

"I don't know. Maybe it all depends on how we relate to God. Or whether or not we lose our faith. It could be our spirituality that's the problem. What do we really know about prayer and any deep, mystical contact with God?"

Santek laughed. "And what do we really know about women?"

At the end of a week, they both had a deep tan and had gained five pounds from elaborate meals. Santek talked Beauvais into the first golf game of his life. By the fourth hole they were both laughing so hard at Gerry's swing they couldn't stand up.

"Shit, there won't be a gopher in Florida that's not terrified!"

They managed nine holes despite a litany of curses from the serious linksmen who dodged Beauvais's missiles. Santek shot forty-two. Gerry lost count at one hundred and nineteen.

The final weekend they were in Florida, Beauvais attended a Beethoven concert and Santek went out bar-hopping. Beauvais arrived back at the hotel around midnight after mediocre music and great corned beef on rye. He sipped a beer and finally fell asleep around two. Santek showed up the next morning around ten while Beauvais was making coffee.

"Don't tell me you got lost in the Everglades." He poured himself a cup of coffee and stretched out on the couch.

"I'm in real trouble, Ger. Real trouble!"

"You're still alive. It can't be too bad."

"I hit a few bars and was having a good time talking the usual bullshit, my ranch in Texas, my soap factory in Wyoming. A million laughs and half a dozen invitations to bed.

"I didn't drink that much, and about midnight I was ready to come home. Horny, but victorious and kind of proud of myself. Anyway, I was a little restless and I decided on a nightcap at a little Polynesian bar just down the way. A few couples were dancing to a combo, and there was one woman chatting with the bartender. He was trying to make time with her. Finally she looked over at me. I couldn't believe her face. It was like a madonna, I mean a warm, sensitive, real face like you dream about. Kind of honey hair, these light-blue eyes, perfect skin, nice body and all that, but just some quality that blew me away. Maybe it was a kind of innocence. I don't know. She's a Canadian from a small town in Ontario and came down just to think things over. We danced for a while and I felt like I was falling in love. I mean, I didn't think about taking her to bed or talking bullshit. I just couldn't leave her.

"At first I told her I was a DJ at a small station in Detroit and she never questioned it, even though I knew she didn't believe me. We walked along the beach, watched the waves, just kept talking. I didn't even touch her. We finally kissed gently a few times, but it was like I didn't want to spoil some mood. Sometimes we just looked at each other without a word. It was more than chemistry. It was crazy: physical and spiritual all at once. Honest to God, I'd have married her on the spot if I'd been free. No questions asked!

"By four o'clock I was in love. We got something to eat, took a few blankets from her place, walked back to the beach, and lay there snuggling and talking like old friends until the sun came up. I wanted in the worst way to tell her the truth, but I just couldn't. It would have ended everything. But for the first time in my life, Ger, I didn't want to tell one more lie about anything.

"She lay there in my arms and gradually told me her whole story. Her name is Angela Fortier, and she's been a devout Catholic all her life. She even flirted with the convent for a few years. Her mother's dead, she raised a couple of brothers who are now married, and she lives alone with her father and teaches school. She planned on marrying a guy last year, not really in love but wanting kids of her own and believing it was her last good chance. He was a decent, dependable, kind man she'd known since childhood. Then damned if he wasn't killed in a lumber-camp accident and she started thinking about the convent again. She's almost thirty and this is her first vacation since high school. She really came here to get away and

84

make up her mind about the future." He paused and spoke softly. "I think she's falling in love with me too, Ger. I'm not sure but I've got to find out, so I'm gonna stay here another week. You cover for me. Tell Slowinski I got the flu or stayed out in the sun too long. He knows I burn like a hot dog. Christ, tell him anything!"

Beauvais got up from the couch and poured Ted a cup of coffee, then put his arm around his shoulder. "You can't stay, Ted. You've come too far. You'll be over her in a month. If you stay, you just screw up two lives. I want you to come back with me."

Santek stood up and stared into Gerry's eyes. "I can't do it. All my life I've been doing what I was supposed to. It may not look like it, but I well may have become a priest because that's what my mother and Father Al wanted. This time I'm going to make up my own mind. I'm no kid any more. Angela Fortier is in my damn blood! This isn't your horny, confused buddy talking. I know the difference, for Christ's sake!"

He lit a cigarette. "All night long I met half-drunk losers: lonely, divorced, abandoned, aggressive, depressed, clinging women ready to go to bed with damn near anyone. Then I met Angie. Ever since she came down here, she met the same kind of people I did. Married men, crazies, drunks, gigolos, playboys, veteran bartenders, even a friendly dyke. She couldn't believe I was real. I felt the same way about her. I'm not going back, Ger. I can't! I've got to find out. And I've got to tell her the truth, no matter what."

Beauvais knew Santek well enough to realize that nothing would change his mind. There wasn't anything else to say.

Santek drove him in the rented car to the airport. Neither of them spoke until the flight was ready for boarding.

"I'll see you in a week." Santek smiled sheepishly.

Beauvais nodded softly. "You were born to be a priest, Ted. More than anyone I know. Don't throw it all away. This will pass."

"I guess I've got to find out for myself." He embraced his friend warmly and made his way out of the terminal to find Angela Fortier. And Ted Santek.

Ted wondered if it wasn't the happiest week of his life. Angela had no doubts. They did it all, sipping frozen daiquiris and dancing almost alone till dawn to the music of Glenn Miller at a small beach-front bar they adopted as their own. Later they walked along the strand in the moonlight, building their dream house in the sand, splashing and hugging, leaping like children, clothes and all, into the warm water and then silently watching the waves turn silver and gold in the dancing light of a peaceful, now sacred night. At last they returned to her room, holding each other as if they feared to let go, then fondled and kissed hungrily like adolescents until they fell asleep from exhaustion. They awoke laughing, only to embrace again and again as if time and place meant nothing, as if they were the last two people left on earth. Only when he tried to make love did she resist him, gently and then almost firmly.

"It's not right," she said quietly. "It's only for marriage."

Yet she did not resist his touch when he massaged her breasts and thighs, nor did she move away when she felt his hardness against her legs, or even when he brought her curious, excited hand to his groin. Somehow, in her French-Canadian morality, none of this was wrong because she knew she loved him. Only intercourse was denied him, the mortal sin that could tarnish their love and incur the wrath of their God. And surprisingly, Ted Santek made no seductive moves to change her mind or threaten her ancient ethic. As long as she was with him, it was enough. He had not laughed like this in months.

And they talked and talked, afternoons and evenings and far into the night. She told him of the children she wanted, at least three boys who would look like miniature versions of Ted so that his whole life would pass before her every day they were together. And he told of his desire to run a home for young men who knew nothing but the streets. To give them a new vision of life, to challenge their minds and reform their hearts.

"We could do it together," she said softly.

"Who the hell's gonna take care of the kids?"

She laughed. "We'll do that together too."

He talked of his old neighborhood and the kids who never really had a chance, of the blacks who gave up on life, and the hollow eyes that lived on dope and booze because they knew no other way.

"All my life I've wanted to be a helper. It's the one thing I'm good at. People listen to me. They know I understand. They know I care."

"It sounds much more exciting than the convent," she said. "We could do whatever we want."

When he leaned to kiss her he felt her very soul and young idealism blend with his own. He held her for several minutes, then began tickling her, and they were laughing again.

She mocked his clumsy French; he imitated her accent and elegantly feminine gait. They gathered shells, fished unsuccessfully from the pier, then ate shrimp and drank beer and talked to the pelicans that waddled nearby to beg for bits of French bread. Everything made them laugh, every kiss seemed fresh and inviting, every touch brought new life and a rush of sensuality. At times he only stared at her as if he could not believe her beauty. She traced her fingers across his hands and lips and the rugged, angular nose. Then they kissed softly as if for the very first time.

It was after such a kiss, and enough daiquiris, as the sun was setting on their last night, that he looked at her sadly and told her the truth about himself.

At first she laughed. "A priest! And I'm really a nun!"

But his eyes told her he was not joking. She turned white, then began to tremble and retreated to her childhood French.

"Mon Dieu, mon cher Dieu!" Then her eyes filled with tears and her whole body was convulsed by sobs.

He tried to hold her, but she pulled away and covered her eyes as if it were now forbidden to look at him. She continued to cry and moan softly in an unintelligible French patois. Again he reached to put his arms around her and she resisted, calling him *"mon père."*

Finally she was able to walk and took his hand like a small child as they made their way back to her room. In semidarkness she made tea without a word. Santek sat on the couch and tried to talk to her.

"I can get a dispensation, Angie. I want to leave. I never really wanted to be a priest in the first place! I was going to leave before I ever met you."

She continued brewing the tea in silence.

"Damn it, Angie, talk to me! For God's sake, I love you! I need you! Don't ignore me. I'm still your friend, no matter what. You can't just turn away like I don't exist." He was shouting.

She looked at him with hurt, innocent blue eyes, still stained with her tears but now, finally, lusterless and defeated, as if there were no joy left for her on earth. She shook her head. It was all too much. There was no longer anything or anyone to believe in.

"But what if I weren't a priest?"

"But you are," she said softly, some gentle strength returning. "God found you first. You belong to him." She spoke simply, like a child.

"There must be some way, Angie!" He was pleading as never before.

"There is. I go back to Canada, and you return to your priesthood. I can't see you again. I just can't. I only hope that God will forgive us."

"But we didn't do anything!"

It was no use. She wasn't listening. When he finished his tea, she got up and moved toward the door. She opened it and extended her hand.

"Goodbye, Father Santek, I will never forget you."

He went out, too weak to protest any more. He heard the door close and lock behind him. "Angie. My God, Angie, we can't end things like this. . . ."

There was only silence. He sat on the steps outside her room, his head in his hands, convinced that he had let the most important person in his life slip away. He knew her conscience. He had helped to form a thousand just like it. An entire history was against him, and no amount of Polish charm could ever change it. He got up slowly, sadly, and made his way back to the Deauville in a daze.

Behind the locked door, Angie began packing her bags. Her eyes now flooded with tears as her whole life seemed to pass before her. Everything till now had been pain and responsibility. She thought of her mother's death when she was twelve, with two little brothers to raise. For weeks her father had not spoken, and he had refused to pray or attend Mass. She had held the family together. There was never time for ice skating or swimming, dating or parties. Her teaching had become her only joy until she decided to marry and have a family. It didn't matter if she was not in love. He would give her children and be good to her. Then the man she had chosen was dead and her father was as despondent as she was.

There was a curse on the family, some spiritual blight. She must enter the convent. God had now spoken clearly.

Florida had been the last chance to clear her head. And Ted Santek had briefly made all her dreams come true. She had thanked God a hundred times as they walked on the beach. She finally understood her life of pain and sacrifice. She would have married him the very next day, no questions asked.

Then came the horror of knowing he was a priest, and she fell into the worst gloom she had ever experienced. She wanted to die, briefly hated God and her religion, wanted to desecrate her body and lose her virginity to anyone. Finally she just fell on the bed and cried. She could never see him again. There could never be anyone else. Even to remember his face, his kiss, his gentle touch would be to offend her religion. Now she knew she must be a nun, even though the convent was never an escape but rather a great, priceless gift for the chosen few. And even though she could only with great effort cling to her faltering God—whose face was that of Father Ted Santek.

Chapter 8

Ted Santek was obsessed with the memory and radiance of Angela Fortier. He returned to Flint from his Florida vacation with a deep tan but with a deeper pain in his chest and a lack of interest in much of his priestly work. He had to see her, to get something resolved. Her memory clung to him like his own skin and breath. Her eyes seemed to stare lovingly at him from the congregation when he said Mass. He would hear her voice in a crowd. The pain of missing her was so acute that he could think of nothing else. Had it been a sexual longing, he could have resolved it through fantasy or masturbation, but he missed her very presence and being, and for that there was no relief. It was a new experience for him, an incredibly painful one that had to be relieved. He knew that she lived and taught in Moncrief, a small Ontario town in the middle of nowhere, approximately a four-hour drive from Flint, but it was difficult to take more time off after returning from an already extended vacation.

The gym was in the final stages of completion, school was in session and there were extensive preparations for the three high school religion classes he taught every morning. One of the young nuns was terribly troubled by a lesbian relationship during the summer and could talk only to Father Santek. Men came looking for a job, welfare checks had been stolen, a mother with seven kids was running out of resources to find food, and Buick had laid off five hundred men on the line. There were pregnancies in high school, pending divorces, a father sleeping with his teenage daughter—the procession was endless. Monsignor Slowinski sat in his chair, watched TV game shows, and drank beer, laughing at Milton Berle and spilling ashes over his cassock.

It was no time for Ted Santek to be licking his wounds, but he was powerless to let go of Angie. Plans for painting the recreation center had to be decided on, a Polish priest hired in his absence had accused America of being soft on communism, and a Korean veteran had slapped him in front of the church.

"Go back to Poland, you foreign son-of-a-bitch. I lost two fingers fighting those Commie bastards."

The whole parish was a vortex of problems only he could solve, but Ted could not pull himself together. It was all he could do to say Mass and recite his breviary with minimal concentration. He cursed his own weakness and begged God to free him from the hold that Angie had on him.

At the meeting of the athletic committee on the new gym, he struggled to be enthusiastic and dynamic, but his mind kept drifting to that solitary beach in Florida on a dawn streaked with unforgettable light blue and butterscotch—as if soft morning colors had retextured his whole life. A woman with honey hair and round, guileless blue eyes, long legs, and a deep spirituality had transformed him. He stroked her caramel-colored skin, smiled at her piquant French accent, and was carried away by the child's laugh that lit up her whole being. But more than all this, he loved her.

"I think we should have boxing, don't you, Father?" Ned Gramulski, a graying forty with an athlete's face, was the brightest and hardest worker in the parish.

"Boxing? Yeah, I suppose we should." The enthusiasm and sense of humor were gone. He tried again: "Boxing will be great." He said it hollowly.

Ned continued exuberantly. "We could field a Golden Gloves team that would be the best in the city, give these kids some pride. Lefty Zabelka is one hell of a trainer. He went ten rounds with Graziano and would have beat him if he hadn't cut his eye in the seventh. He can round up five or six guys. Old Jerzy Krinski managed two or three contenders years ago. One of his boys fought Tony Zale."

"That sounds great. It's okay by me." He was pale and listless and complained of the flu.

A few minutes later, he excused himself and indicated that whatever the men decided was agreeable to him. They were dumbfounded. The recreation center had been his dream, and now he acted as if it didn't really matter. Maybe their charismatic leader was seriously ill. Word spread through the parish, and thousands of sudden prayers, black and white, Protestant, Jewish, and Catholic, invaded the heavens.

After leaving the meeting, Santek was too restless to do anything. He paced back and forth in his room, sipped a drink, and smoked two cigarettes. He didn't know what he wanted to do except to see Angie. He had to.

Later that evening he drove the fifty miles to see Beauvais. He slumped helplessly in a chair, declining a stiff bourbon on the rocks.

"I can't get her out of my mind, Ger. It feels like I've been tricked into the priesthood. I was no more meant to be a priest than Frank Sinatra. Why am I so damn angry?"

"Just hang on. You'll get over it."

"I don't think so. I've just got to talk to her."

"What's there to say? You've got nothing to offer her. Even if you left the priesthood, she wouldn't marry you. You've got to throw yourself into your work with more energy than before."

Beauvais was as distressed and pale as his friend, not really knowing what to say and fearing that Ted might really leave the priesthood. He had never seen him like this.

"That's just what I can't do. I don't give a damn about anything but her. She's not just a piece of ass. I love her."

"Maybe you should go to bed with her," said Beauvais thoughtfully, sucking awkwardly on a new pipe he had bought to cut down on cigarettes. "I know that's not priestly advice, but she can be a great illusion. You hardly know her." He tried to relight his pipe. "Maybe if you just screwed your brains out, you'd get some perspective on this. You can't throw away your priesthood. It would ultimately kill you. You're the best there is, man!" He tossed the pipe away and lit a cigarette.

"I've known a lot of women in my life. Even in my priesthood I look around and admire. But this is different. I am on my ass! I can't pull out of this. Ger, can't you hear me?" He was pleading.

Beauvais felt his friend's pain as if it were his own. "Then maybe you have to see her again. Get the hell up to Canada and do what you have to, but don't give up your priesthood, for God's sake! That's what makes you who you are."

Beauvais's encouragement was all Santek needed. He lied to Monsignor Slowinski about a brother in the hospital, made a few essential phone calls, gave money where it was needed, referred a couple of urgent cases to Gerry, and was off the same night. He stayed overnight in London, slept badly, had breakfast in Stratford, and then drove through the little villages and along country roads to Moncrief.

The town was smaller than he had expected. He stopped at a general store, drank a pint of chocolate milk, ate a stale doughnut, took a coffee to go, and was off to the school a mile and a half down the same road. It was not quite eleven o'clock. He waited in his car, listening to music and strange Canadian accents on the news, sipped his coffee, and chain-smoked Pall Malls. Finally he got out of the car and walked nervously through the front door of the single-story brick school.

In his light blue slacks and dark blue nylon jacket, he looked like a football coach. There was no one around. He walked quietly down the main corridor. The classroom doors were open, and an elderly woman was teaching geography to about a dozen nine- or ten-year-olds. She did not look up. Nor did a young man on the opposite side of the corridor, teaching long division to a slightly older group.

Then Ted suddenly heard her voice, and his heart almost stopped. What could he say? He couldn't just knock on the door and start where they had left off. His mouth was dry, his eyes moist; he could feel an emptiness in the pit of his stomach and a sharp pain that refused to leave his chest. He was trembling with excitement and fear. He had no right to be here. She had made her position clear. But he couldn't exist without her. His priesthood suddenly meant nothing. Her very voice tore him apart.

"Adjectives always modify nouns so they go on a straight line under the noun like this. 'The grizzly bear is a mean, hungry, fat bear.'" The children laughed loudly. "*Mean, hungry,* and *fat* all modify the bear. They tell us something about the bear. Adverbs modify verbs. 'The mean, hungry, fat bear walks slowly.' *Slowly* is an adverb."

Her voice was soft and soothing, and he hated her for it. He wanted her to be as desperate as he was and resented the mellifluous flow of soft words and the laughter of the children. He wanted to rush in and hold her in his arms, to scream out his pain, to tear her away, like Errol Flynn in some swashbuckling movie. Listening to her brought it all back more acutely: the first gentle embrace and quiet conversation as they had waited for the dawn; then the sobs, deep and wrenching, that shook her body in sudden spasms as he held her protectively while twilight had appeared as a

93

rude intruder, erasing the sun. Now he wondered if her nights were as miserable as his, if she saw his face staring at her from every cloud and tree and heard his voice in every silence.

A bell rang and students came pouring into the corridor, giggling when they saw him. He stood awkwardly as they rushed by, snickering at this novelty in their school. He moved against the wall like a vagrant, then was blocking someone's locker and moved awkwardly again, still staring at her classroom door, not knowing what he would do or say if she came out. He could hear the screams of children as they raced outside with their lunch sacks. Cautiously he moved toward the open door, peered in, and saw Angela arranging a display of autumn leaves on the bulletin board. His heart almost left his chest as he studied her face, her long legs, the outline of her breasts. God, he loved her! She stood back to admire the display as he moved into the doorway. She looked up and her whole body flushed. For several seconds she was speechless. He moved toward her like a shy new student. All his bravado was gone.

"You shouldn't have come!"

"I had to. God, Angie, I had to! I've been going nuts! I haven't been able to do anything but think of you. I can't do my work. It doesn't mean anything. Nothing means anything." His eyes watered. "God damn it, I can't live without you! I won't, I won't! You can't do this to me. What the hell's it doing to you? Christ, how can you teach?"

He moved toward her to take her in his arms. She stiffened and kissed him lightly on the cheek. Her whole body trembled. He felt rebuffed and foolish and did not know what else to say. He fought his emotions, lest he blubber like a little boy. Most of all he hated her Catholic control that could think and reflect.

"We can't stay here. I know a place, but we only have an hour."

He wanted to kiss away her coolness, to reduce her to his passion and anguish.

They walked through the crowded schoolyard to his car. The children buzzed with excitement and more giggles. She did not acknowledge them and got into the car stiffly when he opened the door, clutching her brown paper lunch bag and small thermos, still totally in control of herself. Only when they moved away from the schoolyard did she begin to weep.

With difficulty, she directed him a mile down the road beyond a bridge over a small stream and waterfall. They got out slowly and leaned against a large oak at the edge of a grove, the leaves tinged

94

with red and gold. A startled fawn stared briefly, then ran awk-wardly away in the midst of a drink. A squirrel chattered. Then it was silent except for distant crows and the fresh water chuckling softly over the rocks. He noted that the color of the water matched her hair, but still he could not talk. He stared almost fiercely to control his pain. She opened the lunch bag and pulled out an apple and a single sandwich. She spoke softly.

"Not much of a picnic. It's cheese. I hope you like it. The bread's homemade. I'm not hungry." She spoke quickly, as if her voice would take leave. She handed the sandwich to him and he munched slowly, thoughtfully, then almost cautiously put his arm around her as he ate. She relaxed partially and opened the thermos, sipping the iced tea briefly. A truck drove by, stirring up dust along the road, and instinctively she turned her head away.

"Angie, I want to marry you." He blurted it out without inflec-tion or passion.

"You can't leave your priesthood." Her voice was aghast. "I can't take you from God. I would be doomed forever." She paused. "Maybe I could handle that, but you would be lost as well."

"There's nothing without you. I never should have been a priest. Don't you love me?"

"More than I thought possible. More than myself. I've thought only of you. But you love your priesthood. You told me you did."

"Not without you! I didn't plan on falling in love. I wasn't looking for you, for God's sake. You just were there. I hardly know you, and I can't get you out of my head. This never happened to me before. Damn it, Angie, I'm not a boy! I'm thirty-five years old and I'm in love. You can't just turn me away. I'll try for a dispensation, no matter how long it takes. I'll leave for Rome tomorrow! I'll—"

"No," she said firmly. "Never! I couldn't live with myself." Her face flushed, her chest swelled. She was beautiful, as her whole French-Catholic inheritance rose up in her to do battle. He knew why he loved her: the integrity, the beauty, the total loyalty. Some control returned to him, realizing that everything in her that was human wanted him.

He leaned over and kissed her firmly on the mouth. She stiff-ened, but did not move her mouth away, and soon softened. They kissed for several minutes as her whole body seemed to open to him. Gently he stroked her hair and cheeks, her neck and breasts, with all the love of his being. She clung to him, protesting nothing. Then they lay down gently on the soft grass and embraced tenderly, as if the least passion would be an intrusion. Only then did the pain in Santek's side go away. He continued to caress her with the tips of his fingers and felt her lips softly exploring his. He had never known such pleasure, such gentleness, such total absorption without thought of time or pleasure. He felt totally helpless, as if he could not move. Only gradually did her breathing become labored, and her body trembled in tiny spasms as they continued to kiss. Now he wanted her and knew that she wanted him. He moved his hand down her thigh and under her dress and felt her flowing wetness. For once in his life it was not a conquest or an invitation to some personal pleasure. It was her total love.

Gently she began to resist. "Oh, dear God, I want you so much, so much! But I just can't! I've got to get back. I've . . . oh, God, you're a priest, a priest. . . . You're a priest!"

Only then did he begin to panic. He held her fast and continued trying to kiss her and touch her, not really wanting sex but her surrender. She pushed him gently away, then firmly, almost frantically, and turned her face toward the stream. Then, with heroic effort, still trembling, she stood up and walked weakly a few feet away from him. Ted was still sprawled awkwardly against the oak tree as she adjusted her dress. An eager leaf fell to the ground, its life abruptly ended with a final frail murmur on the grass.

"I'm entering the convent for certain. My doubts have disappeared. I think our meeting was a sign from God." She spoke in a whisper, as if she had no energy to fight him. Her whole body wanted to surrender to his wild love.

"Oh, no, for Christ's sake, no!" A chill breeze stabbed him, and two or three more leaves fell from the tree. He still could not move and for the first time in his life wondered if his life had any meaning.

"I've already made my decision. I'm joining the Daughters of Mercy in Toronto." Her voice was flat and unconvincing. She still could not look at him, lest she dissolve in his arms, choosing him over her distant Christ.

There was nothing Ted could say. He felt the blood drain from his body; he could barely move. She continued to stare at the stream, as he lay sprawled against the tree, for ten minutes of silence. Her body still trembled.

"I've got to get back to class." His obvious pain made her breathing labored. "I'll always love you." She said it with every ounce of her being.

He could not respond. He stood up like a robot and moved toward the car. Listlessly he opened her door, still unable to speak, and drove back to the small brick school. The children were moving from the play yard into the building, a small spotted dog looking mournfully after them as if startled to be suddenly all alone. The sun had disappeared, and the whole area seemed shrouded in the grayness of the sky.

He parked the car in front of the building. Neither of them moved. Finally he spoke with new energy dredged from somewhere. Ted Santek had never been rejected by a woman.

"Let's have dinner tonight! I'll wait till after school." He knew she could not refuse. He needed more time and the caresses of evening. Darkness would be his friend and powerful ally. He knew she wanted him. He just needed more time to dissolve her guilt.

"No, it would only be harder," she said. "Goodbye." She feared to look at him. Her heart pounded wildly.

She opened her door, then leaned over and kissed him softly on the cheek. She held his hand and kissed it reverently, summoning all the strength of the peasant blood that had beat the forest land into subjection a century ago, the strength that had made her dry her tears and, still a child, raise a family. She had denied herself as Santek never had. Her courage could move glaciers and forests.

"No one but God could take you away from me!" But her God had spoken for eons, and his voice was unchanging. Santek was finally defeated. There was no victory over a peasant's God. His own mother was proof of that.

She slid out of the car and walked slowly toward the school. The dog approached her, and she patted him briefly on the nose. Then she turned once more, her face pinched in pain. She stared longingly for a few moments, then turned and walked resolutely into the building.

Ted watched her disappear, fought an impulse to rush inside, then lit a cigarette and smoked it slowly, staring off into the distance. Finally he started the car and drove away. Only the dog watched him leave. His strength was gone, his mind blank; there was nothing to say or do. In a stupor, he found the highway and somehow kept the car on the road.

As he rode back to Detroit, a quiet rage replaced his deep hurt and filtered slowly through his body. He still did not understand his love for her and his incapacity to walk away with any grace, but by the time he reached the tunnel under the Detroit River he knew only a wild, crazy anger. At first he thought of stopping to see Father Al and attacking him for pushing a young idealistic man into the priesthood. But what was there really to say? Father Al could tell him nothing. Even Beauvais had pious clichés to offer. He hated God and the Church, hated his whole misdirected life, which had destroyed his freedom and chained his manhood with a pointless celibacy.

He stopped at a small bar and ordered a couple of beers. There was no one he knew who could help—except Angie, and some medieval God had stolen her. There was no reason to go back to the parish. There was no reason to do anything.

He continued to drink like a Ham Town thug. A thin, blond woman of forty with a sad, worn face and plump figure sat one barstool away. Her skirt was pulled up to the middle of her thighs and her man's shirt showed too much cleavage. She addressed him playfully as "Scaramouche" until he forced himself to smile and move next to her. They exchanged pleasantries, and he told her the usual lies as if he were an actor playing a part from some distant memory and she a meaningless mannequin. Immediately attracted by the animal sexuality he exuded, she took him to her small, neat apartment in Highland Park where she offered him red wine. Within minutes he was undressing her. Neither of them said a word, she overwhelmed by this sudden violent passion, he lost in the confusion of his own pain.

His anger and hurt exploded into a devouring sensuality which met her own loneliness and desperate need. He let go completely, with all the passion of years of self-denial and the unbearable rejection by the only woman he had ever loved. His rage came pouring out in the merging of mouths and groins, arms and legs without gentleness or reflection. He could not stop, nor did she want him to. No one had ever desired her like this, loved her like this. Toes, eyes, ears, breasts, thighs, mouth, he was like a starving man who finally found food, and she flowed with his every attack. He grabbed and sucked, rubbed and bit, pounded like a threshing machine, fiercely unaware of the whole scene. Had he chosen to fight a man rather than make love to a woman, he would have fought to self-destruction.

Then it all ended as abruptly as it began. Three hours had passed like fifteen minutes. Without a word, in a total daze, he put on his clothes. She lay watching him, naked and helpless, pitifully aware that she barely existed to him. It was as if he had been alone.

He walked to his car, removed a ticket from the wiper blade,

98

tore it to bits, and drove slowly away, realizing even more acutely that he didn't want to be a priest, that he had been trapped by God and the Catholic Church, whose inane idealism had begun to destroy him, and that the only woman he had ever really loved was the victim of this same historic and superstitious God.

He drove straight to Lansing, somehow freed by his anger. It was early morning when he walked in the back door of the cathedral and up the stairs to Beauvais's room. He sat on the bed. Gerry looked up groggily, then smiled warmly and looked at his watch.

"You keep strange hours, man."

Santek said nothing. He walked into the other room and sat down next to the stereo cabinet and poured himself some brandy. Beauvais slipped on a robe, sat down opposite him, and lighted a cigarette. He offered one to Ted, who declined it.

"I want out, Ger," he said quietly, though rage shone in his glazed eyes. Beauvais was terrified. He remembered another man a year ago, with the same glazed look, who had murdered his wife and children and asked Beauvais to call the police.

"What the hell happened?"

Ted told him in a monotone of Angie's refusal and her plans to enter the convent. "She could just walk away! I mean, my God, she could just turn and walk back to school like a vacation was over. I don't understand that kind of strength and coldness."

"It's called 'God,' Ted. It's the God we gave them. Human feelings don't count."

Then Ted recounted dispassionately the whole tale of the blond woman, from bar to bed. "It was like she meant nothing! That's the worst damn sin of all! She was probably hurting as much as I was, but I didn't give a shit."

"Do you want absolution?"

"Hell, no! I don't feel sorry for anything except losing Angie." His voice sounded as if a dark, demonic spirit had taken possession of his soul and reduced the irrepressible Santek to a corpse.

Beauvais sucked on his cigarette, then lit another from the stub, struggling frantically to say something to exorcise his friend's ugly, shrouded evil spirit.

"It would take months to get out of the priesthood, maybe years, maybe never. Even if Pope John were still alive he couldn't simplify that. The Curia would have you for lunch."

"I'm not talking about going through channels. I just want to get the hell out and start over. The only thing holding me back is my family—my mom, really." He was beginning to sound like himself as the fierce anger gave way to the empty monotone of sorrow.

"I think this will all pass, Ted. You've just got to throw yourself into your work. You're as great a priest as I know. The people need you. They really love you. I mean *love* you." Beauvais knew his words rang hollow, but he said them dramatically to break through the steel fog that separated them.

"That's all changed, Ger. I feel completely empty inside."

"Kneel down and I'll give you absolution. You'll feel a hell of a lot better." Gerry was pleading.

Santek looked at his friend sadly. "It would be bullshit. I've got to think things over." His voice had lost all inflection again, as if pain and anger enveloped him in a diabolic presence.

He made his way to the door. Beauvais put his hand gently on his shoulder. "I'm here if you need me." Then he smiled. "You could always go in the service. At least you wouldn't have to babysit your pastor. It could be a distraction and a time of healing."

Santek looked at him and nodded. Gerry wondered if he had really heard him.

Chapter 9

Theodore Santek was commissioned a first lieutenant in the U.S. Air Force in the winter of 1963, a few weeks after President Kennedy's death. The tragedy had seemed to bring him back to his senses and give some purpose to his life. The people of Sacred Heart parish and on the north side of Flint were crushed with additional sorrow after losing their President. No priest had ever made such an impact. It was as if Christ had left his people. Santek could not face their deep disappointment and refused a going-away party. Even Bishop Wieber, now growing extremely feeble, was torn by his decision, but he knew the crying need for chaplains.

"I hate to lose you, Father. You've done tremendous work in the north of Flint. But the men in service need someone like you."

Santek was embarrassed by the praise. In the months of rage and confusion since Angie, he still had not been to confession. He had paid only token attention to the new recreation center at Sacred Heart, but had received full credit for what the men of the parish had been able to accomplish. He had ignored priests, even Beauvais, drinking and brooding and finally giving free rein to his seemingly endless appetite for sex. It was as if his devotion to the priesthood and the service of the people had been transformed into a massive binge of sex and self-indulgence.

He even became involved with one of the high school girls, a buxom brunette of sixteen who had not so innocently flirted with him ever since he had been assigned to the parish. One night after a school dance, they had driven to a secret spot, hardly twenty minutes from the rectory. After too much wine, he had fondled her full young breasts and begun exploring under her skirt before he realized the consequences of what he was doing. Then guilt and shame overwhelmed him, and he was able to get her out of the car.

He continued to brood and drink, slept fitfully, then again felt the massive guilt. Finally he would feel the hurt of Angie again, and his own rage against the Church. Then the guilt would dissolve, and like an alcoholic, the vicious circle of the sexual drug would begin again.

He withdrew from his painful reverie and heard the bishop's soft voice.

"The men in Vietnam really need you, Father. It's an insane war. You will give them something no one else can. God has given you great and special gifts. Your people love you."

Santek could only nod and smile appreciatively and remember the married women who had loved him in the past weeks.

Ted had been warned in the seminary, priests joked about it—in fact, it was a truism—that the celibate cleric was for some women a prized trophy, for others the spiritual kind of man who fulfilled a romantic dream. The feminine affection for Santek had not only been expressed in homemade bread and gifts on his birthday, frequent phone calls, and visits to seek counseling. The women also pursued him after novenas, parish suppers, or even during football games, or volunteered to chaperone high school dances, knowing he would make an appearance. They attended his Masses, lingering afterward to commend his sermon or invite him to breakfast. All he had to do was make the first move and they were his, and if it felt like love, it superseded all the ecclesiastical bans that made sex with a priest the unpardonable sin.

He was, for them, the ultimate norm of all morality. Otherwise, why would they have tolerated the Church's inhumane position on birth control and sex and divorce? From the start, he had exuded animal charm, but the rage that now burned inside him created an intensity that made him irresistible. He made impulsive love with a secretary in a darkened parking lot, caressed and fondled and explored a passionate young mother in the church sacristy. Oral sex that a beautiful Lebanese woman had denied her husband was not only permissible but almost holy in a darkened church basement. No place was too dangerous: a garage, behind a bush in the backyard while the husband was fixing drinks inside. He took any chance, and the women, as hungry and confused as he was, threw all caution aside. It was as if the lonely and unloved could refuse him nothing.

His own sexual appetite, long disciplined and seemingly diminished in his active ministry, now came hungrily alive. Sex was on his mind from morning till night. He reactivated his relationship with an attractive Mexican woman he had met on a Buick picket line. Her own culture and sophistication saw no real point in a sterile celibacy. He called her from his office.

"Cerita, what time are you through work?"

"In about an hour, Father. Do you need me?"

"I have some work."

"I will come sooner."

They would begin working in the office, and he would end up undressing her—in his rectory bedroom or in the school infirmary—and enjoying a flowing, flaming, explosive sensuality that ignited him for hours—once for a day and a night in a discreet Detroit hotel. She was like a hallucinogen, her every undulating motion a total sensuality, her full olive breasts and grinding hips and her healthy appetite releasing every inhibition to create an unending panorama of pleasure. But no stimulation, no matter how absorbing and imaginative, was ever enough. A dying man, he clung for life to her groans and softness, the moistures and varieties and paroxysms of her sensuality. Every taste and touch, every spasm and beckoning orifice with its attendant rewards, only pleaded for more. And she was a veritable goddess of love whose needs and appetites, history and sensitivity, were as wild and insatiable as his own, because she had fallen deeply in love. But he wanted sex to do what only love could, and each woman in turn, even the curvaceous, loving Mexican, finally abandoned him to his sexual madness if he had not first tired of her.

Then guilt would overwhelm him, and the blackest kind of despair. He wanted to call Angie, to get her to rescue him from this madness, but feared greater rejection. He tried desperately to pray, to make his Mass mean something, to reactivate his parish work. He drank as much as the pastor he had criticized, avoided any social contact with parishioners unless it might lead to some sexual alliance. He stalked the women he wanted like a private investigator, then blamed his priestly commitment when he tired of them or needed new stimulation. That he did not go over the edge was only a testimony to the depths of his hurt and hunger and the strength of his Polish constitution. He continued to say Mass without great guilt, neglected his breviary, and generally discontinued private prayer and meditation. He taught his classes perfunctorily, without preparation, or called them off at the slightest provocation. Sex had become an all-absorbing master.

Nor were non-Catholic women in the parish out of bounds, when once he would have feared the massive scandal that he gave, the scandal that Christ had so stringently forbidden with ominous words of condemnation. When he was assigned to seek marriage testimony from a tall, sultry brunette young woman a few blocks from the parish, his very presence had the same sensual effect. It was late in the afternoon when he rang the bell to her apartment.

"Marjorie Standish?" He liked her long brown hair and the loose way she stood in the doorway.

"Yes?" She said it slowly, almost seductively.

"I'm Father Ted Santek from Sacred Heart. A friend of yours wants to marry a Catholic, and I have a form for you to fill out establishing that she was never, to your knowledge, baptized or married by a Catholic priest."

She had never seen a priest up close before. All her own fantasies were unleashed to mesh with his. She let him in, offered him coffee, and sat beside him on the couch. Within a few minutes he began a spontaneous seduction. He seemed powerless to do anything else, lost in an endless depression that threatened to destroy his very soul. Sex, like any drug, gave him brief respite, then tore at his mind and body more fiercely.

"It's really good of you to give me the time." He looked directly into her eyes and then boldly explored her body.

She was already flustered. "Really, I don't mind at all. It's kind of exciting just to meet a priest."

He extracted the form from his briefcase and moved closer to her on the couch. Their arms touched. She did not move away. He continued to explain the form, what the Church required, and then began inquiring about her. His very work had become but an interlude that led to more imaginative sensuality.

She was completely captivated and did not stir when his elbow moved firmly against her breast. She felt her excitement grow as the air between them became thick and explosive.

After they had talked for almost half an hour, he glanced at his watch. "Wow, it's getting late. I wonder if I could come back later and fill out the form." He laughed. "We eat by the bell at the rectory."

104

"Of course," she said.

"It may be a little late," he said, looking deeply into her eyes and staring at her mouth. "I have some convert instructions—"

"It doesn't matter," she said hurriedly, nervous and excited.

They both knew what had passed between them, and it mounted to an impossible pulse during the intervening hours. When he returned at ten thirty, dressed in mufti, she offered an expensive Pinot Noir. Candles were lit on a coffee table, a nice selection of hors d'oeuvres had been laid out, jasmine incense sifted lightly through the room. Marjorie Standish was dressed in pink lounging pajamas which revealed the top half of her breasts. Her long brown hair hung loosely over her shoulders.

They filled out the form at the dining room table. It took only a few minutes. Then they settled down on the couch to sip wine and munch hors d'oeuvres. As earlier, they moved closer together until his arm was again resting against her breast. He turned and looked at her, then put down his wine and kissed her hard. She pulled back slightly, sensed his urgency, and returned his kiss more softly. He took the wine from her hand and began undressing her, slowly, almost reverently.

She had no power or desire to resist him as he made warm, rhythmic love to her. He was gentle, as if the deep rage and hurt were softening. Then they sipped more wine and rested naked on the couch, occasionally touching and kissing. They made love again, slowly, tenderly. Finally she could speak, comfortable with their nakedness and feeling the warmth of their embrace, almost an impossible closeness for a beginning experience. Yet she knew he was only half present.

"You're beautiful," she said. "Your soul is beautiful. But you are terribly troubled. I want to help."

It was all he needed. Her tenderness touched something in his manhood. The Catholic women had been lost in the excitement of his priesthood. He told her the whole story of Angela from beginning to end, as if he could finally admit that he needed more than sex could give.

"You must go to her. You will never rest until you do. Your love is made in heaven."

"But I'm celibate," he said. "She won't have me."

"She will, she must. Such a love cannot be dismissed. I could love you easily. Many women could. Strong and sensitive men like you touch women deeply and painfully. But to love you would be frustration as long as there's an Angie. Your love was an explosion, the unique love that's a kind of destiny—even though you hardly knew each other." She laughed softly. "It's in the stars, though you probably don't believe that."

He looked at her warmly. "I believe I'm a mess, and I can't keep going on like this. It's not just a love I can't seem to get over. It's ruined my whole damn priesthood!"

"I told you, it's from heaven," she said quietly. "I don't know much about your church or your priesthood, but I know about love."

He kissed her softly and again she felt his arousal, as if there were no end to his need. "You are so lonely," she said. "I'll be here whenever you want me. Whenever. Day or night."

He nodded his gratitude and meant it, picked up his briefcase, kissed her gently, and left. It was five thirty, and he had the six o'clock Mass in the convent.

The bishop's voice again interrupted his reverie.

"Seek the company of other priests as much as you can, Father Ted. The service can be a lonely life for the chaplain. If the boys become your companions, they will lose respect for you. I remember a chaplain in France. A great priest. But he started drinking with his men. . . ."

Then he was off on the use of gas warfare. His own lungs had, according to rumor, been severely damaged, and that explained the soft voice with which he spoke.

"This Vietnam is a different kind of war, Father. The issues are not clear and the battles are not straightforward. It will be a hard war to win. And it can never be won if the morale of the troops is low. I think you can be of great help, with your uncanny ability to relate to the young. . . ."

Santek was still lost in the nightmare of his own thoughts. Finally, he let himself remember the nun at the hospital. It was the most painful memory of all. It could not have happened.

The Sister's complexion made him think her a redhead. She had sent word when he was making his rounds that she wanted to see him, and when he went to her office, she had requested confession. Then she told him a sordid story of a prominent psychiatrist who had seduced her more than a dozen times while treating her with drug injections for an emotional and hormonal imbalance. The story was surreal. After the injections, she felt totally helpless to resist sex

106

in any form and had become addicted to every variety of sexual pleasure. Since her training as a nun had taught her to respect authority beyond all else, the doctor had become a kind of distorted high priest of pleasure, and she looked forward to the sessions with him more than anything else in her life. He told her everything that she wanted to hear: that sex was not sinful but a part of her healing, a road to a closer union with God, genuine sexual contact with Christ himself. As if to give support to his spiritual theory, he took great pains to disrobe her each time and whispered biblical verses, Catholic prayers, and religious aspirations in the process.

But one afternoon, when the physician had been crazy with lust, he changed the script and had her play the part of a totally unspiritual whore, complete with wigs and sexual instruments and a variety of seductive lingerie. Even in her drugged state, she realized instinctively with embarrassment and shame that the entire treatment had been a hoax. She was barely able to break away, feeling like a complete fool and on the verge of a total breakdown, but there was no way she could report him, for no one would believe her, and she had been a willing participant. Since Father Santek had a reputation for compassion and worldly understanding, she chose him as her confidant.

He heard her confession with only phrases of support, aware of her deep emotional confusion and massive embarrassment. When she had finished the list of her sins, he spoke softly. Her voice had recalled the musical lilt of Angie's.

"This terrible humiliation has been penance enough, dear Sister. God understands and forgives you." Even her eyes reminded him of Angie. "It is only natural that it will be hard for a while to resist sexual desires. Just do the best you can." He found himself getting excited, just talking about sex, and angrily strove to resist the urge with all his strength.

"But Father, I must atone for such terrible crimes."

"These are not crimes, Sister. They are only pleasures forbidden you by your vows. They are very human faults. We are all subject to them. But you should seek some emotional help from a therapist who will not take advantage of your mental state. Find the genuine help you need. Don't worry about sin. You must find health!"

He blessed her and rose to leave. She approached him impulsively and threw her arms around him. He felt her body close to his and realized he had never experienced the body of a nun before, not even in fantasy. Suddenly she was not a nun at all. He was on a

107

beach in Florida, then in a meadow outside a small schoolhouse in Canada. Beneath the nun's trappings, her body was overwhelmingly soft and round and seductive. It was as if she had lost all control and the next move was his. Lost in a fantasy of Angie, he began kissing her passionately, and their bodies merged into a rolling, groaning surge of increased desire. It was as he eased her back on the couch and felt his hands begin to move under her long skirt that he came to his senses.

He drew back suddenly and spoke aloud. "My God, what am I doing?"

Perhaps it had been his memory of Angie or some subconscious desire to attack the Church which had emptied him of all joy. Or simply the novelty and strangeness of being with a nun. All his rage and hurt, anger, anxiety, and revenge, even his hatred, had suddenly mounted into one great passion.

Even as he held her away and stood up to regain his composure, she struggled to embrace him. He calmed her with gentle words.

"We must not compound the problem. God will help you. He has forgiven you and you will find the strength."

She was not put off easily. Her whole being had been raped by the sick doctor and her emotions were raw and confused.

"I want you. I need you! God sent you!"

She had found her spiritual lover, all she had ever dreamed of during the sordid ministrations of the doctor. Here was compassion and dedication and genuine love, a love that would not abuse her or tear her from Christ. Her face was suffused with joy, while Santek was now tense and angry at himself, as if he could not believe that he had almost surrendered to such depths of sin and bitterness.

Gradually he began to calm her, holding her hand and speaking softly of God's forgiving love, even as he continued silently to reproach himself. To seduce other women in lust and anger and hurt had been tragedy and travesty enough, ruthless scandal, but a nun! He felt the pain at the back of his eyes and wanted to run away, to run anywhere. She sensed his deep hurt and tried in her own way to soothe him.

"You are a wonderful priest," she said. "Our closeness felt good and spiritual and holy. I'm sure God is not displeased. We can make love."

He shook his head. "No, dear Sister. God has forgiven you and he will forgive me, but I cannot take advantage of your pain. I will find a doctor who can help you. Meanwhile, be patient with yourself and your sexual urges. You will find beautiful outlets for your loving heart within the bonds of your virginity."

She beamed with the joy of a very young woman in impossible love. Her face and eyes shone, her skin was almost translucent. Her whole being seemed on fire with all the pure sensuality that had been repressed for so many years. She looked about sixteen. Already she had been cleansed from the doctor, freed from some diabolic possession. He found it hard to say anything.

He stood up awkwardly, deeply embarrassed, like a boy in school.

"I'm . . . I'm sorry. Please forgive me! I'm so sorry I let you down."

"But you didn't let me down. We need each other. We are good for each other. Our whole mission to souls will be enhanced. Just to know you are coming to me again—"

"No," he said, more firmly. "It's wrong for me, and you must find your health again, in or outside of the convent." He kissed her hand reverently. "I must go. I've got to go." He had lost all poise. "Father Beauvais is a good confessor," he said. "He would come to see you. . . . Forgive me. Please, forgive me!"

Before she could stand up to restrain him, he had opened the door and let himself out, saying only over and over, "I'm sorry, I'm so very sorry."

He walked out into the corridor. An elderly nun rushed up to him and he turned white, fearing that she knew what he had done.

Tears flowed down her face. "He's dead, Father, he's dead. They shot him."

He only looked puzzled. "Dead?"

"President Kennedy . . . they killed him!" Her face dissolved in grief.

It was then that he had run to Beauvais, knelt at his feet, and told him everything about the long nightmare of vindictive anger at God, the prolonged binge of sexuality, the hurt and fear and unrelenting rage, the scandal and irreparable harm, and the nun who had somehow brought him to his senses. Now he was ready to be a dedicated priest again, to recapture the excitement he had known. His pursuit of sex was only anger and selfishness, drug and flight, immaturity and revenge, futility and childish resentment. He had made a promise to God and he intended to keep it. He had not really laughed in months. The sense of humor that had sustained him in the darkest hours seemed gone. His mouth was firm with resolution, the blue eyes shone like steel agates, his muscles tightened and swelled with promise. He would write letters to everyone he hurt, beg their forgiveness. He would do penance, "Chastise his body and bring it into subjection," with Saint Paul.

A week later, still crushed by Kennedy's death, he had enlisted in the air force.

Chapter 10

Bishop Wieber gave Santek a final admonition. "We've got to be on the side of our government, Father Ted. I know there are a lot of people opposed to this war, but they're the young people who don't understand the philosophy of godless communism. We have to fight communism everywhere in the world. Vietnam is more than the site for a war in Southeast Asia, it's a battle for a whole civilization, a battle that conceivably could be fought in space. God is on our side. We have to believe that and not be deceived by those who distinguish between communism and Marxism. You are fighting a Holy Crusade, Father Ted. The future of the world depends on it."

Santek nodded, knowing he was no crusader but well aware of a deep love for America and its people and a deep commitment to the kind of world that John F. Kennedy had dreamed about. There was talk already that Kennedy wasn't much of a president, but Ted didn't listen to it. Such talk was the profound ignorance of those who confused politics and personal power. A dozen more Bays of Pigs would not have demeaned Kennedy to Santek. Kennedy had given him hope in the future, even as the air force gave him a chance to find his priesthood again. To find his life.

He and Beauvais had talked long hours about the service. Gerry recalled the great times with Father Misch.

"There will be the companionship of the guys and the other chaplains, a good salary and opportunity to travel, and the problems of a young congregation you're really suited for. Besides, parish life is getting to be a mess.

"You can make your own decisions in service," Beauvais had

gone on. "Each chaplain can be his own bishop if he uses his head. And you can get out of the rut of parochial life."

Lieutenant Santek was sent to Scott Air Force Base near St. Louis, where he was briefed on his new duties. Resplendent in his air force uniform, he felt excited and newly ordained. He was assigned to the BOQ and introduced to a friendly Methodist, Major Irwin Dawkins, who had been expecting an authoritarian Pole with a rosary around his neck and met instead a charming, laughing, energetic young man who hoped that the council called by the late Pope John XXIII would make the Catholic Church more open to ecumenical dialogue. Dawkins couldn't have been more pleased and invited Santek home to meet his plump, round-faced, and smiling wife, Millie, devour her chicken and dumplings, and pledge his cooperation in joint services. Dawkins and his wife were terribly impressed, and Santek had found a home in the air force. And when the young men at Scott discovered him—open, understanding, and incredibly real, a totally different kind of priest from what they were used to at home—they flocked to him. The senior Catholic chaplain, Major Antonelli, a gentle, quiet little man with thinning hair and sad, dark eyes who kept to himself and read incessantly, was all but relieved of his duties. And even he was totally charmed by the irrepressible new chaplain.

"You're like fresh air in a mausoleum, you grinning Polack!"

"You heard the one about the lady who went to the obstetrician and came back home beaming to her husband? 'The doctor said I have the breasts of a twenty-year-old.' The husband groaned. 'What did he say about your fifty-year-old drooping ass?' The wife grinned. 'Your name never came up, darling.'"

Antonelli wheezed and poured a glass of good wine as the veteran and the neophyte became unlikely friends. At first, Santek was concerned about fitness reports and deferred to Antonelli, "humbly" giving him credit for many of the convert classes and premarital instructions he himself handled. But when he got to know Antonelli and spent time chatting and drinking wine with him, his respect grew for this quiet, self-effacing man who had devotedly served his God in the service for twenty-seven years. Santek gladly covered for him on days that should have been his own free time and made light of how hard he was working, knowing that hard work and prayer would bring back his priesthood. He gave up hard liquor and rose early every morning to make an hour's meditation before his Mass. Antonelli complimented him quietly.

112

"You've got the right idea, Ted. It can be a great life if you keep your head and ass on straight."

Santek laughed. "I've had problems with both."

"Who the hell hasn't? But you've got to do it yourself. The air force doesn't really give a damn about you. They don't really respect religion or the chaplains. It's all just tokenism."

Ted made seventy-five converts to Catholicism his first six months at Scott. The national average per priest in the United States was approximately three a year. He resolved marital conflicts far into the night, talked young men into or out of getting married, promoted medical discharges with great tact and energy, prepared sermons that soon became characteristic of his special appeal to young or old, cynical or naive, and redoubled his efforts at prayer. He began to recognize that he had used the priesthood to sate his own need for affection and attention and power, and he banished sexual thoughts and memories like rattlesnakes, pledging his body and mind to God every day at Mass. Even his breviary, from which he could have been exempted, was now a devout prayer rather than a chore to be endured. And Antonelli was a great balm for loneliness.

They played racquetball, went to movies, spent a weekend in Chicago, a few fun days in New Orleans, and gambled in Las Vegas. Santek felt like a priest again, and his friendship with Antonelli filled in the gaps. But in the fall of 1964, Antonelli was moved to Lackland, and Ted gradually began to drink again and to spend more of his free time with the men.

It was as if he could no longer cover his pain in hard work and prayer, and time spent alone frightened him. He recognized that to most of the men he was a religious "official" who punched their "visit-the-chaplain" cards. A handsome ruddy-faced young Irishman from Boston summed it up.

"When I went to parochial school and believed in hell, Padre, the Catholic Church meant something. It was something to hang on to, even though it really screwed up my adolescence. You're cooler than most, but you still are trying to sell the same damn product. Once you've faced the gooks and watched your buddies die in a helicopter that looks like an incinerator, you don't worry about hell."

He said it without malice, but it hurt Santek deeply. He had tried his best pitch on the young man but it hadn't worked, and he realized that the novelty of his new life had worn off to reveal a deeper wound, still unhealed. On a weekend in Chicago, while celebrating with a couple of Notre Dame graduates from the base—who were delighted to be with "Father"—he drank too much and almost got involved, for the first time in service, with a nondescript woman he met in a bar. His buddies were as drunk as he was and all but pushed him to spend the night with her. Despondent at his behavior and feeling at a low point in his life, he missed Beauvais profoundly. He went to confession to a stern, unsympathetic Franciscan at St. Peter's Church in downtown Chicago and was lectured violently.

"If you want to be a priest, be a priest! If not, take off your collar and have all the booze and women you want. Make up your mind. You chaplains are all alike!"

Santek tried to protest. "I've been playing it straight for a long time, Father. It's just that a priest friend of mine was moved and—"

"Look, God doesn't give medals for doing what you're supposed to do. Don't tell me about improvement. Christ said it simply: 'Let him who can take it, take it!' If you can't, get out!"

Santek said no more. He muttered, "Screw you, fart face," under his breath, received a reluctant absolution, and left the confessional in a rage. Then he concluded his leave in a kind of drunken stupor by himself and returned to the base in a state of emotional collapse. For the first time in his life he had suicidal thoughts. He felt too old to leave the priesthood and begin a life in some other profession and too depressed to live the life of a chaplain. He talked to Major Antonelli's replacement, a dapper, gray-haired Irishman named Steve Beahan with a flushed Van Johnson kind of face who had a reputation for liking the ladies. In 'Nam he had been seen regularly with a breathtaking Oriental beauty. A kind man, he was brief and to the point.

"You just hang on any way you can, Ted. I'm three years from retirement. That's what I hang on for."

He grinned easily, and Santek smelled the bourbon on his breath without feeling the least judgmental.

"I've got a place picked out in New Hampshire where I'll do nothing but fish and read and pray and watch the world go by." He said nothing about the Oriental woman who had promised to live with him. He looked at Santek as an errant, sincere son. "Just hang on. The crisis will pass and the years go by quickly. God won't let you down!"

Then Beahan poured them both a healthy drink and they began a long evening, during which Beahan grew increasingly more melancholy until he finally slumped in his chair and slurred a final admonition.

"You'll wake up in thirty years and there won't be any Church! I'll either be fishing or pushing up daisies. It won't matter. . . ." Then he was asleep.

Santek let himself out, for some reason feeling better about the angry Franciscan in Chicago. Whatever he was, Beahan was a warm human being with the right priestly faults.

The following day, after Ted had struggled to say a devout Mass and given listless instructions to a group of prospective converts, he picked up his mail, deciding at the same time to drive up to see Beauvais for a needed lift. There was a letter from his mother, another packet from the schoolchildren at Sacred Heart in Flint . . . and a battered letter from Sister Marietta Fortier in Toronto!

His heart stopped and his hands trembled. Angie's letter had been sent to Flint, then to the chancery office, and finally to Scott Air Force Base. His hands continued to shake as he fumbled with the letter, and his heart resumed pounding as if it would leave his chest. He couldn't believe what he was reading, as he devoured each word and then read them all again. Her very handwriting tore him apart, but the message was more than he could handle. And all the old feelings of love and need came pouring back into his mind and body.

In the months before Angie's letter, Gerry Beauvais had managed to visit Santek only once at Scott between Ted's schedule and his own. The long weeks without much contact put some strange emotional barrier between them that precluded any personal questions. Gerry shared a little parochial gossip about Monsignor Slowinski falling asleep while assisting the bishop at confirmation, then recalled that Father Ed Hennessey, a notorious gambler from the diocese, had bet the entire Christmas collection on a four-to-one shot at Hazel Park—and won.

"He bought a new Buick and lost the rest on a sure thing at Santa Anita. Now the parish finance committee has taken over the reins, but they love the guy so much they allot him three hundred a month to spend at the track of his choice."

It was just priest talk anywhere, the talk of strangers who might have met on a train or at a hotel bar. Santek wanted to talk about his sudden new loneliness since Antonelli's transfer and the frustrations of his work. He began to realize that even his numerous converts seemed to be either scared kids who feared hell or "fuck Catholics" who wanted to get laid by a Catholic girlfriend. Instead, he talked about life on the base, and Beauvais countered with memories of his naval service, the growth of the musical program in the diocese, and more clerical gossip. They listened to some blues on the east side of the river, pretended to be having a lot more fun than they were, and drank excessively. Ted made one last effort.

"I miss the hell out of you, Ger. Something's still lost in my priesthood, and I don't know where to find it. I quit drinking for a while, worked like hell, but there's a deep loneliness I just can't get rid of. I keep thinking about leaving, but I don't know where to go. If I talk to any chaplain about it, it seems to scare the hell out of them and they change the subject. Most of them are more air force than Catholic."

Then he had laughed as though the conversation had grown too heavy. "Maybe I should take up the flute or learn card tricks."

"You gotta learn how to play par golf." Beauvais was slurring his words. "That's what keeps all the pastors in the Church. You'd probably be a general if you had a scratch handicap."

Even as he spoke, Beauvais hated himself for treating his friend's concern lightly, but he had drunk too much to be of any help. His thoughts wouldn't congeal but floated through his brain helplessly.

They had embraced at the airport and were gone—two men who loved each other deeply, but in the priestly way of personal privacy could never really say it. With a lump in his chest, Ted had watched his friend disappear and felt that some deep seminary friendship had been fractured by the reality of the priesthood and the stress of time and distance. He felt totally alone and depressed.

That week Gerry had a customary Tuesday-night dinner with Ed Sanders, who had become his only real friend. They went to the YMCA to work out on the weights, boxed a little, took some steam, then showered and made their way to the Jack Tar Hotel, their favorite and familiar spot. Beauvais mentioned the highlights of his trip to Scott. Even as he talked, he found himself regretting the emptiness of the occasion. Santek had badly needed to unload. Sanders noted his friend's preoccupation but chatted politely and seemed more concerned that the early dinner hour not interfere with Beauvais's priestly responsibilities.

"I thought there was a Forty Hours tonight and the usual gathering of priests."

"I decided to pass," said Beauvais. "There's one every week, and

I get tired of golf scores and gossip about who's going to die and who's going to get what parish. The word is that I'm up for monsignor."

"You'd look good in red."

"Well, at least my family would think I had arrived. My musical success doesn't really thrill them. I'm not even sure the priests are that excited about it any more. With all the liturgical changes, no one knows what's happening from week to week, including the pope. The pastors don't accept the fact that good music costs money. They don't like new organs, the cost of sheet music and hymnbooks, and the salary of a really good director. They've always had volunteer help and the choirs have all sounded like it, but as long as Bishop Wieber's alive, they'll spend the money."

Ed lifted his wineglass. "May he have a long and hardy life. By the way, I have tickets for *La Traviata* in Detroit Friday night. Can you make it? And let's stay overnight. I don't welcome that drive at midnight."

"I can swing it," said Beauvais confidently. "I don't have to be back until a wedding at eleven. So if I can get you out of bed at a decent hour Saturday morning . . ."

They finished a brandy and Ed looked at his watch. "It's still early. You want to head over to my place and listen to some music, or are you going to make an appearance at the priestly poker game?"

"No, I promised a couple of kids from the choir that I would play some ancient baroque choruses for them tonight. I'd better get back."

"You can choke on baroque."

They both laughed, and Beauvais headed back to the rectory. As he fumbled for his house key, Monsignor Kelley, the chancellor, opened the door. He smiled and rubbed his skinny hands together nervously.

"You missed a great Forty Hours, Father." There was criticism in his inflection. "The priests were asking about you. You're getting to be quite a loner."

"I'll catch the next one, Monsignor. There seems to be one every week."

Kelley grimaced slightly. He had not missed the sarcasm. He did not like the sophomoric clerical gatherings any more than Beauvais, but he was determined to do the appropriate thing. Kelley had expected to have a diocese of his own by now, but his very efficiency in running the chancery office—accountant and clerk *extra-*

ordinaire—had prevented Bishop Wieber from ever submitting his name for consideration. He was still an impressive man, though tense and balding, with darting eyes that were still forever on the lookout for anyone in the diocese who might rob him of the episcopacy. Gerry was probably not an immediate threat, since the heads of dioceses rarely came from musical ranks; such types were more prone to peculiar hobbies and nervous breakdowns. Yet Beauvais bore watching, because he was extremely gifted and had won such a deep place in the bishop's affection. But if push came to shove, his decided preference for lay companionship created an aura of suspicion. Not to mention the time spent with his choir.

"There are a couple of young boys who have been waiting for you, Father. It's a little past their bedtime, isn't it?" He grinned.

Beauvais smiled too. "Just members of the boys' choir. I promised to play them some music we've been studying. I won't keep them late." He wondered why he felt guilty in Kelley's presence.

Kelley wrapped his arms in the sleeves of his red cassock, shrugged his disdain, and was off to his room.

Santek would have said that Kelley was sticking pins in aging bishops and masturbating to statues of cherubs and plaster saints. Beauvais realized how much he missed his friend and, more instinctively, that the Lieutenant Santek he had visited at Scott was not the same man.

In retrospect, Beauvais was deeply troubled. He entered his office, almost forgetting that young Alberti and Foley were waiting for him. They rose to greet him with that look of admiration that only a boy can give to a man he admires beyond all words. Beauvais broke the silence.

"Well, are you ready to be transported by the oddities of Monteverdi and Scarlatti? And maybe a little Bach and Handel?"

"Yes, Father." They were shy in his presence. He had never achieved Santek's easy manner.

They followed him upstairs to his room, far more eager to please him than to comprehend the strange twists and contrasts of baroque music. It was his passion that inspired them. He offered them a small glass of wine as a unique tribute to their maturity. He dimmed the lights, made certain they were comfortable, gave a passionate explanation of what they were about to hear, and then was himself lost in the beauty of another world.

It was after eleven before he realized the lateness of the hour.

He offered to call their parents, but they insisted there would be no problem.

"They know we're with you, Father."

He walked them to the door, embraced them warmly as was his way, and again apologized for the prolonged evening. He saw Monsignor Kelley move out of the shadows and descend the stairs as he ushered them out.

"I get carried away. You're both excused from the eight o'clock Mass tomorrow. If Mother Dominic gives you any trouble, have her consult me."

They blushed and thanked him again and were gone. He walked back into the rectory and moved toward the kitchen for chocolate grahams and milk. Monsignor Kelley startled him by emerging as he walked past the parlor and TV room. Apparently, the evening news was over. He must have imagined that Kelley was upstairs.

"You keep late hours with your boys, Father." He did not look at Beauvais.

Beauvais was briefly embarrassed. "I lose track of time when I'm sharing my music."

Kelley nodded and disappeared upstairs in the darkness. Beauvais again reflected on Santek's imaginings about the chancellor and chuckled softly on his way to the kitchen. For a brief moment he was depressed; then he remembered *La Traviata* on Friday night with Ed and began humming softly.

Kelley walked by the open bedroom door and noticed the dim light and candles, the empty wine bottle and glasses. He shrugged and moved slowly down the dark corridor toward his bedroom, a sad figure, all alone. He began unbuttoning his cassock as he approached the door—disproving another of Santek's theories: that he slept in it.

Chapter 11

Angela Fortier had entered the Daughters of Mercy at Good Shepherd Convent on the outskirts of Toronto with fiercely mixed feelings. From the moment that Ted Santek had dropped her off at the Moncrief schoolhouse, she had not been able to get him out of her mind. She had excused herself from teaching that afternoon of his departure, feigning illness, and returned to the meadow where he had last held her in his arms. She buried herself in the soft grass near the oak tree and wept as if there were no longer any reason to live. Late in the afternoon, she returned home and prepared her father's favorite dinner, roast pork, mashed potatoes, and home-made applesauce. Later, she sat in the tiny living room, with its overstuffed furniture, and told him unemotionally that she was entering the convent. Her father drew deeply on his pipe and finally looked up from the paper over his glasses.

"It is what you want?" He spoke in French.

"Yes, Papa."

"Marriage and children do not appeal?"

"God is calling me, Papa."

He scoffed quietly. "It could be your own fears. You have seemed sad since your Florida vacation."

She knew that he hated the Church, which had denied Christian burial to his beloved father, and that he refused to believe in God or attend church since his beautiful wife's premature death of cancer. At times he made bitter comments about the Church's wealth or the lazy life of clerics, but usually he said nothing at all.

"The nunnery is for failures and outcasts, you know, for country

120

girls who have known nothing else since childhood. You are college educated and have been to the States. Why not take more time for such a decision?"

"I have already taken too much time."

He puffed his pipe almost angrily, realizing that she was as stubborn and willful as he was. "Where did God speak to you? From a cloud? Or a smokestack?"

"On a beach in Florida. It was all very clear."

"You will bear no grandchildren." He said it with a sigh. Then, sadly, "Most of all, there will be no life here without you." It was hard for him to admit it. His two sons had married and moved to Nova Scotia to fish, but Angela was his life, his last contact with his wife.

"Perhaps you will marry again, Papa."

"And perhaps not," he said. Then he buried himself in his paper to hide his emotion.

He drove her to Toronto three months later, almost in silence save for observations about what they saw along the way. When he entered the grounds of the Good Shepherd Convent, he briefly acknowledged the beauty of the trees and tailored lawns, the grottoes and statues scattered about, and the massive stone buildings which had been erected to endure forever.

"It is beautiful here. Perhaps you will find peace." He paused and looked at her. "I look at you and see only your mother today. You have some radiance. But if you are not happy, do not stay. Life goes by too quickly."

It was far more than he was accustomed to say. He gently refused her invitation to explore the chapel and library and kissed her softly on both cheeks, then looked away as if he could not bear seeing her face.

"I love you very much, Papa. I will write as often as I can."

He only nodded. There were tears in his eyes waiting to fall. She had not seen them since her mother's death.

She watched him as he walked away, smaller than she had realized, now shrunken and alone, the proud steps she remembered as a child become the shuffle of a defeated man. The Church she looked to for solace was his eternal enemy. It was a final defeat. She turned away and hurried to the chapel to bury her own pain in the heart of the suffering Christ. It was a strange beginning for a Daughter of Mercy.

The postulancy lasted for six months and was a friendly, gentle introduction to the life of a nun. Most of the girls were just out of high school, giddy and excited about their new life. The majority of them, as her father had said in anger, were from farming communities or fishing villages in remote areas of Canada. After an initial few weeks of great joy and peace in her new surroundings, Angela began to feel out of place and isolated among these giggling high school girls, but the busy schedule allowed her little time to brood about the past. A kind of benign numbness gradually enveloped her, and she went through the daily schedule in a kind of gentle daze.

She rose with the others at five thirty, still in the "grand silence" of the night before, had twenty minutes to complete ablutions, then morning prayers and meditation followed by Mass and a breakfast of bread and oatmeal, during which the postulants were allowed to talk. Occasionally Angela would mention her travels or teaching experiences, but usually she only listened to the exuberant conversations of her young classmates and wondered what their exuberance was about.

During the day, college classes were held, most of which Angela had already completed. While the other postulants complained mightily about "not enough time," Angela found the weeks refreshing and healing. She assisted several of the girls puzzled by trigonometry or English literature but found most of them to be simple peasants with loving hearts and dull, untrained minds. Two or three of the girls had adolescent crushes on Angela, and the directress warned Angela about this privately.

One girl in particular, dark-eyed, petite Marcella Pelletier, would cling to her during recreation periods, often staring at her and telling her how beautiful she was. She loved to touch Angela's hand, even to stroke her face, unaware that her feelings were anything more than simple affection.

Once, in a field hockey game, she collided with Angela and they fell down together. She embraced Angela lovingly and kissed her innocently. Later, she came to Angela's cell at night and tried to crawl in with her.

"I'm so lonely."

"Just sit here for a moment, Marcella, and you will feel better."

"I always cuddled with my sister at home. It helped so much."

"But it is forbidden here, dear sister." Angela felt sad for her and wanted to hold her.

"Why? What is wrong?"

122

"We could be attracted sexually to each other, I believe." The desire to embrace the beautiful young postulant was stronger.

"Is that so bad?"

"Yes, my sister, you should return to your room. If you were caught, both of us would be dismissed." Angela felt herself trembling.

There was a noise in the corridor, and Angela's heart almost stopped. She feigned sleep as Marcella slid under her bed. The directress glanced in the door and then moved quietly away, but Marcella waited almost an hour before she returned to her room. Angela felt she should report the incident, but, knowing it would mean Marcella's dismissal, she couldn't do it.

Three weeks later, the young sister was detected in the hall at night and was sent home. Curiously, Angela missed her far more than she could have anticipated, but it was forbidden by convent rules to discuss her absence. Her name was not to be mentioned again, lest her departure unsettle any of the other young women struggling with their own vocation. Angela found it painful not to inquire about her young friend, since even the adolescent crush had been a kind of emotional support. Anything to keep Santek from her mind. She mentioned her feelings for Marcella in confessional, and the gentle priest told her it was only normal affection but not to allow that kind of proximity again.

"It is testing God," he said. "We must not do that, or none of us could be pure. You must forget about her as your holy rule requires."

It was during the postulancy that Angela learned to walk and talk like a nun. Colloquial expressions and identifying accents were gently corrected, exuberance of any kind was subtly corraled. Arms were not to swing, eyes were not to look about, legs were to glide in a gentle motion. There was to be no attention-seeking individuality. The postulants found all this almost impossible and giggled at the least provocation, but there was great patience with them until they entered the so-called "seminary." The postulancy had its outings and picnics, its tolerance of almost anything but sinful tendencies, its exciting feast days and noisy recreations, its frequent laughs and its innocent novelties.

The seminary, however, was a different experience, in which the young girls became women of strong faith and total dedication—strong, committed nuns, ready to give up the world no matter how

123

seductively it beckoned; shaped and disciplined by the long experience of the Catholic Church, which knew how to turn out brave believers.

The seminary was a year-long program to foster the spiritual life and contemplative side of the Daughters of Mercy by means of solitude and inner discipline. Angela was given her religious name, Sister Marietta Fortier, and having graduated from giddiness, as it were, she was thrilled by her own personal development and the mature, loving atmosphere of convent life. Never had she experienced such kindness and warmth. Each of her sisters was determined to achieve sanctity through unselfishness and prayer and the whole atmosphere was charged with love and caring. Several of the young women became warm friends in an environment of true family.

She also learned to sew her own habit, the complicated dress of the seminary sister modeled after that of a Frenchwoman of many generations ago. A chemise was worn next to the skin, along with a half slip, pockets tied on like holsters, a chaplet, and a two-piece dress; the headgear also consisted of two parts. The end result was not unlike the little girl on the Old Dutch Cleanser can. Angela's face, always beautiful, was now almost exotic. Each sister had two chemises. One was worn to bed and even in the shower, since a sister was never to see herself fully unclothed.

Even though the garb was strange and complicated and gave Angela fits trying to get ready in the allotted time in the morning, and even though the food was starchy and unpalatable for the most part—the same meal served on its own day of the week, including the "Monday mystery meat"—it was the seminary program itself which gradually wore her down.

Endless spiritual talks, spiritual reading at all the meals, frequent sermons by the kindly and compassionate Sister Directress, classes in Gregorian chant, church history, and more spirituality by French writers—all of it, to Angela, boring and uninspiring. The training forced the young women to examine each facet of their personalities to root out the tiniest vice. For some, this was a spiritual challenge that excited them. They were young and malleable, much more docile than the independent Angela, who had raised a family in her early teens and graduated from a co-ed college. In a weekly chapter called "spiritual charity," each sister confessed her petty vanities or minute lack of consideration, then kissed the floor and knelt before the directress and the community asking forgiveness. It was also appropriate to request that another sister report a spiritual charity that one might have overlooked. To Angela it was gossipy and ridiculous, especially when one of her friends reported, "I saw Sister Marietta Fortier glancing at her image in the refectory window."

Then more floor kissing and bowing and begging of forgiveness. For some it was a perfect way of life. It was a preparation and a discipline for what they had always wanted: to be a nun. Angela struggled with all she had to understand, begged God to make her more suitable, more patient, more generous in her love, more willing to meet the supreme test of her vocation. But meanwhile her whole being and body protested the picayune spirituality and the overwhelming boredom. In a private conference with the directress, Sister Raphael, she wondered if she was suited for religious life. She told of her memories of the dark-eyed Marcella, who had come to her bedroom at night, of her own longing to be held by two or three of her friends, and even of her attachment to a man and her decision to enter the convent because he was unavailable.

The kindly directress, fortyish, with her luminous eyes and unchanging expression of love, was not put off.

"Christ calls his brides a number of different ways. That is why each has a particular beauty. You are an extraordinary young woman with a fine mind and generous heart. You will be an outstanding teacher and superior. Even now your younger sisters look to you for approval and support. Yet you chose Christ over man and woman. Your choice is real and special. You can be his most beautiful bride."

Sister Directress stared lovingly at her, then gently touched her face.

"You have deep, sensuous, inquisitive eyes. In the world they could cause you great misunderstanding. Here you must learn to control your gaze. There will be many more Marcellas if you do not learn to turn your eyes away. God has led you here, with your great talent, and he will work wondrous deeds through you—perhaps more than any of your sisters."

There was not as much concern over Angela's eyes or her beauty after she gained thirty pounds and her face, ballooning out of the tight headgear, broke out in rashes and pimples that resisted all tending and medication. When she blushingly admitted that she had had no period for eight months, she was told by Sister Raphael that this was not unusual.

"Leave all this in God's caring hands, Sister. The seminary is a spiritual test to try one's faith like steel—to meet the many temptations and stresses that lie ahead. I too once knew such stress and tribulation. You remind me so much of my once-struggling self. Now there is only joy." Sister Raphael's smile looked almost beatific.

Angela believed that she too could make it, if only she could handle her thoughts. For Sister Marietta Fortier was increasingly plagued by maddening sexual fantasies and troubled dreams. The dreams, in particular, kept her in a state of growing anxiety. Frequently she was back in Florida, cuddling next to Ted on a blanket by the ocean, his hands fondling her bare breasts, with Sister Raphael, long-haired and with piercing eyes, transparent against the sky, smiling at her from the distance. Ted stood up and walked naked out into the waves up to his shoulders, then called to her over and over again with the same expression on his face that he had when he dropped her off in front of the Moncrief schoolhouse. Then he disappeared into the water. She called his name, but he was gone. She awoke in a cold sweat, terrified, believing she would have to confess her feelings.

She talked to her understanding confessor, insisting that she was not meant for this life. He told her these were only temporary trials sent from God himself to test her faith and strengthen her resolve and were, in fact, evidence of God's love for her. Her struggles with chastity would ultimately free her for a universal motherhood to bring love and understanding to all humankind. She talked again to Sister Raphael, whom she had grown to love like the mother she had never had. But the Sister Directress only smiled and insisted that she must practice greater penance and mortification to "chastise her body and bring it into subjection.

"Of all the young women in the class, you have the greatest gifts to bring to our order. You are my very own assurance that our work is God's work. Yours is a mature choice, made after much experience."

Angela denied herself favorite foods, said more prayers, sacrificed sleep, and spent her work hours with greater devotion to the job at hand. Still, she could not banish Ted Santek from her mind. No one told her what she knew in her heart that she wanted to hear, so finally, fearing that she was falling apart, she was compelled by a deep yearning for life to get in touch with Ted. She knew she could not have him as a man, but she desperately needed him as a priest to give some perspective to her tortured life. The convent confessor was a deeply spiritual man with no awareness of the world or of

126

sexual love. He could not help her. Father Ted Santek could. Her need to see him became an all-absorbing obsession.

She had no intention of jeopardizing his vocation or her own, but she needed to know if he agreed with her counselors. Since all incoming and outgoing mail was inspected and not received or sent if it was considered unsuitable for a seminary sister, there was no way she could make her plight known to anyone. She feared staying, lest she die of loneliness and emptiness, and feared leaving, lest she lose her soul. She had to write to Father Ted. He would know what to do. She wrote the letter very simply.

Dear Father Ted:

      I need to talk to you most desperately. I do not think the convent life is for me, but I don't really know what to do. Would it be possible for you to visit me here? Special arrangements are made for a priest visitor. You can really come any time. I have to see you! Even though I am afraid of my feelings for you, I know God will protect us from any wrong. You will probably not recognize me, since I have gained much weight and my face is all broken out. Every day seems endless. My prayers seem pointless. I fear I am not growing closer to God but losing my faith instead. Please come. I hope you do not hate me for causing so much pain. I do not know where else to turn. Do not write, for my mail might be opened and I could be in more trouble.

                    My love to you in Mary Immaculate,
                         Sister Marietta Fortier
                         Ad majorem Dei gloriam

It was a real problem getting the letter out. Her father, still hurt by her entrance into the convent, had not yet been able to bring himself to visit her on any of the assigned Sunday afternoons. After a lengthy explanation, she prevailed upon a young Sister and dear friend to sneak the letter out with her parents, since the envelope was obviously addressed to a priest. After the letter had been sent, however, the Sister felt compelled to mention her "sin" in the chapter of faults. Later Sister Directress talked to Sister Marietta privately.

"Why didn't you come to me, my child?"

"I was afraid you wouldn't let me send it." Angela sounded like a timid child.

"Were you ashamed of it, my child?"

"No, Sister. It was a matter of personal conscience."

That was the right thing to say. Sister Raphael bowed graciously and smiled warmly, nodding understanding. Angela kissed the floor, bowed low from her knees, and wondered how long she could wait without going mad.

It was almost a month before Ted received the frayed letter. Meanwhile, Sister Marietta Fortier truly feared she was losing her mind. The frightening dreams continued. She slept feverishly, was frequently forgetful, developed a slight stutter, still did not have a period, and, no matter how little she seemed to eat, could not lose weight. She grew almost paranoid. One night she dreamed that she was standing on a high cliff above the ocean, scanning the water for Ted. She saw his blond head disappear in the waves and leaped off the cliff. She awoke breathing frantically, suppressing a scream.

"Oh, dear God, please send him to me!"

Then she buried her head in her pillow and sobbed in the loneliness of her tiny cubicle, sobbed as if there were no end to her sorrow.

In the morning she approached the Sister Directress and told her with great firmness that she no longer felt suited for the religious life. She was totally honest about her dreams and continuing anxiety. She felt that she was losing her mind as well as her health. She did not admit that Ted was a priest, but she felt her dreams were a "sign" from God—even as in the Bible God spoke through dreams.

Sister Raphael was deeply troubled and consulted the Mother General, Sister Evangelista, to determine if Angela needed special medical care. The Mother General reassured her that she was doing the right thing.

"She is an extraordinary young woman, and thus she will have greater trials than most. Remember what John of the Cross and Teresa of Avila suffered, even the Little Flower. The seminary time is difficult. Soon enough she will be freed from its rigorous demands. You might give her more to do, Sister. The mind can cause sicknesses all its own."

"Do you think there might be some psychological help?"

The Sisters of Mercy had not yet accepted such help as a viable course, despite the recent writings of Gerald Vann and Dom Thomas Verner Moore, which accepted psychotherapy as an asset to religious life. Such opinions were still considered novel and dangerous in the less enlightened orders, even a dangerous denial of God's providential care.

128

The Mother General shook her head emphatically. "Our sacred order has been molding young women for centuries, Sister Raphael. God does not need the help of learned atheists who explore the mind and neglect the soul."

Sister Raphael bowed profoundly and returned with confidence to direct the spiritual struggle of her beloved Sister Marietta Fortier. "These are only normal temptations, my child. 'God will not suffer you to be tempted beyond that which you can endure.' You must rise up each morning and do his will. Our dreams can be the voice of Satan as easily as that of God. I myself was once tempted for two years, and it only succeeded in strengthening my resolve. When the fury passed, I knew the greatest peace and joy of my life. I felt as though I had entered the Holy of Holies."

"But, Sister, I have no strength left. Two years of this is impossible. I cannot tolerate the pain and confusion. I feel I must leave. The misery and unhappiness I am experiencing tells me that I must try another kind of life."

"You cannot throw away your vocation, my child, you above all the rest," she said kindly. "If you were to leave, it could result in the loss of your soul. And many other sisters might follow your example. We must not trifle with God's gifts. Besides, the trying seminary year is almost over and you have been very brave." She stroked her face gently for several moments, then held her hand warmly in her own.

Angela was finally defeated. She loved Sister Raphael. She was her mother and best friend, and without her support she could not find the strength and confidence to leave. She could not bear to lose her, so she hung on with a new and firm resolve, begging God to give her the courage to endure the life of silence and prayer, boredom and anxiety. Even though she would never see Ted again, she could not erase his face from her consciousness. But with all the strength of her French peasant heritage and generations of deep faith, she was determined to emerge whole from this black and endless nightmare.

Chapter 12

When Bishop Wieber died of cancer late in 1964, the life of Gerald Beauvais was destined to change radically. The solemn requiem, attended by fifty bishops, seven archbishops, and two cardinals, was sung by the boys' choir, with special offertory and communion hymns by the adult choir. It was Beauvais's finest hour. After graveside obsequies, Beauvais sat with Ed Sanders at the clergy dinner. Later they slipped off to the Jack Tar Hotel for a drink.

"An incredible performance," Ed said quietly. "You'll finally get the recognition you deserve. There wasn't a bishop who wasn't knocked right out of his pew. I heard dozens of raves at the cemetery and at the dinner."

Beauvais shrugged. "Bishop Wieber was a great man and a real friend," he reflected sadly. "I never appreciated the liturgy as much in my life as I did today. It was the only real way to express creatively the loss we were all feeling. Today I felt that all my work really meant something."

"There's no way now that anyone can discontinue what Bishop Wieber started." Ed had deep fears about losing his job as choir director, now Wieber was gone.

"I don't know about that, but I think I have the energy to make the liturgy live all over the diocese, if the Liturgical Commission can only make up its mind whether we're Catholics or Baptists. Every week there's a different directive. The new directive on English really upsets me. I hate to see Latin go, I think it's a critical mistake."

"Well, it may be a way of keeping the young people interested."

130

"While losing everyone else. It's not a language change that's needed, it's compassion and understanding and getting rid of a sex-obsessed morality that's out of touch with modern life."

"That sounds like heresy, Father." Ed smiled when he said it.

Beauvais was not smiling. The success of the liturgy had given him new strength and confidence to speak his mind. "It's common sense! The Church is saying, 'Let them eat candles,' when people are starving. There was a chance under Pope John, but Paul VI is running scared. People are going to walk away. So are the best priests, the ones who aren't scared."

"What's the answer?"

"I don't know the answer. I just know that I'm going to live my priesthood the way I see it. And divorce and birth control and a celibate view of sex aren't going to stand in my way. Otherwise only the ignorant and frightened will remain."

He paused and spoke more softly.

"There were three admitted homosexuals in the steam room the other day at the YMCA, guys from our parish. What have we got to offer them? I can hear their confessions. Some of them help me get out the bulletin and go to daily Mass. But they're expected to be celibate the rest of their lives."

They were silent for a full minute until Ed interrupted. "Who's going to be the new bishop?"

"The odds are on Kelley. God knows he's earned it, and he suddenly looks years younger. He'll have me baptizing Siberians." They laughed heartily.

Two months later, with a handsome and crisp new Irish ordinary, Michael Patrick Sullivan from conservative Philadelphia, in charge of the Lansing diocese, a crushed Monsignor Kelley recognized that he would never become a bishop. But Sullivan was his kind of man, traditional and unequivocal, so Kelley became Sullivan's confidant and informed guide to the problems of the diocese.

A few months after Bishop Sullivan was installed, and a series of pastoral changes had been made to prevent liberal priests from introducing personal tastes into the liturgy, Father Gerald Beauvais was called in for a private conference with the vigorous new bishop. Sullivan, built like a bricklayer, with thick hands, broad shoulders, and a full head of auburn hair, had been nicknamed Moses in Philadelphia because he was said to keep the law on stone tablets under his bed. He never seemed to lose the faint smile on his full, ruddy,

Irish face, even when his dark eyes were angry or distant. He had a reputation for being eminently fair if he could be made to listen—which was difficult.

Beauvais entered the bishop's large red-carpeted office, which emphasized his episcopal powers. Monsignor Kelley sat behind the desk with the bishop, nervously toying with a pen on a yellow legal pad, looking intimidated and almost embarrassed. Beauvais kissed the bishop's ring, took the only vacant chair, and started to make conversation, but the bishop did not waste time on amenities.

"I'm moving you to St. Mary's of Farmington, Father."

Beauvais was stunned. It was an insignificant parish in the corn and cattle country of southern Michigan and offered no challenge.

"I also want to remind you that the teaching authority of the Church, the magisterium, does not reside in individual priests who have modern ideas about birth control and divorce. There have been reports, Father, that you play pope in the confessional. I hope I will not have to suspend you to mend your ways!" Sullivan stared directly at Beauvais. A fearless and fiercely conservative man, his only concern was to preserve orthodoxy, no matter what the personal cost.

Beauvais, red-faced and trembling with anger, nodded silently. Monsignor Kelley, eyes down, scribbled on the yellow pad. He had paled considerably.

"The transfer is effective immediately, Father."

"Is that all, Bishop?" Gerry had finally managed to find his voice and was determined not to show any weakness or disappointment. If this was God's will, he would accept it.

"Not quite, Father." Bishop Sullivan continued to smile. "You are not to be in the company of one Ed Sanders, or to spend time with the young men from the boys' choir. Or to hang around public baths in the YMCA. These actions are not in keeping with priestly decorum, and there has been some talk I'd rather not discuss." His dark eyes focused directly on Beauvais and did not move away. Kelley dropped his pen and looked as if he wanted to crawl under the table.

Beauvais was angry. "What kind of talk, Bishop?"

The smile tightened and Sullivan's lips and eyes narrowed.

"Just talk, like sharing a motel room with Sanders on several occasions, and working out at the YMCA, nude and in questionable company, and frequenting public showers in the presence of known

132

homosexuals, and inviting young boys to your room to drink and listen to music at all hours. Would you like me to continue?

"It is not my prerogative to assert that anything untoward is going on, Father. That is between you and your confessor and, of course, God. I will not invade that realm. I deal with that which has the appearance of evil. These are difficult times, Father Beauvais, and the priest must not give anyone reason to question his virtue. Is that crystal clear?"

The thick hands had clenched into fists. Sullivan's smile had not wavered, and he looked directly at Beauvais. Monsignor Kelley picked up his pen and continued writing but still did not look up. Beauvais's face was flushed and his voice full and resonant as he spoke.

"It's very clear, Bishop. But your suspicions are in no way warranted. Ed Sanders is an outstanding Catholic layman, planning marriage in the very near future. And as regards the YMCA and the members of the boys' choir, there is—"

The bishop spoke gently and with great sincerity, as if the whole matter were terribly distasteful to him. "I am not here to debate, Father, nor am I here to ask you to defend yourself. I have no reason to believe that you are anything but a good priest. I have given you a new assignment, and I want you to accept it as God's will."

Beauvais stared back at him with a rage he didn't know he possessed. He was afraid to speak or move lest he leap over the desk and choke this powerful hierarch who was so convinced of his own sound leadership. Beauvais hardly heard the rest of the bishop's words. His voice was now soft and compassionate.

"Father Davidson will replace you as director of the adult and boys' choirs. You will continue as diocesan coordinator of music. I wish you well, Father. This change will give you an opportunity to examine the roots of your own priesthood and the promise of obedience you made at ordination. St. Mary's of Farmington is one of the oldest and most devout parishes in the diocese, and there is a simple faith there that believes solidly in the Holy Father and the magisterium. I think you will be renewed there." He stood and gave his episcopal blessing and offered his ring. Beauvais made the sign of the cross, kissed the apostolic symbol coldly, and left without a word.

The very next day, without the customary farewell party, Father Gerald Beauvais packed his books and clothes in his car, said goodbye to no one, as he had been instructed, and drove the seventy-five miles southeast to St. Mary's of Farmington. Monsignor Grady, heartbroken at Beauvais's transfer, had given him a check for a thousand dollars for "a little trip or something" and promised to talk to Bishop Sullivan about Beauvais's outstanding work. There were tears in the kindly man's eyes.

The pastor of Farmington, Father John Niedermeyer, who was retiring, greeted him at the door of the rectory. Niedermeyer, past seventy and crippled with arthritis, had a reputation for profound sanctity. A kind of quiet joy shone in his eyes despite his constant pain, and he was startled that such an obviously competent man as Beauvais would succeed him.

"You will learn to love it here, Father. I know it may seem a comedown from the cathedral, but these are truly good people. My thirty years here have been the happiest of my life. It is my hope and prayer that you will love St. Mary's as much as I do."

Beauvais nodded warmly, then followed the old man around the house, learning about heating and cooling systems, the combination to the safe, parish records, ushers and custodians, parish societies, and whom to call for what. Everything had been prepared in an orderly way, anticipating any difficulty Beauvais might have. After a visit to the church and more explanations, the old man knelt in front of the Blessed Virgin's altar and let the tears come. After a few moments of prayer, he got up stiffly with Beauvais's help.

"You'll have to excuse my emotion, Father. I'm an old man, and this has been home for a very long time. If you have any other questions, I'll leave you my sister's number in Detroit, where I'll be staying. And from time to time, I may come back just for a visit."

"You'll always be most welcome, Father."

"One more thing. I could never really afford a housekeeper, so I had a woman from the parish come in every night to fix my dinner and take care of the laundry and cleaning. She's in about the same shape as I am, so I have arranged for Mrs. Margaret Santini to take over until you decide what you want to do. She calls herself Peggy. She works as a secretary at the Dairy Cooperative and teaches in our catechism program. You will like her. She's an extraordinary and sensitive woman with a heart of gold, but don't feel obligated to keep her on. I told her it might be only a temporary arrangement."

Then the old man was gone and Father Gerald Beauvais, new pastor of St. Mary's, made his way to the ancient brick church. He knelt in the sanctuary in front of the gold tabernacle and gazed at

134

the wooden crucifix above the altar, dramatically portraying a blood-spattered, dying Jesus. Gerry prostrated himself on the floor as he had on ordination day and lay there for almost an hour, then again knelt looking at the crucifix.

"*Fiat mihi secundum verbum tuum, Domine.* Not my will but thine be done!"

He said the prayer several more times. Then he got up and made his way across the parking lot to the rectory. Margaret Santini was waiting for him. She was a petite woman with square, strong shoulders and a look of sadness in her eyes. She had a peasant quality, with high cheekbones framed in long jet-black hair, dark liquid eyes, full lips, and olive skin. She spoke softly and shyly, with a rasp in her voice as if she had been a smoker. She appeared to be in her mid-thirties and found it hard to look at Father Beauvais.

"I'm Peggy Santini, Father. I'd like to be of service."

Gerry bowed graciously, trying to put her at ease.

She smiled warmly but still shyly, playing awkwardly with her fingers, then rearranging her hair. "If you'd give me some idea of what food you like. . . ." She rearranged the white collar of her full maroon dress. The color was not appealing and exaggerated her darkness.

"I don't suppose you can make pasta."

Their laughter broke the tension, and her smile made her look like a teenager.

Peggy Santini retreated to the kitchen, and Beauvais began to feel the shock of the move. His whole body ached. He wondered if God had not taken all meaning and happiness away. He wished he could talk to Santek and Father Misch. He would call them soon. He also needed desperately to talk to Ed Sanders, but that had been forbidden and he could not think of what to say. As Peggy moved about the kitchen, he lit a cigarette and slumped into an easy chair in the living room, wondering seriously for the first time if his whole priesthood were not a grave error. He turned on some music and thought of Vienna and Ursula and the offer of Karl Metzen to direct a choir there or sing professionally. Ursula had written regularly, and her affection for him seemed to have grown. It would be a perfect escape from the pain of his new appointment, but he still needed to talk to Santek. He thought briefly of California and his brother Louis. He wished he were not too old to reenlist in the navy. He also was beginning to despise Bishop Sullivan with a rising hatred he did not know he possessed. It frightened him to feel this kind of murderous rage.

Late that night he called Father Misch, now retired in California, and told him as honestly as he could what had happened. "Sullivan's a consummate son-of-a-bitch, Gerry! Always has been. I know about him. Don't do anything rash, just hang in! He'll discover what kind of man you are!" Just hearing Misch's voice helped. Soon they were reminiscing about old navy times, and Beauvais promised a visit to California. He also decided that a cantankerous and militant Irish bishop could not break his spirit, no matter what!

Father Ted Santek reread Angie's letter for the tenth time and pondered what to do. His promotion to Captain the day before had given him new incentive to dedicate himself to his work. The promotion was a rapid one and offered solid proof that his counseling and convert work had not gone unnoticed. Major Steve Beahan had arranged a little party and joked about his own slow progress in the military. It had taken him nine years to achieve the same rank.

"This dumb Pole will be a general before I get my bird. It must be his sex appeal. It sure as hell isn't his brains or ability."

Santek roared with the rest of the chaplains. It felt good to be among friends again, to share the camaraderie of men who labored in an almost hopeless struggle to make God mean something in the military.

Angie seemed part of another life. After the first rush of emotion he felt upon receiving the letter, he wondered what he had to offer. His chaplaincy, though marked by loneliness and occasional depression, had in reality given new direction to his life. He was respected—no, he was loved—by enlisted men and officers alike. He was the born chaplain, a man of power and eloquence with the street toughness and basic savvy that jet jockeys admired. Angie meant pain and confusion, a pain that had almost destroyed him and threatened his very priesthood.

He spent an hour in the chapel asking God's guidance. He felt an inner peace and somehow knew he could not abandon her to the troubles that marked every sentence of her letter. She had been his friend, and Ted Santek, if he was anything, was loyal. He would go to her and offer what help he could. Then he could get on with his priestly work.

He arranged time off, allegedly to share his new rank with his family in Michigan. To avert suspicion he caught an air force junket to Detroit and rented a car, and after a day and night with his parents and family he drove to Toronto, not really certain why he was going or what he was going to do. The next morning he made his way to the Good Shepherd motherhouse of the Daughters of Mercy, some ten miles outside the city. He hardly noticed the impressive grounds and well-tailored acreage as he drove through the stone gate and up the long drive, flanked by flowers and shrubs, to a visitors' parking lot at the side of the main building.

He rang the bell, which resounded half a dozen times, and a beaming older Sister appeared in the winged headdress of her order while the doorbell was still chiming. She recognized his chaplain's cross after a moment's hesitation and gave him the bow and smile that nuns reserve for priests. Her eyes had the twinkle of a joyful, dedicated nun.

"Welcome to our home, Father. Can I get you some coffee or a cold drink?"

He looked around. "Coffee would be fine, Sister. It's really beautiful here."

Actually it was like any other motherhouse he had visited: terrazzo floors and marble corridors and a smell of incense and wax. She ushered him into a parlor with familiar overstuffed furniture and an assortment of bleached holy pictures on soft green walls. A statue of the saintly but human Curé of Ars gave some mild warmth to the setting.

The portress went in search of coffee and returned to serve it to him with a fresh homemade doughnut. "Is there someone you wanted to see, Father?"

"Yes," he said almost offhandedly, "I would like to talk to Sister Marietta Fortier. She is a former penitent of mine."

The nun bowed graciously, smiled cherubically, and was gone without a sound. In a few moments, another Sister came in, bowed, and sat tensely on the edge of a couch opposite Ted. There was a strength and glow about her as if she had some mystical contact with God and had been destined to the convent from her very birth. She reminded Santek of the nuns who had taught him in grade school, and he smiled warmly.

"I am Sister Raphael, the directress, Father. You wanted to see Sister Marietta Fortier?"

"Yes," he said. "I happened to be in Toronto for a chaplains' conference and decided to pay a visit. She is a former penitent of mine."

137

Again she bowed graciously. She stood up, then asked awkwardly, "I forgot to ask your name, Father."

"Just tell her Father Ted is here. She'll probably be in shock." He laughed heartily.

The nun started to depart, then smiled lovingly. "It's a good thing you've come, Father. Sister Marietta has been most distressed of late. She has only a few weeks left in the seminary year and has talked of leaving. I think your presence will be a great blessing."

Then she bowed again, smiled thinly, and was gone. Her stare was overwhelming and seemed to go right through him. He reflected on what a powerful directress she must be and what influence she must have on young nuns.

Ten or fifteen minutes later, he heard the soft shuffling of feet and looked up. Sister Raphael had returned with Angie, now dressed all in black with the cap of the Daughters of Mercy. Only her large blue eyes, though wounded and glazed and looking terribly frightened, seemed the same. He hardly heard the departing words of the Sister Directress, but he felt tremendous relief when she left, as if some vast power had moved away.

Ted could not take his eyes off Angie. As soon as the directress was safely gone she burst into tears and rushed to him. He stood up and held her gently. She turned her head.

"Don't look at me," she sobbed. "Please don't look at me. It's horrible."

And it was. Her face was bloated and broken out. Her lips were cracked, and there were tiny sores at the edges of her mouth. Even her hands were puffy and chafed. He continued to hold her without saying a word. Then gradually he led her to the couch and sat down next to her.

"My God, Angie, what the hell has happened to you?"

Finally she was able to look at him, and the words came. "I'm going crazy," she said. "Maybe I already am!"

"Then why haven't you left? You've taken no vows."

"I'm afraid to leave," she said. "Sister Directress said it would be against God's will."

She sounded like a little girl. Even the Canadian inflection was gone. It was as if she had been transformed into someone else.

"God's will?" he said angrily. "God doesn't will anybody to destroy themselves. You've got to get the hell out of here. The convent's no prison! You can leave any time."

"But I can't seem to do it by myself. Even Mother General says I should stay. I don't want to lose my soul. I need you or someone else I respect to tell me I can leave!"

"Hell, yes, you can leave! You'll leave now, with me. Your health is at stake. Your superiors will understand that." He realized the power over her that the Sister Directress had—even with the best of intentions. Her eyes seemed an indelible memory.

"But I can't leave with you. They would stop me." Despite her fear, she already seemed stronger in his presence, and some of the remembered sparkle returned to her eyes. "How can I know it's not my vocation?"

"For Christ's sake, Angie, your whole body is telling you. The rest of your class didn't gain forty pounds and break out in acne!"

"Some did," she said softly.

"Then that's their problem. Your whole being is protesting that this life isn't for you. You wanted kids and a husband and a home! You can't hide out here. Even God won't let you do that. You're crazy if you don't take a stand."

"Will you help me? Sister Directress doesn't seem to listen any more."

"Of course I will. That's why I'm here."

He continued to caress her swollen hands until the Sister Directress reappeared. "Would you like lunch, Father? Sister Marietta can't eat with you, but she can rejoin you after she has eaten."

Santek stared deeply into Sister Raphael's eyes until he saw a glint of fear and doubt. "I want to take Sister Marietta home to her family, Sister. She no longer wants to live the life of a nun. I think her very health is threatened. I would like to pick her up this afternoon."

The directress flushed. "This is not the first young woman who gained weight and was troubled, Father. I had my own difficulties and have found great peace here."

"But she wants to leave, Sister! Perhaps you didn't."

"I thought I did," she mused. "I thank God every day that I stayed."

Santek grew impatient. He felt strong in his uniform. "I'm not here to debate the issue, Sister. I am her spiritual director, and it is my judgment that she wants to leave. I will pick her up this afternoon and drive her to her father's home."

Sister Raphael twisted her folded hands in some pain. "Her own confessor did not give such advice, Father."

"What does he know of her, Sister? I am convinced that Angela has made her decision, and while I have great respect for your order, I see no reason to cause her further mental distress. I want to take her home while she can still walk out and talk coherently."

Sister Directress smiled. "I don't think it's as bad as all that, Father." She turned to Angela. "Do you choose to leave, Sister Marietta?"

Beads of sweat appeared on Angie's forehead. She wanted to cry but controlled herself. "Yes, Sister Directress, I do. I want to leave with Father Santek. I no longer feel called to be a Sister of Mercy."

"You realize that this could all be a temptation, Sister?"

Santek was ready to explode. "I'm sure she's been over all of that, Sister. I'll be back this afternoon to pick her up. What time will she be ready?"

Sister Raphael flushed almost angrily, then regained her composure. "Perhaps sometime around five thirty, when the others are at prayer." She paused. "She has no clothes, Father."

"I'll buy some, Sister!" he said impatiently.

As he made his way out, the portress quickly reappeared and led him to the main door. She had obviously found her place in life and continued to smile with an ecstatic look of pure beatitude. "You're always welcome, Father."

He bowed graciously, walked briskly to his car, and wondered what would happen when he was finally alone with Angie.

Ted Santek had two bourbons and a leisurely lunch at the Charcoal House in Toronto. The place suited him, with its plush red booths and mahogany wainscoting, its large stone fireplace and powerful beams stretched across the ceiling. He liked real tablecloths and elegant waiters in formal dress and felt a strange excitement in living that he had not known for months. The smile and charm returned. He chatted with the maître d', savored his steak and salad, and ordered a brandy after his meal. He would have preferred a beer but felt it would be out of place in such surroundings.

He wondered what Angie really wanted. It did not seem likely that she would go home to her father. There was nothing there for her except more security and loneliness. And it did not seem possible that she would go with him. She had made that clear in Florida, and her guilt would be impossible for her to live with.

Even if she agreed, what did he really want? Could he leave the priesthood when it had begun to mean something again, despite his lapses and periodic unhappiness? He ordered more brandy and a fresh cup of coffee. His priesthood had at times grown stale and impersonal and seemed increasingly less exciting, but the promotion had given him new energy. Besides, to leave would destroy his family and corrode his own future. He was trained for nothing but the priesthood. In reality, he loved being a priest when his loneliness and sexual needs were under control. He could become an Episcopalian. He laughed. Impossible! Angie would never let him leave the priesthood on her account. Would she stay with him? He doubted it. Her Catholic conscience would never permit it. Nor would his. He couldn't lead a double life.

He needed Beauvais. He hadn't heard from him since a few weeks after he was transferred to Farmington. Farmington? The move totally puzzled him. Beauvais in Farmington was like Santek in Hyde Park. It made no sense at all. Beauvais had joked about the move: finally enough time for music and reading. Maybe he and Angie should drive to Farmington and talk. It would give some perspective. There were too many unknowns to make an immediate decision. It was only important to get Angie out before she spent another night in the seminary. She was falling apart.

He paid his check, complimented the staff, and made his way out. The parking attendant brought his car, and expansively he tipped him five dollars. He found a woman's clothing store and purchased slacks of two different sizes and a couple of loose-fitting sweaters. He found a movie theater and watched *Zorba the Greek* and loved it. Somehow it strengthened his resolve. Maybe he couldn't leave the priesthood, but he had to be free. That's who he was.

A little before five he drove slowly back to the motherhouse and into the visitors' parking lot.

Angie had been a nervous wreck ever since her conversation with Sister Raphael. She had toyed with her asparagus soup and nibbled at a puffy sugar cookie while she sipped tea, grateful for the silence. After lunch she scrubbed the back stairs leading to the kitchen, peeled potatoes for almost an hour, and then did some spiritual reading in the library, all in silence. She returned to her cell briefly to pick up a small picture of her mother and a holy card commemorating her death, a box of matches from the Florida bar where she had met Ted, and a letter he had sent her professing his love. She hid these in her missal and, together with a small golden crucifix she had received on her confirmation day, tucked them into the holster pockets strapped around her waist. She wondered if Ted would remember to bring underwear.

She was startled when Sister Raphael appeared soundlessly at her door. Her face was pale and her usual serenity was missing. There was a redness around her deep-set eyes.

"I think you are making a grave mistake, Sister Marietta. You are not an adolescent like the others. You are a mature woman who chose to be a nun. You cannot walk away from God as if you never made a commitment."

Angela was surprised at her own strength. "I am not walking away from God, Sister Directress. I am only choosing to serve him in another way." Somehow Sister Raphael did not seem to have the same old hold on her, but Angela was troubled by her obvious pain. "I will always remember you, Sister Directress. I love you. You have been my very good friend. I would like to write to you one day."

Sister Raphael trembled noticeably. "And I have loved you, Sister. Perhaps it is because you are so very special to me that I find it hard for you to go. Perhaps I have confused God's will with my own. If so, I am sorry."

Angela moved toward her and embraced her lovingly. Sister Raphael kissed her on the cheek. "I hope you will find the peace and happiness you seek." Then, with some secret source of strength, she regained her composure and became Sister Directress again. "You are to tell no one of your leavetaking, Sister Marietta."

"Could I not just say a brief goodbye to Sister Louise and Sister Damien?"

"It is forbidden, Sister."

Angela was well aware of the usual procedure. An empty chair in the refectory meant that someone else had left. That was all. No goodbyes, no tears. The absent sister's name was not mentioned again. It was the custom of the order lest a departure undermine the vocation of another nun. Angela was to leave and not look back. Her refectory chair would be filled, her cell would be given to another sister, and the ripples of her presence would soon disappear like a stone in a serene lake.

"You will leave during Benediction, Sister Marietta, after everyone is in place. They will think you have taken ill. I presume your priest will be waiting for you outside. Please avoid any contact with anyone when you leave."

She turned to move away. Her face softened. "Goodbye, dear

142

Sister, and may you grow in Christ's love." She pressed her hand gently, her eyes moistened and she glided away down the corridor.

Angela made a point of finding a place at the end of the pew on the outside aisle so that her leavetaking would create as little disturbance as possible. As the familiar prayers began, she rehearsed her escape, hoping against hope that when she entered the professed sisters' corridor no one would be around. She began trembling again. How long should she wait? She heard the organ music as the nuns' voices rose in a giant sibilant sound to sing the "O Salutaris Hostia." This was the time to make her move! She hesitated for a few moments, struggling to keep her composure, then left her pew slowly, genuflected on two knees to the Blessed Sacrament, and made her way to the Sister Directress a few rows behind. She approached her nervously and spoke softly.

"I don't feel well, Sister Directress."

"You don't look well, Sister Marietta. You may return to your room." Her lips trembled as she spoke.

Fighting the urge to say goodbye to her friends, Angela went slowly down the aisle, her head discreetly bowed, her hands hidden in her sleeves, and moved out into the vestibule. She opened the door slowly just as one of the cooks made her way to the chapel. She let the door close and watched through a crack until the cook disappeared. She could hear the "Tantum Ergo" of Benediction being sung and knew that she had only a few minutes before the chapel service was over. Where had the time gone? She looked again; there was no one in sight. Trembling in her whole body, she opened the magic door of freedom and walked down the long corridor. There was still no one in sight. Somehow she walked swiftly, feeling as if she were a thief or renegade about to be caught by the police. The corridor seemed endless. She could see the main entrance and prayed that no one would be around. She heard voices and ducked back into the shadows of a small office alcove. The voices moved away, and she slipped back into the corridor. She walked toward the marble entranceway and slid across the terrazzo. Only a few more feet.

Suddenly an old nun appeared at the top of the stairs. Certainly she would see her and wonder what a seminary Sister was doing in the main corridor. The nun looked right at her and spoke.

"A lovely day, Sister."

It was one of the gentle, senile nuns who were permitted to come and go around the building as they pleased. Angie could only

143

nod in relief and make her way to the front door. She pushed it open and heard the sound of an engine. A green Oldsmobile pulled up in front of the steps. She raced down. The door opened. Out of the corner of her eye she could see three nuns coming from the college toward the entry. She ducked down next to the car and slid inside.

Ted drove out toward the main gate. The college sisters smiled warmly and waved at him as he drove by. They looked as if they belonged. He waved back. Then Angela and Father Ted Santek were out the main gate and gone.

Chapter 13

Father Gerald Beauvais decided he liked St. Mary's of Farmington on his very first Sunday there. Though the choir was abysmal and the church in need of repair, the people were warm and friendly like his own family. He still felt the shock of transfer and anger at the implied reasons for it and at Bishop Sullivan's seeming arrogance, but now he began to realize that the busy life at the cathedral had taken its toll on his priestly spirituality. There had been no real time for private prayer and meditation, his breviary had been recited perfunctorily and distractedly, and he had given little time to preparing his sermons. Nor had he had much time for the people, since he was too frequently on the road. He quickly discovered that the changes in the liturgy had created confusion and resentment in Farmington, where tradition was everything. New hymns, wordy English prayers: all of it upset the people and their pastor and made them wonder if the Church were not finally surrendering to the world.

The people of Gerry's new parish were largely of German stock whose forebears had emigrated to Michigan in the nineteenth century. The fertile land and vast acreage of southern Michigan provided them with all the farmland they needed, and they raised families of nine or ten children who worked diligently to raise corn, potatoes, onions, the nation's finest tomatoes, apples, peaches, grapes, and cattle. Their dairy farms were as fine as any in America. These were not poor truck farmers eking out a living but a prosperous community of strong, intelligent, successful agricultural experts who enjoyed a hearty life. They took to the smiling Beauvais immediately.

Since most of the people of the area were Catholics, there were few converts or mixed marriages and practically no divorce or birth control. The parishioners supplied the pastor with meat and vegetables, a variety of home-canned goods, and an assortment of pastries and breads. Gerry Beauvais might miss the excitement of cathedral life and his deep friendship with Ed Sanders, but he assuredly would not starve. Peggy proved to be an outstanding cook, and in the first few months of his stay he gained twelve pounds. More than that, she appeared to be a deeply spiritual woman who attended the early Mass every day before work at the Dairy Coop and spent some time in the church after her evening work was done.

Beauvais had managed to avoid Ed Sanders with a variety of excuses of how busy he was without an assistant and how important it was that he not stray too far from the rectory. Ed drove over one night for dinner—there was no way to put him off—and found Beauvais strangely preoccupied and distant, despite his warm hospitality and congenial conversation. The bonds of easy friendship and totally honest communication had been interrupted. Ed attributed it to his friend's disappointment in the new assignment but found it impossible to draw him out.

"Is there something you're not telling me? Heart trouble? Cancer? Otherwise this is the stupidest move in the world!"

Beauvais smiled softly. "Maybe they thought I was working too hard. Or maybe the new bishop isn't a music buff. I know I haven't received any orders from the chancery to visit any parishes. Allegedly I'm still diocesan director of music, but I don't get any assignments. That part just doesn't make sense. But I like it here. It gives me time to read and reflect and reassess my priesthood."

"But for how long? Davidson can't fill your shoes. He's a nice young guy with a real love for music, and he plays a good guitar, but he's not even in your league. The people don't want Bob Dylan and Joan Baez, they want a powerful, prayerful, ancient liturgy. All your work will go down the tubes. Several of the boys have dropped out already. The adults are more patient and need the outlet, but I'm only going to give it another month or so. Pope Paul is replacing the Latin and chant with crap."

"It's not the pope, it's the Liturgical Commission. They wouldn't know a real human being if they ran over one. I wish you'd hang in, Ed. Maybe Sullivan will recognize what's happening and recall me."

146

Ed was totally puzzled. Normally, Beauvais would have recited all the fresh gossip about the move. Now he was feigning some ignorance that seemed totally unlike him. When his smile dimmed, there was a profound sadness in his eyes that Ed had never seen before, as though some light had gone out permanently. But there was nothing he could do. Beauvais would not be drawn out. After dinner they shared a little brandy, listened to Bach, whom they both loved, and spent the rest of the evening in silence or awkward conversation. Beauvais, increasingly uncomfortable, brought the dying camaraderie to an abrupt halt by announcing that he had an early Mass in the morning. Even Ed's announcement of the date of his forthcoming marriage did not have the impact he might have anticipated.

"I'm expecting you to do the honors."

"I'll do my damnedest to get there."

"You'd better. Your presence is as important as Rosalie's."

Beauvais laughed briefly at the remark and walked his friend to his car. Ed looked at him sadly.

"I wish you could share what's really going on. We've been friends for a long time. I'd like to be a real friend now. You're hurting badly!"

Beauvais did not avoid the issue. "I wish I could tell you everything. I just can't do it."

"Maybe next time?"

"Maybe next time." He laughed. "At least I'll know how to operate a corn picker and a threshing machine."

But they both knew that something had changed radically and there might not be a next time. Some intimacy had disappeared.

After a few months of too much inactivity, when Gerry had caught up on his reading and listened to Brahms far into the night, when the church had been repainted inside, the roof repaired, and most families visited, he began to experience an occasional despondency. He tried to ignore it, struggled to get involved, but no matter what he did to overcome it, nothing seemed to absorb his consciousness or control his black moods. They startled him because they were unfamiliar and beyond his control. They came like a sudden wave, then were finally gone after a few hours or, gradually, only after a day or so. On such occasions he felt not only strangely helpless but almost terrified.

Whereas formerly he would take leisurely drives in the afternoon to visit his parishioners, and even occasionally stay for dinner, when the despondency hit he did not seem to have the energy to move. He said his Mass in the morning and recited part of his breviary, keeping his mind on what he was doing with difficulty. Two afternoons a week he conducted religion classes for high school students, but his own classes gradually grew listless and uninspired when he was depressed, and fewer students attended, even when he struggled to talk about Bob Dylan, the frequent missile launches as America began challenging the moon, or even the military buildup in Vietnam. He was not himself and could not put energy into his classes or anything else.

Much of Beauvais's work was optional. Thus he could make regular visits to the hospital, chat with the aged in convalescent homes, visit the state prison nearby, or make himself available for high school retreats. But none of this was really necessary, and increasingly he found it difficult to summon up the energy. In the beginning he had enjoyed dropping in on the six- and seven-year-olds preparing for their First Communion, but soon he was not up to making even a token appearance except during his "good" days.

He began to spend more time with Peggy after the evening meal, encouraging her to sit with him and sip wine. It was as if he feared to be alone or even to move. Her serene air and amiable outlook seemed to restore his energy. He began to realize that her real beauty was a reflection of a profound inner serenity. They watched TV, something he had rarely done before, played Scrabble, or just talked, usually about his past or her concern about the poverty in Appalachia or the confusion of the Church. She rarely talked about herself unless he asked, and then only an occasional word or two. His time with her was the one thing he really looked forward to each day, and when she left for home the heavy weight of depression often descended upon him without explanation. He chain-smoked, turned music on and off, picked up a book or magazine and soon lost interest, and drank more wine than he ever had before. Alcohol, which once would have calmed him, seemed to depress him more. Finally, he could only pray. And he prayed more intently and more frequently than he ever had before.

He prayed that God would come closer and make his presence known. Prayed that he might be rescued from the dark night of the soul that inexplicably had descended upon him. Prayed with Christ in the Garden of Olives and on the cross that this chalice of sorrow would pass away. Often, late at night, when the depression was most severe, he walked over to the church and lay prostrate in the

148

sanctuary begging for deliverance. More than once he fell asleep there and was awakened by the janitor unlocking the church.

At times there were refreshing moments of peace and serenity when he surrendered himself totally to God's will and he again visited his flock and felt joyful in his new assignment. But the mood would soon pass as inexplicably as it came, and he was lost in a recurring, often unrelenting depression. It was as if nothing could rescue him. He tore at his own psyche, questioned his motives and behavior, wondered if he was being punished for some attitude unwittingly assumed in life, begged for the humility and resignation that might make of his pain a loving sacrifice to God. Only the moments with Peggy seemed to give him some relief, and this, too, gradually became more sporadic. It was as if nothing and no one could really rescue him. And that was the most terrifying feeling of all.

Again and again he tried to force himself, with all the accumulated willpower of his seminary training, to become more active in the parish. He made another attempt to work with the choir, but the lack of talent was so obvious he soon gave up and allowed them to continue in their accustomed ways. In the past he would have worked with them individually until he had created what was needed for a choir of quality, but now, if things did not work out almost immediately, he lost interest. It might have helped if there had been assignments from the chancery office to work on the musical programs of larger parishes, or to solidify the work that he had already begun, but Gerry Beauvais was an isolated and forgotten priest in St. Mary's of Farmington. Even though he was invited to the usual dinners for priests after Confirmations or Forty Hours Devotions, he did not have the energy or interest to attend. The smiles that had been ever-present on his face, the easy laughter, became far more infrequent.

"I had such dreams," he said to Peggy one evening. "But they all centered in music. Maybe I was never meant to be a priest."

"I doubt that," said Peggy. "Maybe God is just asking you to change directions. Suffering can purify and heal us if we don't fight it. When my mother died and my father became my responsibility, the last thing in the world I wanted to do was to come back to Farmington. I loved Chicago and my job in the Furniture Mart, meeting stimulating people, getting ready for shows, eating on Rush Street and at the Palmer House. I had dates, excitement, dancing, all I dreamed of. I had forgotten all about my two-year marriage to an alcoholic."

"Here in Farmington?" asked Beauvais.

"No, I left Farmington at seventeen and moved to Detroit, working days and taking classes nights at Wayne State. I married a very horny Catholic medical student at High Mass, and he thought that drinking and slapping me around was part of the contract. Actually, he wasn't any more ready for marriage than I was. He just wanted a part-time momma and sex partner. And I was a busty, round little Dago girl who loved to make love. Leaving him and going to Chicago was like entering heaven. Probably for him too."

"The adjustment must have been terrible, to come back to Farmington, to care for your dad, and—"

"It wasn't so hard at first. I felt I would be going back soon, so I took a leave of absence from the Mart, but when I discovered that my father had no money and his health was going fast . . . well, it was hard to be the 'noble daughter,' sacrificing her happiness to support her father. And then, when I had to get a job at the Dairy Coop, the divorcée returned home, I wasn't ready for the men. They all knew I had been married, so I was kind of the blue-ribbon prize to get into bed."

"My God! How did you handle it?"

"When they made filthy remarks, I ignored them. I wasn't a grinning little hot-blooded Italian Catholic girl any more; I had plenty of experience with a sophisticated, wife-beating drunk. But when some of the men began looking damned attractive, and my entire social life centered around going home to my dad and watching TV, my morality was really put to the test. In Chicago, no one seemed to care if I lived with a man, two women, or a turkey, but here everyone knew everything that went on, and sex was a big deal! One married man in particular really attracted me. I had dinner with him a few times, slept in out-of-the-way motels, and then decided that sex didn't solve my problems and I couldn't do it any more. I needed love, to give or receive and preferably both, and that's when I started helping out here at the parish."

"Would you marry again?"

"Not in Farmington."

"In Chicago?"

"If I met the right man. That's why I never receive the sacraments, as you may have noticed. I don't accept the Church's position on divorce. My 'holy marriage' was a nightmare." She laughed.

"God and I annulled my marriage a long time ago. We're just waiting for the Church to catch up."

She paused and looked at him directly.

"I do wonder how you hang on. Or maybe why. I think I have come to understand my suffering. Chicago was really leading me nowhere. At least now, if an opportunity came along, I would recognize it. I never would have met you if God had not brought me home. But your pain seems to be destroying you."

Beauvais, really for the first time in his life, talked of his own vocation, of his admiration for Father Misch, and of the days in the seminary, especially the friendship with Ted Santek.

"It all seemed so simple. Happiness was assured. I just kind of floated into the priesthood. No great drive for it, but it seemed to offer me the kind of life I wanted."

"Were you never in love with a woman?"

"No, not really. There were a couple of brief crushes in the navy and a very attractive young woman in Austria I still think about, but I guess I feared down deep that women would not find me attractive."

"I doubt that," she said quietly, blushing softly. "But I had the same feeling about men. I always felt like a squat little Italian with a future in too much pasta."

He laughed nervously, hardly able to reply. "The pasta looks good on you, Peggy."

She refused to detour into small talk. "I would like to stay in the rectory here with you. I think I could help. Your loneliness is destroying you, and I feel the same loneliness. It's been three years since I had to leave Chicago, and God sent me here for some reason. I think you're the reason. My time with you is good time for both of us."

Her dark eyes shone, her olive complexion seemed almost golden in the soft light of the living room. Her long dark hair framed her plain face and fell gently across her shoulders. Some inner light seemed to refashion her simple grace into a kind of childlike beauty. There was no boldness or seduction in her manner, only the simple honesty of one who had known a great deal of life and pain.

Beauvais found it hard to look at her. "What about your father?"

"I can look in on him, and there's a woman next door who could help. I think your need is a greater one." Beauvais hesitated. She anticipated his fear. "I know you are celibate and I respect that. I will be no threat to your virginity, but you must have love and caring if you are to survive!"

He could not answer her. Mozart's Clarinet Quintet played in the background. He twisted nervously in his easy chair and sipped his wine. Peggy continued to gaze at him from the couch across the room, her shoes off, her legs yoga-like under her body. Then slowly she got up and moved across the room and sat in front of his chair.

"I want to stay with you tonight," she said. "I have watched you suffer too long, and I want you to know you have me. I will always be here as your friend as long as you want me."

"No," he said. "I would need you. I would not be able to let go of you, and then I would have nothing left."

She continued to look at him, studying his face. For five or ten minutes neither of them moved. Then Beauvais spoke softly.

"Maybe you should go now, Peggy. I need to be alone to think."

She got up slowly and stared at him with great tenderness. "I care about you very much, and I would never interfere with your priesthood. I don't understand your God or your religion any more. My own pain has given me a new understanding of God. He has a plan for me, and I am ready to follow wherever it may lead. I don't know what else to do. I am only a very ordinary woman, but I understand pain and hurt and caring. You are a truly good man, worthy of my concern, and I want to stay with you in any manner I can. You are being destroyed and I won't permit it!" She grinned. "You'll have to throw me out on my ear. I warn you, I'm not gorgeous, but I'm tough."

He looked up at her. The words came slowly. "I need you, Peggy. I'm just so afraid . . . like I'm losing control . . . of my life. . . ."

She picked up her purse and made her way to the door. Then she returned and kissed him softly on the cheek. Her expression told him that they would together conquer this strange demon. He could not move from his chair. Then she was gone.

He lit a cigarette and sipped the last of the wine, finally moved to the stereo and shut off the music. He turned out the light and smoked his cigarette in darkness. Only the dim reflection of the moon through a side window in the small dining room gave any light. With great effort, he finally got up and made his way to the church, prostrating himself in the sanctuary with his face down and his arms outstretched. He was alone with his God. Slowly he began to feel again the power and meaning of his priesthood as he united himself with Christ on the cross. He wondered about Peggy and his own feelings—admitting to God that he wanted her, that he needed her, but promising with his whole heart that he would never violate his celibacy, even if he didn't really understand it.

It was only then that he felt some semblance of peace, but he shuddered with the awful awareness that the overpowering blackness would soon again descend.

Chapter 14

It was after nine and Peggy was clearing away the remains of a veal scallopini dinner, served with an expensive Valpolicella to celebrate a brief lifting of Beauvais's depression, when the doorbell rang. Gerry checked his watch. Who could be calling at this hour? Probably a transient who needed food or bus fare to visit a sick mother. He pulled a few dollars from his wallet and slipped on his roman collar and black coat over his T-shirt, wondering if his breath smelled of wine. Then he flipped on the front porch light, stuffed the money in his coat pocket, and opened the door.

Ted Santek and a strange woman stood in the doorway. Santek beamed one of his broadest smiles. Gerry hadn't laid eyes on him in more than two years.

"I was betting on you being home, baby! God, you're thin!"

They embraced spontaneously, exchanging an assortment of expletives, and only then did Ted introduce his companion. "Gerry, this is Angela!"

Beauvais extended his hand warmly. "Welcome to your home away from home."

Beauvais found it hard to hide his shock. She wasn't the beauty Ted had described. The brown hair was cut ludicrously like a GI's. Her face was swollen and pale, and a rash covered her cheeks and forehead. Her incredible blue eyes were sad and frightened, and she clung to Ted's hand. Her gray slacks were too tight and her blue sweater was at least two sizes too big. She stood in mock contrast to the debonair Santek in his air force uniform, looking trim and full of life. Beauvais noticed the captain's bars, which gave him a chance to recover from the shock of Angela. He whistled admiration at his friend's promotion.

"Somebody up there loves you. A few years premature, lad. You must be impressing the brass."

"It was nothing. I just pulled three guys out of a burning jet and played poker with a couple of generals."

They laughed as if nothing had changed. Peggy heard the commotion and came in from the kitchen, still in her apron. Recognizing Father Santek from his pictures, she started to move back into the kitchen. Beauvais motioned her into the room and introduced her to Ted and Angela. Santek grinned mischievously.

"I see why you like it here, Ger. Doesn't canon law suggest an older woman, a *superadulta*, if memory serves me?"

"It's all in the translation," said Beauvais. "The modern translation is a 'neat lady.'" Beauvais's depression seemed forgotten in the excitement of his friend's presence.

Peggy blushed appropriately.

"Have you eaten?" Beauvais asked.

"Yeah, we ate in Detroit."

"Peggy, bring in some wine and take off your apron."

"I'll take bourbon rocks," Santek said.

Peggy nodded and disappeared. Ted carefully settled Angela on the couch next to him and slid off his coat, while Beauvais took his favorite leather chair, slipped off his collar and coat, and lit a cigarette.

"God, it's good to see you, Ted. I was just thinking about a trip to Scott." He wanted to talk of his depression, but it seemed an inappropriate time.

"I'm being moved to Lackland next week."

"Where's Lackland? In Texas?"

"Yeah, near San Antonio. Not exactly an easy drive."

"Well, bring me up to date. What the hell's happening?"

Santek settled back and talked about springing Angie from the convent, while Peggy passed drinks around. They laughed about Angela's haircut and she blushed violently.

"Another month in that place and she would have hung herself from the main altar. I had a bit of a struggle with the Sister Directress, but it all worked out."

Beauvais was momentarily alarmed. "Do they know who you are?"

155

"Not really. Nuns ask few questions of priests. Actually, I could have been an imposter!"

"Maybe she should call her family."

"She already did. There's just her dad, and he was relieved that she had left. She told him she had a job arranged in the States and would write as soon as she got settled."

Peggy, sensing that Beauvais needed to be alone with his friend, led Angela into the kitchen. Santek retrieved the bourbon bottle and more ice from the dining room table and poured himself a generous drink. Beauvais continued to sip his wine.

"What the hell are you going to do with her?"

"I don't know yet. Maybe marry her." He laughed. "I'm not really sure what to do, Ger. She needs some help to get on her feet."

"You can't leave the priesthood."

"I'm not even sure of that. The service has been good duty, but half the time I'm just going through the motions. Too often, I'm drinking too much, and at times I'm confused as hell. Then I reform and work my ass off out of loneliness. I notice every attractive woman in the congregation on the base and wonder if we could have something. You know I still love the priesthood—but without a woman I just don't seem to make it. God knows I try! As bad as Angie looks, I think I'm still in love with her. As we drove down here, all those old feelings came pouring back. Even her effort to run from me only proves her character. She's an incredible woman, Ger."

"Then why don't you just continue seeing her without deciding to leave the priesthood? What the hell kind of work would you do? There's not a big demand for ex-priests. Not even charming, good-looking ones." He had been reflecting on his own departure for several weeks. Ursula had even agreed to come to America when she read of his depression.

"Shit, I'm not worried about getting a job. That's no sweat! I just don't know if I have the guts to leave. I'm afraid for all the wrong reasons. Mainly my family. It would embarrass the hell out of them."

Beauvais lit another cigarette. "Just take your time, Ted. You don't have to do anything right now."

"I have to be back at the base tomorrow. Then I have to move to Lackland. It'll take a few months. I don't know what the hell to do with Angie."

156

"Then leave her here. She can stay with Peggy until she gets herself together and you get some clarity on it all. She looks like she needs about six months of good food and R and R. She can't even laugh."

"That's asking a lot of Peggy."

"You don't know Peggy. Besides, I can find her some work around the parish. I like the idea of having two women wait on me."

"Christ, I can't tell you how much I appreciate it. I just can't—"

"No speeches! It's done. You get moved to Lackland, do what you have to do, and we'll get Angie back in shape. You have an important decision to make, and I don't want it to be Polish impulse. She'll be fine!"

They heard laughter from the kitchen.

"See? It's already happening."

Santek looked directly at his friend. "How are you doing here?"

Beauvais stubbed out his cigarette slowly and sipped more wine. He waited a long time before speaking. "I'm just hanging on. I've been depressed as hell, and when the blues hit, I too just go through the motions. Then the depression lifts briefly and I'm okay. I don't know what's wrong. Peggy has been a lifesaver. On the bad days, I look forward to her coming. Nothing else makes much sense. Sometimes I'm able to say Mass with real devotion, usually begging God's help. But there's not really a lot to do, and the way I've been feeling, I don't really create work."

"Why the hell did Sullivan send you here? It doesn't make sense. You were doing great things with diocesan music!"

Beauvais looked off into space. "I guess he thinks I'm a fag."

"A fag?" Santek almost screamed the words. "How the hell did he come to that conclusion?"

Beauvais told him of the formal confrontation at the bishop's office and Monsignor Kelley's obvious embarrassment.

"Kelley's a creep. But I wouldn't have believed he'd blow the whistle. The poor, miserable bastard! I guess everyone gets desperate in his own way." Santek stood up and walked across the room to his friend. "Why the hell didn't you tell me sooner?"

"I was too damned embarrassed."

"Hell, I wouldn't give a damn if you were a total fag, complete with silk stockings. I love you. Nothing makes any difference. You're dying in this place. Are you in love with Peggy?"

"In a sense."

"In what sense? Do you sleep with her?"

"No."

"Why the hell not?"

"I don't think sex will solve my problem. It may only compound it. My celibacy is one of the things I've got left. It still means something—or did when I wasn't depressed. Or maybe I'm just afraid, Ted. Hell's bells, man, I don't know! I've never really slept with a woman."

"Maybe you ought to. But one thing for sure, you've got to start playing politics. You need a parish that challenges you or you'll go nuts. Why don't you start going to Forty Hours and Confirmation dinners? Pop in at the cathedral and have a drink with Kelley or Grady. Kelley probably feels guilty as hell. Sullivan too. Make sure the bishop sees you. You'll get a parish where you can use some of your talent. Meanwhile, there must be something you can do in this place. You can't just lie down and quit. That's why you're depressed."

"I've tried, but I just don't have the interest. They're good people, but I don't have much in common with them, and they really don't need me except to marry and bury and baptize. They're busy people with few problems."

Santek whistled softly. "That's rough. Well, you just gotta start circulating and get the hell out of here! Why don't you go to the bishop directly and tell him that you need something more challenging?"

"C'mon, Ted, he thinks I'm a screaming fag! He'd have patience if I were screwing ten women or even chasing little girls, like that Franciscan who helped out at the cathedral. But a fag? You know that's the number-one sin to Bishop Sullivan. He pictures me running around nude at the Y, getting it going in the shower, the whole ball of wax. Nothing will change his mind. It's not even his fault! Even the fact that Ed Sanders got married didn't count for anything."

"Do you still want to be a priest, Ger?"

"With all my heart, but I don't know if I can hang on when this depression hits. Everything seems so blank and pointless. What about you?"

"I really love the work. I love preaching and counseling, forgiving sins and saying Mass, but I realize I can't seem to live without a woman. After ten years, it still doesn't make any sense to me. I could keep Angie well hidden, and no one would be the wiser. Then I think I could make it. Otherwise, there's not enough to live for."

158

"Lately I've been wondering what the hell a priest is," said Beauvais reflectively. "Sometimes here in the country it all seems like something we've inherited from another era. The magic man for frightened people."

"Well, a hell of a lot of people need the magic man! It makes as much sense as any other life." He said it as if to convince himself.

Beauvais nodded assent. "I just wish I had the simple faith these people have. Or my mother."

"How is your mother?"

"Failing a little, but still strong as an ox. I get down to see her when I can, and it restores my faith in life and the priesthood."

They continued to chat for another hour before Peggy interrupted. She had already assumed that Angie would be her houseguest. Santek said he would get back as soon as he could.

"I'll take good care of her," said Peggy. She laughed. "She'll feel a lot better when her hair grows back and she loses some weight."

Santek approached Angie gently and kissed her on the cheek.

"You won't be long?" she asked. "I don't want to interfere with your life, but I do need you."

"One step at a time. I've got to get moved. Meanwhile, I'll call you every day I can." He laughed. "And next time I see you, you'll look more like your old self."

Angie blushed and smiled, then followed Peggy out the back door to her car.

Santek and Beauvais filled their glasses and settled back down. There was a long silence.

"Do you think there's a God?" Santek asked.

"Yes," said Beauvais, after hesitating for several seconds. "If I didn't, I don't think there'd be much to live for. Sometimes he just seems so far away."

"It's all so complicated. So damn complicated!"

"I know. It seemed so simple once."

Then they were silent, each staring off into some private space in the semidarkness, each feeling unable to resolve his own conflict or that of his best friend.

Lackland was just another air force base, as bleak and spartan as all the rest. The same problems of marriage and divorce, adultery and masturbation, booze and whores and broken hearts. Ted Santek had difficulty maintaining interest. Beauvais's depression had unsettled him. His mind was on Angie and his future, and he wondered if the priesthood was possible for him—with Angie or without her. He heard his confessions while almost half asleep, listening to all the repetitive grocery lists of insignificant sins. The most interesting sinners didn't go to confession, only those who had been scared half out of their wits in Catholic grade school. "In another twenty years there won't be any confessionals," he mused. "Once hell is not a reality, why would anyone go?"

He instructed his converts listlessly, took short cuts, covered the basic lessons haphazardly, and answered questions without real enthusiasm. He had repeated the instructions so many times. What did he care about Confirmation or Extreme Unction? What did he care about the identifying marks of the true Church or papal infallibility? It was all so many words. He was burned out. He had seen it happen to other chaplains. There was a saying among them: "Keep the faith." In reality, it meant you were lucky to come out of the service still believing in God.

All Ted really believed in was Angie. He called her every night when Peggy was attending to Father Beauvais. As the days passed, she told him she had lost the extra weight and her skin had begun to clear. He talked of his love for her, of leaving the priesthood to get married, of starting over in some strange town far away from everyone. Maybe they would go to Florida, where they had first met. Or New York. Or New Orleans. Nothing was impossible. He had saved money and could eventually get a teaching certificate. She had secretarial skills as well as her teaching ability. Their hour-long conversations reviewed one fantasy after another, even when Angela had misgivings and realized how little they knew one another.

"Maybe you wouldn't be happy unless you were a priest."

"No way. I'd be happy with you, pumping gas."

"I feel responsible," she said. "Like I'm taking you from God."

"It's my own decision," he said angrily. "I'd leave with you or without you. My God understands!"

Finally they hung up, pledging their love. He would see her in a few weeks. They would have a month together. He had arranged the time. Meanwhile, after the phone call he tried to read or watch TV, but nothing held his interest. Usually he went out to some lonely bar and sipped beer until he was tired enough to sleep, then he headed back to the BOQ and thought of Angie. He made none of the contacts at Lackland that had endeared him to the men at Scott. The senior chaplain, Colonel Briggs, was concerned.

"Are you feeling well, Captain?"

"Just burned out. I need time off."

"You've got it coming. There's no thanks around here for over-time."

But he could tell from Briggs's inflection that he was not sympathetic and that it could be reflected in his fitness report. He laughed bitterly to himself. The service was just like the Church. There was always someone looking over your shoulder offering a gratuitous evaluation. And nine times out of ten, the evaluation was the work of someone who had never extended himself for anyone. In a few days it would all be over. He and Angie would settle somewhere, and he would resign his commission. His commission was only as valid as his priesthood, and he had lost interest in that.

He had already fabricated the tale he would tell his parents. He had volunteered for missionary work in Africa or Asia. What the hell did it matter? All he had to make sure of was that they would get a letter once in a while. He could arrange that. To them he would still be the devout priest they could boast about, and no one would be the wiser. Certainly no one would tell them any differently. Finally he could start over and live the life he would have lived if Father Al had not pushed him into the priesthood. The ironic thing was that Father Al had himself left six months before.

And, rumor had it, with a guy! The Church was going crazy. Santek made up his mind that he wasn't going crazy with it, no matter what.

Chapter 15

In the months they were together, Angela and Peggy gradually became devoted friends. It was an unusual experience for both of them. Each had lived as a kind of loner, but in reality they were very different kinds of people: Angie, a sensitive, sheltered girl struggling to be a woman, and Peggy, a strong, disillusioned, experienced woman struggling to believe in something. They enjoyed listening to Joan Baez and Peter, Paul, and Mary, tried the new styles in shorter skirts, enjoyed *Mary Poppins* and *My Fair Lady*, and shared confidences over wine coolers. It was easier for Peggy, who had been raised in the intensity of the Italian ghetto, where feelings poured out like wine. Angie was a controlled French-Canadian who had always kept her own counsel and buried her feelings in the tradition of centuries of restraint. Peggy's openness gave Angie new permissions.

After a brief, unsuccessful marriage and a miscarriage, probably because of physical abuse, Peggy had found work in Chicago as an assistant to a broker at the Merchandise Mart.

"It was like I never had confidence in myself till then. I wasn't just a nondescript, stubby little Italian from Hicksville any more. I was bright, funny, and even sexy. I had a good income and a whole new circle of friends. I began to go to the theater and to different restaurants, and I fell in love with my boss, Dave Smathers. He was in a tragic kind of marriage with a polio victim, and even though he loved her we began sleeping together the first night we went out. No man had ever treated me with such love and respect. The Church meant little or nothing to me—it was just a historic hangup that had scarred my childhood and pushed me into a miserable marriage. If my mother hadn't died and my dad been suddenly incapacitated, I never would have come back here.

"I might not even have come back if I had known my dad was going to live so long. His condition was critical, and I felt my stay would be brief. But somehow he hung on and kept me locked in Farmington."

"Would you have married Smathers?" Angie asked.

"I don't know. I didn't really love him. I liked the beautiful sex and someone who treated me well and took me places. Looking back, it was kind of empty, but a fun period of my life and it got me over my Catholic guilt. Maybe that's why I don't have as much patience as I should with your ethical worries. If you love Santek and he loves you, just get married. It wouldn't be easy, marrying a priest, but you would learn about life together. Life's too short to debate and delay and wait for the Church to catch up with you." She laughed. "Besides, Santek would be great with kids."

"It's not as simple as that, Peggy. God makes demands on priests, and there are solemn vows you just can't ignore."

"I think people make demands on themselves, Angie. I wonder if we can know what God expects. For sure, he doesn't want us to ignore love. It comes so rarely. I was so confused when I married that I thought my vows should keep me tied to a madman, and the Church reinforced my ignorance. I guess I can never forgive that. It's hard not to hate the Church for helping make me lose my baby!

"I should have known better. I could have run away, but the priests and nuns were such know-it-alls in my day I was afraid to decide anything for myself. They tried to tell me it was God's will that my baby died!"

Peggy's face flushed from anger and wine.

"That's pure horse shit! I hate that part of the Church where everything becomes God's will, even Gerry's pain. I hope it's different now. Maybe Pope John helped clear things up. You just weren't meant to be a nun, Angie. So you leave or you go nuts. You're no different from any other person in the world, just trying to make it. In fact, you really had it better than most: plenty to eat, time to yourself, respect from others, a community that cared. You created your own torture. We all do. If you start thinking you're special, you can ruin your life. That's the Catholic nonsense that almost drove me whacko."

"It wasn't nonsense to me. I gave it all I had until I was worn out," Angie said.

"But it's not such a tough life if you don't take it all so very seriously. You were just running away rather than facing your feelings for Ted. That's what made it tough."

"But I don't even want to pray any more. It's like I lost God, somehow. All the silence and discipline made no sense. There was no connection between what I went through and the service of people. It was an endurance contest."

Peggy laughed. "Sometimes I think religious people are like little children. All your problems are in your head. I'm not laughing at you, but you didn't really have to endure anything of any real substance. No kids to take care of, no financial problems, no husband, no men trying to get in your drawers, no real pain and tragedy beyond what you create in your own mind. That's why I could never get excited about saints. They were all priests or nuns. Why not bartenders or auto mechanics or strippers in cheap nightclubs supporting a bunch of kids? Now *there's* pain and suffering and reality!"

Angie could only nod. "But the pain seems real."

"It is real. You gained weight, you didn't have a period, your face broke out. But it was all in your head. You could have just said 'The hell with it' and walked out. The fact that you didn't tells us a lot about you and me and the Catholic Church. Why did I wait around in a brutal marriage until my baby died? Our heads murder us."

Peggy was wound up.

"A few years ago I read a book called *Let Us Now Praise Famous Men*. It told about really poor cotton farmers and miners in Alabama and Kentucky. It was so beautiful and revealed the nobility and beauty of these people despite their poverty. The pictures tore my heart out. I was surprised that very few of them were Catholic. At that time, I thought Catholics were the only really good people in the world. But these Appalachian Mountain people didn't see themselves like nuns or priests or very special at all. They just had a job to do and they did it. They rarely had enough food, their kids died like flies, they worked in mines and choked from black lung, they never really had anything. Except love and a sense of their own value. They were happier than most people I know. I never forgot the faces in that book.

"I made up my mind that I was going to spend my life among them. It was like God was really calling me. But somehow life and

164

work got in the way. And yet, it was these people, strangers, that helped me with my own religious struggles and put God and the Catholic Church where it belonged."

No one had ever talked to Angie like this before. Suddenly the pain of the convent didn't seem so significant. In fact, it now seemed very distant. Peggy fascinated her.

"Even the names of the towns were as wild and strange as the people. My girlfriend, Millie Purvis, and I took a bus down there one summer on vacation. I didn't want to come back, but there was just no work or way of staying."

She laughed.

"One toothless old man offered to marry me. I darn near took him up on it. It was all so simple and beautiful. The people had nothing, but they really had everything. We rode through tiny places like Betsy Lane and Grethel, Flat Lick, Stoney Fork, and Jeremiah Latcher. They weren't martyrs or saints, but they moved me a lot more than any Italian virgins and Roman martyrs. Beneath the loose overalls and unbleached cotton dresses there were wise and beautiful people. I loved them. They were nothing like our Italian clan, fighting and hating and judging, all in the name of God. I didn't care whether these people were Catholic or Protestant. I only knew they were honest and friendly. I still miss them and wonder what would have happened to me if I stayed.

"Now I end up here, after so many great dreams and hopes that I would really do something worthwhile with my life. It just never happened. So when my dad needed me, I considered it a challenge to think of someone besides myself. Maybe it was a chance to make my life mean something. And at first it was okay.

"But then it was like I had no reason to get up in the morning. I couldn't really date because I was a divorced woman—at least not in Farmington—so I kept telling myself that God was preparing me for some great work. It was a game I played with myself to keep from going nuts."

Angie put a sympathetic hand on Peggy's arm.

"It wasn't easy around my dad," Peggy went on. "It never was. He's really a self-centered old tyrant. I always felt his anger and rough ways led to my mother's death. She wanted more kids after me, she wanted to have friends and to travel, to read and learn, and he laughed at everything she wanted, called her stupid, ultimately broke her heart. That's how the men in our family were in those days. Some of them still are. So she dies and he lives and I end up taking care of someone I really despise. He still laughs at her, the same way he laughs at me, only I ignore him.

"He doesn't appreciate anything I do. It's all expected. He's the real macho Italian male with no regard for anyone but himself. Maybe if he had a son it would be different. But I'm nothing but a lazy cunt who owes him everything. It's all expected. I can work all day at the Dairy Coop and nights at the rectory, and if his TV isn't working perfectly he screams at me. He doesn't say a word about his perfect lasagna; that's taken for granted. I'm his daughter, a piece of spaghetti. A dozen times I wanted to murder him. I could have done it with a dish towel. Then I cry and tell God I'm sorry and promise to do His will, even if it means taking care of this old man who fathered me. But when I really think I can't take it any more, I don't think of God or the martyrs or the nuns I work with, or even the priests. I think of Alabama and Eastern Kentucky and the pictures I looked at in that book, where the people had nothing and the least consideration was appreciated. And I think I'll go down after my dad dies and end my days there."

Angie was deeply moved. There was really nothing to say. Her own pain seemed inconsequential in the light of Peggy's suffering. Peggy sensed her deep compassion and made light of it.

"It hasn't really been that bad. The hardest part was taking the job at the Dairy Coop, where I felt like I was being undressed by a hundred pairs of eyes every day."

Angie wanted to share her convent feelings, but they seemed childish and inconsequential, so she let Peggy continue. It was as if she had never had a chance to tell anyone.

"In Chicago, I guess I felt like Dave's wife. Yet I knew he would never be mine, even though we vacationed in Acapulco, in Spain, in the Bahamas, and in Alaska when his wife was in a sanitarium or staying with her parents. He was heartbroken when I came back to Michigan and cut him off, but I couldn't saddle him with my dad as well as his wife. I knew he needed someone else and I guess I was also looking for a way out, knowing that I'd really get hurt some day. He drove over a couple of times, but it wasn't the same.

"After Dave was gone, the men at the dairy started looking better to me. That's when I knew I'd been in Farmington too long. But I was no longer the scarlet divorcée I'd been. Gradually they started respecting me. And when my dad hung on endlessly, I finally began dating one of the married men on the sly. I thought I was in love with him and gave in on the very first night, I was so damned starved for love. He had practically undressed me before I could resist him. Then I didn't want to.

"Later I told him I couldn't see him any more—but I did, several times, until finally I went to confession here to Father John. I thought I was pregnant and couldn't live with myself. He got me involved in doing parish work and teaching the kids. I guess he saved my life, always gently encouraging me, never judging me. The kind of Christlike priest I needed. Now, with Father Beauvais, it seems like a whole new world. He really needs me."

"Are you in love with him?" Angie asked quietly.

"Who knows? I'm happy being around him. He's the kindest man I've ever known. When he hurts, I hurt. I'd do anything for him. My whole day begins when I come here in the evening." She paused. "I guess I'm confused now. I used to dream about going back to Chicago to make enough money to take a trailer and work among the people of Appalachia. I can still join the Peace Corps. But now I'm torn. I want to stay with him, to work with him."

Her voice grew soft.

"For some reason he's fighting for his very life. He won't tell me why. I just know he is, even though I don't know what his struggle is. I don't really want anything from him. I accept his celibacy and appreciate it for what it is. I know there's a hell of a lot more to love than sleeping together. Dave was dying of loneliness, so I know it can happen. I think that God sent me here. It's funny to say that because I have so little respect for the Church and its God. It's all gone. If Pope John hadn't appeared, I think I'd have lost all faith."

She laughed.

"In Chicago, I didn't think about the pope or the Church. Sex and life was my own decision—to pray or not to pray, to love or not to love—and the Catholic Church was like a museum in Farmington. Now I think of Father Beauvais all day long. Do I love him? I don't know. It doesn't seem important. He needs me desperately, and I'm here. And I don't want to be anywhere else!"

Peggy filled their wineglasses and took a long sip before she continued.

"Maybe I want to do God's work and have him too. We could devote our lives to the poor or whatever we decided. I keep telling God that we would be an unbeatable team with or without his priesthood." She laughed. "Beauvais knows nothing of these conversations."

Angie was stunned. "Has he talked of leaving?"

"Not in so many words, but he experiences such anguish and depression I don't know why he stays. I can't believe God wants a gifted, sensitive man to live his life in misery."

"What makes him hang on?"

"I really don't know. Maybe God or his priesthood, maybe his family in Ohio. Especially his mother. Most priests have a thing with their mother."

"What kind of thing?"

"They were the chosen son, and they want to be taken care of for the rest of their lives. I don't think men really grow up in the priesthood. A lot of attention is paid to them, their collar admits them to hundreds of homes, and people in the parish are willing to do anything for them. Their whole life is a kind of clergy discount. They're mothered from birth till death. If any group of men should be married and have children, the Catholic clergy should head the list. And their wives should be half mothers." She laughed.

"I think Ted just wants to leave. He says he's lost interest in his priesthood."

"Maybe, Angie, and maybe not. What if he decides to remain a priest? Will you stay with him?"

"A year ago I couldn't have. But I don't have the same kind of faith I had before. Or maybe I grew up. Like you said, I was running away, and the kind of spiritual challenge they offered me in the convent just dried me up. Some girls blossomed beautifully, but I was dying there and almost lost my faith in everything. All I knew was I wanted Ted. Not my father or friends in Moncrief, just Ted! And from the moment he came to the convent, I started breathing again. It no longer felt like I was taking him from God. The whole world of the convent seemed petty and unreal, like a bad dream to me. I was always living inside my head, keeping track of my spiritual progress, trying to solve the problems that community life created. I didn't even see the trees or the flowers, I didn't laugh or sing or act wild and crazy. I was determined to be a saint and lose my personality in Christ."

Peggy smiled. "I can tell. You still walk like a nun. You even talk like one. Shoulders high, head down, a measured gait, a discreet laugh, a controlled inflection—you've got it all, girl. You were going to do it all by willpower, and you just didn't belong there." She laughed heartily. "Maybe we should just get drunk."

"One more glass of wine and I will be."

"Good." Peggy reached for the bottle on the coffee table and

168

again filled Angie's glass and her own. She slipped off her shoes and settled yogalike on the couch. Her olive complexion looked more deeply sensual in the dim light of the living room.

"Have you ever made love with Ted?"

"I've never made love with anyone. I wouldn't know how. I've never seen a man naked. I'm a thirty-one-year-old virgin."

"Aren't you curious?"

Angie blushed and stammered briefly at Peggy's directness.

"I-I don't know what I am. It just doesn't seem as wrong any more. I don't know why it doesn't, but convent life changed something in me. I guess it all seemed so unreal to me that I'm beginning to trust my own feelings."

"I can almost look back on my Catholic school," said Peggy, "and be grateful for the good things it taught me. Like patience and simplicity and a love of solitude, and especially some kind of idealism I've never lost."

"I have the same feeling about doing something important," said Angie. "But every time I think about it, I remember my bloated face, the pimples and the silence, the boredom and the self-absorption, making trivial faults into serious character flaws."

Peggy grinned broadly. "That will pass, and convents will change too. Even the nuns who teach catechism here are alive and different. It's a new world now. Pope John was smart enough to realize we need a new Church. His successor doesn't seem as aware, but you'll get over your anger and even appreciate some things you learned. You'll even find yourself loving the nuns again, and you'll realize that they're just women like the rest of us. Usually dominated by men, too. It's funny. I fought every invitation to the convent. I knew I wanted to help people, but the convent never seemed right for me. Even the Church has always seemed strange. When you're Italian it all kind of mingles with your background."

"I fought the convent since third grade," said Angie. "Every nun I ever had told me I was the perfect candidate. And when my mother died, the nuns were like my family. But I doubt I ever would have entered if I hadn't met Ted. I didn't know any other way to get away from my feelings."

They sipped more wine in silence, each enjoying a comforting closeness with another woman that neither of them had really ever known. There was nothing they couldn't admit to each other. It was a new, refreshing freedom.

"Maybe I would like to make love to him," Peggy said after sev-

169

eral minutes. "Or maybe I'm drunk." She laughed. "I'd just like to see the smile on his face when he let it all out."

She paused reflectively, her voice now gently slurred from the wine.

"Maybe I'll seduce him. What do you think? Do you think I'll go to hell in a handbasket?"

Angie had fallen asleep. She looked like a peaceful little girl.

Peggy surveyed her carefully. "If you survive Ted Santek, you'll grow up in a hurry, my sweet baby."

Then she covered her with an afghan, brushed back her hair, and kissed her gently good night.

Chapter 16

When Ted Santek arrived at St. Mary's rectory in Farmington on a beautiful May evening, almost six months later, no one would ever have suspected he was a priest. Resplendent in tapered brown slacks and cream-colored cashmere sport coat, he could have been a doctor or a lawyer or a jazz musician, for that matter. Anything but a priest. He was flushed and exuberant before his first drink.

"Christ, I'm out! I can't believe it!"

He grabbed Angie, draped in an elegant chocolate chiffon dress that showed a touch of cleavage and rose a few inches above her knees, and hugged her warmly. The pimples and extra pounds had all but disappeared, and he had never seen her more beautiful. She stiffened briefly at his embrace and then surrendered in his arms. For the first time in her life, she allowed herself to feel almost like a woman with a man.

Beauvais, in his finest red and black silk dinner jacket, beamed with pleasure at his friend's delight and was able to forget about his own black shadow, which seemed more insistent every day. He looked momentarily grave.

"You didn't resign your commission?"

"Hell, no. I got settled in Lackland and worked my ass off. Nobody suspects anything. I want everything that's coming to me. After a month in New Orleans or wherever the hell else we want to go, I'll go back to Lackland and take care of that. We might as well use the air force as long as we can."

"I just hope you don't move too fast, Ted."

"Don't worry, baby. I'm moving a step at a time. I just wish to hell you and Peggy were going with us. We'd kill 'em on Bourbon Street." He started to sing, "Oh, when the saints . . . go marching in . . ."

Beauvais couldn't resist joining him, and the rectory rocked with a joy it hadn't known for a very long time. Peggy, tending a roast in the kitchen, rushed in for the second verse, while Angie, not familiar with the English words, sang along in French.

The meal was perfect, with the rib roast medium rare and a smooth Pommard that Beauvais had saved for the occasion. Even Peggy's first attempt at chocolate mousse was superb. While the women cleared the table, laughing like sorority sisters, the two priests settled in the living room with cigars and Chopin.

"It's good to see you laugh again, Ger."

"I thought I'd forgotten how."

"I know the feeling. I feel like I've been reborn. God, I love her! And no one to answer to any more. I was almost afraid to take a drink on the way here, I was so damned high already. It's like everything I've been holding in just exploded. I walked out of the BOQ with my suitcase and started jumping up and down like a six-year-old kid. I've never felt so free in my life."

"I still can't see you leaving the priesthood. I keep remembering what you did on the north side of Flint. You were something else!"

Santek sucked his cigar slowly and blew a fragile smoke ring. "I'll miss saying Mass and preaching. Even hearing confessions. Those were the times I really felt connected with God. I guess that's never really changed."

"I'd be afraid to leave. This damn depression immobilizes me, but I wouldn't know where to look for a job or what the hell to do with myself."

"What's the depression like?"

"It's like I'm at the end of a dark tunnel and I can't see any light. Nothing interests me except the time I spend with Peggy, and even that doesn't always work. It's like I'm living in a deep, dark cloud and I can't find my way out of it, and I'd like to cry or scream or beat my head against the wall, I feel so damn helpless. Every morning I hope it's gone and it just sits there. I start thinking about it when it's gone and get terrified, knowing it's coming back. At Mass I can offer it to God and feel a moment's peace. Then it comes roaring back and I seem powerless to fight it. Most days I feel suicidal as hell. Like there's nothing to live for."

"Suicidal? Jesus, Ger, you better talk to someone."

172

"To whom? And what will I say?"

"Maybe a shrink or something. It wouldn't hurt to try."

"I don't think it would help. I know my relationship with my father was a bad one, that I slid into the priesthood, that Sullivan angers me the same way my father did. But this doesn't seem psychological. It feels almost physical. I have no control over it. I know what's wrong. I just can't commit myself to my work. I miss you and Ed and all the tension and excitement of the cathedral and traveling around the diocese, but nothing touches me any more. I just watch the days pass and can hardly wait until it's bedtime. I drink enough wine with Peggy to finally fall asleep. When I wake up, it's like the 'dark night of the soul,' only I'm not John of the Cross. I don't want to get out of bed, but if I stay there I'm tormented with fragments of distorted and disconnected thoughts and I feel like killing myself."

Santek twirled his cigar around in his fingers, crossed and uncrossed his legs, then slid down in his easy chair.

"Jesus, man, you've got to get the hell out of here! I don't care if you have to kiss the bishop's ass and take an hour to draw a crowd. This place is driving you nuts."

Beauvais nodded. "Maybe I'll talk to him directly."

"Or talk to Kelley or Grady or someone in the chancery. He might do you some good. And start moving around in clerical circles like I told you."

"Well, I have Confirmation here in two weeks. Maybe I'll talk to the bishop then."

Santek nodded. "Hell, yes! He wears dirty shorts like anyone else. Don't let 'em kill you, Ger. There's a whole world out there, and it's beautiful. It really is." He smoked his cigar and blew a perfect ring.

"It's hard to believe it when this damn depression overwhelms me. It's like I'm drowning or suffocating. There are no words. . . ."

"Then it's time to swim, baby, swim like hell!"

New Orleans has a magic character all its own, like San Francisco or Boston or Paris, created to capture and enhance the excitement that Ted and Angie were feeling. Angie was like a little girl when they checked into the Royal Orleans of St. Louis Street in the French quarter. The wrought-iron lace on the overhanging balconies, the sense of mystery and intrigue behind locked iron gates, the narrow streets and courtyards, the Gay Nineties carriages and the winding Mississippi, the serenity of Jackson Square and St.

Louis Cathedral, the excitement of the French Market and Pat O'Brien's, all of it dazzled her. Even Ted, who had been to New Orleans two or three times before, was now seeing it through the eyes of a glowing Angie. She had never been more beautiful and alive, and if he learned to love her almost instinctively on a beach in Florida, now he was ecstatic with love in his newfound freedom from the priesthood and a lifetime of responsibility.

It is hard to describe what a man feels when he has been locked into a religious vocation ever since high school and then suddenly finds release. For years there had been no way out. His very salvation depended on his fidelity to the priesthood. Even if he knew he had made a mistake, there was his family, the parishioners, and his own salvation to consider. Even another priest wouldn't really understand. There was no one to talk to, or at least it seemed that way to Ted. Priests didn't even talk honestly among themselves. If a rare pastor was sleeping with his housekeeper, no one said anything, and if a priest slipped sexually, he usually sought out a strange confessor or the weakest or kindest man in his own area.

A priest knew he was chosen, set apart, not of this world, and Ted had prostrated himself in the cathedral sanctuary and pledged to God himself, the bishop, and the Catholic people that he would be a priest forever "according to the order of Melchizedek." Now, after knowing for so long in his heart that he was bound eternally, Ted Santek felt the sudden freedom of a prisoner removed from solitary confinement, a lifer or a man on death row released unexpectedly. There were no words to describe what it meant to be immersed in the sensuality of Creole food and fine French wine, the thrill of the Dukes of Dixieland and Al Hirt, the elegant splendor of Brennan's and Arnaud's, the romance of the Court of the Two Sisters and the early morning doughnuts and coffee at the French Market. And above all else, the overpowering experience of an incredibly passionate love.

The first night in New Orleans, Angie had been almost too frightened and embarrassed to speak and he held her gently in his arms and caressed her lovingly.

"You're disappointed," she said.

He continued to caress her and kiss her softly. "There's no hurry," he said quietly. "I love you. It's a whole different thing for me."

And it was. He was startled. Had he really ever made love with anyone before? Holding her naked in his arms was more exciting

174

than most sex he had ever experienced. Love was different, and it seemed so impossible. In reality, what did he know of her? A few days in Florida when they had shared their dreams of children and home and a life of service. A few sad, treasured moments by a brook in Moncrief. A few hours in a car that rescued her from the Daughters of Mercy and took her to Beauvais's rectory. And now the explosion of New Orleans.

And yet he knew everything and had from the moment he met her. Perhaps great loves are always that way: impetuous, instantaneous, instinctual. He knew her Catholic girlhood, her hopes and ideals, not unlike his own; he knew her fears and scruples, her beautiful naiveté and spiritual hunger. He knew that for both of them life had to mean something beyond one's self, that there had to be some passionate commitment to some great service and love. He also knew that the very touch of her skin excited him, the fragrance of her body and the taste of her breath pleased him beyond all telling, the long tapered legs and oval breasts with a virgin's nipples tormented his endless appetite for her. And he knew she loved him as well. It was in the glow of her eyes, the touch of her fingers, the almost hysterical tears when she believed she could not have him. So much in love that she ran to the convent to escape him and risked her very health to preserve his priesthood. Hung on when she thought she was losing her mind.

On the second night in New Orleans, after a quiet dinner in the hotel's Café Royale and flaming coffee in the Esplanade Lounge, they made their way upstairs in silence. He moved toward the bed and knelt before it. Silently, she did the same. He took her hand gently in his. The room was dark save for the glow from the street below. He looked lovingly in her eyes. "Before God, I take you as my wife," he said. "No matter what!" She whispered her own consent. "And I take you—before God—forever!" Then they stood up and embraced.

Without a word, they slipped off their clothes in the darkness and he led her, naked, to a lounge chair near the window overlooking a corner of the Vieux Carré. He stroked her soft brown hair and kissed her shoulders as she rested on his lap. She shuddered at each kiss until gradually, without stress or fear, her whole being was open to him. Like a child he led her back to the bed and continued kissing her breasts and stroking her thighs, telling her how much he loved her, how beautiful she was, how his whole life he had longed for her.

175

He had never spoken this way to anyone before. He was not conscious of technique or a planned program of arousal as he always had been before. He was absorbed in her, beside himself, as unfamiliar with such feelings as she was. Soon they were making love, both of them for the first time. The only sound was a startled gasp when he entered her; then she moved slowly in perfect harmony with his body. Her freedom amazed him, and an expertise he had not expected. It was as if there were no barriers, as if the depths of their love crossed every boundary of kiss and caress and passionate explosion. He had no memory of how long they made love. It was as if they explored every crevice of soul and body, drowning in some ultimate pleasure in the midst of space and clinging to each other lest they be cast away in some impossible orbit.

Finally, exhausted, they fell asleep in each other's arms, and when the morning sun roused them torporously from sleep, they loved gently and longingly again and again. Santek felt as virginal and startled as was she. He had no clever words, no sudden jokes, no well-rehearsed ploys to ensure his continued pleasure. If he'd ever doubted God before, he never would again. Before he had known lust born of anger or pain, pleasure enough to silence a persistent ache at the farthest corner of his heart, or proof that he was an attractive man of the world.

Now his whole being had merged with her like "two in one flesh." He wanted to scream or shout or preach to the whole world. He wanted to climb mountains and clouds, to let oceans and hills cover him, to make the heavens and earth resound with the joy he felt. Finally, he was able to hold her face a few inches away from his own and to stare into the deepest, purest, most loving blue eyes in the world.

"My God, my God!"

It was all he could say. And in his heart, he knew he wanted to be the world's most loving priest. But said nothing.

The Confirmation dinner was Peggy's finest. She had enlisted the help of two women of the parish to prepare a standing rib roast, broccoli and green beans, baked potatoes, a Waldorf salad, and an assortment of homemade pies, warm home-baked bread and rolls, and fresh butter churned that day.

Fifty invitations had gone out to priests within reasonable driving distance, and Beauvais said she could probably expect from twenty-five to thirty. A local bartender and usher, Jim Stanley, had

176

taken the evening off to tend bar before and after the ceremony. Peggy herself had prepared an elegant assortment of hors d'oeuvres, including fresh shrimp and blue point oysters from a Detroit fish market.

"We'll just let them know these farmers have a little class," Beauvais had said. In reality he wanted Bishop Michael Patrick Sullivan, who loved his food and Irish whiskey, to be in the best frame of mind for his planned confrontation.

The Confirmation was scheduled for five o'clock on Sunday afternoon. The bishop and his secretary arrived about four thirty. They were met at the car by two high school students in suits and ties, who took their bags and led them graciously into the rectory. The bishop was suitably impressed. Beauvais greeted him warmly at the front door, knelt to kiss the ring, and led him into the living room, where the bar and hors d'oeuvres awaited them.

"It looks wonderful, Father Beauvais!" The Irish eyes were smiling their most gracious smile, and any past differences between the two men seemed at an end. Santek had been right. Sullivan was charming. Beauvais knew why most lay people were totally captivated by him.

Gerry nodded to Jim Stanley, who was poised and waiting with the Old Bushmill, and offered Sullivan his drink.

"Just a light one before the ceremony," the bishop said, already sampling the oysters and shrimp. "Wonderful, wonderful!"

A gregarious man, he moved out into the kitchen, where the flustered women interrupted their work long enough to blush and kiss his ring. It was a rare privilege. Beauvais tagged along to introduce the ladies.

"It looks like enough food for an army," the bishop said laughingly. Beauvais, sensing his superior's expansive mood and feeling confident of his own mission, was glad that he had accepted the new assignment without rancor.

The ladies giggled and scurried back to work as the bishop returned to the living room. He began changing into his red dress cassock with Father Beauvais's assistance and directed his young, darkly handsome secretary, Father Kincaid, tall and hurried in his movements, to make preparations in the sacristy for the ceremony. Beauvais noted that Kincaid was the kind of priest who would fit in, seemingly destined for the clerical life since childhood.

At four forty-five Monsignor Kelley and Monsignor Grady arrived. Grady graciously accepted a shot of Bushmill, and Kelley requested a little soda water for a nervous stomach. He still could not look at Beauvais, but Grady embraced him warmly and took him aside.

"God, I miss you, Gerry. So do the people! I didn't realize our time together was the happiest of my life." Then, more quietly, "I think I understand your move and am working on things. This is no place for you. Are you doing okay?"

Gerry wanted to melt in the gentle, fatherly man's arms and tell him everything. Why hadn't he gone to Grady for help? The old man loved him. Why had he kept his distance? Even now he could not be honest with a genuine friend.

"Everything's great. The people, the kids, even the cows."

All Grady could do was laugh, and Beauvais was left with his private pain.

At ten to five, four priests arrived together from Jackson. They were too late to drink and followed the bishop over to the sacristy to act as his assistants in the ceremony, holding cotton and oil to anoint foreheads and a silver bowl to receive the used cotton and consecrated oil. Young Kincaid rapidly announced the name selected by each child to be confirmed, taking the slip of paper held in nervous young hands and translating the name of a favored saint or relative into perfect Latin. Proud parents looked on joyously from the crowded pews. There were barely enough priests to man the necessary positions, but Beauvais had reassured Peggy and her assistants before rushing over to the sacristy to join the bishop. "A lot of priests just come for the dinner. There's nothing very inspiring about the ceremony. It should be over in an hour."

And so it was—but no more priests arrived. It was the smallest number to attend a Confirmation in the history of the diocese, despite probably the best food served anywhere. There was a kind of unwritten custom among priests that they attended the Confirmations and Forty Hours celebrations of those priests who had been present at theirs. So it was not really a malicious slight to Beauvais that only seven priests and the bishop sat down to a splendid dinner. Priests were not like that. It was rather that Gerry had so isolated himself in Farmington that his dinner was easily overlooked. The more popular and gregarious pastors would often have fifty or sixty priests present, even in a small diocese like Lansing.

Gerry Beauvais had not known such humiliation since Bishop Sullivan had sent him to Farmington. He was unable to face the women in the kitchen or even Jim Stanley, who had given up an

178

evening's work at his own Wolverine Bar to serve a couple of dozen drinks, including an after-dinner liqueur. Beauvais was tense and had all he could do to make certain he talked privately with the bishop, who customarily had one stiff drink after dinner, then thanked his host and the women in the kitchen and was gone. When the meal was finished, and a mere four pieces consumed from the ten homemade pies lined up in the kitchen, the bishop and his priests filed into the living room. The bishop ordered his usual, Monsignors Grady and Kelley excused themselves and left, and the priests from Jackson talked of early Masses the next morning. They, too, consumed a cognac or Drambuie and were gone before the bishop had finished his Bushmill. Only the bishop, the young, hand-some Kincaid, and a frightened Beauvais remained. Beauvais ner-vously kept looking for the precise moment to talk to the bishop privately. He need not have worried. The bishop suggested that Kincaid pack the vestments and make a couple of phone calls. The secretary departed quickly, and before Beauvais could say a word, the bishop addressed him gravely.

"There's a matter I want to discuss with you, Father Beauvais."

Gerry's heart bounced in his chest. Maybe there would be no need to ask for anything. Maybe Sullivan finally felt that he had done his penance and served his time. Half smiling, his hands sweating, Beauvais waited for the bishop to finish the last of his Bushmill. He stood up and offered him a refill, but the bishop waved him back into his chair. The hierarch seemed nervous and searched for the right words. Beauvais's heart continued to pound wildly. The bishop fidgeted with his empty glass, then placed it on the coffee table at his left.

"Father, it is important for a priest not only to do good and serve his flock but at all costs to avoid even the appearance of evil. When I sent you here from the cathedral, I really did not accuse you of anything but dangerous indiscretion. The rest is between you and your God."

He paused and looked reflective. Beauvais's heart had quieted and he waited for his new assignment, feeling that the bishop's in-troduction was a proud and pompous man's apology for what had happened. The bishop straightened his episcopal ring and chose his words carefully.

"Now it has been called to my attention that there is another matter which reveals a similar lack of good judgment."

Beauvais turned white and thought he might faint.

"Apparently, your young and attractive housekeeper has been seen several times leaving the rectory at a very late hour, long after her work has been concluded. Again, Father, I am not suggesting anything beyond appearances, certainly not *malum in se*. But the life of a priest is a hard and challenging one, and we must always be on the lookout, as Christ said, lest we 'give scandal to little ones.' I'm afraid, Father, this situation can give great scandal, especially in a small town. So I want you to dismiss your housekeeper, relieve her of all parochial duties, and find, as canon law suggests, a *superadulta*, which according to Bouscaren and other commentators should be a woman well over fifty, of sterling reputation and deep faith. Do I make myself clear, Father Beauvais?"

Gerry could barely nod. The sweat appeared on his forehead and his legs were trembling. Wild fantasies raced through his brain. He wanted to kill the domineering, fat-faced bishop with his bare hands. Then he wanted to take Peggy in his arms and desert this whole maddening scene of the priesthood. His mind continued to reel, and he felt the suicidal thoughts again force their way into his consciousness. He was still unable to speak. He wanted to cry, to scream out, to pound the bishop and his canon law into a mass of unrecognizable pulp.

The bishop stood up to leave and extended his hand to Beauvais, who knelt docilely and kissed his ring. It was the final ignominy.

"We must have strong faith, Father, to serve God's will," Sullivan said. "I never expected to be a bishop. It was the farthest thing from my mind. But God chose me through the will of my superiors. God wants you here to serve these people, but he wants you to be 'a light upon a mountaintop.' Perhaps we can arrange for you to spend some time in a Trappist monastery, Father. It could be a spiritual renewal." He paused. "Is there anything else you want to talk about, Father?"

Beauvais shook his head. His mind was racing madly in a thousand directions. The bishop most graciously thanked him and the ladies in the kitchen and quickly followed his poised and self-assured secretary out the door and into the car. Beauvais stood in the doorway, paralyzed, and nodded his goodbye. As the bishop drove away, he followed the black Cadillac with his eyes, then stared off into the darkness of the night. An old couple walked by, hand in hand, and nodded graciously at the priest. He smiled and still stood staring. He heard a dog barking in the distance, then two or three more. He could hear the frogs and screeching crickets in the marsh across the street and the sound of children's voices laughing and arguing. He felt a sickness as his own lonely childhood flashed before his consciousness. His whole life meant nothing. He had never learned to live. He found himself wishing desperately for Father Misch or Santek. Tears of anger and hurt pounded behind his eyelids, but he would not let them flow. Slowly he walked out the door and made his way in a daze to the church. He entered the side door and stumbled into the sanctuary. All was in darkness save the flickering of vigil lights in a Lourdes grotto at the rear of the church and the glow of the tabernacle lamp in the sanctuary. He knelt down stiffly on the floor, then prostrated himself in front of the lonely tabernacle. He could smell the incense from the Confirmation ceremony and heard the roof creak ominously in the wind. His body began to tremble, and slowly he grew rigid. He wanted to pray, but nothing but empty words came as he lay there, gradually turning to stone. He cried out for his mother. Tears continued to pound at his temples and jaw, but he refused or was unable to release them until his face and neck were as rigid as the rest of his body. Again, he called out his mother's name, then Jesus and Mary. He tried to move but could not. He tried to call out for help, but nothing would come. So he lay there helpless, hopeless, finally a beaten man, and felt urine trickle down his legs in some final degradation.

It was almost midnight when Peggy found him. She had cleaned up the kitchen with the other women, packed up the extra food to be delivered the following day to the orphanage in Lansing, thanked them for their assistance, and had begun searching for Father Beauvais, anxious to hear the outcome of his conversation with Bishop Sullivan. At first she thought he might be out on a sick call, but when she saw his car in the garage, she checked his bedroom and the study and assumed he had gone for a walk. After nervously watching TV for a while, she decided to check the church. She almost missed him in the darkness, but the tabernacle light revealed the outline of his prone form in the sanctuary. Not wanting to intrude on his solitude and prayer, she approached cautiously and thought that he had fallen asleep. She fumbled for a light switch in the sacristy and turned on a light over the altar. Still he did not move, but his face was turned toward her and she could see the tears on his left cheek and the puddle of his urine on the sanctuary floor. She knelt beside him and saw the rigidity of his face and body.

"Oh, Father! Dear God, what's wrong, what's wrong?"

She began rubbing his neck and shoulders and felt the massive tension that seemed to reduce him to stone. For more than an hour she massaged his back and legs unceasingly, until finally he stirred feebly. She helped him to sit up cautiously, but he still seemed dazed and unable to speak and his staring eyes did not really focus on her. Carefully she led him from the sanctuary over to the rectory. He shuffled like an old man, and tears began to fill his eyes and flow gently down his cheeks. He looked ten years older, the light gone from his eyes, his mouth drooping slightly open, his whole posture stooped and rigid.

With great effort she led him up the stairs to his bedroom and eased him down on the bed. She began taking off his shoes and socks, then his cassock. When she tried to slip off his pants he resisted her and fell back on the bed, embarrassed as much by the stains of urine as by his own nakedness. She rearranged his body so that his head rested on a pillow and managed to cover him with the blanket and bedspread. She leaned over and kissed him gently on the forehead, and the tears flowed more copiously. He was trying to speak, but his mouth seemed parched and sealed shut. She brought him water and he sipped it cautiously, spilling it on his chin.

"I'd better call Dr. Hengesbach," she said.

He shook his head.

"But, Father, something's wrong! You need help."

Again he tried to talk, but the words wouldn't come.

"Then I'll stay with you tonight. I'm not leaving!"

He shook his head vigorously and mumbled, "Bishop said . . . you must go." Each word emerged like a death rattle.

"I don't care what the bishop said. I'm staying here!"

"Go!" he said almost firmly. His eyes rolled back in his head, then reappeared.

"No!" She spoke even more firmly and began stroking his head and massaging his shoulders. He did not resist her. Finally, his eyes seemed to focus.

"Peggy?"

"I'm right here," she said.

He smiled briefly and closed his eyes. In moments he was asleep. Peggy took off her shoes and lay down next to him, continuing to stroke his face. He cuddled against her like a small child. It was only then that she realized how deeply and completely she loved him. She would not let this beautiful man be destroyed. No

182

bishop or celibate vow or God himself would stand in her way. He had become her reason for living, and her own beautiful dream of working among the poor would attend his primary need. She belonged to him. God had sent her—even if she never possessed him in total love. Holding him like this was the greatest joy she had ever known.

Chapter 17

After a week in New Orleans, eating and drinking and making passionate and languorous love, sampling exotic Creole dishes and soaking in the addictive jazz, even touring the strange aboveground cemeteries and necking like teenagers on the roller coaster at Lake Pontchartrain, Ted and Angie finally had enough diversion. Over dinner at Brennan's they began to make plans for the future.

"This is a great place to live," said Ted. "It makes Ham Town look like a prison."

"I love it," said Angie exuberantly. It was hard for her to stop smiling.

He sighed softly. "I guess it's time to settle down and start looking for work."

Her smile faded briefly. "I can't think of you as anything but a priest. I'm so afraid you're going to wake up in two or three months and think it's all wrong. Then you'll blame me or hate me and—"

He interrupted her. "For God's sake, Angie, I know what I'm doing. I love you. I can't live without you. I just wasn't cut out to be a celibate. God knows it. Beauvais knows it. I've known it my whole life. I just got carried away with the idea of helping people and being someone important. I never really became a priest for the right reasons."

"But who does anything for the right reasons? You love it. You told me that. Father Beauvais told me! You love forgiving people and saying Mass. You love preaching and counseling and consoling and being respected. That may not be easy to replace. You're a wonderful priest—the kind we all need."

"I can still teach or counsel or whatever. As long as I can have you, I'm willing to pump gas! I don't have to be a priest to serve God and people."

"Sometimes I wake up in the morning and feel guilty that I've taken you away from God."

"I haven't left God. I'm just changing jobs. Priests have left before. I'm not the first or the last." He thought of Father Al, probably desperate and lonely, not only leaving the priesthood but having to face his homosexuality. Santek had tried to contact him, to no avail. He also thought of Beauvais and wondered about his impossible depression.

The next day they found a suitable apartment on St. Charles Avenue about two miles north of the Vieux Carré. They rented furniture and a TV and shopped for pots and pans, dishes and silverware, bedding and groceries. They laughed and teased like excited newlyweds.

Their first meal at home, by candlelight, was his favorite filet mignon, baked potatoes, Roquefort salad, fresh lima beans, and a good bottle of Chateauneuf du Pape.

"A toast to Pope John, who knew what the hell it was all about. May he and JFK rest in peace and play touch football together," said Ted almost solemnly. Then he grinned broadly. "And here's to Pope Paul, who can't decide whether he's liberal, conservative, or Baptist, and will set the Church back a hundred years during his visit to the United Nations. Christ! He thinks he can scold the whole world! Which reminds me, are you on the pill?"

"I went to the Planned Parenthood clinic before we left Michigan."

"Good. We don't want any surprises. Not yet, anyway."

The following morning, after a hearty breakfast of sausage, pancakes, and eggs, Ted scanned the want ads.

"It's getting harder and harder for me to read the small print."

He squinted and circled two or three possibilities, and together they set out to look for work.

"It feels strange," said Ted. "I haven't looked for a job since I was in high school. Suddenly I don't even know what the hell I can do. I'm really not up to selling cars again."

"You can do anything you set your mind to."

"I wish I had your confidence."

At the Orleans Parish School Board on Corondolet, Angie, with her bilingual ability, found immediate employment as a substitute teacher, to begin the following day if her degree and credits checked out. She requested a few days' grace to get the apartment in order and agreed to begin the following Monday to replace a junior high French teacher who was out with hepatitis.

"You should have no difficulty getting full-time employment within a few weeks if you want it," she was told.

"That would be wonderful. I think I can have my transcript here within a few days," Angie assured the principal.

"I have no doubt that it will be more than adequate, as you explained. What about your husband? I'm sure you have a degree."

Ted was caught unawares. He blushed briefly. "My B.A. is in scholastic philosophy. I was in the seminary for a few years, but I doubt that I have enough credits in education."

"My brother is a Jesuit," she said. "I knew there was something about you two that I liked. If you want to send for your transcript, I'll let you know what you need. Meanwhile, the parochial schools are not quite as demanding. The pay's not as good, but it would get you used to teaching."

Ted nodded gratefully. "I appreciate your suggestion."

Later that afternoon Ted was hired by an employment agency on a commission basis.

"Once you get the hang of it, you can make thirty or forty thousand a year," the oily manager said. "You make a nice appearance and speak well, and with a college education you should have no problem. You're not afraid of a little competition, are you?"

The athlete in Ted was aroused even as intuitively he despised the man. "I think I can handle it," he said modestly.

"Good. We'll see you tomorrow morning and teach you the ropes. If you need a little advance, we might be able to arrange that too. Usually you get your money when we get ours."

"I can wait," he said confidently. "I'll see you tomorrow."

That night they celebrated with a special dinner at Antoine's and later enjoyed Lee Marvin in the outrageous *Cat Ballou*. At dinner, Ted was high after a second glass of wine.

"Well, baby, we're off. After we get settled in our jobs, I'll fly back to Lackland, resign my commission for health reasons, and then we can get married." His mood changed briefly. "I'll stop by and see my folks and tell them my missionary story. Then an occasional letter and a trip home in my collar should do the job."

"I wish we could get married in church. It would make it all seem better somehow."

"There may be a way. Send for your baptismal record, and I'll pick up mine when I get home."

"Won't it say you're a priest?"

"I'll see that it doesn't," he said. "It's no real problem. If that doesn't work, I'll take instruction and become a convert."

He laughed briefly and Angie looked worried.

"What the hell's wrong?"

"It just takes a little getting used to," she said. "It's like playing games with God. It scares me."

"The Church is not God," he said angrily. "God's God. He understands. We're married before God—forever! Pope Paul should scare you, trying to impose Catholic morality on the whole damn world. The man must be crazy." Ted had realized there would be no married clergy during Paul's reign and it angered him.

Angie nodded docilely without changing her worried expression. Ted lifted up his wineglass to change the mood.

"To us."

"To us," she said, finally able to smile.

Angie loved her teaching job at Corondolet Junior High. The students were bright and well behaved, and a few of them had spoken a version of French at home as children. They laughed at her Canadian accent as she mocked their patois. Within a few days she felt a part of New Orleans. She found the people warm and outgoing, loved the shopping and the Creole food, and found her knowledge of French an immediate advantage in a strange environment.

Ted's progress was not satisfactory. He was scarcely aware that he had received special treatment as a priest. It had not mattered where he went, the collar had provided immediate friends, built-in respect, and an innate courtesy not extended to the rest of the world. He had never even received a traffic citation, had not been cursed at in years, and, most of all, had never really been ignored. Even when he was in uniform, the officer status had provided him with a certain respect not unlike that of the priesthood. It was a strange feeling to be treated as just another member of the Crowell Employment Agency.

As a beginning employee, he was to receive one third of the company's fee, which was 55 percent of a client's first month's gross, payable when the person he placed had been thirty days on the new job. The manager encouraged him to get the money as soon as he could.

"Once a firm gets to know you, and realizes that you send them

187

only good people, they'll pay almost immediately. When we get paid, you get paid."

His smile was all teeth. He reminded Ted of an assistant coach he had had in high school with his mop of greasy hair, pointed jaw, small, nervous eyes and a potbelly that hung loosely over his belt. He was a large man who talked with his hands even when he held a cup of coffee, which was almost always, and a cynical smile never left his lips. He wore a green plaid sport coat and loose brown pants and a white shirt that could have made money in a detergent ad.

He handed Ted a list of which businesses needed what personnel. It was his daily delight to tease the staff before he released the lists. The six other employees, all women, grabbed the lists like a school of piranha, then feverishly began dialing numbers and looking through their files. Ted, of course, was at a distinct disadvantage because he had no files of suitable personnel who might be right for the job. Nor did he realize that the receptionist, a thorough man-hater, could send the better candidates to any counselor she chose, more often than not to an attractive Chinese girl named Linda Lou, who was far and away the most successful staff member.

Aggressive and unscrupulous, Linda was also an outstanding counselor. When she found a good prospect, she taught that person grooming and the correct way to respond to the personality of the employer and even rehearsed questions that were likely to be asked. If the prospective employee proved inept, which Linda Lou could decide in two minutes, she usually referred that person to another agency right away. Ted was not capable of this.

Even though he was a good judge of character, he was still the complete priest, moved by the unfortunate life experiences of his clients. A middle-aged woman, whose husband had left her for a twenty-five-year-old secretary, had no marketable skills and was terrified to begin life again. Linda Lou would have given her three minutes at the most. Ted was with her for more than an hour, made a dozen unsuccessful phone calls, and took her problem home with him. Even when he had an outstanding prospect, by the time he called the employer, three or four applicants had already applied, often from his own agency.

There were bitter quarrels among the staff, particularly over Linda Lou's tactics. Ted had never worked under such tension before, a kind of continuous marathon race and cat fight almost every day. He was as discouraged as Angie was exhilarated. In an entire week of constant work, he placed only a janitor and a ware-

188

houseman. The warehouseman was a chronic alcoholic who proved to have a bad back and quit after one day, and the janitor was fired the third day for smoking marijuana in the women's restroom.

The manager approached Ted and suggested that he might do better as a social worker, but before he fired him, Ted was clever enough to set himself up an interview with a radio station looking for a commercial salesman. Again he was on straight commission, and even though the pace was more relaxed and the other salesmen more encouraging, the leads he received were new businesses opening up with little or no money for radio advertising. His confidence dwindled rapidly, since he had never been treated as just another peddler. Receptionists were often rude, managers were "too busy" to see him, and once, when he persisted, a small fat man with thick glasses whom Ted could have floored with one punch told him to "get the hell out before I throw you out."

The first week he made approximately ninety dollars for fifty hours' work and was let go by the station for not being aggressive enough. It was the most painful humiliation he had ever suffered, and with it he lost almost all remaining confidence. Ensuing interviews for jobs were incredibly painful and lackluster. He was turned down by two auto dealerships, a pest control company looking for a manager, and a law enforcement agency—even though he lied and said he was a policeman in Detroit for three years. In desperation he admitted to having been a priest and a chaplain. The angular, cigar-smoking private detective grinned without removing the stogie.

"If we were looking for angels and not wayward husbands, Padre, you'd be our man!"

A salvage company offered him a job driving a truck, which he turned down, and an insurance company agreed to pay him while he went to school. He lasted two days, was completely bored by the pseudo-enthusiasm and found it impossible to be treated like a college freshman. After he was chided for not knowing the basic coverage of a homeowner's policy, he got up and walked out. When Angie returned from school on Friday evening, he was watching a replay of the Clay-Liston "one punch" fight and well on his way to getting drunk.

"I don't know where the hell I fit. I'm scared to death to go on one more interview. It's so damned humiliating. If I don't tell them I was a priest, they wonder what the hell I've been doing for the past twenty years. And if I do, they treat me like I pee holy water and read the Bible during my lunch hour."

"You have to be patient, darling. Something just right will come along. You've got to find something that's not unlike the priesthood. You were meant to help people. It's all you've ever done. You can't change your heart just to get a job. Besides, what's the hurry? We've got enough money. You can take your time."

He flipped off the TV and lit another cigarette and poured more bourbon. "Money's not the issue," he said angrily. "I'll go nuts just sitting around. All these assholes treat me like a piece of shit! The going rate for ex-priests is four bucks an hour and a sweet smile like you're a goddamned angel-fucking fag!"

Later that same evening, after he had barely picked at his lamb chops and baked potato, Angie went over to the couch where he was sprawled disconsolately and began stroking his hair and gently touching his face.

"Maybe you can only be a priest," she said.

"I don't know what to do," he said quietly. "I miss the priesthood already. It's like I'm nothing without it, but with it I end up losing you."

"I miss it for you, sweetheart, and I doubt very much if you will lose me no matter what you do."

"I can't live a double life, Angie. If I'm going to be a priest, I've got to play it the way it was written."

"Why? You've already told me what happens when you try to be a priest all by yourself. What's better, to be a married truck driver or a compassionate and loving priest who can't live without his woman?"

"I can't believe you! You were the one running away from me three years ago."

"I know there will be married priests someday. Just like I know that the Church will finally accept divorce and birth control. It's all common sense. And convents will change too."

"Who the hell told you all this?"

"Peggy and I talked for hours and hours. We agreed about a lot of things. If the changes don't come, people will stop attending. I know more people who have left the Church than are in it. So does Peggy."

"Well, nothing will change under Pope Paul. You can be damn sure of that. He just made a fool of himself before the United Nations. Half the damn world starving and he's worried about birth control. My God! You and Peggy may be right about everything you say, but it's not going to happen overnight."

190

"So we destroy ourselves because we were born too soon. It doesn't make any sense. You want to be a priest. I want you to be a priest. You're never going to find a job that will suit you. What compares with it? Teaching? Selling insurance?"

Ted lit a cigarette, dragged deeply, and stared off into space. After several minutes of silence he finally spoke.

"You know, I really think you're right about one thing. I can't be anything but a priest. And I'm tired of looking for a job I don't want. I'm also tired of trying to have fun. I want to get back to work. With your help I could be one hell of a priest. I just don't know if—"

"Why don't we try it? I'll get a job and an apartment near the base, and you come when you can. If it's only once a week, it's a thousand times better than not seeing you. There'd be nothing to live for."

"What if I decide after a while that I can't handle it?"

"Then I'll just go back to Canada and try to forget you." Her eyes teared at the very thought. "But I'll pray my heart out that it works. Even if we never make love again, I'd rather be near you."

He sat up and put his arms around her, and she nestled against him on the couch. He looked at her tenderly, his own heart overflowing with love.

"If you're near me, we'll make love."

He continued to hold her, then kissed her softly.

"All I really want to be is a priest," he said.

"It was the priest in you I fell in love with."

He took her hand and led her from the couch toward the bedroom.

"We'll have to break our lease," she said. "And all the rented furniture—"

Santek laughed loudly. "Christ, we settle our differences with God, and you're worried about the damn furniture!"

A week later Angie had found an apartment on the outskirts of San Antonio, about five miles west of Lackland. She spent the first week purchasing furniture and dishes, pictures and knickknacks to turn the attractive apartment into a warm home. It was a twenty-unit, almost new, white stone building surrounded by trees and set off by itself. It also had a rear entrance and back stairs if Ted wanted to slip in without entering the lobby or using the elevator. Angie had checked carefully to see that no military personnel occupied any of the apartments. As Ted instructed, she kept very much to herself and ignored her neighbors, save for a nod and smile.

The following week Angie found a job in the office of Welby-Lewis Construction Company, a large, successful operation that built condominiums and commercial buildings throughout Texas. Her secretarial skills, in addition to her attractive appearance, which obviously pleased her boss, William Brockley, got her the first job for which she applied. Brockley, a prematurely graying man of forty with a full head of curly hair and a trim, athletic figure, dressed like an ad in *Playboy*. He was conscious of his Hollywood good looks and, although already tall, wore high-heeled boots, which added two or three inches to his stature. His interview with Angie went in a variety of directions, including his former football days, fishing and hunting in Montana, a grandpa in the oil business, and his faltering marriage. He also explored her background far beyond the employment form he filled out.

"How's your marriage going?" He stared at her breasts.

"Fine."

"What does your husband do?" She felt him undressing her.

"He's in service."

"An officer?"

"Yes."

"What rank?"

"A captain."

Brockley was impressed. "What's his job?"

"He's in classified work. He's gone a lot."

Brockley seemed pleased. "Can you start Monday? I'll teach you the construction business."

"I'd appreciate that." She smiled and got up to leave.

"I can teach you a lot of things." He grinned seductively, put his arm around her, and walked her to the door, his hand brushing the top of her butt and his elbow nudging her breast. "Monday!"

Angie nodded and went to apply for a teaching position as well. Her name was put on a waiting list but with only a slight opportunity of being hired.

"College students from Austin grab anything that comes along. But at least your knowledge of French is an advantage. We'll let you know."

She thanked the matronly woman and wondered how long she could stand the aggressive Brockley. Two weeks later, having successfully kept him at bay, she was promoted to Mr. Ruppel's office.

A grizzled, fatherly man in his late fifties and a devout Catholic, he immediately made her feel at home.

"Your work is superb, Mrs. Fortier. I hope you are with us for a very long time."

She smiled graciously and was glad she had not shared with Ted her concerns about Bill Brockley. He raged if another man stared at her too long.

But Angie gave him little reason to rage. She had matured in her contacts with men and the once naive ex-nun could hold a Brockley at bay with a single glance. When he persisted in wanting to take her to lunch, she explained very simply.

"Look, Brock, my husband is the most beautiful man in the world. If he can dedicate his time to our country, I can dedicate my loneliness to loving him. I think we'll get along just fine if you stop treating me like I'm available. I'm not."

That resolved any problems with Bill Brockley, and more sensitive males recognized the air of remoteness about her that presented no possible opportunity for misunderstanding. Her life with Ted Santek had developed beyond her wildest dreams. She shared his concerns about difficult marriage problems, attended his Masses at the base when it was safe and appropriate, and thrilled when she heard him preach with typical confidence and passion. She delighted in being his secret woman. When he remained on the base for a couple of days, she occupied herself with reading and crocheting, shopping for surprise gifts or additional knickknacks for the house. It was exciting to hear his soft knock on the door, to fall into his arms and make beautiful love far into the night. She had become a relaxed, exciting sexual partner, beyond his imaginings, and he had no reason ever to think of another woman. Loving sex had made all other sexual encounters pale and insignificant.

Because of their time spent apart, almost every meal was a celebration and free weekends meant a trip to Austin or, on occasion, cautious expeditions around the San Antonio area. They had developed a signal if he thought he saw someone who might recognize him. When he said "Pope Paul" it was a signal for her to drift off on her own as if they didn't know each other. If it was too late, she would mention something about a conference and tell him how much she and her "husband" enjoyed his remarks. Once, while watching *Dr. Zhivago*, they moved out to the lobby together during intermission and Angie kissed him on the cheek just as he said "Pope Paul." She blushed furiously when he introduced her to a young airman, Mike Ennis, as a cousin from Toronto. It was doubly difficult when the young Ennis asked her out for dinner the following evening. Still blushing, she informed him that she would be staying with an aunt in Dallas. Ennis insisted on watching the remainder of the movie with them while a playful Santek occasionally pinched Angie surreptitiously.

The weeks and months moved swiftly. A two-week leave in Aruba gave them a total sense of freedom from any pressures of recognition. They were able to have dinner with other couples, to dance and lie on the beach, to gamble and enjoy long, relaxed dinners, to hold hands and kiss in public, even to swim nude on a remote section of the island. It was a total refreshment for them both, but it made life a little more difficult for them when they returned to San Antonio and played hide-and-seek again with the world.

Angie's only real sadness was her yearning to have his baby. After several months together, she admitted her deep, lifelong need.

"It would be so wonderful. It would give me a whole new life while I'm waiting for you to come home." She beamed like a little girl.

"For God's sake, Angie, not yet! There's time for a kid."

Her eyes gleamed. "I keep wondering when the time will come. I'm not getting any younger. My dad keeps wondering about you, and if I'm pregnant."

"Tell him you miscarried. Tell him anything. We're not ready to have a kid yet. It's just too damned complicated!"

She turned away and burst into tears.

"We're moving to Chanute," he said softly when she calmed down. "In Illinois."

She was startled. "My God, when?"

"Next week. I'll be Major Santek."

She felt anxiety and relief all at once, believing that the move and the rapid promotion explained his resistance to a child.

"It seems like we're hardly settled here."

"That's the service," he said.

"We'll have our baby there," she said softly.

Santek sighed and said nothing. Then he got up and flipped on the TV.

Angie moved into the kitchen and began preparations for dinner. She was ready to have a child. It would give real meaning to everything, and she had no doubt that Santek would agree. She was so convinced that she had stopped taking the pill.

Chapter 18

A few days after Peggy found Beauvais on the sanctuary floor, his doctor, Fred Hengesbach, recommended that he be sent to a mental hospital. He had given Gerry tranquilizers and a daily dosage of two hundred milligrams of Elavil. The antidepressant took at least ten days to be effective and had no immediate effect on his condition. He could barely get out of bed, spoke only in monosyllables, and suffered excruciatingly from the torment of his own muddled thoughts. Even the tranquilizers rarely gave him respite, but they did help him sleep less fitfully. He had known melancholy before, even serious depression for two or three days at a time, but never anything like this. He wanted to die. Life had lost all meaning. He was an emotional paraplegic in a long, dark corridor which had no end. There was no light, not a spark of it, no hope of getting well or going on.

All the pain and humiliation, the shattered ego and pointless existence had finally smothered him. He would have killed himself if he had known how. He had experienced suicidal thoughts before, but only in passing. Now he truly wanted to stop living. Bishop Sullivan had won. There was no fear of hell or even an afterlife. There was only the unending yearning to be freed from the most overwhelming pain he had ever known, a pain that no one seemed to understand, a pain he had not known existed.

Hengesbach tried to explain what had taken place. "As far as we know, the body and mind's ability to handle anxiety and depression is limited. When one's private resources are drained by serious conflicts or tragedies, a person often loses the ability to resist despair.

Just keeping alive is awfully difficult until the body and, I think, the spirit can take over again. Medication is just an effort to assist the individual's system to resume some kind of control."

"How long does it last?" Peggy asked.

"A month, a year, two years . . . there're not enough data. We're only beginning to understand it. People that used to be put away in asylums are now often able to be saved. But it all depends on their determination to live, their reason to live when everything inside wants to give up. It takes massive courage. The medication can only help and give the patient some feeling of hope. If it works . . ."

Peggy had not notified the bishop. Instead, she had called the former pastor, Father John Niedermeyer, at his sister's house in Detroit and asked him if he would replace Father Beauvais, who had become ill. Niedermeyer asked few questions, delighted to relieve the boredom of his retirement. Peggy knew she had to act quickly. If the bishop found out about Beauvais's condition, it might mean the end of his priesthood. Men with the background and training of Bishop Sullivan frequently considered mental illness a personal reflection on the moral status of the individual so afflicted. Peggy lied to Dr. Hengesbach and said she had called the chancery to report Father Beauvais's condition and that Monsignor Kelley, with the bishop's consent, had recommended a psychiatric hospital in Jackson, less than an hour's drive away. Hengesbach was startled.

"I assumed they would send him to Mercywood in Ann Arbor. It's no paradise. In fact, I really don't have much faith in any of them, but watch that Dr. Sellers in Jackson."

"I think the bishop wants to keep this matter as quiet as possible."

Hengesbach reluctantly agreed to have him admitted to the psychiatric unit of Voss Hospital in Jackson. He was not to tell Niedermeyer or indicate that Beauvais was a priest. Peggy would accompany him as a sister or wife, take care of the insurance, and be with him as often as the rules allowed. A neighbor agreed to look in on her father if she was gone too long. Peggy felt that Beauvais would come around in a few days, be discharged from the hospital, and then respond to her total care. Nothing mattered but his recovery. She was ready to give up job, home, anything to restore this beautiful man to health, but she was terrified by his morbid condition and had no experience with mental hospitals.

The psychiatric unit at Voss proved to be a nightmare. Dr. Sellers, the psychiatrist in charge, believed only in massive doses of drugs and totally indiscriminate shock treatment, given without any tranquilization. Manic depressives and schizophrenics were lumped with acute psychotics and hopeless alcoholics. There was little if any psychotherapy. Most of the nurses and orderlies had become more like jailers than professionals, yet it was hardly their fault. The patients were maintained in a kind of twilight zone with heavy doses of drugs and too-frequent shock treatments. There was little to do but police the ward, prevent paranoid quarrels and physical fights, keep patients from defecating on the floor and smearing their food on anyone or anything that was available. Peggy was horrified at what she saw, the drooling mouths and empty stares of the patients and the downright cruelty of the staff. When visiting hours were over, she was terrified to leave her dearest friend in this seeming madhouse. But she did not know what else to do.

She need not have worried. Gerald Beauvais did not stir from his bed for several days. Meanwhile Dr. Sellers recommended heavy dosages of drugs, phenobarbital, antidepressants, and, eventually, shock treatment. When Peggy, who posed as his wife, sought information, Sellers was brief and dogmatic, as when she protested Beauvais's loss of memory and confusion after shock therapy and the real terror he experienced as he waited his turn.

"Why does he have to watch?"

"He doesn't. He can close his eyes," Sellers suggested.

"But the sound is enough to scare the bravest man."

"He can use earplugs."

Afterwards, Gerry had great difficulty recognizing her and occasionally confused her with one of his sisters.

"He may come around and he may not," Sellers said resignedly. "It's up to him."

"But the shock treatments don't seem to do him any good. He's just helpless and disoriented. And the drugs only make him more confused and groggy. The terror and depression remain."

"Your husband has had a severe breakdown, Mrs. Beauvais. It's not like he broke an arm or a leg. We don't understand what's going on, so we do what we think best. Trial and error. He's a voluntary patient. You can take him out of here any time you want." He walked brusquely away.

There was nothing more to say. Peggy stood at Gerry's bedside, stroking his face and hair, pleading with him to communicate. Occasionally he spoke briefly.

"It's all dark."

"Isn't there something you want? Food? Music? A drive some-where? The leaves are changing color. We could drive up north. It would be so beautiful."

Gerry shook his head. "There's nothing I want. It's all dark and gray. I can't even enjoy the sun. It's like I'm going to be here for-ever. That's the real horror of it. I'll never be any better. It's always the same."

After he had been in the hospital two weeks, Peggy became frightened. She would have to notify his family. Even the bishop would find out soon enough. Maybe she had taken too much on herself.

When she visited him on a Saturday evening, there were bruises on his arms and a cut on his forehead. No one on the staff admitted knowing anything about it, and Gerry just shook his head. Finally, when she was ready to leave, he spoke.

"I wouldn't take a shower, so they made me get up."

The tears appeared again, more of anger and humiliation than pain.

"I want to get the hell out of here."

"Where do you want to go?"

"Anywhere! If you don't get me out of here, I'll never speak to you again. This is a hellhole! People wander into my room and stare at me. One guy relieved himself on my floor. The orderlies take dope and molest the patients. Sellers is screwing one of the young women patients and one of the nurses. They think we're all crazy and don't see anything. Only a few of the staff care anything about us. Half the time I feel in physical danger. Christ! A young guy said I stole his kids and took them to Texas. He was going to punch me out unless I brought them back!" His anger was refreshing. It was the first real emotion he had shown.

"I'll call Dr. Hengesbach tomorrow."

"The hell with Hengesbach or anyone else. I can't wait till to-morrow. I want to get out of here right now."

His face was flushed. His eyes flashed some awareness and rec-ognition that she had not seen for days.

"I'll ask Dr. Sellers."

"No, damn it, tell Dr. Sellers. He's a grinning, greedy, lecherous butcher who doesn't give a shit about anyone in this place! He's about as helpful as an enema!"

He pulled himself out of bed. Only then did Peggy realize how much weight he had lost. She hesitated for a moment.

198

"I want out of here right now, or I'm going to murder Sellers and a couple of orderlies."

"But your medication—"

"Sellers can give me a prescription for that. If he won't, Hengesbach will. I'm not spending one more night here."

Peggy approached Sellers, who was about to leave for the evening. He was teasing one of the nurses and rearranging her hair.

"There's nothing keeping him." He grinned sardonically. "He'll be back. They all come back." He sighed resignedly. "All of them."

He stopped at the receiving desk, grabbed a pad, and hurriedly wrote out a prescription for Elavil.

"I hope you know what you're letting yourself in for, Mrs. Beauvais. Your husband is suicidal and will remain that way until the depression goes away. Perhaps more shock treatments."

Peggy shook her head vigorously. "No more shock treatments!"

She moved down the corridor to Beauvais's room. He was already dressed and packed.

"Let's get the hell out of here!"

She was amazed at his sudden energy. They signed the release forms at the desk. Sellers stood by awkwardly.

Neither Beauvais nor Peggy acknowledged him. Beauvais's face was still flushed with anger, his fists clenched, his eyes narrow. Sellers started to say something and thought better of it. An orderly with huge biceps unlocked the main door and they were gone.

Father Niedermeyer was just making his way over to the church to hear confessions when Peggy drove up with Father Beauvais. As far as he knew, Beauvais had injured his back. He approached the car with a broad smile.

"How's the back?"

Beauvais was startled for a moment, unaware of what Peggy had reported to Niedermeyer. He recovered quickly, smiled, and stepped cautiously out of the car.

"Much better, Father. I really appreciate your taking over for me. I should be able to help out in a few days."

"There's no hurry. It feels good to be active again. I really missed it. Besides, my sister was starting to get on my nerves. She treats me like an old man."

He laughed loudly.

"I'll be glad to stay as long as you need me. I haven't said much to the people. Just that you suffered a slight injury to your back and would return soon. These people have a lot of affection for you, Father."

Beauvais nodded his appreciation as Niedermeyer walked away towards the church. Peggy led him up the back steps of the rectory and into his bedroom.

"You climb into bed and I'll get the prescription filled before the pharmacy closes."

"I don't feel like going to bed. I'm so damn glad to be out of that place."

"Nevertheless, I think you should rest." She opened a drawer and handed him his pajamas.

"I'll be back in half an hour."

He nodded, took the pajamas, and suddenly felt tired. There was nothing to be angry at any more and he felt the furious wave of depression return like a dark and unrelenting cloud. Peggy noted the change and was alarmed.

"I'll be right back with your medication," she said.

He nodded bleakly and began undressing.

When Peggy returned with the Elavil, he lay motionless in the bed, his face a mask of despair. She poured water in the bathroom, struggled with the container's safety cap, and finally extracted two capsules. Beauvais took them silently.

"It's dark again," he said sadly.

She moved across the room as if she were going to leave.

"Don't go!" he said frantically. "I don't want to be alone!"

"I'm right here," she said softly. She moved toward the bed and began stroking his face gently.

"I love you," he said. "I've got to pull out of this. It's all so frightening and hopeless. I really don't want to live. There's nothing to live for."

"You could live for me," she said. "Without you, there wouldn't be anything left for me."

She leaned over and kissed him on the mouth, then lay next to him on the bed. Instinctively he cuddled against her. She kissed him again, more passionately. His body moved spontaneously closer to hers, and he returned her kiss with some intensity. Then suddenly his eyes filled with tears and he pulled away. He began sobbing like a small child. She sat up and stroked his head and neck.

"I love you," she said.

The tears continued to flow, and his sobs sounded like an abandoned little boy. "It's not right," he sobbed. "I'm a priest!"

"Priests need love too."

"Not the kind of love I want with you. I promised God."

"God is not a tyrant. He understands. If he didn't, he wouldn't be God."

"Maybe he's punishing me for wanting you, but without you there's nothing. It shouldn't be that way. I was ordained to help people, not to please myself. I just don't understand why everything seems so hopeless. I've never stopped trying."

"It will pass," Peggy said. "I won't leave you until it does."

"But you can't stay here. The bishop will find out, and I'll be suspended from the priesthood."

"Don't worry about that now," she said. "Get some rest."

She continued caressing his face and neck and shoulders. Gradually he calmed down and his eyes grew heavy, his words muffled and disjointed. Soon he was asleep.

Peggy walked down to the living room where Father Niedermeyer was finishing up his breviary. He looked up and smiled broadly.

"How's the patient?"

"Not so good, Father. I think I should stay the night. I'll run home and get a few things and sleep in the guestroom. I'll just make sure my dad is okay."

"You sure I can't handle things?"

"You are handling things: the Masses, the confessions, the sick calls. I'll take care of the patient."

Niedermeyer nodded. "I'll stay up until you get back."

Upstairs, Beauvais continued to sleep heavily. His dreams were tortured and nightmarish. He was in a deep pit, like the cistern in the backyard of his childhood home in Ohio. He tried climbing out, but the bricks were wet and clammy. He tried calling out, but his voice would not work. He tried screaming, to no avail. He saw his father at the top of the cistern and pleaded with him with his eyes to rescue him. Then it was Bishop Sullivan, with the same angry expression as his father. Then it was his father again, giving him a scornful look, the look he had given him when Gerry had quit the football team. Suddenly the water in the cistern began to rise. It was already up to his shoulders, and again he tried to scream out. He could hear Father Misch's voice in the background while his father and Bishop Sullivan both continued to stare at him coldly. As the water covered his neck, he cried out and woke up in a cold sweat.

It took him several seconds to realize where he was. The black

cloud again engulfed him. His whole life seemed ruined. His boyhood and priesthood were a failure. The beauty of Europe, of Karl
and Ursula, of Father Misch and Santek were all gone. So were his
dreams of music and choirs. He wanted someone to save him.
Maybe if he had stayed in Europe? He wanted Santek, he wanted
Peggy, he wanted to die!

He felt an unbearable pain in his legs and buttocks that gradually
climbed up his back. It was an unfamiliar pain, feeling as if he
wanted someone to beat his back and legs with a baseball bat or a
rubber hose. His whole body seemed knotted and tense. He
couldn't stand it. He had to end it, but how? He didn't want to die
but he couldn't tolerate the pain. It was too much to bear.

He sat up in bed and looked for the pills that Peggy had purchased. They were not on the nightstand. He got up and walked
into the bathroom and searched the medicine cabinet. They were
not there: nothing but aspirin and cold tablets. He picked up the
aspirin bottle. There were only two left. He took them without
water. The pain continued to throb unbearably. His back felt
twisted and hard as a rock. He had to stop the pain, he couldn't
endure it any more, he had to die! There was no way out. Peggy was
an impossibility, his life and his priesthood were destroyed. There
was nothing left. His movements were stiff and abrupt. He moved
to the closet.

There on the floor next to his weights he saw the elasticlike
jumping rope that he had used regularly when it was important to
keep in shape. He thought briefly of Santek and their days in the
seminary. No one could help him now. He wanted his mother. He
wanted Peggy. He wanted to return to the cathedral and direct the
choir. Then he wanted nothing. The darkness encircled him. Nothing mattered. The impossible pain continued to throb. It was indescribable, as if all the tension in his life were stored in his back and
legs. He picked up the rope and walked into the bathroom. He tried
tying it around the shower head. His hands were rubbery, but he
finally managed a slip knot. He pulled hard against the shower head.
It held firmly. Then he made a noose out of the rest of the rope and
slid it around his neck. He crouched down in the shower until the
rope was tight against his neck. He felt the rope grow tighter around
his neck and the air leave his chest. He tried to let go, just to slip
down a few more inches in the tub and the pain would be gone. The
rope pulled tighter on his neck. He wanted to let go, but he
couldn't. He didn't want to die, he wanted to live, but he could no

202

longer stand the pain. There was no release. Death was the only way. It was not death at all. It was release, only release. It would only take one burst of courage, and the pain and darkness would be gone. He let go briefly, then stood up. There were tears of rage in his eyes.

He called himself a coward as the pain continued to ravage his legs and back. Again he lowered himself against the floor, struggling to let his body fall far enough to choke out every last ounce of air. Something in him still resisted. He did not understand some persistent fear of the unknown. There was little pain. The rope again pulled tight against his neck and he felt his neck and face grow tense, his chest gasping for air, his mouth and nose twisted in some final contortion. Suddenly he slipped on the floor of the shower and the rope pulled tightly against his neck. His body slumped, his legs touching the ground, his head and shoulders and back hanging suspended. He passed out.

He was in the back seat of his father's old Chevy and felt himself fall to the floor and thrash beneath the seat. He was ten or eleven years old. His father was yelling at him. He called him "sissy" and "coward" and "pantywaist." Gerry continued to thrash about the floor. Somehow he slid under the seat and was hiding in the darkness. Then, frightened, he struggled to get out.

He was trapped! He beat against the seat and felt his body grovel on the floor. Suddenly it was silent. Cautiously he felt around with his hands. Gradually he realized he was in the tub.

His whole body was too weak to stand up. The rope, still around his neck, had broken at the shower head, the sharp metal gradually cutting through. He felt his head. It was wet. He looked at his hand. It was covered with blood. He tried to get up but still did not have the strength. With great difficulty, he loosened the rope and slid it from his neck. He felt his neck where the pressure of the rope had left a ring of swollen raw skin. He heard the door open. Peggy's voice called out to him. He was not sure if the dream had ended. Again he heard her voice. The bathroom door opened. She switched on the light and saw him lying there with blood streaming down one side of his face, then saw the rope and the raw, red ring around his neck. She grabbed a towel, found the wound on his head, and tried to stem the flow of blood.

"Oh, Gerry, Gerry, dear God! What are you doing to yourself?" She felt herself grow faint and struggled to maintain her senses.

203

He fell against her as she continued to press the towel firmly on his wound.

"Oh, dear God, what are we going to do?"

Then she held his limp, childlike body next to hers. He felt like a helpless little boy. She began to weep desperately. He looked at her blankly and again felt the pain.

"I want to die," he said. "I've got to die!"

"I won't let you."

Her tears stopped, her jaw was set. She held his face in her hands as the blood flowed through her fingers.

"You're going to live! Damn it, I won't let you die! Do you understand? You're going to live!"

Chapter 19

Chanute was just another air force base. San Antonio had become home after less than a year. Now life had to begin again, and despite the forced move it went amiably along after Angie had located a suitable apartment in Champaign-Urbana not far from the University of Illinois. Although she was not really fond of her clerical job at the Universal Heavy Equipment Rental Company, checking dozers and earthmovers in and out, her time with Santek gave meaning to her life. The weeks passed too quickly, and the weekends when they traveled to Chicago or St. Louis provided the freedom they needed from the constant fear of detection.

Despite Santek's periodic anxiety over their situation and his increasing awareness that religion in the air force was only another facet of the bureaucracy, he had found his priesthood in the months at Lackland, and the move to Chanute only strengthened his resolve. With Angie the only woman in his life, and her love as a constant support, his priestly mission was again exciting and meaningful, especially since he could share his life with her.

"The brass doesn't really give a shit about what I'm doing. They just pay a kind of political homage to religion. Chaplains are simply part of what the American people expect. No one gives a damn if we do anything. That's why so many of the guys are more air force than priest. We aren't really respected. That's what hurts."

"That doesn't matter, darling. Hundreds of the boys respect you. So do many of the officers. What the air force thinks doesn't concern us. You don't belong to the air force. You're like Christ, and the pharisees and Roman officials didn't believe in him."

He loved saying Mass as the spiritual center of his own life. It was the greatest act of his day, bringing Christ down on the altar to lonely and suffering humanity, uniting himself with Christ through communion, and pledging himself to "go about doing good" as had his Master. It was almost a physical rejuvenation for Santek: he felt his muscles flex when he elevated the chalice; his body came alive when he bent low and whispered the words of consecration. He extended his arms at the *Dominus vobiscum* to embrace the whole world, and when he gave his final blessing he reached out to all the Americans killed and wounded in Vietnam in the last week of May in 1967, to their grieving parents and his own parents in Hamtramck, to Gerry Beauvais and Angie, to everyone in the congregation who was struggling in some private way to find peace and meaning. Angie's occasional presence at his Mass seemed to unite them spiritually as their loving sexuality united them physically. Giving her holy communion was a particularly powerful experience which somehow sanctified their relationship.

He had no real quarrel with his faith, never questioning the real presence of Christ as many priests were beginning to do. Nor did he welcome the liturgical changes of Vatican II, which made the service more "Protestant." But he was proud of the Catholic Church, the same way he was proud of the fighting spirit and courage of the air force. He heard confessions regularly and was increasingly gentle and understanding about the usual sexual sins as his own relationship with Angie matured. He went out of his way to make converts, again with Angie's encouragement.

"Maybe they take instructions because they want to marry or sleep with a Catholic girl, but later on it will mean something," she told him.

"I just wonder if they really have faith."

"Maybe faith is like love. It takes time. They like you and they are in love with a Catholic, so they become Catholic. They'll never forget you, and their religion will grow stronger when they really need it. I see the way they look at you. You'll be a part of their life long after the air force."

Angie helped to restore pride in Ted's priesthood and he again became dedicated to his work, relieved that her loving presence in his life took away any need to prowl and wander lustfully on lonely weekends. Her understanding and sensitivity gave new meaning to his life, and her love stood firmly behind his priesthood. Even Pope Paul's backing away from the positive strides of Pope John did not really upset him. Curiously, he did not question even celibacy or the Church's stand on birth control and divorce, as did Beauvais. Somehow he accepted human weakness, his own and others', without needing to take on the doctrine of the Church. A pragmatic man, Santek was content in his belief that the Church was moving in a relentless new direction. That he could not live as a celibate was ultimately his private business with God.

At first he had stayed frequently at the BOQ, but increasingly he was able to stay with Angie in Champaign on free weekends and one or two nights a week. His confreres presumed he was working at a local parish, giving high school retreats, attending theological seminars, or helping out at the Newman Center at the University of Illinois. There was no reason to suspect his liaison, and as long as he completed his official assignments he was free to come and go. The air force could not care less.

As the months passed at Chanute, it was well known that he was a priest's priest, seeking out the lonely alcoholic, the bereaved wife and family of a flyboy, or conducting his convert classes far into the night. His sermons were a down-to-earth joy with punch and a liberal use of the scriptures, often reduced to the street jargon of East Detroit. Angie loved them as much or more than the men did.

"Christ had no time for phonies. Pimps and sinners didn't bother him. They weren't trying to prove anything. They knew their life was screwed up. It was the super-righteous big shots he had no time for. He called them brass coffins, beautiful on the outside and inside full of dry bones. They prayed so everyone would see them. They made a big splash, tipping headwaiters and marching to the front pew in church, because they considered themselves the cat's hips. Christ knew he had nothing to offer them. They were so damned sure of themselves, they didn't need salvation or advice, so Christ went to the little ones like you and me, who understand our weakness and know that we can't make it without his help.

"He didn't throw stones at the prostitutes like the high priests did. He forgave them, changed their lives, and told them to line up and follow him. He didn't pick bankers and generals, lawyers and senators to be his apostles. They were too cocky and self-assured. He picked ignorant fishermen who knew that without Christ they could do nothing. He gave them the power of the keys to unlock heaven and hell. The rich and powerful were content to ask him smart-ass questions to show how clever they were and to see if they could make a fool of him.

"People still do that. They ask, How do we know that Christ is God? Or, How do we know there's a heaven or hell? Or, How can we be sure that the priest forgives sin? Or, Is Christ really present on the altar? The other day a young officer who wanted to marry a Catholic girl told me he was an 'atheist.' I doubt if he could spell it, but he said it with great pride, as if that made him a real intellectual. I didn't try to change his mind. Life will do that.

"Christ has been around for two thousand years. He's seen great nations come and go. But he doesn't change. He's still the shepherd looking for his sheep. He's not looking for giraffes or lions, kings or queens or heads of state. He's looking for the humble people who want forgiveness of sins. You may or may not get your wings in this world. What counts is whether you get them in the next."

He finished his Mass in record time and heard the confession of the young homosexual. "Don't be discouraged. Do the best you can. You are the way you are."

He consoled the young wife whose husband died in Vietnam. "Cling to your children and make them proud of their father. He was a hero. So are you! I'm here whenever you need me."

And he was. He was all things to all men, and with Angela in his life, he had the love and security to be the kind of priest he wanted to be with his whole heart. He knew that she was often lonely, that she desperately wanted friends and a social life, that nights without him seemed endless. But their time would come with retirement. Only her growing desire to have a child seemed too hard to handle, and she brought it up more and more often.

After the aborted weekend at the Oak Grove Resort in the fall of 1967, when he saw a man he feared might recognize him, they had abruptly checked out and returned to their apartment in Champaign a day early. On that evening, she seemed more distressed than the unhappy incident warranted. He knew that she disliked her job with the heavy equipment company and that the Champaign-Urbana area lacked the excitement of San Antonio. Their apartment was smaller and less elegant than the one in Texas, there were few restaurants and almost nowhere to go, but that had never really seemed to bother her as long as she had him.

It was almost four years to the day since he had first met her. So much had happened it seemed like a lifetime. He lay on the couch in his shorts reading the statement of the American bishops supporting Pope Paul's harsh position on birth control. There were reports of dissent from priests and laymen all over the world.

208

Aware of her silence, he looked up from the paper.

"Those boys don't know when a war is lost."

Normally she would have laughed, but she was lost in her own thoughts.

He spoke softly. "You really seem down. What's the matter? The baby?"

She stared coldly at him and didn't speak.

He tried his tactic of staring coldly back at her. "You know there's no way we can have a child now."

Her expression didn't change, and her voice was firm and unyielding. "It will make all the difference. I can accept all the rest, but I want your baby. I waited for months in Lackland, and now here at Chanute. I think of it all the time when you're gone. I don't want to be put off any more. It's time, Ted, and you damn well know it."

He couldn't believe the force of her words. His face reddened and his whole being exploded. He had risked his whole priesthood for her. "Don't I mean anything to you?"

"You mean everything to me," she said softly, "but I'm a person too! I accept the moves, the loneliness, the fear of being recognized, the new job, and trying to be all you need me to be, but I want your baby! Everything in me says it's right. We have so much to give a child. I'm through being put off like some troublesome little girl. We're in this together—man and wife—and I count too!"

Her firmness frightened him, and his voice softened.

"I need you, honey, more than I can say. I can be the best priest in the world with you at my side. But a baby right now is out of the question. What kind of home could we give him? Hiding him, dragging him all over the world, afraid to admit he's ours except to strangers. It's hard enough with the two of us sneaking around like a couple of Russian spies."

"We don't have to do as much. We've played enough and traveled enough. We're afraid to have friends—I try to understand that—but at least I want to give some of what we have to a child. I know it will mean everything to you. I just know it. Even Peggy said so!"

He looked away, feeling totally rejected, as if his own love for her was not enough. And for Angie, although Ted had become her whole life, for some reason it was not enough. Maybe it was living without close friends or any family, but everything in her wanted a child to fulfill something inside her that had felt empty for years.

She was convinced that once the baby was a reality, Ted would adjust and be overwhelmed with love. His own yearning to be a father had only been suppressed. And with a child would come friends they could trust to share their secret. She couldn't live like a recluse any longer, no matter how much she loved him. She would have their child!

But now there was nothing more to say. She knew he was lost in anger and self-pity. It would pass, but she chose not to discuss it till later, to avoid an angry outburst. But she would not be put off. Two years of waiting was enough.

She watched as he finished his drink, dressed silently, and got up to leave.

"I've got to see that dead pilot's wife and kids this afternoon. I'll be back around midnight."

"Will you want to eat?"

"No. See you later."

Then he was gone.

She tried to watch TV but finally turned it off. She slept on the couch briefly but got caught up in terrifying dreams about losing her child to her father and a cranky bishop from her childhood and woke abruptly. It was five o'clock. Finally, begging God to help her, she got up and began to pack. When she had filled two suitcases, she wrote him a note and left it on the dining room table where he couldn't miss it. She called a cab and slowly walked out the door, locking it behind her. The note read:

My darling:

I guess I need some time to make up my mind. When I am with you, I can't think straight. I realize that a child and a normal social life were not a clear part of our marriage, but suddenly a baby and friends means as much to me as your priesthood does to you. I don't know where I am going, maybe back to Canada, maybe not. I just have to think things out for myself. I love you with my whole being. You know that. This is the hardest thing I've ever had to do, harder than leaving you for the convent. I'll write as soon as I'm settled. I love you, my darling, and I always will. I am sorry to cause both of us this terrible pain.

Your Angie

Late the same evening, a contrite, loving Santek made his way to the apartment door with a bottle of her favorite cream sherry. He had called earlier and there was no answer. After knocking twice, a chilling wave of fear engulfed him. He felt for his key and unlocked the door. He called her name, but the very echo of the apartment answered his question. She was gone. He knew it instinctively.

He found the note and read it over three times, looking for an indication that she was not really gone forever. It seemed so cold, so rational. That hurt most of all. He sprawled on the couch, suddenly out of breath, and lay there numb and motionless save for the trembling of his arms and legs and his labored breathing. He wanted to scream out, to beg her to return to him, but he was silent as sadness and fear almost ripped him from his senses.

The very apartment which had become his sanctuary of love and refuge, of warmth and healing, now seemed like a hollow cave, echoing an ultimate emptiness. His eyes, dilated and burning, roamed aimlessly about the room. Everything shouted of Angie: the temperamental Boston fern hanging gracefully in the kitchen window and the African violets on the sill, the cactus they had gathered on a trip to the desert, the dining room centerpiece of giant pinecones and evergreen and oak leaves, the pictures on the den wall of their trips to New Orleans and the Rockies and three days in New York when they saw *Man of La Mancha* and Hal Holbrook in Santek's beloved *Mark Twain,* the mementos of a special weekend at the Palmer House in Chicago and of a Black Hawk game when Bobby Hull scored his fifty-first goal of the season. He loved the statues and miniature metal sculptures, the oil painting of the New York skyline, the carved Buddhas from the antique store in Dallas.

All were placed with her exquisite taste and framed with her gently artistic eye. Even the furniture tore him apart as he thought of his beloved Angie selecting his suede easy chair and the carved oak tables, the Scandinavian area rug and the early American dining room set, all guarantees that he would never be a poor kid from East Detroit again. He was afraid to walk into the bedroom.

He got up to mix himself a drink. He opened the liquor cabinet and slammed it shut. He wanted her to mix his favorite Rob Roy and prepare the hors d'oeuvres she knew he loved. He wanted to see her smile, the honey hair falling over her left eye. He wanted to pinch her ass, to tease her about a few extra pounds.

Nothing was the same. As much as he knew he loved her, he had not realized that she had become the very core of his world. Without her there was no priesthood, no excitement, no joy, no meaning, no happiness. He never really believed she would leave him.

She had been his totally devoted, almost serflike woman. He had been her whole world. She hung on his every word, laughed helplessly at his jokes, listened enthralled to his stories about the daily tragedies and wonders of his priesthood, reveled in their sexuality as if she could not live one day longer without it. She waited on his every wish, anticipated his needs instinctively, surrounded him with a hundred surprise gifts and almost daily manifestations of her all-absorbing love.

And when she had attended his Mass or listened to his sermons, her very face shone with pride and spiritual joy. No one in the world ever had a better wife, a closer friend, a purer expression of everything he cherished and had longed for all his life.

He didn't want a drink. He couldn't even linger in the apartment where her very shadow and odor filled his chest with massive pain. He sprawled again on the couch, and finally the tears came. All the bravado and toughness and charismatic power were gone, all the humor, insight, and compassion that had made him a priest. He was suddenly a helpless little boy from the slums of Detroit, and the tears that came were those of a small child whose heart was breaking with grief.

Nothing could distract him from the pain. All the loneliness of his entire life seemed to descend upon him and congeal like stone in his chest and back. He could not move. He could only continue to cry and call out her name, as if she had left the earth and nothing held meaning any longer. He clenched his fists with pain and determination. He had to find her, give her all the children she wanted, jeopardize his priesthood, even his very existence, if he was ever to know the least shred of joy again.

He knelt down and prayed with his whole heart. "O God, I know I am not your best priest, maybe even your worst. But I do the best I can. I want to do your work, but I can't without Angie. I don't know what's right or wrong any more. I don't know whether you want us to have a baby or if you want me to leave the priesthood. I can't leave Angie. My whole life falls apart without her. You know that, my God!"

The prayer briefly calmed him. Then he picked up her picture and kissed it reverently and wondered why he had feared having a child and a social life. It was the only thing she had asked, her only complaint, despite his absence, his moods, his frequent neglect. But he had refused because he was afraid to face the consequences of being a real husband. He had only wanted to have his own needs met. He had owned her, possessed her totally, and now he might never see her again.

Angie was in no better shape. She had gone to the Greyhound depot with no idea of a destination. The realization that she was leaving Ted did not really overwhelm her until she looked around the bus station at the collection of immigrants, wanderers, and vagrants. Three policemen were hassling a pale, skinny young man with long blond hair, who was rummaging through his wallet to establish his identity. One of the policemen pushed him against the wall in the search position, legs apart and body leaning precariously. After an abrupt attack they dragged him out the door. Angie burst into tears. An Italian woman with a mustache interrupted her rosary long enough to stare at her.

"Men," she said in broken English. "They all trouble."

Angie nodded and looked away. She stared at the schedule posted on a blackboard. She decided on St. Louis, then changed her mind and wondered about Chicago. She tried to imagine what it would be like. She had never felt so alone in her life. No move had been really difficult before because Ted was with her. Now everything seemed frightening and impossible. A black man stared at her. She looked away. Two sinister men, speaking a foreign language, seemed to be laughing at her. She got up and moved her bags to a more isolated spot. It was almost nine o'clock and she had to decide on something. She thought about going home. It was impossible. She had told her father too many lies already.

She had not realized what strength her relationship with Ted had given her. She heard his belly laugh echo in her ears. She saw the boyish pleasure in his eyes when she prepared his favorite meal or his excitement when they were going away for a few days without the pressures of avoiding detection. He was like a child, really, although he would have cursed if she tried to tell him that. It was the boy in him that she adored: the enthusiasm, the joy of living, the delight in his priesthood, his ability to find the humor in anything. She knew she would never find anyone like him. There was only one Ted Santek, the man-child who had made her life—despite secrecy and solitude, despite a lack of social life and even a baby—an adventure she had never fantasized in her wildest reveries.

She decided to call Ted, went to the phone and dialed the number, then hung up. She knew that she had to get away. She thought about visiting Peggy and Father Beauvais. They were really her only friends in the States. But there was no way she could tell them that she had left the ebullient Santek. Besides, they had overwhelming problems of their own. She felt suddenly tired, as if the emotional strain of the last day had enveloped her. She did not want to travel far.

Finally she decided on Peoria, after she noticed there was a 9:30 departure. She liked Peoria. Set along the Illinois River in a broad basin that formed Lake Peoria, it looked rustic and beautiful. There was an abundance of industry, with chemical plants and beer and whiskey distilleries, and Bradley University. The agent informed her that the bus would arrive around midnight and that there was cheap lodging near the station. In the morning, she thought, she could start looking for a job. As she purchased her ticket a surge of loneliness swept through her. It was a feeling she had not experienced since she left the convent, but she boarded the bus and took a window seat near the back. An attractive, well-dressed salesman with a New York accent took the seat next to her. She shuddered noticeably.

"You from Peoria?"

"No," she said quietly. "I'm moving there."

"You'll like it. I've lived there three years. Big enough to have everything you need, small enough to get around. Where's your husband?"

"He's overseas. In the air force."

The salesman edged closer. "Maybe I can show you around."

A chill went through her body. She shook her head and turned to the window, only wishing she were going home to Ted and that he would laugh again and take her in his arms. The salesman looked away.

Chapter 20

After his abortive suicide attempt, Gerry Beauvais again sank into a deep depression and was unable to get out of bed for days. Peggy refused to leave him, once she had shared with Father Niedermeyer what had really taken place and how sick Father Beauvais actually was. She could not have chosen a more compassionate and wise confidant. She admitted to him that Bishop Sullivan knew nothing of Beauvais's condition and tearfully decribed the shock treatments and indifference of Voss Hospital. John Niedermeyer was well aware of Dr. Sellers's reputation, and although he usually had a good word for even the most disreputable parishioner or public servant, his face flushed with anger.

"Sellers has become an extremely wealthy man at the expense of many helpless, frightened people whose terrified, guilt-ridden families feel that a mental illness may be their fault. I hold Sellers responsible for the suicide of one of the finest women in our parish. She was suffering from postpartum blues; Sellers and his barbaric treatments destroyed her. And I know two men, each of whom was given an unnecessary lobotomy without their families' realizing there was any other option. Sellers is a butcher. You should have taken Beauvais to Mercywood."

"I was afraid," Peggy admitted. "I thought it would end his career as a priest and ultimately destroy him. The new bishop seems to lack compassion and understanding." She wanted to say more.

"I can understand. Bishop Sullivan is a sincere, well-meaning man who doesn't always listen very well. It's true of so many men of power. I think we should consult Dr. Hengesbach. Fred's no psychiatrist, but he's a dedicated, knowledgeable doctor who keeps up on things and is one of my closest friends."

"He knows Father Beauvais is ill, but I lied to him too, because I was afraid the bishop's office might find out."

"You did what you thought best, Peggy, under a lot of stress. We all owe you a lot." He pressed her hands warmly. "I'll give Fred a call. There's probably no need to alarm the bishop as long as things are under control. He's got enough on his mind trying to make sense of Vatican Two."

Later that evening, Dr. Hengesbach examined Beauvais compassionately. Back in the living room, Father John explained the problem and the need, temporarily at least, to keep things under wraps.

Hengesbach nodded. "I can keep him on Elavil and maybe some Miltown until we can stabilize his dosage, but he'll need constant care."

"I can provide that," Peggy said. "I'll take a leave from my job and get help to care for my dad."

"It may be difficult for you. A depression this severe usually has deep roots and can last for a long while. There is no way to describe what Father is feeling unless you have experienced it yourself. Everything seems hopeless and unending to him. Progress is so slow that he is not aware of it. The deeply depressed person loses all interest in everything, even the most basic pleasure, and feels powerless to do anything about it. If we can just get him to want someone or something, to show the least interest in anything, the process can be reversed. Otherwise he'll remain anhedonic and suicidal."

"Someone may have to talk to his family, especially his mother. He usually drove home to Ohio once a month or so to visit her. It was something he really looked forward to."

"That may be our hope," Hengesbach said quietly. "Meanwhile, I'll tell the family what they need to know when the time comes. If he shows any inclination to want to see his mother or anyone else, let me know immediately. Desire alone can cure him. And perhaps our prayers. The medication has side effects, by the way, usually a dry mouth and blurred vision. He might have vertigo if he gets up too quickly, and a rapid pulse rate, or there may be some constipation and difficulty in urination, but usually the side effects disappear in time."

"How long do you think the medication will take to have an effect?" Niedermeyer asked.

216

"It's hard to know. If it's a chemical depression—that is, a drain on his system's own antidepressant apparatus as a result of great stress over a long period of time—we may see results in a couple of weeks or months. If not, I just don't know. A lot depends on his will to live. There are so damn many variables. I've watched his enthusiasm wane over the last several months. When he first came, as delighted as I was to have a worthy successor to you, Father, I wondered why they sent him to a small country parish. He obviously has far greater talents and energies than this parish requires."

He grinned at Father Niedermeyer.

"You built the church and the rectory and the parish hall. You didn't leave a lot for a successor to do."

"Enough of your malarkey, Fred. Beauvais has abilities I never dreamed of. He's episcopal timber and wasn't meant to be a country pastor. I think Bishop Sullivan—or, more likely, Monsignor Kelley—made a grave mistake in judgment. They may be punishing him, for all I know." He sighed. "It happens more frequently than I care to admit."

"Punishing him for what?" Hengesbach was startled. It was not his vision of the Church. "If that could be the case, we've got to find out. He doesn't seem like the kind of man who would resist the bishop's authority. If he shows no improvement, I'd be more than willing to discuss matters with the bishop or the chancellor."

"Do you think he'd be better off at Mercywood?" Niedermeyer asked.

"Not really. Mercywood is no paradise. Just being in a mental hospital is its own trauma and can be as hard to get over as depression. The very best are mediocre and impersonal, to say the least, and often attract a bizarre personnel. There's no magic about mental hospitals. They're just holding tanks where some people get well in spite of their surroundings. The 'Catholic' ones are no better. As long as Peggy can give him the care he needs, I think we should spare Father that additional humiliation and shock. Here he'll have love and familiar surroundings. That and his own inner strength are what we have going for us. The medication may help, but Father Beauvais has to fight his way out of this himself. We'll just take things one step at a time."

Peggy wondered if she should share what she knew of the attempted suicide and the bishop's insistence that she not be in contact with Father Beauvais. She decided that now was not the time.

A life-and-death struggle was going on, and she believed herself to be the key to Gerry's recovery.

Hengesbach wrote out a prescription, finished his coffee and homemade strudel, and departed. Niedermeyer walked over to the church to finish his breviary in the presence of the Blessed Sacrament. It felt good to be a real priest again. Only now did he realize how much he had missed it. Even the smell of the country seemed to revive him, and he hadn't heard the melodies of frogs and crickets for months. He only hoped and prayed that Beauvais might recover completely and enjoy the priesthood as much as he had. No other life could compare to it.

Peggy made her way to Beauvais's room with his favorite veal chops and brussels sprouts and his evening medication. When she went in he was staring blankly at the ceiling with a kind of quiet terror and anguish in his eyes. She had never seen that look before. She placed the food on the bedside table. Gradually he focused and looked at her stiffly as if he could never smile again. She was frightened.

"I'm not hungry," he said.

"You've got to try to eat something. Your body has to remain strong to fight this thing."

"I've got nothing to fight with," he said sadly.

"You can pray. God will give you the strength."

"I can't find God. Only you are real to me. And not always even you."

"God isn't gone. Something good will come of all this." She wasn't sure she believed this, but what else was there to say? She never really understood how God entered into her life or anyone else's. She just tried to believe in him as a child would.

"I wish I could feel that way. It's so hard to think that God could want anyone to suffer like this if he could bring relief."

She propped him up with pillows and tried feeding him. He munched part of a veal chop and a brussels sprout.

"It all tastes the same," he said.

"I'll put on a record. What would you like to hear?"

"Maybe Beethoven. The 'Missa Solemnis' or the Ninth Symphony."

She was heartened and leafed through the collection. She saw his eyes brighten briefly at the first colorful notes of the "Missa." He tried another bite of veal but could barely get it down. She took his plate away. He shook his head when she offered dessert and coffee,

218

and lit a cigarette. But then sadness engulfed him again and he asked her to turn off the music. When she returned later in the evening with more medication, he was staring at the ceiling again with a glazed, despairing look in his eyes. She knelt at his bedside and began saying the rosary aloud. At first he answered, then he was silent.

"I can't pray," he said.

"Then just listen." She continued the prayer as he drifted off to sleep. She stroked his head and kissed him gently on the lips. Then she put her head next to his and continued her prayers.

As the days passed she became acutely aware that the medication seemed to have little effect. Even a daily shower was an almost impossible task that he undertook with great reluctance. He seemed afraid to get out of bed but was tortured by anxieties when he didn't. He ate poorly and continued to lose weight, and only when she demanded his compliance did he seem to do anything. He would usually get angry and then somehow have enough energy to do what she asked. She realized that her gentle, motherly understanding was not getting the job done. Her beloved priest was wasting away. Even his mind seemed listless and pale.

Gradually, Peggy forced him to exercise briefly with his weights a couple of times a day, demanded that he eat, read to him from the Detroit *Free Press* each morning, played brief selections from Mozart or Bach or Beethoven's sonatas, and talked to him of God's will and protective providence. Even if she wondered at her own words, she knew it was an idiom that might reach him. And gradually she began to have faith in her own pep talk.

"God is calling you to sainthood."

"I don't like his methods. There must be an easier way. It's so black and futile. I just can't make it."

"You will make it," she said defiantly. "I can't live without you, and I don't want to die."

The same week Santek called and Peggy explained Gerry's condition as best she could. Santek wanted to come immediately but said nothing of Angie's startling exodus. "I can come next weekend."

"Not now," she said. "He wouldn't want you to see him like this. I'll call you when it's time."

"What's he so depressed about?" Santek was too tough and practical to comprehend a depression that could not be put into words.

"There's no single cause," she said. "He's just depressed. Everything seems black. Maybe it's life or death. The bishop . . . the bishop told him I was to leave the rectory for good. That was the night he fell apart. He was hoping for another assignment and never got a chance to mention it."

"That arrogant Irish son-of-a-bitch! I'd like to kick his ass! He has about as much feeling as a dead lobster. Does he know you're still there?"

"No, he doesn't know anything. He's not even aware that Father Niedermeyer has taken over. And the parishioners think he's injured his back."

"Christ, the CIA could use you!" He laughed loudly. "Lucky you're in the sticks. It's a million miles from the chancery. Just don't set the place on fire!"

It was good to hear someone laugh. So good!

"Call me as soon as anything breaks. I may not be here as long as I thought." He wanted to tell her about Angie.

"What do you mean?"

"I'm going to Vietnam." He didn't admit that he had volunteered.

"My God, what about Angie?"

"She'll have to stay around here. Maybe we can meet in Bangkok or Hawaii when I get liberty." He hated the lie, but his pride would not allow him to admit his rejection. "She'll probably get in touch with you."

"Everything's falling apart! Why does it all have to be so complicated? When Gerry's better, we all ought to run away and start over, together. On some island in the Caribbean where there are no bishops or even churches. I think I'd like that."

Santek could not share her dream, without Angie. He was finding it hard to talk and in fact had hoped that Beauvais might give him some direction, or that Angie might have made contact.

"Maybe the priesthood digs too deep, Peggy. Vietnam without Angie will be hell, but at least I have a life with her to look forward to," he lied.

"I wish I could say the same. I'd like to take Gerry away from all this. It's killing him! I don't know if he can make it. Or if I can." It was the first time she had admitted it.

"It's that bad?"

"Yes, it's that bad. And I just have a horrible feeling that when the bishop finds out, it'll be all over. Then I don't know what's left."

There was nothing else to say. Santek was speechless. It was more than he could understand and he had no strength to help anyone. Vietnam was a feeble effort to hold himself together. Or maybe to fall apart. If only he knew where Angie was living, he would promise anything.

Peggy interrupted his reverie. "I've got to look in on the patient."

"Give him my best and don't forget I'm here," he said. Then he was gone and Peggy was all alone with her nightmare.

And Major Ted Santek with his.

Chapter 21

As Bishop Sullivan was obliged to spend intermittent months in Rome, working on the harried Liturgical Commission, Gerry Beauvais had valuable recovery time without episcopal interference. Almost every day, Peggy feared a visit from the chancery, or at least a letter, but the pressures and confusion of Vatican II and a very troubled Catholic world made the problems of Gerald Beauvais inconsequential. Word was leaking from the Vatican and appearing sporadically even in Catholic papers that the fierce conflict over birth control could divide the Church. It was as if Rome—four and a half centuries after the Reformation—had finally lost control of its docile "children." The once powerful and historic Church, just a few years ago celebrating Pope John XXIII, was now fighting for its very life.

Meanwhile, as Gerry Beauvais was fighting for his, Father Niedermeyer read the weekly directives that came from the chancery office and attempted to interpret the liturgical changes to his generally docile flock. Although confessions and collections were down, he noticed no dramatic falloff in Mass attendance, except perhaps among the young. He did not know where the Catholic Church was heading, but he felt in his heart that God would not desert his people, and he tried his hardest to hang on and make the best of the changes.

Gerry Beauvais was not concerned about his Church. Dr. Hengesbach continued to increase the dosage of Elavil, with little noticeable effect, but each time Beauvais was ready to give up, Peggy was there to force him to cling to whatever thread of life she could manufacture. When he received word that his beloved friend Father Misch had died, he was crushed by the loss and also because he could not go to the funeral.

"I just can't take it any more, Peggy. Now Father Misch is dead. There's nothing left to live for. I wake up every morning and hope that I'll be delivered from this nightmare. If only I could understand or know that it will go away in a month or even a year, I could hang on. A dear friend dies and I can't even go to his burial. I owe him my life." There were tears forming in his eyes. "I just can't stand it."

"The medication will have some effect soon. You've just got to hang on until it does. Father Misch would be the first to understand."

"There's nothing to hang on to. I can't think of a single thing I want. Nothing gives me the least pleasure. I feel like I exist just to endure. What kind of life is that? I didn't know there was pain like this."

"Can you write about it? Maybe that will help." She was shocked each time she noted his weight loss.

"I don't seem to have any energy. It's like my mind is locked on itself and I can't lose myself in anything. I just focus on my pain and beg God to deliver me. It all seems so pointless. There's no way out! I just want to stop hurting, and dying seems to be the only way to do it. I don't really want to die, but I can't stand the unending darkness."

"You're not going to die! You can make it. You've got to fight!"

"There's nothing to fight for. Nothing to fight with."

He said it softly and turned away. Peggy continued to sit by his bed, in reality as upset and frightened as he was. But she couldn't give up. Nor could she leave it to Fred Hengesbach and medication. She had to do something.

She combed the local library and went to bookstores in Detroit and began to read everything she could find about depressionRollo May's book *The Meaning of Anxiety* was difficult reading but a tremendous help, as were William James, Carl Rogers, and Abraham Maslow. Psychology was new to her, and her education in it was exciting and enlightening. She pored over the books morning and night.

As she read, she began to formulate her own theories. She saw Gerry Beauvais (far more than herself) as a person who had denied inner feelings and personal needs. She at least had had enough sense to escape Farmington and a destructive Catholic marriage, no matter what anyone said. Even her sexual experiences, limited as they were, seemed beautiful, despite the Church's laws and the unending ration of guilt. She was never driven to accept a Bishop Sullivan as the expositor of God's will, and now her challenge—to save the life of Father Beauvais—was, in reality, a religious work. Her very presence in Farmington and her work at the rectory, a seeming happenstance, were a definitive proof to her that God wanted her to remain where she was.

When her father finally died painlessly in his sleep at eighty and she had no family ties left, there was nothing in life for her but a simple religious faith that centered in her love for Father Beauvais. Curiously, as much as she had defied the Church during her own struggle to survive, she felt more like a nun than anything else. She wanted to share her joke with Angie and only regretted that Beauvais could not presently see the humor of it.

As she continued to study psychology, she realized that the docility and obedience taught in Beauvais's seminary was a denial of his own uniqueness as given by God. Her own mental health, fragile enough in Farmington and during her marriage, had improved in Chicago and even upon her return home, once she began trusting her own experience. Her own gradual break from the orthodoxy of Rome had convinced her that she would never again surrender her own mind and feelings to anyone. In the process of surviving, of caring for her father and Beauvais, she had learned something about her own personal dignity and had no respect for Bishop Sullivan's decision in her regard. She saw him not as a successor of the apostles but as a frightened, unenlightened, inexperienced man, even though sincere and well-meaning.

That Gerry Beauvais saw the bishop as something else was a deep part of Beauvais's present illness. He had denied his own personality and dreams to such an extent that he had lost his desire to live. His great musical talent had been grossly abused in the name of puerile obedience. His great potential for leadership had been buried in the isolation of St. Mary's of Farmington, and even his warm, sensitive manhood had been aborted in the throes of loneliness and unfounded episcopal suspicions. Peggy had seen numerous lives destroyed by the Catholic Church, even in her own family. Now she was ready to do battle for the man she loved, to save him from death at the hands of a modern but equally savage Inquisition. She had never felt closer to God in her life. That she was part of a new Catholic Church being born excited her and gave her strength.

She knew that she had to go slowly, to make gentle inroads on Beauvais's consciousness. Gerry's struggle had only just begun. The priesthood had submerged his anger and aggression, the powers that could save his life, God-given powers that were at the core of his survival. And, more than ever, she finally understood, with a renewed and profound faith far beyond Church or bishop or pope, that her meeting and falling in love with Beauvais were part of God's profound and loving plan. This gave her a renewed strength to battle for his life. She laid out a total game plan. She only had to implement it and he would begin to be saved.

As a result of her study, Peggy began by not being as attentive and understanding. It was painful for her, excruciating. She only wanted to take him in her arms and stroke him forever. But that would not get the job done. There had to emerge some spark from him, some fierce desire to live from somewhere deep inside. She could only trust that it was there, that the natural rhythm and harmony of life would take over with a yearning to live if she could but kindle an almost extinguished scintilla. She felt that psychiatric help would be a waste of time. He did not need a review of his childhood or his relationship to his father or mother. He needed to get involved with life.

She began by resolutely organizing his day. She awakened him at seven and insisted that he shower and dress. When he objected strenuously and wanted to remain in his bathrobe, she laid out his clothes and took his robe away. Gradually she made him select his own clothes instead of doing it for him. When he insisted that he didn't want breakfast, she continued to bring it to him and set a table in his room. She ate with him and let him eat or ignore the food according to his own tastes. At nine o'clock she read the paper to him even if he ignored her or feigned sleep, and at ten she lined up his weights and turned up his music. If he just sat on the edge of the bed, she did the exercises herself. After that she insisted that he go for a walk and would not permit him to resist. He was forced to talk to people along the way, forced to buy groceries, forced to make a visit to the church with her to ask God for guidance and direction. When he balked or complained, she was insistent and unsympathetic. Finally he raged at her.

"God damn it! I can't do all this! You've never experienced anything like this! I'm terrified to go out. Everything's fuzzy and frightening. Half the time I don't know where I am. Stop pushing me, God damn it! Stop it!"

Once she would have given up. Now she was battling for his life and for her own. She said simply, "You can do it. Even priests are not exempt from pain. You must do it. There's no alternative. Your life has not been as difficult as most. You've just never had to fight for what you wanted. Priests are sheltered. You'll come out of this much more human."

He was furious. No one had ever talked to him like this, but he did what she asked. Whether it was the medication that began having some effect, or Peggy's dogged persistence, or his anger at her, bordering on fury, it was hard to tell, but very gradually Gerry Beauvais began to show a slight interest in things. She first noticed it when they were watching the evening news on TV and he protested the stupidity of Vietnam, cursed Johnson and Westmoreland, and wondered about Santek—and even Angie. It was the first time that his mind was not on his own pain.

Almost imperceptibly, he began to be more concerned about his personal appearance, selected a sweater to wear on their walks, even ate occasionally in the dining room with Father Niedermeyer. He began to read on his own at times and to select music that he wanted to hear. But his progress was up and down, and intermittently he continued to snap at Peggy when she prodded him, calling her "the warden," "Madame Torquemada," and occasionally "an arrogant bitch." Later he would feel remorseful and apologize, but she did not let up, even when he had a three-day relapse and could not be forced from his bed. As the gloom cleared, she continued to pressure him.

"It's time you said Mass. I made arrangements for tomorrow."

"I'm not ready. I don't think I can remember how. I don't really want to. Damn it, I just can't. Stop pushing me, you insensitive bitch!"

She dismissed his objections. "You priests are all alike—mama's boys. I'll have an altar boy there at nine o'clock tomorrow."

It crushed her to speak offensively and see the deep hurt in his eyes, but he was going to get well even if he ended up hating her! She waited in the sacristy and watched him vest. She saw the tears form in his eyes and his formidable effort to control them lest the altar boy see his struggle, then turned away to hide her own tears. He recited the prayers hesitantly, but with great devotion, and seemed almost elated when he had concluded the ceremony. He continued to have new energy the rest of the morning. Peggy did not applaud him but capitalized on his strength.

226

"You should drop in on the children who are getting ready to make their First Communion."

"My God, I can't do that! It scares the hell out of me just thinking about it. That drug makes me forget things. I'm not ready."

"It's already arranged. The kids are expecting you."

He forced himself to make the appearance and came back to the rectory smiling. It was the first time that Peggy had seen him really smile in months.

Dr. Hengesbach was overjoyed. "I don't know what the hell you've done, but it's working! When's he going to be ready to say a Sunday Mass?"

"Sooner than he thinks. The more he does, the stronger he gets." Peggy laughed triumphantly.

"There will be relapses for a time," Hengesbach said cautiously. "But I think he's on his way back. I'm reducing his medications gradually without telling him. It's amazing! I've seen these things last for years. You're quite a healer."

"He's the healer. I only had to help him realize that."

Again Hengesbach looked grave. "He needs some overriding passion, anything that excites him and gives him something to look forward to. Then he'll really begin to be healed. This is still the same small parish, which may not challenge him very much. As he improves, he may need more."

Peggy nodded. I'd like to give him more, she thought. I'd really like to give him something to live for. Even as she briefly indulged the daydream, she knew that his celibacy was a sacred, personal promise made solemnly to God and she must respect it. Her own passion for him came in waves, then disappeared when she begged God to keep her pure, but despite her sincere effort, her thoughts were frequently sexual. She dreamed of making love to him, wandering nude on a tropical beach, caressing him to health in long languorous encounters. He would be healed and they would be together. The thoughts frightened her as much as they excited her, and she continually asked God to help her conquer temptation.

Then there were the occasional dark moments of relapse when she had to remind Gerry of how far he had come. He woke frequently tortured with fright, and she had to urge him immediately from bed. And even as the depression grew less absorbing, his overwhelming anxiety seemed to increase.

"You've got to get up and keep going. Lying in bed will only make things more frightening and impossible."

227

He knew she was right and forced himself out of bed with the steel discipline learned in the navy and the seminary. When the cloud began to lift and the anxiety quieted, he could face the day with rare bursts of new energy and occasionally even a mild joy. Finally, he was ready to say a regular Sunday Mass and preach a sermon. Again he was terrified, but now she was at his side, gently encouraging him, assisting him with his sermon, telling him how good he looked, how brave he was, how much progress he had made, promising him that the darkness would disappear.

He made it through the Mass, ignoring fear as an impossible temptation, preaching briefly and comfortably with a new depth to his words. The congregation was delighted to have him back, believing only that he had injured his back and had experienced the pain of a long recovery. Afterward he joined the people for coffee and strudel, even laughed and joked with them, told them how delighted he was to be back and meant it. The same day he called his mother—who was complaining of fatigue—lied about his illness, and promised a visit within a few weeks. He asked about the family, and she told him more than he wanted to hear. Even as he talked to her, the depression and anxiety came and went like a cloud toying with the sun. He did not understand it, but with growing hope and determination he could handle the more moderate confusion and pain.

Dr. Hengesbach continued to reduce his medication, and Beauvais was able to maintain greater emotional balance. The anxiety did not frighten him as much. His appetite was back, and he began gaining some part of the weight he had lost. At times the whole experience seemed like a nightmare that had never really happened.

Peggy stayed on in the guestroom. She had given up her job, and the parishioners seemed to accept her as a part of the scenery. Her devotion to their pastor had brought him back to health and the painful rumors of the past that had trickled to the chancery office were forgotten or at least reduced to occasional private musings of cynics and inveterate gossips. With Father Niedermeyer on the scene, they were like a family.

One cold Sunday night in January, after a full day of Mass and baptisms and novena services, they celebrated Gerry's recovery with a great dinner and a warm evening of wine, a glowing fireplace, popcorn, and a game of Niedermeyer's favorite cribbage. The old priest triumphed as usual, then excused himself, made his visit to the church, and was off to bed. Peggy and Gerry sat down to watch the fire from the couch, then continued to drink wine and listen to Bach.

Casually, he put his arm around her and she rested her head against his shoulder. Wordlessly, they shared the joy of knowing how far they had come together. It was hard to talk about. The room suddenly grew tense with love long unexpressed. Finally she stared up at him, looking directly into his eyes, then leaned forward and kissed him. Spontaneously, he returned her embrace, and soon they were joined almost helplessly in a gentle union of silent love and gratitude. All the pain of the past dissolved as he seemed to lose himself in her. They fell together on the couch, then lay close together in the glow of the fire and continued kissing wordlessly. Peggy felt her breasts against his chest, the warmth of her thighs against his groin, moving gently in the soft persistent hunger of as deep a love as she could know. A quiet warning was easily dismissed from her consciousness.

Gerry felt himself grow hard and could not move away. Never in his life had he held a woman like this! Never in his life had he experienced this kind of pleasure! Nor had she, and they could not pull themselves away.

Now they were in darkness save for a dim, flickering light from the fireplace casting sensual shadows and hissing pleasure. The rising passion of their breathing seemed to keep time with the soft music and the fire. It was as if they were mesmerized, dancing together in the sky or floating on a gentle, flowing ocean of love. She stroked the back of his thighs and gently felt the contours of his buttocks, then pulled him even closer to her. He began massaging her with his hand as her blouse opened to him, and for the first time in his whole life he touched a woman's breasts. His whole body trembled at their size and shape and softness. She drew his head down, and he instinctively began sucking her taut nipples like the starving man he was. Her whole body opened to him. He could feel her flesh soften and give way as they continued to mold gently together in an indescribable love. He had never imagined this in all his celibate curiosity, never knew there could be such rhythm and merging. He struggled with his conscience, but the relief from months of pain reduced his resistance to a fleeting, powerless thought.

His love for this incredible woman who had all but given her life to gain his was beyond description. Love had only been a word to him, a weak religious word, pale and spiritual without passion or flavor. Now he wanted to drown in her, to taste and devour her as if there were no end to his longing. She stirred, then sat up and took him by the hand and looked at him as if for the first time. Her body trembled, and her heart pounded. She tried to remind herself of her promise to preserve his chastity, but her whole being rose up as if to silence her.

She started to speak, then feared it would break the trance they were in. She stood up and lovingly led him to his bedroom. He made no effort to resist. They lay down on the bed and began undressing each other. He unbuttoned her blouse. She continued stroking him as she removed his shoes, then cassock, shirt, and pants. He shuddered again as she removed his shorts and gasped at his erection. He had slipped off her skirt and panties and shook with the unbearable passion of an adolescent. Peggy had felt excitement before with Dave in Chicago and even the man at the Dairy Coop, but she had never imagined this wild desire for a man that she loved with every particle of her being. They lay there naked and trembling and he stared at her body. He had never really seen a naked woman in his life. Her eyes shone with joy, and her whole body seemed to glow. He could not believe what he felt. Nor could she!

Thousands of confessions had not prepared him, all the whispered sins of countless lovers had given him no premonition of what it was really like. The penitents' words had been drained of reality and rapture. There was no experience that compared to what he felt. Hundreds of sinners had described every minute facet of lovemaking in the confessional, and he had not really known what they were talking about. As she lay before him, only their hands touching, her full woman's body completely open to him, it was as if he had never known pain or distress in his life. All self-consciousness was gone, all the dark shadows that had driven him to desperation and near suicide seemed as if they had never been. It was as if his whole life had been lived for this moment. He continued to stare at her beauty, continued to lie helplessly on the bed, unable to move. It seemed that without even touching him she possessed him completely. Her ripe sensuality and love beyond measure lured him to some madness until she seemed irresistible.

She moved cautiously closer and began caressing him, massaging his toes and kissing his thighs, burying her head against his legs. It was as sacred a moment as she had ever experienced. No solemn profession of vows, no wife or cloistered nun in her bridal gown symbolizing her eternal marriage to Christ, could ever have been

230

more profoundly moved than this. She was drawn to him, starved for him as if she wanted to devour him body and soul. When they again moved next to one another and embraced hungrily, he felt her whole body wrapped against his. His heart began pounding as all the softness and tenderness in the world, all the joy and understanding, was gathered in Peggy's being to envelop him. She could not stop smiling and sighing.

In all the decades of his life he had never really known any sexual pleasure before. He had never masturbated, never surrendered to sexual fantasy, never allowed himself to know the commingling of body and spirit which thousands of married couples had experienced. The sordid experience arranged by his father years ago was an unreal blur. He had never really known passion, the helplessness and eagerness and surrender that touched every cell of his body. But now the yearning of their hearts and spirits raised passion to a level of near madness. They were middle-aged teenagers with an insatiable hunger to be touched and stroked, caressed and held and loved forever. Their very lives seemed to change in these few intense moments.

He had never really been celibate, because he did not know what celibacy was. His whole vocation flashed through his mind, the dreams at his ordination, the thrill of Europe and Karl Metzen, a boy's fantasy of Ursula, the adult and boys' choirs and the improved music throughout the diocese, the confrontation with Bishop Sullivan, and the angry innuendo that had sent him to Farmington. He felt as though his whole life had been doomed till now. Peggy seemed the only possible release. He could no longer tolerate the pain, the darkness from which there seemed no escape when his vision was totally distorted during the madness of depression and anxiety: his fears that Peggy would leave him and get married and he would grow old and helpless, his illogical belief that Father Misch's death predicted his own as he worried about hell and wondered about afterlife. In such a state, every least concern was a major crisis, when Peggy alone had loved him, nursed him back to tenuous health, given meaning again to his life. Now he rested naked against her and was ready to abandon his whole priesthood. He wanted her, longed for her, needed her, and yet something inside him stubbornly resisted that final step of total lovemaking.

More than anything else he wanted the pain to go away, the confusion, the distortion, the hazy film that covered all reality like a fog. Even as he lay there with Peggy in his arms, he quarreled with

231

his whole existence. A lesser man would have given no thought to anything, but Gerry Beauvais began struggling with his very core and conscience.

He had chosen the priesthood for whatever noble or unknown reasons, and he had felt the confidence and trust of thousands whose respect for him centered in the reality that he was not like the rest of men; he had promised God never to know the beauty and ultimate tenderness of a woman. Up to this point, his promise had been only the words of an altar boy. Now it was the overwhelming reality of a man deeply in love. Somehow he knew that his final surrender to his beloved Peggy and his throbbing body was the end of his priesthood, and at the far reaches of his soul he could not let it go. He would not. His love for her could only be the impossible, soul-wrenching, spiritual love of a celibate, a love that might make no sense to anyone else in the world.

He knew that priests sometimes slept with women. He had heard enough confessions of fallen and repentant clerics, of the rare, lonely priest who had lived with his housekeeper and somehow satisfied the demands of conscience. Or the few who strayed briefly and then returned to their vows, scarred, humbled, more understanding, and determined anew to serve God as they had promised. But despite the suspicions of the Church's critics, the great majority of religious never experienced sex, many of them reduced by the seminary to a kind of bland asexuality that made celibacy no real problem. There were occasional homosexuals, more of them in recent years, who found the priesthood a release from the private torture they could admit to no one. Usually they were celibate, occasionally they were not. There were even a few priests who had fallen in love with nuns, priests who had made love with married women they were counseling, priests who had seduced teenagers, even priests like Santek, the rarest of all, who finally saw celibacy as a meaningless impossibility and lived a kind of clandestine marriage with all of its deprivations and occasional joys.

Then there was Gerry Beauvais, who had known every kind of rejection and humiliation, clerical jealousy, and punishment he did not deserve. Somehow he hung on until he collapsed in the darkness of a life without light or hope. Was Peggy his salvation? Unquestionably she was his friend, the dearest he had ever known. But he could not make love to her until he had resolved his priesthood in his own heart and mind. Even as they clung and kissed, Peggy felt his uneasiness.

232

Curiously it matched her own, as hungry as she was. Despite all the loneliness she had felt since leaving Chicago, she found it impossible to let go. A persistent voice had to be heard. She could not simply surrender to this purest, deepest love without reflection and prayer. As much as her body and soul screamed for him, as much as she trembled and felt the moisture of her longing well up and flow like a pure spring, she had to draw back almost instinctively. It was not the least shred of guilt or fear but rather her very love that made her hesitate, and the discipline of a difficult lifetime gave her the strength that few could have had. Her love for him was somehow founded on her own profound love for God. From that love—mysterious and confused by the Church's pettiness—it drew its massive strength as well as its sudden fear and holding back. Even as she felt his chest rolling gently against her breasts and his legs pressed against hers, and longed for him to take possession of her, she resisted. Impossibly, she resisted in response to some ancient habit of love and self-discipline, love and personal denial.

And even as she fought for control, she felt his body grow as suddenly taut as her own. Spontaneously they continued to writhe gently as if coming down from a cloud, then slowly moved a fraction apart and continued to touch subtly and lovingly as if their brains could not convey restraint to longing hands. Finally, Beauvais was able to speak, almost in a groan. "I love you, Peggy, I love you. . . ."

Unable to speak, she nodded silent agreement but could not move away. Her hands continued to stroke him, more slowly, tenderly. He spoke in a whisper.

"I want you more than anything else in the world. I don't ever want to live without you. I'm not sure I can. And every ounce of me wants to surrender, to make love to you again and again. I want to forget everything, all the pain and humiliation I've felt, but somehow I've already possessed you more deeply than any physical bond. . . ."

She began to tremble, then shake almost violently, releasing the tension she had felt for so long, fighting every day for his life. She gasped softly as he continued to hold her.

"I don't want it to be impulse or loneliness and pain or too much wine. I have no doubts about my love. For the very first time I've known love, but my celibacy is the only thing I've salvaged from my priesthood, the only thing that makes me feel strong and worth-

233

while. I don't know if it even makes sense, but if I give up, it's almost as if Bishop Sullivan would be right about me."

Peggy put her finger to his lips as if words spoiled something and nodded agreement with her eyes and gazed even more lovingly at him before she spoke. "I love you so much. I can never leave you! I want to be with you forever, to work with you, to laugh with you. And I want to keep your vow as much as you do."

She paused.

"God will direct us. I only want your love and to give you mine."

There were no more words. They continued to hold each other for a very long time; then, exhausted, Beauvais drifted off to sleep, a deeper, more serene sleep than he had known in years.

Peggy got up quietly, kissed him softly and lovingly tucked him in, then gathered up her clothes and moved out of the room. The fears had disappeared and there was a look of rapture on her face. She walked back to her room and fell on her knees.

"Thank you, my God. Thank you! Please tell us what to do and we will do it. I only wanted to help save his life and win his love, and you have given it all to me. Nothing else matters!"

Chapter 22

Peoria was a much larger city than Angie had expected. She walked quickly to the dingy Avon Hotel near the bus station to avoid the ever more insistent advances of the aggressive salesman who hoped to be her tour guide and "protector." When she had tried to sleep, his elbow was exploring her breast, his knee was against her thigh. She felt briefly relieved as she stepped cautiously through the dim lobby to the front desk, but everyone she observed seemed a potential danger. Two portly black men in their forties, already withered and scarred, were arguing drunkenly about the relative merits of Joe Louis and Muhammad Ali, and their boisterous, angry tones, verging on violence, frightened Angie, especially when one of the men, with a fresh pink gash on his left cheek, surveyed her with warm approval. Even the burly, graying desk clerk in a stained black turtleneck, who looked like an ex-cop with his close-cropped hair and Dick Tracy jaw, seemed to leer at her over a double chin and badly shaven face when he asked if she would expect visitors in her room.

"We lock the front door at nine o'clock. If you're out after that, the night man will let you in. Or your visitors." He grinned knowingly. "This is a rough neighborhood."

His expression showed he thought she was a prostitute, maybe chased out of Chicago.

"If you need anything, I mean *anything* at all, just let me know!" He rubbed his beer belly and grinned again, revealing badly capped teeth, as he surveyed her body like a menu. Several men in the lobby overheard the desk clerk and laughed. She heard one of them mutter something about "prime pussy," then more laughter. There were no women in the lobby, only a collection of used men who seemed to have nowhere to go.

A short bellman in his sixties, balding and pock-faced, picked up her two bags and limped toward a decrepit elevator. Angie noticed the caked dirt and worn spots in a gray carpet that had once been green and felt nauseated when a bearded old man with moist, red-rimmed eyes spat his tobacco into a paper sack. Then he wiped the drool from his liver-colored lips with the sleeve of a dirty beige sweater with one remaining button. Even he appraised her with the feeble lust of some ancient fantasy.

The elevator creaked and groaned its way to the fourth floor. The gimpy bellman struggled with the bags and wheezed down the brown linoleum hallway to room 411. He fumbled with the key, cursed at it, and finally pushed open the door. Angie felt her heart sink and her knees grow weak. Her cell in the convent was a luxury suite next to this decaying coffin. On the right wall was a stark, single bed with a sloping mattress and a soiled brown-chintz bedspread. On the other wall was a warped card table and a single chair with chipped blue paint. A dim light bulb overhead gave the room a ghoulish appearance. There was a coverless Gideon Bible and two stained glasses on the card table. A single bold roach emerged from one of the glasses and scurried across the Holy Writ. Near the window was an upholstered chair, covered with a stained brown material speckled with faded red coachmen and carriages, resting on linoleum of the same brown, decaying badly. Around the door and near the bed the flooring was worn through to the black adhesive, and the whole piece covered the floor like a rotting layer of gingerbread. A musky, mildewed smell filled the room, a brief relief from the stale smell of sweat that exuded from her companion.

The bellman, lingering for his tip, pulled back thick green drapes, stained with age and dust, to reveal an enclosed courtyard. On the opposite wall was a deserted brick office building with boarded windows and FUCK NAM and *De Colores* scrawled in white paint. The courtyard was littered with crumbled bricks and beer cans, splintered boards, and an assortment of newspapers and broken glass. Angie wondered why the bellman didn't leave. He opened the closet door and pointed out a shelf covered with yellowing newspapers and a few bent hangers. She noticed small chunks of plaster on one corner of the floor. The bathroom door opened to a rusted sink and dripping faucet, a small spotted mirror and a narrow shower framed in gray linoleum, and a sticky plastic curtain with a

236

worn floral pattern faded into red pencil marks. Two more cockroaches stared at her, then disappeared behind the sink. The stool against the far wall had rotted away the brown linoleum at its base. Its seat was apparently coated with the same chipped paint as the blue chair.

Finally the tour was over and the bellman looked straight at the now-pale Angie. He grinned nervously, leaning awkwardly on his good leg. "We usually get a tip."

Angie blushed and fumbled in her purse for a dollar. Finally he took his leave with a final glance at her legs, then limped and sweated his way to the door, mumbling as he went about a pay phone in the lobby and no food above the ground floor.

"The roaches will find anything," he said matter-of-factly.

Nothing in Angie's sheltered life had prepared her for this, and she found herself reflecting on and admiring a courageous Peggy until she fell asleep.

An explosion in the courtyard awakened her. Someone had fired a gun or tossed a whiskey bottle out the window. She looked at her watch. It was already seven o'clock, and the gray light of a lackluster midwestern morning sifted through the dirty window like stale flour. Angie washed and dressed quickly and made her way with her bags into the dark, musty hall. She pushed the elevator call button and, when the door opened, shoved her bags to the rear and pushed the DOWN button. The lobby was empty, except for the desk clerk, snoring soundly on a battered couch, his potbelly stretching a dirty gray sweatshirt to the limit. Miraculously the door was unlocked, and she slipped quietly through with her suitcases.

Outside, in the chill drabness of the morning, the traffic was just beginning to move. Angie walked wearily with the heavy bags for several blocks until she saw a coffee shop. Quite ordinary, it looked immaculate after her night's lodging. A man held the door open as she stumbled awkwardly through. She found an empty booth, set the bags down with great relief, then ordered tea and toast and scanned the want ads in the morning paper the waitress brought her.

She felt overwhelmed. She needed a decent place to live and a job to support herself, but she didn't even know where to begin. Again she wanted to call Ted, but she suppressed the thought. The dark-haired waitress came with more hot water. She looked Italian or Greek, was twenty pounds overweight, probably thirty years old.

"Will there be anything else?" Her voice was warm and inviting.

237

"You seem troubled. Maybe I can help." Her dark brown eyes looked concerned and sympathetic.

"I've just . . . well, I'm moving here and I need a place to live. I really don't know one end of town from the other."

The waitress sat down with her briefly and scanned the ads. "Do you want a furnished place?"

"I think so. At least at first."

The woman circled half a dozen apartments with her pen. "These are nice areas if you can afford a hundred fifty a month. Maybe you can get one of these places furnished and gradually replace their early plastic with your own stuff." She laughed. "I've still got early plastic. Do you have kids?"

Angie shook her head. "I'm not married." It was hard to admit.

"Divorced, eh? Well, I've been down that road. It's worse when you got kids like me. Waitressing is the only thing that gives me any time with them."

Angie was finally able to look at the woman and notice how tired she seemed.

"I really appreciate your help," she said.

"I'll give you my phone number here and at home. If you need help, just call. If a kid answers, you'll know you've got the right place. If a man answers, it's a wrong number." She laughed without changing expression, then looked admiringly at Angie. "If I looked like you I wouldn't worry about a thing. The guy that let you get away must be nuts."

Angie blushed, gathered up her paper, and started to leave a tip. The waitress shook her head.

"Keep it. You probably need it as much as I do."

Angie thanked her warmly and was back out on the street with her bags. It was hard to believe that anyone could be so kind for no reason. She had always associated helping with God and religion— she'd had so little contact with ordinary people. This woman had nothing and wanted to share it.

Angie had to get rid of the bags. She addressed two college girls shyly, asking directions to the bus station. Fortunately it was only two blocks away. She deposited her bags in a large locker, avoided the appraising looks of an assortment of men, and was back out on the street. She had never noticed the insistent, hungry glances of men before, old and young; they chilled and angered her.

By late afternoon she had located a furnished apartment in a brick building a few blocks from Bradley University. The apartment

238

manager, an elderly man with small nervous eyes, a whiskey nose, and an impish grin, warned her of noisy parties.

"You don't look like the type, but people change. I run a nice quiet place and aim to keep it that way. You don't have any pets, do you?"

She shook her head, gave him a fifty-dollar deposit, and paid her first month's rent. He gave her the key to 210 and offered to help her with her bags.

"The elevator is on the bum. Like the manager." He grinned and stared at her breasts as she bent over to pick up the bags. He liked what he saw. "Here, let me give you a hand."

"I can make it," she said quietly.

She climbed the cracked concrete stairway and made her way to an open hallway. Halfway down she found 210, opened the door, slid her bags in, and fell down on the couch. This time she let the tears come, sobbing as if her heart would break, but after an hour she felt better and was able to look around the room. It was like a thousand apartments everywhere: a small living room, a tiny dining area off the kitchen, a single bedroom and bath off the living room. The beige carpet showed wear and clashed with the green couch. The yellow end tables did not match, and she noticed that one of the lamps needed a new shade. There were two green plastic chairs at a light yellow table in the dining area and a cheap glass fixture hung from the ceiling. The kitchen was bright and inviting, the nicest room in the house. She examined the scattered, mismatched pots and pans and dishes. An old toaster and an electric coffeepot rested on a small counter. The refrigerator was clean and empty save for a bottle of ketchup and a jar of pickles. She laughed to herself. No convent "poverty" was ever like this.

She walked into the bedroom. The bed sagged in the middle and was unmade. A few blankets were folded neatly at the head of the bed with a single stained pillow. She would have to buy sheets and cases and a new pillow. She would also have to buy a shower cap, since there was no tub, only a narrow white painted shower without a curtain.

She sighed, walked back out into the living room, picked up her bags and opened them on the bed, and began to unpack. It was hard not to think about the beautiful apartment she had left behind with its curios and oil paintings, expensive suede and leather furniture, and a thousand memories. Finally she lay down fully clothed on the bed. She was exhausted. She drew one of the blankets over her body and fell asleep.

Two days later she had a job at another heavy construction leasing firm near the Illinois River. Her boss, Hal Markeley, was a kindly, barrel-chested family man with dark-rimmed glasses, in his early forties and devoutly Catholic. His sandy hair was almost gone on top and he stuttered when he got excited, which was frequently. He wore blue jeans and an assortment of colored Hawaiian sport shirts. The office was nothing but three wooden desks, a file cabinet, and a counter that separated Angie, a mousy old bookkeeper who rarely spoke, and Mr. Markeley from the contractors and salesmen who walked in and out. As much as she hated the noisy, drab office, she was grateful to have a good job and a gentle, honest boss who was not making passes at her. She was also grateful for the counter separating her from the customers, whose eyes revealed immediate interest in the new secretary with the long legs and full breasts, honey-colored hair and serenely beautiful face. She decided to wear the wedding ring that Santek had bought her in Texas, even though she had told Mr. Markeley that she was divorced.

A month later, having settled in, she leased a Toyota with her boss's help and enrolled in a literature and history course at Bradley. Finally she decided it was time to call Santek at the base. She was channeled to one of the chaplain's assistants.

"Major Santek? I'm sorry, he left last week."

He laughed softly when Angie asked for a forwarding address.

"He may be a little hard to locate for a while. He's been sent to Vietnam."

"To Vietnam?" Her heart almost stopped. She had wanted to tell him how much she had grown up and how exciting it was to go back to school. Most of all she wanted to hear his voice. It was one thing to be separated from the man she loved more than anyone else in the world. It was another to know that she could not contact him. Now she felt completely alone. She barely managed to speak.

"I'm his sister," she said. "He didn't say anything about Vietnam."

"He requested it, ma'am. No doubt you'll be hearing about it from him. Probably didn't want to frighten you. That's the way he is. You must really be proud of him. They can sure use him in 'Nam."

"I am proud," she said softly.

"I've never known a greater priest," he said exuberantly. "They

240

just don't make them like Father Ted. He saved my ass—I mean, he helped me a few times. I'm sure he's in good shape and you'll be hearing from him in a few days. Don't worry about a thing. He's the greatest! And he sure can take care of himself." He laughed at some memory and was gone.

She continued to hold the phone after the young airman hung up. His final words seemed like the ultimate rejection. Finally she slumped down on the couch. All her newfound strength and sense of adventure seemed to have dissolved. She had wanted to share it with Ted. She now realized that psychologically she had not really left him. She was trying to prove her independence to him, and he had been with her every moment of each day. The nights had been the most difficult of all. She fell asleep thinking about him and woke up the next morning still wondering about him. She had strained with her whole being to be settled before she called him, knowing that he would come to her the very next weekend. She had never imagined that he was no longer a part of her life.

Vietnam. He had requested it. She suddenly realized that she might never see him again. She had not been able to look at another man, even the attractive young ones at Bradley, or talk to anyone beyond polite and sterile conversation. She had not even bothered to learn names. All her dreams still centered in the intense, laughing, beautiful Santek. Her very body ached for him. And his laugh, his wild Polack laugh! God! One day with him was worth a lifetime with anyone else. She did not know if she could go on. There was no reason to work, to grow, to live, no reason to do anything without Santek.

Why had she left him? Now it seemed childish and impulsive. They could have worked things out. She made her way to the bedroom and snuggled under the covers, holding her pillow close to her breasts.

"Dear God, help me. Help me! I'm so sorry about everything. Please tell me what to do."

When she woke in the morning, she felt the beginning of a determination not to give up. There was a feeble but real feeling that she could create a life for herself, with or without Santek. All the strength of her French-Canadian blood and the courage of her faith and willpower began to buoy her up. She had to make it. There was no other option. She would get involved socially, maybe even begin to date, as difficult as that would be. She would go to dances and lectures, plays and outings on Peoria Lake. There was so much she hadn't done. She had to come alive. She challenged herself. She had never endured what others had. She thought of the waitress with two small children. And of Peggy.

What did she know of life? It was time to stop feeling sorry for herself, to stand on her own two feet. As much as the thought of Santek tore her apart, she would go on—"boot by boot" as her father always said.

A week later, she learned that she was pregnant.

Chapter 23

It was not happenstance that Ted Santek's request to be sent to Vietnam in 1967 was immediately granted. There was massive concern for troop morale as the fighting men increasingly resisted further participation in what millions considered a civil war. It had become clear that the American soldiers were no match for Charlie, to whom war and deprivation had become a way of life since 1946.

American military personnel had almost given up, since it was not a war they really believed they could win. They simply hung on with the help of heroin and marijuana and the persistent hope that their tour of duty would soon be over. What was to the disciplined and impoverished Vietnamese an accustomed way of life, all they had ever known, was to the Americans a pointless and hopeless political mess. Even the fighting spirit of Ted Santek would hardly be a match for the anger and indifference of the dispirited American soldiers. War, always a horror and a personal sacrifice, becomes total futility when one's own nation removes its support.

Santek felt the emptiness of his confreres and found it difficult to encourage anyone, especially when he was still recovering from the intense, almost unbearable pain of Angie's departure. It had been more excruciating for Ted to endure Angie's absence than he ever would have believed. It was more than missing her. She had belonged totally to him and was the one thing in his life that gave him direction and stability. He had not realized how much strength and support he derived from her presence, especially her loving, unquestioning desire to please him. She had given him a swaggering confidence that turned to timidity and emptiness when she was gone. He had taken her love completely for granted and found no suitable object for his own deep affection.

For the first few days after her departure he was in a kind of helpless daze. He didn't feel like drinking or chasing, or even working, as though all past forms of escape were denied him. If Angie could leave him, what kind of man was he? He began to realize that in his whole life he had never really been rejected by a woman. He was always in charge, always sought after, always waited for, no matter how insensitive he was to a woman's feelings. The priesthood, with all its benefits to the lonely and distressed, to the confused and heartbroken, was not always a boon to the man who wore the collar and black robes. Santek became aware that he could remain a child emotionally, with no one having the courage to challenge him, especially if he was well liked or gained hierarchical status. Priests and nuns rarely heard the truth, bishops and popes never! The priesthood usually helped even a good man remain self-centered and immature. Thus Santek had been thanked a hundredfold for the least consideration, excused for his tardiness or forgetfulness because "Father is so busy," and catered to by Catholics and non-Catholics alike. Even his sexual indiscretions were wiped away by the gentlest of confessors. Lay people did not receive such privileged treatment unless they were a Kennedy or a Crosby. The collar was a magical key to open a hundred doors.

It began with a priest's own mother. Ted was his mother's entrance to heaven, her guarantee of honor and respectability in the parish and neighborhood, and she had attended to his every wish from the time he entered the seminary. It was little wonder that Santek expected Angie to behave the same way. Ted had gradually become aware of a long tradition in the Catholic Church of anti-feminism, which subtly infected both priestly ministers and theology. The birth control issue, for example, was only a reflection of the downgrading of women.

At the core of the whole madonna-whore complex of so many Catholic men and women were the notions that sex was dirty at its best, and dirty sex was best. Ted Santek became aware in his pain and reflection that these ancient, insidious attitudes were also at the root of his own neglect of Angie. She had been raised to serve men, to honor priests, to be the lowly "handmaiden of the Lord." Her finally leaving Santek was a courageous thrust for life, a brave and powerful resistance to her whole tradition.

Santek was ravaged by her departure, but his macho mentality rose up to save him. He didn't need her! Fuck her! He hated the dependency that had made him helpless and despondent without her, and his anger became fury, and fury became energy. Vietnam was the answer. He needed to be in the thick of things, to rage and fight like a street urchin, to risk his life and transform the weary, frightened men who had lost their vision some thirteen thousand miles from home. He requested 'Nam. No, he demanded it. Within two weeks of her departure he had stored the furniture, given up the apartment, spent a week at Travis near Fairfield, California, and was on his way to Bangkok and a chaplains' conference in preparation for Vietnam—still in a private rage to make it all by himself.

At first he waited anxiously for a letter, waited nervously for a phone call, but when finally there was no word, he cursed her savagely, got roaring drunk, and determined to live without the goddamned woman. Vietnam was the very best way to begin. War was all male.

But Ted Santek was not prepared for the Orient. He had intended to visit the struggling Beauvais before he left, but his orders came through so quickly there was no time. He called instead, felt good to learn about his friend's incipient recovery and new determination, and promised to write.

"I'll bring you back a couple of gooks to take care of your yard. Yeah, and maybe a cook."

They had laughed together like old times. Beauvais promised to look after Angie as soon as he had her new address.

"She hasn't decided where to live yet," Santek had lied. "But she'll be in touch soon."

"Give her our love and tell her she's welcome to stay here."

Then he was suddenly in the confusion of Bangkok after a brief stopover in the comfort of Hong Kong. He was scheduled to attend a conference for chaplains in Thailand and then go on to Saigon. After the tedious twenty-hour flight, he was met by gracious, smiling hotel representatives and was soon on his way from the sweltering airport to the Indra Regent Hotel for the conference.

From the airport to the hotel in the heart of the city, there was one massive, steaming traffic jam of cars, buses, taxis, motorized bicycles, and rickshas of every description. The unbearable heat defied even the air conditioning in the limousine in which he rode. The smog of Los Angeles seemed almost transparent by comparison. At times there was hardly any motion of traffic at all, yet no one seemed at all impatient except Ted. The tawny, serene faces of the

Thai people belied the conditions in which they lived. Despite tropic heat and more than two million people crowded together in Bangkok like a Manhattan noon hour, the smiling, gentle faces moved along almost joyously, as if some secret reward awaited them in one of the thousand stalls or shops of the open-air markets.

He could not believe the serenity and joy of these people who had never known Christianity. He did not know what he had expected, but certainly not this joyous, almost childlike ambiance. There was none of Manila's discontent, Mexico's hysteria, or New York's preoccupation and abrasiveness. Schoolgirls giggled in their blue and white uniforms, vendors called out from their assorted hibachis where the aroma of pungent, spicy wooden skewers of meat and fish mingled with the persistent smell of raw sewage. Bangkok, despite heat and smog, dirt, and a massive population and abysmal poverty, seemed a city of color and laughter, as if life itself was either a great, enduring delight or the largest joke of all. The Buddhist monks, bald and begging in their saffron robes, tossed gifts of rice and fish and eggs from the people to their obviously humble assistants, who followed silently with large sacks and baskets to gather the simple offerings. Occasionally a monk paused to free two urchin sparrows from a tiny cage and wordlessly accepted the *baht* offering of a devout shopkeeper or a withered old lady. The drone of the language, an offshoot of the Sino-Tibetan family, sounded soft and musical enough to merge harmoniously with the irrepressible good humor of the people.

Why were they so damn happy? Christianity, with all its heavenly dreams, could never have created joy around such squalor. The multiple shop signs, in letters of Sanskrit origin, gave an eerie effect with surprisingly little evidence of English save in hotels and obvious tourist shops. Misspellings were frequent and comical.

Despite an endless flight and little sleep, despite the anguish of a sudden decision and Angie's disappearance, Santek felt released from some pressure which had troubled him for the last few months. He wondered if his compromise with Angie had been worth it. As much as he loved her, there had been the ever-present need to be on guard, to watch what he said, to be certain that no one was aware of his life-style. Constant pressure, conscious and unconscious. Now, suddenly, in a foreign environment which seemed a million miles from Illinois, he felt a freedom and serenity he could not explain. There was a joy and simplicity, actually a spirituality, in the very air, which defied explanation or description. Who were these tiny, tawny, busy, smiling people who seemed to work and play and eat as if all life were a carnival?

The limousine in which Ted rode stopped in the circular entrance to the attractive Indra Regent Hotel with its large pillars and impressive lobby. Ted and the two Thai officials who had met him at the airport emerged into the tropical heat. The men, all in white and flanking him like two tiny altar boys, directed a uniformed doorman to remove the visitor's bags. They tipped him graciously and urged Ted back into the limousine.

"The conference does not start until tomorrow. Perhaps you would like to see something of Bangkok." It was part of the hotel's official tour for prosperous Americans or Japanese.

"The traffic's a little heavy and I'm a bit tired. . . ." He was dying for a shower, a drink, and a nap but found it hard to resist their warmth.

"We will go where you can relax, have a massage if you like, eat and drink as much as you want."

They laughed with guileless delight. They did not seem like agents of the hotel but rather like two happy children. It was not only their small stature, but some irrepressible joy which Ted struggled to understand. As they made their way slowly from the hotel, several passersby stopped briefly, stared in the windows of the limo, and smiled warmly at the tall, blond officer with blue eyes. Young girls seemed to giggle almost in embarrassment. Ted was puzzled by their laughter and asked about it.

The shorter and pudgier of the Thai men, Sarit, explained the giggles in his chopped, musical English.

"They giggle because they think all Americans have a very big cock."

Sarit's companion, a handsome, well-built man, Boomprajak, laughed briefly. Only Ted seemed embarrassed.

The black limousine slid slowly through the random glut of traffic, which moved without lanes or obvious order, but there were no shrieks or horns or curses. The helmeted policemen who made some show of directing the jungle of motion smiled frequently and waved their white gloves with military deftness. The limousine received no more preferential treatment than the lowly rice farmer in his basket-shape straw hat and sputtering, smoking motorbike. Had Santek understood the Oriental mind, it would have helped him in his comprehension of Vietnam.

Before he left Travis, he had been roughly prepared by a marine chaplain, Colonel Mike Shea from Boston, rugged and cigar-chewing, who had finally learned in two rugged years in 'Nam that the Army of the Republic of South Vietnam (ARVN) had no real hope of winning the war. Increasingly the soldiers felt more loyalty to their brothers in the north than to any American battle against the Communists.

"In Saigon and Hue," Shea said, biting on his cigar, "thousands of our kids and Oriental students drift in and out of opium dens to avoid the entire conflict. There's no choice, no future, no possible victory. Bombing North Vietnam has accomplished nothing except pointless destruction. This despite the constant American propaganda fed to the people back home.

"And the American boys never know who the hell's a friend or enemy among the villagers, who lived a guerrilla life long before the Americans arrived. They just smile stoically and blow you apart."

This was the Orient, and it would take time to understand it. Santek was in no mood to understand anything. He was here as a priest, to buoy up American morale, to serve the spiritual needs of American soldiers who were losing their identity to dope and despair, but as he rode in the limousine he found himself wondering about the seeming serenity of a people who had never known Christ. He was dumbfounded.

After endless stalls and hair-raising switchbacks, the limo stopped sleek and unscathed in front of a large, attractive restaurant fronted by a mosaic fountain splashing exuberantly over statues of playful, naked Thai maidens and circled by marble stairs with brass rails. Ted walked quickly to keep up with his laughing hosts and moved inside a Las Vegas-like lobby where a tuxedoed Thai with slicked-down hair approached them with a great show of affection.

After an exchange of *sawadis* with folded hands and bowed heads, faces grew briefly serious but always gentle, as an apparent business proposition was made. The transaction was brief. Sarit drew a thick roll of colorful bills from his black leather purse, peeled off a few with deft experience, again exchanged smiles and bows, and directed Ted to follow the elegant tuxedo to a circular red leather booth in a surprisingly small restaurant of twenty or thirty tables. The aromas were tantalizing. Santek, exhausted by long hours in the air, had hardly eaten, and the food in Thailand is among the world's finest, as he would soon learn. Weak tea was served, then brandy and strong cigarettes that made him cough, small bits of fish and beef prepared with hot spices, and the finest shrimp Ted had ever tasted. Another brandy, and he began to relax and realize he was in Thailand.

The man in the tuxedo appeared again, congratulated Ted for his enjoyment of the traditionally hot food, then whispered to Sarit. They laughed, whispered some more, then directed Santek up from the table.

"There will be plenty of time to eat," Sarit said with a kind of childlike glee. Ted moved out into a spacious corridor and followed the tuxedo and his hosts through clumps of grinning Japanese businessmen, American navy men, and more well-dressed Thais. He noticed there were no women as he slipped off his chaplain's cross. It was the first time he had done it since Angie left.

After about a hundred feet down the corridor, Santek turned and saw one of the most unforgettable sights of his life. Behind a series of large, department store windows were perhaps a hundred and fifty young Thai women assembled in ascending rows, dressed in brief colorful bikinis and wearing an arabic number around their waists. To Ted, most of them seemed exotic and almost breathtakingly beautiful. Sarit delighted in his guest's shock as Ted continued to stare and gradually understood what was taking place. Two Japanese executives pointed and called out numbers to the attendant. A loudspeaker directed two of the young women to leave their perch and move forward to an exit door that led into the plushly carpeted corridor. Their faces blushed with pleasure and several of their companions clapped and congratulated them as they made their way down the levels of the stage toward the door. They took the arms of the portly Japanese men as if encountering special lovers, and the executives were suddenly all smiling teeth from nose to chin as in the stereotype. Then followed exuberant giggles until they descended plushly carpeted steps at the far end of the corridor.

Sarit extended his arm toward the display windows.

"Take your pick!" he said magnanimously in his singsong English.

Ted, motionless, looked imploringly at Sarit, then at his companion, Boomprajak. He had not been prepared for this, hardly twenty-four hours after saying a final devout Mass in America. He had known no woman but Angie for a long time.

"Some are better than others," Boomprajak volunteered.

"Numbers forty-seven and sixty-three are very good. And fifty-four. Yes, I think you would like fifty-four very much!"

Ted, exhausted from his trip but moderately excited by weeks of celibacy and a foreign novelty, nodded a weak assent. Immediately he felt guilty. The loudspeaker boomed and number 54 moved amid loud shrieks to the exit door. Even the girls knitting or reading or engaged in friendly conversations took notice. It was obvious that the tall American was an unusual attraction. Several of the girls who had been gesturing their willingness to serve Santek expressed brief, sullen disappointment. But by the time 54 moved through the exit door, the giggling conversations and knitting had been resumed. An American sailor peered in at them and there were more dramatic pleas like schoolchildren begging to be called on to recite. None of the women seemed outraged or misused. Indeed, it seemed that they had been selected to play an important role on a national stage.

Ted moved awkwardly toward the exit door, and 54 took his arm with warm enthusiasm.

"Ooooh, you are so pretty!"

The dark-haired beauty, petite with sparkling eyes in the briefest red-flowered bikini, squeezed his arm, and Ted glowed with a perfectly proper priestly blush. Then he looked pleadingly at Sarit.

"What's it all about? I mean . . ."

"It is the famous Thai body massage. Don't worry, you'll like it." He smiled broadly.

"We'll see you in an hour or so, then eat . . . if you're still hungry."

"But it's like a meat market," Ted protested, trying not to smile at Sarit's accent.

"Not at all," said Sarit, suddenly without his accustomed smile. "These are not whores, these are beautiful girls, mostly from the country, who come here to support entire families. They are treated well and take great pride in their work. But you will see. It is not like New York or London where you must guard your wallet, if not your life. These are warm, loving, talented ladies, not angry greedy whores!"

He patted Santek's shoulder, then grinned broadly.

"It is our official welcome to Thailand, the land of freedom and love." He chuckled aloud. "The Japanese executives come here on excursions for the massage, only pretending to do business."

Ted moved down the corridor, descended the steps, and looked carefully at his companion in the floral bikini. About five feet tall with the usual dark brown hair and beige skin, she had features that

250

were barely Oriental, and her figure was full and perfectly shaped without the thick ankles and stubby legs that were more usual. Actually, she was not from Bangkok, but from Chiang Mai in the north, a city of delightful climate, said to produce the most beautiful women in the world.

"My name is Moon," she said in the same musical English. "What you?"

"Ted," he said. "I am Ted."

She bowed graciously with folded hands. "*Sawadi-krap.*" Ted nodded and she paused to show him the proper greeting. Gently folding his hands as if in prayer, she bowed again.

"To lady you say, '*Sawadi-ca.*'"

"*Sawadi-ca.*" He bowed gently with folded hands, feeling briefly like the priest he had been a day ago at Mass.

Her pleased laugh at his performance interrupted his reverie about his whole culture. There was some warmth and freedom in Thailand he had never before experienced.

"You good Thai, Ted."

She repeated his name several times until it began to sound like the gentle cadence of a distant drum. An American sailor and his Thai companion moved quietly from another corridor. Moon smiled without taking her attention from Santek. She continued to cling to him like an enraptured child, turned a corner, and led him down a dimly lit corridor with a series of carved teak doors on either side, then paused and opened door number 54 with a key.

Chapter 24

Once inside room 54, Moon flipped on a light switch, then stepped back to let Ted enter first. The room, carpeted in rich maroon, was surprisingly large, like a comfortable studio apartment. To the right was an attractive pink marble tub on a white marble floor. Opposite there was a small table and two chairs. In the rear of the room was a circular bed all in white velvet and, adjacent to it, a low, sloping chair in gold velour. Moon motioned him to the chair and moved to a locker near the door. Unselfconsciously she removed her bikini as Ted approved quietly the perfect twenty-year-old contoured body which contrasted dramatically with her child's face. She slipped on a white robe, kicked off her sandals, glided to his chair, and began taking off his shoes and socks almost caressingly. She removed the rest of his clothes in reverent ceremony, folded them carefully, and placed them on top of a small table next to his chair. His curiosity mounted. Surprisingly, the experience allowed no room for moral judgment or a struggle with his conscience. It was spontaneous and natural.

A sudden knock on the door interrupted them. Moon quickly covered Ted with a large red towel and admitted a young girl with a tray of drinks. Santek selected a brandy and Moon a Coke. As soon as the girl left, Moon removed the towel.

"She too young to see a man." She frowned as she said it, a mother protecting her daughter.

When Ted had finished sipping his brandy and smoking a cigarette at the small table, Moon extinguished his cigarette and gently pulled him from the chair. She rubbed her fingers lightly over his

chest and down his thighs as though his body were that of a distinguished god. Then she knelt briefly before him and tenderly kissed
his feet. Ted thought briefly of Christ and his apostles in a Gospel
story, then was back with Moon when she stood up and whispered,
"You are very beautiful." Her expression was relaxed but studious,
as if she were about to paint his portrait in oil or sculpt his image
from clay.

Silently she led him to the tub and began filling it with water. As
he stood waiting she massaged his legs and entire body with an oil
that reminded Ted of the lilac trees of his childhood in Michigan.
Once she brushed his erection and laughed with a child's delight.
When the tub was half full she helped him to sit down in the water;
then she began massaging his upper body with the same oil, sighing
with deep pleasure at his broad shoulders and at the abundant hair
on his chest, so unlike the Thai male. When she had completed her
ministrations, she pressed him lower into the tub until his entire
body was immersed, then shampooed his hair and rinsed it several
times with warm water. She dried his hair lovingly and massaged his
forehead and cheeks firmly. Ted felt a release of the massive, stored-
up pain of his separation from Angie. Then she walked over to the
locker and removed her robe.

She returned to the tub area and filled a large galvanized bucket
with warm, sudsy water, and from against the wall took a small rubber raft and placed it on the marble floor at the side of the tub. She
splashed it with the warm suds, led Santek from the tub to lie on the
raft face down, and poured more warm suds over his entire body as
Ted groaned softly with pleasure. She poured suds over her own
body and prostrated herself face down on his back, her breasts
against his back, her groin pressed against his buttocks, and legs
against legs.

Ted felt a rising excitement, more sensual than sexual, but was
startled by her sudden rocking motion as she began massaging him
with her entire body, rolling with amazing speed over every muscle
and joint, in and out of his thighs and legs and arms as if her body
were one soft, loving, exotic vibrator. The whole magical act seemed
impossible as Ted gradually realized how much talent and training
was required for this unbelievable rubdown. For a brief moment he
stiffened, fearing she might knee him in the groin. Gradually, he let
himself go completely as her body found every thread of pain and
tension and stroked it into relaxed oblivion. Welcome to war!

He had no idea of time as he drifted from near sleep and then to total pleasure. Twenty minutes, a half hour, longer? She only paused momentarily to lather herself and Ted with more of the warm suds. Never in his life had he felt such a combination of reverence and pleasure, and this from a woman he didn't even know. It was far more than a body massage. It seemed a religious act of abandonment and love. His thoughts traveled from the streets of Detroit to a boy in the seminary. Then he was eating at his parents' table with his brothers or shoveling an icy sidewalk to make twenty-five cents. Flashes of his whole life passed before him like a movie—Angie, Beauvais, his entire priesthood, the rec center in Flint, women he had loved—but most of all Angie and how he missed her. He recalled a massage in San Francisco when he had wanted the loving touch of a woman to ease his loneliness, but the cold, harshly calculating masseuse only bargained with him for the more expensive pleasures of a "local" until he got up angrily and left the bitch without showering.

Moon had paused in her sensuous rhythms to rub his still prone body with hot towels. Ted again drifted off to dreams and sleep, only to awaken when she gently lifted him to his feet and began drying every crevice of his body with a large soft towel, grinning again with innocent glee when his erection reappeared. She led him to the circular bed and stretched him out on his back as she began gently massaging his face and shoulders, then his whole body, with a light, silvery touch. Ted Santek, devoted chaplain, thought he would die of the loving warmth and pleasure.

Finally, Moon looked at him with deep affection and asked with great seriousness, "Do you love me, Ted?"

"Oh, God, yes, Moon, yes, I love you!" And he felt it.

It was the final permission as she began covering his entire body with soft, deft strokes of tongue and lips and fingers. Santek had experienced every variety of sex before, but never in his entire life had he known such complete sensual pleasure. His mind fought with his body. It couldn't be. This was just a paid actress, an ignorant peasant girl in a foreign culture he would never understand. But his body and spirit protested and quieted the insistence of reason. Suddenly, impulsively, irresistibly, he wanted her almost as much as he desperately missed Angie. She continued her slow, gentle kisses as if each particle of his body contained some hidden, sacred force that demanded special homage. His tense flesh, dead for several weeks, now experienced a sudden resurrection.

Then like a loving child she lay next to him and began kissing his

254

face, drawing her body tightly against his. Suddenly his whole being was drowned in sadness, as if he wanted to cry. All the pain of Angie's abandonment came rushing in upon him. He let himself miss her, love her, long for her.

He hardly knew the moment when he entered her body or, more exactly, when she tenderly led him inside. Time disappeared. With other women he had awaited orgasm, pushed for it, demanded it, working himself up to some vast passion as if the greatest pleasure was in a final release. This new embrace, like a quiet bubbling spring or the sun warming his body on a San Diego beach, was beyond all passion. He was lost in her, a stranger, as totally involved as he had ever been in his life as the tears began to well up in his eyes. He felt that he had never allowed himself to be totally loved by anyone else. Always he had held back a part of himself, even from Angie, fearing to let go completely. His very priesthood was a kind of insurance against closeness. He had never really been close to anyone. He had held back from Beauvais, denied Angie the total sharing that she longed for, that a child symbolized and perhaps realized. Now there were no words for what he felt, save a language drawn from the depths of his priesthood.

It was reverent, godlike, sacred, ecstatic, until finally there were no words at all, merely the ebb and flow of moon and time, planets and ocean, a rediscovering of the beginning of life when some primeval order emerged from chaos, and he continued to cry softly, with no apparent end to his tears. His body floated with hers down the Detroit River, splashed gently in the healing waters of Lake Michigan or the splendor of Bermuda's beaches, drifted reverently through the most sacred moments of the Mass, trembled and sighed in the flush of a midwestern spring, grew hushed and still in the serenity of twilight. He was a laughing, earnest boy in Ham Town, a seminarian struggling with theology and Latin, a priest depressed and troubled by his inability to be celibate. He was lying in bed with Angie, always somehow in control, always on his guard, afraid of a pregnancy, afraid of being discovered, afraid of letting go, of surrendering some vague sovereignty that threatened to devour him. Afraid of the ultimate closeness of friendship. He was a priest and no one would really know him, and until now, no one had broken through the barrier of his real fear of commitment. His priesthood had been an escape from commitment and closeness, a guarantee that he would never have to grow up. Angie had known all the time, but Ted had never realized till now that he had wanted her totally without giving himself. Somehow the pain of Angie's rejection and the reverent love of this stranger had broken some inner barrier, and he saw himself with new clarity as a lonely man afraid of personal love.

When he finally came, his heart and soul melted into Moon's, his whole being finally surrendered to whatever was or could be. And in the ecstatic experience, lasting several minutes, he knew that his life with Angie and his priesthood could all make sense in some circular act of love. Moon had revealed it to him unwittingly.

Surprisingly, he felt no guilt, not a shred of it, no disloyalty to Angie or his priesthood. It was as much a spiritual experience as it was physical, a deepening of his own awareness that celibacy made absolutely no sense for him, that it contributed nothing to his priesthood and only deprived him of the depths of human friendship and joy. His very vows had only been an excuse to avoid total love and closeness, and even as he had been denied the experience of his total humanness, he did not allow Angie hers. He had used her, enslaved her, manipulated her for his own convenience and comfort. He had been neither priest nor husband, had surrendered neither to Christ nor to Angie. Her hunger for a child was her instinctive hunger for him. He had held back and she knew it. He was forever the priest bachelor who thought someone more suitable might come along. It was his "celibate" way to live forever in fantasy no matter who got hurt!

Now some barrier had been crossed with the help of an unChristian stranger, a pagan by all Catholic definitions, a sinful scarlet woman who could only earn contempt and scorn in his culture. To him she was more "Christian" than any Bishop Sullivan—or Major Ted Santek.

Now he was ready for the chaplains' conference, ready for Vietnam and the disillusioned, embittered troops that Colonel Shea had described. He was ready to serve his God with a full and generous heart, anxious to do the priestly work he loved and more than ever anxious to contact his beloved Angie, but without some adolescent compulsion, as if he finally loved her! He could hardly wait to tell Beauvais about the revelation of a "body massage." It seemed reason enough for his recovering buddy to make a trip to Thailand. Then they could finally discuss celibacy in honest detail. He laughed aloud, tipped Moon generously, and was off to sample more Thai food with a joy and understanding he had never felt before.

Two nights later, back in his hotel room and still pondering his experience, he lay silently on his bed, fully clothed and listening to the soft American music which seemed to be everywhere in Thailand. He was still struggling with his American Christian culture, which had always claimed to contain answers to the most profound questions of life and death. The chaplains' meetings of the last two days now seemed wordy and ambiguous, and the canned spiritual answers were as "sounding brass and tinkling cymbals." The theological quarrels seemed to be nothing but empty historical absolutes, to which he had given intellectual assent without emotional harmony.

Instead of going to the chaplains' dinner, Ted had visited a monastery, the Wat Arun, the Temple of the Dawn. In the *bot,* or main shrine hall, he watched the devout Thais make public offerings to Buddha, and even Sarit and Boomprajak, his guides at the body massage and here as well, seemed lost in some serene inner contact with God as naturally and simply as they were lost in food and the massage. They did not shift gears to be suddenly "religious." They talked of a holy man they had visited several days before as naturally as they talked about food and air. They talked reverently of death without apparent fear or concern, as if life merged into death like sunset into dawn. Santek, the product of a totally Western experience, was overwhelmed. The Thais produced a warm, generous, loving populace who seemed to have none of the bitterness and religious arrogance, the confrontations and historical hang-ups of religious history everywhere. Religion here was devout and symbolic, private and public all at once, a part of the culture rather than some alien excretion that spent most of its time proclaiming its own rectitude.

Who cared about the rightness of a religion when those who were its modern proponents were lost young men fighting a hopeless war? Drowned in dope and confusion, clinging like children to whatever they could. Certainly the Hinayana Buddhism of the Thais made as much sense. Certainly Thailand had contact with God as real and graceful as the most devout Jew or Christian. And Moon, who had graciously attended him in a small, private room, was as loving and spiritual as any nun Santek had ever known. Certainly Angie's devotion to him was as Christian as anything he had ever experienced. And if he, a priest, and the priests he had known, not to mention chaplains of every denomination, were the true expression of religion's power and impact, there were a hundred questions the chaplains' meeting had not answered and a thousand more answers that Santek's whole life had not provided.

Still grateful to be a priest, he would never again be the priest he had been. The tears came as he thought of Angie's devotion, of how much courage and love it took to leave him, of the chauvinism and selfishness that had marred his manhood and discolored his priesthood. The culture shock of Thailand had almost released him from some private prison of Western Catholic thought and made him begin to understand clearly that God's relationship with man was too personal and mysterious ever to be encapsulated in a single religion or a narrow, proselytizing point of view. Maybe Christ was only his own "holy man." Maybe Catholicism and Christianity, Judaism and Western thought were only the products of a single track on a giant stereo of a hundred different sounds.

One thing for sure, as the world grew narrower and wars escalated, the insulated, bickering sects of ancient Christianity, from Catholics to Calvinists, from Baptists to Lutherans, would understand their own limitations and unite in some common visceral reality of love and forgiveness and understanding, or religions would dissolve even as had Rome and Antioch and Constantinople. Santek had experienced from a beautiful young woman, in an impoverished, crowded land that knew not Christ or the Old and New Testaments, as much love and truth and beauty as anywhere in the world. And it had created in him a new spark that had changed his whole life. If only it was not too late.

Chapter 25

Gerry Beauvais was still struggling with his own priesthood. He awoke, after his rapturous encounter with Peggy, refreshed and alive and newly and completely in love. He was instinctively relieved that they had drawn back from total carnal love, not out of some guilt—he felt none—but because he had experienced a melding of spirits he had not known before. It would have been easy to surrender, to know the total pleasure of a wondrous sexual union with Peggy. And yet he now felt some spiritual joy which escaped all description, a closeness he had never known in his life. There were no words for what he felt, but he knew that his celibate love had not been a mistake.

At first he found it difficult to face Peggy the morning following their loving encounter. Although his celibacy had some genuine significance, now that he knew what it meant, he had experienced a new dimension in his relationship with her, as if some dangerous, exciting boundary had been crossed. His desire for her, once controlled by a lifelong discipline and absence of experience, had now reached the point of an absorbing free love. He knew he could possess her in total sexuality if he chose. She would not deny him, yet he had no hungry need to invade her bedroom to prolong or complete the beautiful, loving tryst that had been so gently aborted the night before. He could not forget her olive breasts, the pressure of her thighs against his, the devouring kisses that had blotted out his overriding depression and set him on fire. Nor did he want or try to, as he would have in the past.

He knelt at the side of his bed and gazed at the crucifix on the wall. He knelt there for a long time in silent contemplation, as if finally beginning to know what love really was, what his life was all about. He could not stop smiling. Simply to consummate their act of love could never have the meaning that his profound, loving gift of himself had created. A sense of peace came over him. They had done the right thing. He only had to know that Peggy would feel as exhilarated and joyful about their experience, and not frustrated or disappointed. Or embarrassed. They would talk about it. Her friendship was the most important thing in his life. As close as Ed Sanders and Ted had been, there was always some barrier to intimacy. That was gone with Peggy. There was nothing he could not share with her.

In reality, he had to admit that he had never really understood celibacy. It had merely been a part of the priesthood. Had it been virtue that kept him from any involvement, or was it merely fear? He was not sure that he had ever met the responsibilities of a relationship. The priesthood had given him an out. He was not more dedicated because he was alone. He was only alone. All the reasons for celibacy given in the seminary in reality made no sense. If celibacy was his own imitation of Christ, he had not been able to connect with it emotionally. If it meant that he would give more time to the people, this had not been his experience. His relationship with Peggy had given him something to live for; without her he would have given up long ago. Now his love for her, his soul's surrender to give and accept love, had grown in some giant understanding, as if a door closed since childhood had sprung open. How did she interfere with his priesthood? Was he more devoted than the local Episcopal priest, Ed Davis, who seemed a gentle, compassionate man, committed to his parish and his people? Yet he had a wife and four children. They were obviously a source of energy for him and a touch of reality that gave more depth to his ministry.

But on the other hand, Gerry realized he had never tried celibacy. If celibacy meant a particular kind of dedication, a special gift, he had never experienced it. Maybe it was time to begin. He talked hesitantly with Peggy as she served his breakfast.

"It was hard not to invade your bedroom this morning. I really wanted to, and yet I felt a closeness to you and a profound joy in remaining celibate."

"I understand," she said quietly. "I feel closer to God than ever before, and yet I love you more than I thought possible."

"I just wonder if I've ever been celibate. Maybe I've only

avoided all closeness—with women and with everyone. I don't see any benefit in that. No one ever helped me to understand celibacy. It was just there like a block of wood. Easier for me than Ted because I had closed myself up to so many emotions and lost myself in my music."

"I know that my closeness to you makes me feel loving in a lot of new directions, and yet I want you more than anything in the world. I would die for you. I don't want to take away your priesthood or lose my own vocation to do God's work. Would you be any less a priest or I less a good woman if we had made love last night?"

"I don't know," he said. "I don't think it's goodness or badness. Our love could only be good. But I want to understand what celibacy means. I want to be a different kind of priest than I've been the last few years, and I need your help."

"I'll do whatever you want as long as I don't have to go away. I always felt empty without regular sex. Now I feel like a virgin again, and my virginity is beginning to make some sense. At least I don't want to surrender it till I understand. I've already given myself to you with every ounce of my love. Maybe there is a higher love for us. I don't know, but I want to know. I just can't leave you. To leave you would destroy me."

"I don't want you to leave me." He caressed her hand gently. "I want you to help me be a real priest. I want to help you with your vocation, and I want us to get involved together in our work."

Once again he began to visit his flock as he had when he first came to St. Mary's, only now with greater understanding of human suffering. When Ben Douglas committed suicide in his barn, Gerry spent an entire day and half the night with the widow, dealing with her massive guilt, and asked no one's permission to bury him from the Church. After the funeral, he spent a lot of time with the three younger children, doing everything he could to assuage their loss and to help them understand Ben's private pain. Peggy prepared food, tended to the children's school and laundry needs, and told them stories about the joy and happiness in heaven. She was ecstatic at sharing in God's work, not standing outside his priesthood as a dedicated servant but being a part of it.

He began visiting the hospital every day, and when he had occasion to visit young men in Jackson prison, the overcrowded state facility in southern Michigan, he volunteered his services two afternoons a week to relieve the elderly Catholic chaplain. He listened to the men's complaints about a parole board which only retried them for their crimes, and with Peggy's help and advice wrote letters to the governor about the antiquated methods that deprived prisoners of every shred of hope.

"They don't ask you what you've done for eight years, Padre. They just go back and talk about every crime you committed since you snatched an old woman's purse when you were fourteen. They recite every car you snatched, every petty theft, every disturbance in juvenile hall. Then you get a two-year dump for no reason at all and you're back in the joint trying to keep your sanity."

"What about psychological reports or educational progress?"

"If there are any, they don't even acknowledge them. The crime doesn't ever change, so you don't ever change. They think all criminals are the same."

Gerry and Peggy succeeded in having one person removed from the parole board and were able to increase the psychological staff by their persistence. They began writing letters to the Detroit *Free Press*, the Lansing *State Journal*, and the diocesan weekly, to inform people of what was taking place. They headed a group of concerned citizens who organized a committee for prison reform and met monthly at the rectory. He felt more alive than he had since his ordination, and his new enthusiasm only deepened his loving relationship with Peggy. Their love for each other was warm and affectionate but, almost miraculously, had moved beyond sexual need to a kind of spiritual bond they had not thought possible. They prayed together, read scripture, continued to enjoy their music, and talked far into the night about activities in and outside the parish. Often they embraced warmly and held each other in a kind of ecstasy, then kissed gently and lovingly and were off to their separate bedrooms.

It was especially in the confessional that his priesthood reached new heights. Whereas before he had been content to listen to a well-rehearsed list of sex and trivialities, he gradually taught his people about the possibility of personal growth.

"God has a special mission for each one of us," he told a middle-aged woman with dark eyes and graying black hair who was discouraged with her family and housework. Her doctor had advised Valium and dismissed her abruptly as a self-pitying neurotic.

Beauvais listened patiently to her before he spoke.

"The love you give your family is God's own love. I know it gets difficult. Often you are not appreciated. But God is counting on you and wants you to enjoy your life. You've waited on everyone but

262

yourself. Your presence in the world makes a difference to many people, but you have needs to meet too. Try to take a little time every day in private meditation to understand how valuable you are to yourself."

To a young man troubled with sexual sins, he said, "Sex is something confusing at first, but with experience and prayer together you will understand it is a way of showing love, not guilt. I don't think God resets his computer when you masturbate. Feeling good is important to love. If we begin to understand that, sex will not grow dull or commonplace. We try not to use another person, but to love that special individual as God loves us and to love and enjoy yourself. Increasingly, sex will be a great joy."

To a weathered old farmer, he said, "Christ was a workingman. So was Joseph. In those days, being a carpenter was heavy, hard work. I'm sure God has a special love for you, living close to the earth and respecting the land. Try to whisper a little prayer from time to time as you do your work and unite yourself with God."

A nun was troubled about a beginning lesbian relationship. "There is a great bursting love in your heart. You must let your work expand so that this burning love can find new and more exciting outlets. You and your friend can do great things for God and one another. Do not be drowned in guilt or lost in shame. Celibacy cannot be imposed, it must be embraced in joy. Come and talk to me as often as you like, and gradually you'll find a greater peace in your own work."

To a young homosexual living with his friend he said, "Do the best you can according to the light God has given you. You have done nothing shameful. You are only hungry for love like the rest of us. God understands and will help both of you grow in love, if that is what he intends. If not, he will let you know. Have faith and patience and be gentle with yourself and with each other."

Gerry Beauvais had found a new celibate life. Now he worked diligently on his sermons, taught the choir the new English hymns, some his own and Peggy's compositions, and increasingly made of the Mass a warm experience for all the people. Even at the prison, there was evidence of a spiritual rejuvenation among some inmates who had found, in their active participation in the Mass, a new relationship with God and a new determination, where possible, to make amends for their crimes. He and Peggy also wrote special hymns for them that made contact with their own prison reality, and Beauvais's talks inspired hope and confidence and an understanding of the Gospels that Christ had special energies for the weak and imprisoned. Meanwhile he continued to work for prison reform while Peggy supplied him with important articles, typed letters, encouraged people to bombard the governor with mail, assisted with every facet of his work, and deepened her own spiritual life with daily meditation and dedication at Mass. Even the nuns from Jackson who taught catechism noted the change: "You have become truly beautiful," they said. "We'd like to become nuns like you are!"

Their whole life together had become a kind of impossible dream, radiating a new kind of psychic energy and joy as they explored a celibate life of service and dedication by living it rather than theorizing about it. They could express deep affection for one another without threatening their personal promises to God. Often, when the phone and doorbell had stopped ringing, he held her in his arms, listening to music.

"I love you, Peggy, beyond all words." He whispered it.

"I love you too," she said softly.

There was nothing else to say.

Until the appearance of an official letter from the chancery office late in May of 1968. It was typically episcopal.

Reverend and dear Father,

You are requested to appear at the Chancery Office at 10 a.m. on May twenty-fifth.

We trust that you are in good health.

Sincerely yours in Christ

It was signed in Bishop Sullivan's strong hand.

Later that night, after a parish dinner and the usual friendly chatter, they returned to the rectory to listen to music. There was no way to put their fear into words. After an hour of silence, Beauvais spoke softly.

"This time I'm not bowing my head."

"Maybe it's something else besides us," she whispered.

"And maybe not," he said, without smiling.

His face was locked in a kind of strength and determination she had never seen before. He leaned over and kissed her gently on the lips.

Santek was wounded by a mortar shell in the Tet offensive early in February 1968. He was lucky not to have been killed. He had already endeared himself to the troops, risking his life saying field Masses in the jungle with snipers on all sides, riding in helicopters to comfort and administer the last rites to men trapped in pockets surrounded by the Viet Cong, rescuing terrified deserters who had hidden themselves in the villages surrounding Saigon, dragging young kids from dope dens where they chose a slow suicide to an impossible jungle warfare.

But the Tet offensive was a radical turnabout. Suddenly a jungle warfare was transformed into an attack on every important American base and every city of South Vietnam. The surprise offensive began at three in the morning on the first night of the Vietnamese New Year, when nineteen NLF commandos blasted their way through the walls of the American embassy. It was several hours before the U.S. troops could regain control. Some ten or eleven NLF battalions entered Saigon and changed the complexion of the war and Ted Santek's life.

Vietnam was beyond all imagination. American teenagers had been transformed into crazed killers. North, South, NLF, ARVN, old men, women, children—nothing made any difference. Soon they were all the enemy. Charlie was everywhere: in the guise of an innocent child or an attractive woman, in a sampan or a decrepit hut, wherever there was tawny skin or slanted eyes. Minds destroyed on dope and cheap liquor of every variety became twisted and mad.

Santek set out to rescue a nineteen-year-old blond boy from Wyoming. He finally found him in a stinking, disheveled hut in the village of Zen Lu. An old woman and a twelve-year-old girl were caring for him as he drifted between vague consciousness and fearful hallucinations. He had been an altar boy, had served Santek's Mass in the field, and was once captain of his high school football team. Now he was a vegetable. Santek stayed with him for two days, risking his life with the omnipresent snipers and desperate, suspicious villagers. This was not war but an unending nightmare. Finally, after Santek had fed him and got him on his feet, cautiously walked him through the village, the boy was able to talk.

He pointed to the twelve-year-old girl with large, brown staring eyes. She looked about nine. "I raped her, Padre. I didn't know what the hell I was doing. Why they didn't kill me I don't know."

"God understands and forgives. You weren't yourself."

"That's not all, Padre. Two of us paid for half a dozen young girls over the last week. Their parents gave them to us for food. My God, I was like an animal. I just wanted someone to hang on to."

He began sobbing again. Santek held him like a child. "It's all going to pass. You'll be out of here soon. Keep thinking about your favorite place back home, your parents, your friends, that stream where you used to catch trout, the pheasants in the fall."

The boy began to calm down, and Santek was able to sneak him to safety, risking his life every step of the way.

It was never-ending. He felt like a bounty hunter, cautiously following leads, giving away food for information, wondering when Charlie would put him away with a single bullet. Every noise became a threat, every movement in the bushes was a potential enemy. In a cave outside another village, he found two boys from Ohio who were hysterical with fear and grief.

"We didn't mean to, Father. We saw some shrubbery move while we were out on patrol and just blasted away."

He couldn't finish. Gradually Santek heard the story. After the smoke had cleared, a woman and three little girls of six or seven had fallen from the bushes, ripped to shreds. The boys had been living on dope and roots and were almost delirious. Again Santek stayed with them, talked to them, and led them back to tenuous safety. The taller boy, from Cleveland, a former basketball star who had once had a scholarship to Notre Dame, could not stop crying unless he was stoned out of his mind. Then he could not stop laughing. He was only one of dozens that Ted extricated from some personal horror.

It was as if My Lai were confessed in miniature every day. Every strange yellow face became the enemy. Every least movement was a threat to life. Every young female body with a bare hint of "tits and ass" became a sexual object that could salvage some animalistic contact with life and forgetfulness. It was hard to look into the young eyes of terrified boys and listen to what they had done.

A chubby lieutenant from Florida with buck teeth and sad eyes told a horror story when he was just coming out from under a week-long drug ordeal. His voice was flat and sepulchral.

"We tied these young girls to posts and seven or eight of us gang-raped them, Padre. It seems like it never happened. It's all like a crazy dream. Then we shot up the village, killing anything that moved. We stole and destroyed houses. Two guys raped a couple of older women and blew their husbands' brains out. You could

266

hear guys coming and moaning while women and kids were screaming and men were dying. I can't believe it. I just can't!"

Then he was lost in his own grief and madness, still looking as if
he should be surfing on a Florida beach or building a homecoming
float. Santek could not absorb it all. He just kept talking and moving
ahead. He had heard no tragedy before to match any of this. Death
everywhere. Hopelessness and adolescent terror. Orgasmic groans
mingling with screams of death and horror. Men turned to beasts by
dope and fear and despair. All of it unbelievable. These were not
the actions of fourth-century barbarians or the retaliatory behavior of
a brutalized populace. These were the deeds of middle-class, religious, American boys from the land of elm trees and boulevards,
Little League and Pepsi-Cola, pom-pom girls and den mothers—
driven out of their young minds by an eternal, pointless, finally
mindless war.

One youngster from a small town in Oregon had seen his
buddy's red curly hair severed from his brains and watched his closest friend's guts blown out before his very eyes. He had opened fire
on everything in sight and wanted to kill himself. He had shot children, women, animals, anything to blot out the memory. Finally he
had simply settled into dope and hiding, hoping it would all go
away.

Men told of entering whole villages rotting with stinking corpses.
They had seen Hue decimated and Saigon literally flowing with
blood. They had seen flamethrowers dissolve shrubbery and huts
and shrivel people.

"They looked like hot dogs or marshmallows, Padre."

They smelled napalm in their sleep. They had seen ramshackle
huts protecting trembling, toothless old ladies and kids treated as
serious military objectives. They had seen brave strong young men
turn tail and run like five-year-olds, officers hiding out in terror for
weeks, comrades willing to do anything to get the hell out of Vietnam. And Major Ted Santek, with all his experience and street
savvy, with all his humor and private strength, had never known
anything like this in his life. Not even close. Vietnam was a madness
he was not prepared for. Nobody was prepared for it. Yet it went
on.

Santek was furious. Furious at America for refusing to face up,
furious at American Catholic bishops for not denouncing this atrocity
in the name of God. His own mind was drifting in and out of reality,

267

not from dope but from pain and horror. He had seen serenity in Bangkok he never witnessed in Chicago or even San Francisco. He had seen a discipline and determination, a courage and an ardor in Charlie that no American demonstrated. But most of all, he wondered excruciatingly about his Church and his Christian God who made so much of sex and so little of war.

Almost without preparation he was immersed in a war of napalm and flamethrowers, of snakes and sweating jungles, of deadly cops-and-robbers with no meaning, of pointless bombings which decimated hamlets and civilians. But now, with the Tet offensive, a bloody jungle skirmish became a war of the cities, a war he would not have believed if he had not seen it.

Corpses littered the streets, doctors went into hiding before the massive destruction of human life, and when the Americans returned to Hue, hundreds simply turned tail and hid out to salvage their own scarred lives. The official American position was that the Tet offensive had finally destroyed the power of the North Vietnamese, who had engaged in a far-too-broad offensive war. And while that may have been true, the American people had finally endured enough. Nixon and Humphrey in their campaigns for the presidency both promised to end the war. They had no other choice.

Ted Santek had seen enough. Enough bombing of hamlets, enough destruction of innocent human life, enough refugee camps, enough young men destroyed by dope and horror. The war had to come to an end. Santek was no longer trying to raise the morale of the troops, as the chaplains in Bangkok had naively planned. Nor was he trying to forgive sins and save souls. He was only concerned with salvaging the minds and hearts of young men who were going mad in the confusion of Southeast Asia. And instinctively he was furthering his own conversion to a God beyond sects and history. His whole land and culture had gone mad, and he did not know where to take root. Even Angie seemed almost inconsequential amid the horror of what he saw and felt.

Santek was wounded by a lobbed mortar while speeding in a jeep toward the American air base at Da Nang. The North Vietnamese troops had occupied villages nearby and were content to toss mortar shells into the base to reduce the American air strikes. The mortar shell destroyed the jeep, killed two young men, and sent Ted Santek to the base hospital with a wound in his back. That he was still alive was a miracle of inches. Late in the spring he was sent back to Hawaii, a wounded, weary, disillusioned man who never wanted to see a corpse again. He had witnessed more horror in a few months than he thought possible, and his own emotions had been strained to the breaking point.

Vietnam completed Santek's metamorphosis. He had always been a team player, loyal to his school and family, defender of the Catholic Church and America, ready to fight at the least slur uttered against president or pope. He had been the true believer in the purest sense. Now he was disillusioned, ready to charge Lyndon Johnson, Robert McNamara, Clark Clifford, and William Westmoreland with political machinations and treason. For a time he had been able to urge young pilots on, to inspire them with some sense of dedication and honor. But when he began to see the pointless and unending horror with his own eyes, he, like the others, just wanted to get the hell out alive.

But he had not lost interest in his priesthood. He saw far more clearly than ever before that his job was to serve the young men who were helplessly and unwittingly involved in a war that not only could not be won but which never should have been started. Practically the entire American hierarchy had been hawks, and Cardinal Spellman had died still thinking America could win its "holy" war. He, like the rest, had naively bought the political line that a defeat in Vietnam meant that communism would rule all of Asia—as if communism itself could be more destructive than a vindictive, bullying America. Santek's Church had been neither prophetic nor creative, assuredly not faithful to the vision of Christ, and his government had sold out to the military madness of the generals and the Pentagon.

Suddenly his new awareness brought him a double freedom. His fragile chaplaincy was only a platform to help the young men keep their sanity and balance in an unjust and insane conflict. It had nothing to do with patriotism or loyalty to America. And his priesthood, which had been complicated by his relationship with Angie, was no longer compromised. The Church was not infallible or all-wise, nor was it the perfect reflection of Christ or God. It was a wounded, limping, half-blinded, stumbling institution of often righteous men who helplessly and fearfully thought more of their own tired traditions and myopic projections than they did of a solid, honest renewal of the Church. The Church was as weak and confused as Santek, and only in acknowledging that weakness was there the least shred of strength.

Ted had grown up. Vietnam had removed the scales from his eyes. Once he had believed that his Church and his country were the finest and strongest and purest in the world. Now his feelings were the same as those of a young man emerging from boyhood who realized that his father was only a factory worker with a limited education. And his Church and his nation were only feeble symbols of what could be. As a result, some cocky intensity was gone, but in its place there came a renewed dedication to his personal conscience and the spirit and vision of Christ.

The Church's mission to heal wounds and recharge hearts, and American's responsibility to share with the world what God had provided, was blurred by an obsessive preoccupation with communism. When Santek recovered enough to work with the wounded in Hawaii, he was a different Major Santek from the priest who went to Vietnam. He would never preach or hear confessions in the same way again. He was not concerned about human frailty and assorted peccadilloes of errant sexuality. His focus was love and courage, passion and dedication, not the wrong that was done but the good that had been or could be accomplished. He started to write Beauvais to talk of his new vision and of his wound, but there seemed to be too much to cover by mail.

Most of all, he wanted to see Angie, to tell her how he felt and what he had learned. Beauvais had heard from her some weeks ago and said she was "busy and well," but he had offered Ted no address. Secretly he had hoped that she would be waiting for him in Hawaii, but then he caught himself.

"For Christ's sake. She has her own life to live."

He pictured her face and felt his cheeks ache with the pain of unshed tears. He wanted her. God, he needed her! He needed to talk to her, to listen to her like he had never done before. He didn't want a servant but a friend. The back wound had almost healed. He was on his way to Travis Air Force Base and Beauvais. He only wished with his whole being that he was on his way to Angie as well.

Chapter 26

The day that Santek left for Travis in late May 1968, Gerry Beauvais was due in Bishop Sullivan's office in the chancery. He had said the seven o'clock Mass with great devotion, given communion to Peggy and a handful of parishioners, and spent fifteen minutes in private prayer after Mass. Now he glanced at the Detroit *Free Press* and picked distractedly at the sausage and eggs that Peggy had prepared.

"You can't face the bishop on an empty stomach." She was nervous and didn't know what else to say.

He spilled his coffee and Peggy moved to repair the damage and offer him another cup.

"God, I'm nervous!" He felt the aura of the old depression, which still afflicted him, though much more mildly, and was frightened by past memories.

"I'd really like to drive in with you. I could shop or pray while you're there."

He reflected slowly. "I want to do this by myself. Just so you're waiting here when I get back."

"I'll be here," she said softly. "Please eat something. You'll think better."

He munched on a piece of toast and got up abruptly.

"It's time."

She moved into his arms and they embraced wordlessly for several minutes. "I love you, Gerry."

He kissed her gently, picked up his breviary, and walked out the front door. She followed him to the car.

"God is on our side," she said. "Don't forget that. We belong to Him."

He nodded, smiled briefly, and backed his black Chevy out of the driveway. Soon he was on Highway 96 toward Lansing. The day was clear and still cool, and the sky gave a promise of summer. The long Michigan winter, symbolically the longest day in Gerry Beauvais's life, was over. This could be his greatest spring or his most painful. He tried not to anticipate the bishop's conference. He could already picture the sallow Monsignor Kelley fumbling nervously behind his glasses and yellow pad. But it was not the same Gerry Beauvais who was being called on the carpet. A long painful dark night of the soul and the total love of Peggy had changed all that. So had a secret ceremony in St. Mary's Church the night before—which he and Peggy had agreed upon as important to them.

It was almost midnight when they had entered the church. Peggy brought two bouquets of yellow roses and placed them on the Blessed Virgin Mary's altar. Beauvais arranged two small golden candles and lit them. There was no other light in the darkened church save the flickering of the red tabernacle lamp. Beauvais, in the simple white alb of his ordination, brought the golden monstrance from the sacristy. He ascended the steps to the main altar, genuflected devoutly, placed the small golden pyx containing the sacred host in the monstrance and carried it to Mary's altar, placed it gently on the corporal, then removed the humeral veil and knelt with Peggy at the foot of the altar. She was dressed in a simple white dress and carried a single red rose. A veil fell from her dark hair, and her olive skin was golden in the lambent light of the candles. She had never looked more beautiful. Her eyes glowed with joy, and her whole being seemed to shine with some inner light. Beauvais drew back her veil and kissed her softly on the lips. Then both of them turned reverently toward the golden monstrance and the carved wooden statue of Mary. A soft rain was falling outside and seemed to whisper against the stained glass windows as if there were a gentle congregation of friendly spirits in attendance. The roof and floor creaked intermittently as they recorded another event in an eighty-year ecclesiastical history. Beauvais spoke quietly.

"My God, I want to renew my promises of celibacy and dedication. I think I've begun to know what celibacy is and, as much as I love Peggy, I pledge that our love will be chaste, that it will be creative and productive for both of us, even if we hardly understand what we are promising. We take this step to dedicate all of our energies to you. I don't exactly know why I want to be celibate. Maybe it's because it is the greatest gift I can offer you, or a proof of my service. I can't promise it forever, just for now and as long as it seems a genuine source of love and dedication. Help me not to consider celibacy a noble sacrifice or a cause for personal pride, but a way to love you and Peggy and your people with my whole heart and soul. Amen." He gripped Peggy's hand tightly and could feel the moisture in her palm. Her whole body trembled, and she looked at him through a thin film of tears. He kissed her gently and she spoke very softly.

"Dear God and Jesus and Mother Mary, I promise my chastity, knowing how difficult it will be when I love Gerry so very much. But with your help, I lovingly offer this gift that all my energies may be spent in your service as long as I can be the woman you want me to be. I want to live with Gerry a life of simplicity and service, dedicated to helping those whom you loved most of all, the poor and the old, the distressed, the prisoners, the lonely and suffering on the earth. I pray that we can work in the Church where so much needs to be done. Many are giving up, but we want to stay and serve. We know the Church must change, and we humbly offer ourselves to bring about the kind of reforms that are necessary in the world in which we live. Amen."

They knelt silently for a long time. Beauvais's face looked strong and serene. Peggy, weeping softly from joy, was still radiant. Slowly she got up and placed her rose on the altar, bowing to Mary and genuflecting to the Divine Presence as if there were no one else around. Beauvais rose to assist her on the way down the steps; then they knelt together in private prayer, each conscious of the personal promises that were made, each lost in memory and meditation on the countless painful events that had led them to this moment and this paradoxical dedication.

Their private prayer lasted for almost fifteen minutes of the most intimate colloquy with a loving, caring, personal God. Then Beauvais began the divine praises:

"Blessed be God." Peggy repeated the invocation.

"Blessed be his Holy Name. . . ."

Then together they sang softly the ancient "Salve, Regina": "Hail, Holy Queen, Mother of mercy, our life, our sweetness, and our hope. . . ." Their voices echoed in elegant, soft harmony throughout an empty church. Gerry Beauvais and Peggy Santini finally belonged to each other and to God.

Later, for an hour or so, they shared champagne and music, then kissed warmly and said good night. Peggy went off to her private quarters, which had been newly remodeled as her own small convent. Beauvais went to his bedroom, like Peggy, transfused with more joy than he thought possible.

Now, the following morning, Beauvais pulled up in front of the familiar brick building that housed the Irish successor of the original fisherman. He fumbled for a cigarette, then ignored the urge and tried in vain to rehearse his lines. He prayed briefly and made his way to the somber carved-oak door that had played such a dramatic part in his life. A young, tall, dark-haired priest whom Beauvais recognized from the Confirmation let him in.

"It's good to see you again, Father Beauvais," he said almost shyly and too quickly. "You may not remember me. I'm Father Kincaid. The bishop is expecting you. It will be just a few minutes. Can I get you a cup of coffee?" He seemed more nervous than Beauvais.

"No, thank you, I'll just have a cigarette."

The young priest brought him an ashtray, then busied himself with some papers at his desk. He seemed gentler and much less officious than Gerry had remembered. Beauvais noticed a detective story and smiled. There was hope for the Church. The door to the bishop's office opened and Monsignor Kelley, grinning nervously, motioned him in, then withdrew to his oak table and chair next to the bishop's desk. He looked like a docile, embarrassed schoolboy. Sullivan stood up to shake hands with Beauvais, who attempted to kiss his ring. Sullivan pulled his hand away.

"That's not necessary, Father."

Beauvais wondered at the apparent change in Bishop Sullivan. He seemed thinner and older in his simple black suit and collar, and some of his Irish arrogance had been modified. The bishop sat down slowly as if he were very tired and motioned Beauvais to take the captain's chair that matched his mahogany desk. The desk was completely clean. No sheaf of notes. Even Monsignor Kelley was not scribbling on his yellow pad. The bishop seemed drawn, as tense as Beauvais, and fumbled as he began. Then some of the old confidence seemed to return as he tightened his lips and looked directly at Beauvais.

"I understand you've been very sick, Father." His voice was warm and concerned.

274

Beauvais nodded. He wanted another cigarette but thought it out of place.

"You're feeling better?"

Again he nodded. His heart was beating too loud.

"I'm glad for you and your parish." He paused and looked down. "There has been some talk in your parish, Father." He spoke softly and almost too kindly. "Increasing complaints about the presence of your housekeeper. I thought I had made myself quite clear on that subject, but I am now aware that your illness was extremely incapacitating and Dr. Hengesbach was kind enough to explain matters to me and the valuable assistance your housekeeper gave. We are grateful for her help."

Christ! Beauvais thought. Her name is Peggy.

The bishop proceeded slowly, smiling kindly. "Canon law, however, has not been discarded by Vatican Two, even though it is in process of reform. And the Vatican Council decree on the Life and Ministry of Priests is quite clear." He picked up a book from his lap and read slowly:

"Celibacy is to be embraced and esteemed as a gift. Perfect and perpetual continence . . . is a sign and stimulus for pastoral charity and a special source of spiritual fecundity in the world."

He put the book down. Beauvais noted that he did not read the following lines, which approved a married clergy in Eastern Catholic churches, urging "all those who have received the priesthood in marriage to persevere in their holy vocation so that they may fully and generously continue to expend themselves for the sake of the flock." To Bishop Sullivan, the contrast represented no contradiction.

Beauvais saw his lips tremble slightly. He brushed back his hair and coughed nervously as he quoted the ancient Latin edict which turned suspicion into condemnation.

"*Contumaces concubinarii praesumendi sunt.*" He translated obligingly. "The disobedient priest is presumed to be living in sin."

It was a weak translation of a fierce judgment, and Beauvais was tempted to correct him. Instead, he lowered his head and saw Monsignor Kelley do the same. Sullivan continued to speak kindly.

"I am willing to forget the past, Father Beauvais. But I want you to make immediate arrangements to dismiss your housekeeper now that you are well and Father Niedermeyer is gone. You must know my hands are tied. It is a source of scandal. Great scandal!" The

275

words seemed to echo hollowly, as if the bishop were no longer sure. "If you are to continue as a priest in this diocese, you must dismiss her." Again, the words seemed to lack conviction.

Beauvais felt sweat under his collar and pulsing tension in his hands. He stretched them briefly, then clasped his knees. The bishop was not expecting an answer and continued with a touch of some reborn ancient swagger that now seemed misplaced.

"These are difficult and confusing times for the Church and the People of God. Transition is always painful, Father, but the People of God do not need their priests to add to their confusion."

He smiled briefly as if pleased with his own Vatican II rhetoric and opened his eyes widely, elevating his eyebrows, nervously awaiting Beauvais's departure as if all had been said. It had been a painful confrontation for Sullivan, a painful week, but he could not share his pain with Beauvais. Two more young priests had left, talented men, and three teaching nuns. One of the priests had married a former head of the altar society who had left her husband, and it was impossible to keep the information out of the paper. It was rumored that one of the nuns was engaged to a Jewish dentist who had a child in her school.

The bishop leaned back in his chair and cleared his throat to signal an end to the interview, but Beauvais did not move. He couldn't. He wanted to speak but didn't know how to begin. His stomach and chest were screaming like sirens, his hands ached to choke the motionless bishop and the silent, sallow Kelley. Then he stared at them and felt only sadness and pity. He crossed and uncrossed his legs and badly wanted a cigarette. Finally, he lit one as Kelley found him an ashtray and then spoke kindly and patiently, wanting the bishop to hear him.

"I've always been celibate, Bishop, even before, when you—"

Sullivan waved his hands rapidly, like a traffic cop. "This is not a court, Father. Nor is it a confessional. It is an administrative decision. I would not presume to accuse you of sexual sins." He smiled briefly, looked off in the distance, and flexed his prominent Irish jaw. "I'm not judging you." He reached down to scratch his ankle. Beauvais's face flushed, and he felt a rush of anger rise to his temples.

"You are judging me!" Beauvais insisted. "You've always judged me!" His face reddened and the bishop quickly ignored his ankle.

Beauvais heard his voice come out in a higher range and felt some residue of depression pass away with his anger like a sullen cloud. He felt briefly cleansed and remembered Dr. Hengesbach saying that his depression had its roots in stored-up anger.

Sullivan, still startled by his outburst, drew a cigarette from his pocket. Monsignor Kelley again leaped to provide an ashtray from the bookcase. The bishop's hands trembled as he lit the match. Beauvais had not known him to smoke and felt that he was getting through. His anger continued to free him.

"I won't be judged! I won't be dismissed like a frightened altar boy! Maybe there is nothing else you can do. Maybe our position is untenable even now, when the Church is in crisis. But I want you to hear me!" He spoke more softly. "Peggy and I took vows, pledging our bodies and energies to God." He had not intended to mention this.

The bishop saw a safe place to intervene. "Your private vows are your own business, Father Beauvais, and your housekeeper does not concern me. *You* are my responsibility."

"Like hell!" Beauvais said. "I'm *my* responsibility. Doesn't Vatican Two mean anything? Haven't we learned anything? You still treat me like a seminarian, Bishop. You don't even discuss my relationship or ask me a single question. How many priests and nuns have to leave, Bishop? Will we keep suggesting that they are sinners and failures? The Church is not a hierarchy any more. It's not even Pope Paul. It's all of us. We're changing, and the institution is going to have to reflect that change or it will die! People won't take it any more. Neither will I!"

"That's your decision, Father." Sullivan tightened his lips, smacked them briefly, and looked off beyond Beauvais, readjusting a too large collar. "God did not ask me to be popular. I did not seek the episcopacy." He played with his lower lip.

Contradictory word from Philadelphia had said that he had done everything but campaign for the office. He began to speak with more authority, now on the safe familiar ground of pre-Vatican II theology.

"Christ promised to be with his Church until the end of time, Father Beauvais." He nodded as he spoke, scripture lending dignity to his office.

"I question your interpretation of scripture, Bishop. I repeat. The Church is no longer the pope and the curia and the bishops. It is the priests and nuns and people as well." Beauvais spoke too quickly, and his hostility fanned Sullivan's fear into anger.

Again Sullivan waved his hand impatiently, as if to dismiss Beau-

277

vais like a mosquito. "The sacred magisterium is not a Gallup Poll, Father Beauvais." His inflection was now cynical and angry. "Nor is the Holy Father the Queen of England. He is the successor of Peter, and '*Ubi Petrus est, illic Ecclesia.*'"

"I haven't read that quotation in the reports of Vatican Two, Bishop. I thought the human conscience was given new currency." It was all-out war. Monsignor Kelley wanted to hide under the bishop's chair.

"I'm not asking for your approval, Bishop. Or maybe I am. But I think what Peggy and I are doing has a place in the Church. We need the Church, and the Church needs us. We don't want to leave; we want to stay and save God's people."

Sullivan finally exploded, rising from his chair and shaking his finger at Beauvais like a stubborn child. He shouted his words, the veins standing out on his face. He had never been confronted like this before.

"There is an objective law, Father Beauvais! And a teaching Church! We don't stand around and let the people or the modern theologians make up our minds for us about birth control and sex and abortion. Nor do we allow our priests to debate their bishops! Your behavior is out of order, Father. Out of order! You will give up this woman or give up your priesthood. You must know the law. It is as simple as that!"

"Then I will give up my priesthood, Bishop."

Sullivan seemed to lose all control. He had lost more than a dozen of his best priests and over twenty-five nuns in the last three years, all of them disillusioned by the failure of Vatican II's implementation on the home front. Beauvais regretted the impossible tone of the dialogue. All his hopes went out the window as Sullivan became almost hysterical with the strength of his anger.

"That is proof of your guilt! You are involved with this woman. The people are outraged! If you want to leave, then leave and take her with you. The devil is still at work, 'seeking whom he may devour,' and eternal hell is still a reality! Of course, you have probably managed to dismiss hell as a medieval myth!"

Sullivan laughed bitterly, almost maniacally, staring into the distance as if he had lost contact with reality.

"It may be too late when you discover it's not a myth. And your private conscience will have a long time to reevaluate its attitudes! As long as the Holy Father is in charge, Christ will continue to speak to his Church! So if you must walk away out of cowardice and

278

fleshly concerns, it will not be the first or the last time that a chosen Levite has turned his back on God."

He went on more quietly, as if reason had begun to return.

"If you choose to leave, I request that you put it in writing. If you decide to remain, then your housekeeper *must* leave, and I will be consulted before you replace her."

The bishop stood up like an executive dismissing an errant manager who should never have been allowed to air his complaints. Kelley rose to his feet, a docile shadow. He had not looked at Beauvais during the entire dialogue. Beauvais remained seated, seemingly unable to reply. A thousand thoughts raced through his mind. The bishop, now totally in control, spoke slowly, biting each word.

"Let me know your decision, Father Beauvais. I do not want the people to be without a shepherd. That will be all," he said curtly and walked toward a rear exit door.

Beauvais got up very slowly. He had lost. After the long, impossible struggle, he had lost. Just as life had become exciting and fulfilling again, he had lost all that made it worthwhile. He should have known he had no chance. Vatican II was only a direction, a hope. Bishop Sullivan was the victim of his own educational experience, even as was the pope. The only clear thought he had was to grab the bishop and shake him like an episcopal doll. But he knew his fantasy was childish and in vain. Still angry and trembling, he walked awkwardly toward the door. Father Kincaid, aware of Beauvais's distress, stood up as if he wanted to offer comfort and understanding. He followed Beauvais out the door.

"Is there anything I can do, Father? I want to help."

Beauvais shook his head sadly. "There's nothing anyone can do. I should have known."

"Things will change," Kincaid said kindly. He had lost all the starchy righteousness Beauvais had noted before. "It just takes time." He seemed to be pleading.

"I don't have time, Father. I've suffered enough."

Kincaid nodded sympathetically. There was nothing else to say.

Beauvais walked out into the warm spring air. There was a sudden smell of lilacs from the yard as he walked toward his car and felt his familiar depression again begin to settle in. His heart sank and he wanted to scream. He had lost everything he ever wanted, and there was no way to regain it.

*

Bishop Sullivan sat rumpled and bewildered in a leather recliner in his private study, his head in his hands. Kelley stood nervously by. Kincaid had been invited in.

"Maybe I was too hard. Hengesbach said he has been to hell and back. Maybe I should have listened more. Damn my Irish temper!" He whispered the words as a man in agony. "I just couldn't control myself. He seems like such a sincere, good man. So many have left, yet he wants to remain a priest."

"You had no choice, your excellency. Beauvais is a modernist. A good man, but a hopeless modernist. I thought you gave him ample opportunity to defend himself."

Kincaid only looked sad and did not venture an opinion.

Sullivan ignored Kelley's approval and looked away. "Do you really think he and the woman have taken private vows to sanctify their relationship? That would be quite remarkable!" He still spoke as if in a trance.

"I think it's very possible, Bishop," said Kincaid softly. "Beauvais seems a remarkable man."

"That's internal forum, Bishop. That can be no concern of yours. 'A Church without law is a Church without love.'"

The bishop looked up as if he had awakened, startled at the epigram. "Who said that, Monsignor?"

"I'm not certain, your excellency. I think it was said by an Italian cardinal to Galileo."

The bishop again stared off into space. "How many priests have left this year, Father Kincaid?"

"Seven, your excellency. Beauvais is eight."

"That's more than ten percent in two years," the bishop mused. "I haven't liked losing any of them, but especially I don't like losing Beauvais. He wants to remain. He wants to serve. He took his disappointments like a man. He seems completely honest and totally dedicated, and Hengesbach says he is extraordinary and that the woman is devout and intelligent."

He paused, looking defeated.

"I hope he chooses to stay, but I may have made it impossible for him. Could he and the woman really have taken vows?"

The bishop continued to prop up his head in his hands and stare blankly at his desk as if he had lost a dear friend. Kelley knew it was time to leave and slipped out quietly.

The bishop motioned Kincaid to stay and looked up at him. "What would you have done, Father? You understand the modern Church."

Kincaid flushed briefly. He was still not accustomed to offering advice to a bishop. "I'm not sure, Bishop. I think we all do what we have to do." He paused reflectively. "Beauvais is requesting another kind of service, if I understand it. Maybe the Church will have to consider such options at some point."

"Do you, too, think of leaving?"

"Not really, Bishop. But I look forward to changes that can help the Church. Every time a priest leaves, I die a little. Beauvais has so much experience and talent. I've just begun. I wish there were a way of keeping him."

Sullivan nodded his thanks and Kincaid took his leave. The bishop stared silently at his hands, looking very old and weary. Then he began playing with his episcopal ring.

Beauvais drove back toward Farmington like a robot. The fine Michigan spring day was wasted on him as he swam in a maze of private thoughts. He would leave. There was his brother Lou in California. Or Karl Metzen at St. Stephen's in Austria. Peggy would go with him, and they would serve God somewhere else. He had to talk to Santek.

His mind raced wildly. His fingers held the wheel in a death grip. He was furious at himself for not saying everything he wanted to say. He should have prepared, brought notes. He cursed himself for not properly planning the confrontation. He should have remained calm and demanded a reasonable hearing before the deans and older priests. Challenging Sullivan was impossible. It had been a childish pissing contest: who was the stronger?

He wondered who had reported him from the parish. It could have been one of a hundred. Probably some frustrated, overburdened mother who was furious with the current suggestions that the Church would finally change its positions on birth control and divorce. Or her angry husband, who didn't want his pastor to experience some sexual freedom that he had been denied. He felt fury toward the parishioners of St. Mary's.

The miles ripped by. He had to talk to Peggy. She would be waiting for him. He would calm down and talk quietly, far into the night. He would never go through the horror of depression again. He could not survive it. They would make their plans, beyond Farmington and Lansing diocese, beyond Kelley and Sullivan and a dying, archaic, arrogant Church. Nothing in the Church would ever really change. Only words, more words, gutless, pale, theological, effeminate, boring words that said nothing. One hour with Peggy was worth their whole damn theology!

She rushed from the house when his car pulled into the driveway, looking drained as if she had anticipated his defeat. He looked at her like a worn-out warrior. The battle had been lost. She stared at him sadly, tears in her eyes. She spoke before he could open his mouth.

"Your brother called from Ohio. Your mother died last night in her sleep."

Chapter 27

By May of 1968, Angie was six months pregnant and was no longer able to hide her condition. She had finally admitted to her boss that she was separated from her "husband," who was fighting in Vietnam, and he had then insisted that she spend time with his family on weekends. His wife, Ruth, a thin, dark-haired, intense woman, was familiar with the stresses of pregnancy and treated Angie as if she were her own sister. Even the four children, ranging in ages from five to thirteen, began to call her "Aunt Angie." At times Angie was tempted to reveal her secret, to share with Ruth the beauty and pain of her relationship with Santek. But still she held back, even though the Markeley family had wondered openly about clerical celibacy, and Ruth had confessed that she thought it an incomprehensible burden.

Angie was able to talk at length about her own experience in religious life, which Ruth found totally fascinating, but as much as she longed to talk about Santek's priesthood, she found it impossible. Ruth's solid marriage and happy children had an overwhelming impact on Angie, and she was all the more determined to have her baby, even if it meant Santek was gone forever from her life. She still loved him deeply, and the few dates she had had, before her pregnancy became really apparent, only increased her longing for Ted.

She had gone out with Dale Pernot, an assistant professor of modern literature from Bradley, whom she had met when he lectured on contemporary literature at St. Michael's Church. Tall, dark-haired, and witty, with a Bill Buckley accent, he was an extreme contrast to Santek. He introduced her to the poetry of Anne Sexton and Edward Albee's *A Delicate Balance*, as well as the refinements of Chinese and Japanese food. It was only after a third date, when she had eaten her first sushi and watched Taylor and Burton and Sandy Dennis in *Who's Afraid of Virginia Woolf?* that he made his move.

They were holding hands to sensual Chinese folk music while lounging on large, colorful floor pillows in his seductive apartment when he turned to her almost abruptly. "I want to go to bed with you."

Angie was startled and blushed furiously, still pondering his previous ideas about the destructive elements in the male-female relationship.

"I don't think I'm ready for that."

"Let's find out. We might as well get it out of the way. Sex can be either a barrier to intimacy or the primary road to it."

He leaned forward and unbuttoned her blouse. At first she made no move to stop him as he started to fondle her enlarged breasts and then released her bra and gently began kissing her swollen nipples before she was really aware of what had happened. It had been weeks since she had experienced any sexual pleasure, and under the hypnosis of wine and music and his softly mellifluous words, she was momentarily lost in his tender ministrations. When he began exploring under her stylish short beige skirt, however, she laughingly moved his hands away. But he was not about to be put off and more firmly slipped his hand across her thighs and under her panties. Even as she trembled with the memory of excitement, she stood up and challenged him. Her face was red.

"I told you I wasn't ready, Dale," she said, even though she found herself wanting him to continue.

He eased her back down. "You'll like it. Just let yourself go. You're as starved as I am." Again he attempted to undress her. Finally she moved away again, hating Santek for having such an impossible hold on her and not wanting to hurt Dale.

She spoke softly. "I guess I wasn't totally honest with you. I didn't tell you I'm pregnant and have a husband in Vietnam."

It was the last she heard of Edward Albee.

When she learned a short time later from Peggy that Ted had been wounded in Vietnam, she desperately, almost compulsively wanted to rush to him, but knew that even if it were possible, she couldn't confront him with the additional problem of her pregnancy.

But she had to talk to Ruth in her pain and confusion. Slowly, nervously, she told the other woman the story of her relationship with Santek. Ruth was the ideal confidante.

"But you still love him. Maybe you shouldn't have given him an ultimatum. He would have accepted the child."

"I wanted him to want the child, not accidentally to discover it."

"My God, Angie, he's a priest. He took every chance out of love for you. Life doesn't happen all at once. You should go to him when he returns."

"I can't take the lies any more. I want friends and a family."

"He's your family. Few people ever find the kind of love you have."

"You have!"

"Not really. It looks that way. I fell in love before I met Hal and have never forgotten him. He was a wild, crazy artist, full of surprises, and loved me in a way Hal never could. I wanted roots and predictability. I got them. Despite the kids, I am usually bored out of my mind. I don't think you should let go of him. He's in your blood."

"He may not want me."

"Then you'll have to take another course. But dating is never easy. Men are going to want to take you to bed. You're not a teenager. You're a very attractive woman."

It felt better just to tell someone, even though it solved nothing. She admitted that she also feared the brutal pain of acutely missing him if she were again to involve herself and lose him. She had learned to live without him, and she had matured enough to know that she had to create a life for herself. And she could do it. Men liked her. So did women. She just wasn't ready for sexual intimacy until she freed herself from Santek's hold.

At Bradley, Angie took an extension class in the literature of war, reading Hemingway and Dos Passos and Mailer, and another course on the novels of John Steinbeck. The contact with new people and fresh thoughts was exhilarating, and her pregnancy protected her from any aggressive male overtures. She taught a course in conversational French at a junior college and also made a few girlfriends. Margo, a Home Ec teacher from Toronto, warm and laughing, was a fun companion for movies and plays. Angie joined a bridge club with a woman named Helene and went to a few basketball games with other young women, who were in love with the players and wanted to watch the magnificent bodies, even though they knew little about the game. These were warm, interesting companions for entertainment and shopping sprees and friendly lunches, if not for close intimacy. She had created a whole new support system and was finally prepared to begin dating seriously again after the baby came. Even the memory of Dale excited her on lonely nights, listening to music, and she wondered what kind of lover he might have been. Perhaps she would find out.

The hardest part of her life, of course, was not being able to share the excitement of her pregnancy with Ted, but as vulnerable as she felt, and as emotionally dependent, she continually reinforced her resolve not to contact him or to let Peggy and Beauvais know of her condition. They had asked her several times to visit them, but she had put them off until the weather was warmer and she was more secure in her new life. She had told them of her separation from Santek, without great elaboration, and felt the pregnancy would keep until she met them face to face.

"He didn't want me tied to him while he was in Vietnam. Besides, I've enjoyed the experience of being on my own and teaching some classes. I felt I lived too much in Ted's shadow."

"I think he's matured too," said Peggy. "I hope you don't grow past each other."

A sharp pain touched Angie's heart. "I hope so too." It had not really occurred to her before that Santek would change as well.

Yet she loved Peoria, because it was the city that framed her emergence as a person. Always before there had been her father, the Sister Directress, or Ted to lean on and please. She had never been on her own. Home was wherever Ted was, and real friendship with anyone else was an impossibility. Now it was exciting just to hear her phone ring, to plan an evening out to a good local theater or a weekend trip to Chicago to visit the art museum, the planetarium, or to shop along Michigan Avenue, or enjoy a meal at Berghoff's or the Pump Room.

And for the first time, she really liked her job. It was fascinating to learn about the heavy equipment business, and Hal Markeley explained every facet of the work. Gradually she began to talk easily with contractors, even had made suggestions to resolve their problems when rains were exceptionally heavy that spring. And she learned enough from listening to them to develop an advertising program that increased sales 12 percent.

"The radio ads are dynamite," Hal told her. "The humor is great. I guess you're due for another raise. We've landed business a hundred miles away and the drivers are crazy about the weather service we're providing."

Most of all, Angie learned to respect her own abilities and increasingly began to take responsibility for her own life and happiness. With the help of a local banker, she found a small house with an extra room for a live-in housekeeper and began the search for the right person to help her raise her child. A month ago she had not known a mortgage from a down payment.

Her realtor, Dave Phillips, a devout Catholic and a close friend of the Markeleys, had been particularly helpful in listening to her plans for the future. Tall and well-built, with light brown hair and an easy smile that reminded her of Santek, Dave attracted Angie, and she talked to him about everything from the convent to her childhood in Canada. One night after her French class he accepted her offer to stop by for dinner. It was exciting to prepare a meal for a man, and she dug out the silver candlesticks Santek had bought in Chicago for their anniversary. After a delicious meal of lamb chops, fresh spinach, and rice, they continued to drink wine and share the secrets of their personal lives. He had been divorced two years previously when his wife had admitted to an affair with one of his best friends.

"I guess I was too involved in my work and didn't pay enough attention to her. Next time my work won't become the whole of my existence. It gets too damn lonely!"

"You must have been hurt terribly," she said, caressing his hand.

"At first, but then I realized I wasn't in love with her, that I hadn't been for a long time. She was socially far more adept and sophisticated than I was, but we had different values. I dreamed of spending time in South America or Asia working with the poor and she wanted to have a mansion on the lake with servants and gala parties. When I found out that we couldn't have children, the bottom kind of fell out of our marriage. There wasn't anything to talk about. The only thing that excited her was making plans for our new house."

After a second bottle of wine, Angie was for the first time able to talk with a man about Santek. Dave, sensitive and caring, didn't push her sexually. When the tears began to flow, he walked across the room and held her tenderly on the couch and kissed her gently as she continued to talk and cry for almost an hour.

"I would like to be loved like that," he said quietly. "I always felt I was being used, that Margie had constructed a fantasy and I was the bank account that could bring it about. Everything excited her except me."

"Didn't you tell her?"

"At first, but after a while I just withdrew. It was a lonely, empty experience."

"I know that loneliness," she said softly.

There was an awkward pause until Dave leaned over and kissed her passionately on the mouth and pulled her body next to his own. She was startled at her excitement and returned his kiss hungrily. For weeks she had felt unattractive and bloated, tired of her wardrobe and weary of acute morning sickness. Dave's kiss made her feel alive and beautiful again, and she relaxed in his arms, continuing to kiss and caress.

"I liked you the minute I saw you."

"So did I." She laughed.

She did not want him to leave, and as soon as the door closed behind him and the warmth of a final kiss drifted away, she took off her clothes and lay naked on the bed, caressing her body as she tried to imagine making love with Dave. She grew excited and orgasmic, but then Dave's face and body were replaced by Santek's.

"Dear God, why can't I forget him?"

She heard his laugh, felt his touch, wanted his lips on her swollen breasts, wanted to surrender in his arms. She wondered if she should have told Dave Phillips that she was in love with a Catholic priest. The phone rang. It was Dave.

"I had a great evening." He paused awkwardly.

"So did I," she said. She wanted to tell him to return, but couldn't.

"I'd like to see you again. Soon. You're very special."

She didn't know what to say. "Thank you." She hated her shyness and confusion. "I . . . I miss you." She hoped he would suggest coming back. She wanted to give herself to him.

He paused nervously. "Let's get together real soon." He seemed as awkward as she was. Then he was gone.

She lay there thinking of Santek, wondering if she could ever really forget him and get on with her life. And knowing that she had to.

As soon as Santek returned to Travis, he called Beauvais immediately. Peggy answered.

"My God, are you okay?"

288

"Polacks are too tough to die. It's nothing. How's Angie?"

"We haven't talked for a while. We've been trying to get together. We're planning a picnic on Lake Michigan on Sunday. But, Ted, Gerry's mother just died!"

She was upset and tried to tell him everything at once.

"Ted, it's awful! The bishop said I had to leave or Gerry would have to give up his priesthood. He thinks we're sleeping together. We never have; we promised God we wouldn't. Gerry left a few hours ago for Ohio. He was so depressed. Just like before. God, Ted, I'm so worried! I don't know what to do. Can you come to the funeral? It's day after tomorrow."

"Damn, there's no way I can get out of here till the weekend. I'll fly to Chanute and drive over. Will he be back Saturday?"

Peggy promised to fix dinner on Saturday, her special pork roast and mashed potatoes.

"Gerry can't leave the priesthood. It's finally beginning to mean something. To leave would kill him. And we just can't walk away from each other. I don't know what to say. I'm almost as depressed as he is. He even took on Bishop Sullivan and fought back, but it didn't do any good. The bishop told him to get rid of me or give up the priesthood. There's nothing left for Gerry but to throw me out or to leave the priesthood."

"Don't get all torn up. I'll be there Saturday, and things won't look so bad. I've got some ideas." He paused. "Do you have Angie's number?"

"No," she lied. "She wouldn't give it to us." She had promised Angie not to reveal the number.

"If she calls, tell her I'll be in Farmington Saturday. I want to talk to her. Just talk, nothing else. And don't worry about Gerry. Let me figure it out."

He put down the phone and sat on the couch in the chaplain's office. He had to find Angie. There was so much to say. All the pain of her absence had returned as soon as he landed at Travis. He couldn't lose her. If only she would listen to him, believe him. A wave of fear engulfed him. What if she had found someone else? The thought paralyzed him! He couldn't be a priest without her. He couldn't be anything without her. Vietnam had taught him more about love than the combined experience of his whole life. He stretched out on the couch and finally, with the help of the codeine for his pain, was able to drift off to sleep thinking of Angie.

It was after midnight when Santek walked back to the BOQ. He would not be released until Friday at noon. Then he would have a week until reassignment at Chanute. He wanted to attend Mrs. Beauvais's funeral, but there was no way. Gerry must be in the pits. Sullivan had delivered the final blow and now, without his mother, and cut off from Peggy, there was nothing left.

Suddenly it occurred to him to talk to Sullivan. Before 'Nam it never would have been possible. Now it was the only course. No more games, no more little-boy docility. Sullivan liked him. He wasn't Irish, but Santek was his macho kind of man, tough and to the point, the best kind of priest. His fitness reports had been outstanding, and the heroic rumors from Vietnam were to the bishop just further proof of Ted's courage and dedication.

The next morning he called the chancery at Lansing. Father Kincaid answered.

"Can I see the bishop Saturday morning?"

"He's not in on Saturday, Father. Would Monday be okay?"

"Not really. Why don't you check with him? Tell him my schedule is a little confused with the back wound and all."

Father Kincaid disappeared and Santek held the line. He was surprised to hear Bishop Sullivan's voice.

"Father Santek, we're sorry about your wound, but we heard great things. How in the world are you?"

"At least my head is reasonably intact, Bishop. I thought that would be the first to go."

Sullivan laughed heartily. "How would nine o'clock Saturday morning be? Why don't you come to the house for breakfast? I'm anxious to hear about Vietnam."

Santek made his way to the base hospital to have his back checked out. Two of his fingers were still numb, but the pain was now almost tolerable. Save for ten extra pounds he felt almost like himself. He made arrangements for the flight to Chanute, to arrive late Friday. With a rented car he could easily make it to the bishop's house the following day. He felt his anger rise when he thought of Sullivan. Unwittingly, the bishop had succeeded in almost destroying Beauvais. This could be the final blow. Sullivan had to know what was at stake. They had never really had an honest conversation before, only an occasional chat when Ted was in the area.

There was something direct and honest about Sullivan that Ted liked. He had come from the same world as Santek, the uneasy peasant clinging to his faith against the assorted enemy. Ted knew the apparent arrogance was only fear, that beneath the red cassock and firm jaw was a warm, gentle heart. It was a new world for which Sullivan was ill prepared, a wholly different church since Vatican II. Santek was also very different since Vietnam and had no illusions about Beauvais's condition. He had seen too many strong men fall apart and drug themselves to death. Santek knew instinctively that Gerry needed his help. His own priesthood would never have existed without the generous, giving Beauvais. It was time to help his friend regardless of the cost, and this emergency took priority even over his own need to see Angie.

On Saturday morning, Santek passed the rows of red and yellow tulips and the towering lilacs and rang the bishop's doorbell. Sullivan answered himself, led him to his study, and brought black coffee. He was delighted to see Santek resplendent in his air force dress uniform.

"We have some homemade coffee cake, Father."

"I've been approached three times to play Santa Claus next December, Bishop."

Sullivan laughed, made small talk about painting the cathedral and the difficulty in finding a good mechanic for his Oldsmobile, then admitted his anxieties to Santek.

"We've lost a lot of priests and nuns, Father. It's frightening."

"I know, Bishop. Word gets around fast. And we've lost some damn good ones like Flaherty and Martin and Kowalsky. Now I'm really concerned about Beauvais. He's reached the end of his endurance. I think you've broken his spirit."

Sullivan was startled at Santek's awareness. He had planned to talk the priest into leaving the service and returning to the diocese to help fill the growing vacancies. Ted's words were an unexpected tack, and Sullivan could not immediately think of anything to say. Ted dived right in.

"He's a good priest, Bishop. He always has been. I don't want to lose him too."

Sullivan hesitated. He did not want to violate Beauvais's right to privacy and was not sure what Santek knew. Ted anticipated his dilemma.

"I know Peggy," he said quietly. "I have for some time. I think as much of her as I do of Gerry. She led him through hell."

"But the parishioners are concerned. I've had calls."

"Maybe the parishioners have to realize that this is a different Church from the one we grew up in, Bishop. When you have a Beauvais in your diocese, you don't cut him off. You can't afford to lose him, he has too damn much to offer, but you've cut him up pretty bad. You probably had your reasons, but I wish you had talked to me. I've known him for most of my adult life."

Sullivan looked gravely concerned. Tiny beads of sweat appeared on his forehead. He sipped his coffee noisily, the episcopal ring sparkling in the light reflected from the windows. He toyed with it and fumbled with his pectoral cross.

"I can't risk the scandal to the people, Father Ted. An attractive woman in the rectory is bad enough, but they are almost insepara-ble. The scandal could be disastrous." Sullivan sounded as if he were pleading.

"It's only a scandal if we make it one, Bishop. Vietnam is a scan-dal. The pope's refusal to change the Church's stand on birth control is a scandal. There are kids starving all over the world. South Amer-ica is a disgrace. Our position makes a mockery of God, and millions of intelligent, compassionate, good people are laughing at the Church's leadership or cursing it. We have to be concerned about the real issues that are destroying the Church. I've given more than twenty years of my life to the Catholic Church, and I'm not ready to hang on to the past and go down with the ship!"

Santek spoke with the great assurance born of his own most pain-ful experience. Bishop Sullivan found it difficult to argue and hedged anxiously.

"What about the faith of your parents and mine, Father? They hung on. The world has gone mad the last ten years."

"Our parents were immigrants, Bishop. The Church was their whole life. They hung on because they didn't know what the hell else to do. I don't think that the new spiritual maturity is madness. The strong, creative people will leave the Church. So will the strong and creative priests. The frightened will hang on. We'll have noth-ing but cowards and clerks. I see it every day in the service. The Church should be leading the protests against 'Nam and challenging the Pentagon. We need the Father Beauvaises who are concerned about real issues, such as prisoners and the aged and the poor!"

Bishop Sullivan felt his customary anger rise and fought to con-trol it. He would never get used to confrontation or a challenge to his authority. He wanted to shout that eternal life was a real issue, that sin and sex, free love and easy divorce, selfishness and greed and worship of the flesh were all real issues, but somehow the words caught in his throat.

"These are difficult times, Father," he said. "The new liturgy is an effort to communicate with the people. We've worked thousands of hours on the changes. I'm worn out!"

"It's only a different language, Bishop. The real changes are not taking place. That's why so many are leaving in disappointment. The Church is dying."

Bishop Sullivan struggled for his composure. "The Church can't die, Father! It has been challenged before. Christ has promised his assistance until the end of time. He doesn't expect us to compromise."

"I'm not talking about compromise, Bishop. I'm talking about contact with people. It's hard for all of us to change, but we're no longer confined to the experiences of our own town and neighborhood. Vietnam is real! Having too many kids is real! The loneliness of the priesthood and the isolation is real! I don't want Beauvais to be dismissed. He's too damned valuable to all of us. He took the assignment at Farmington like a man. If his kind are rejected, what's left?"

Santek paused and looked directly at Bishop Sullivan, studying him. The swagger and confidence were gone. Apparently Ted was reflecting the bishop's own secret doubts, and the fact that he was an infrequent visitor gave the bishop more freedom to listen. Santek had not intended to lay his own vocation on the line, but the conversation had moved him profoundly. He had never spoken to a bishop like this before. And Sullivan was listening. Ted paused before he spoke and reflected briefly on the consequences of what he was about to say. Then he looked directly at the Irishman and saw his lips tremble slightly. His eyes looked sad and frightened.

Santek's heart went out to him, but he went on. "If you can't find a place for Beauvais, Bishop, then I doubt there's a place for me in the Church either."

The bishop sat stiffly upright and started to protest, then moved his hand in the familiar wave of dismissal. Santek paused briefly to let his words sink in and continued very quietly.

"I lived with a woman for several years, Bishop. I couldn't have been a priest without her. I actually went into the service to get over the pain of her refusal to stay with me. I wanted to leave, to do anything but lose her. Finally I was able to convince her."

The bishop squinted as if he had entered a public women's room by mistake. "Why are you telling me this, Father? I can't give you my blessing—"

"I'm not asking your permission. No one is. Celibacy didn't help me be a better priest. I needed Angie to be a priest at all. I was just too damn immature to appreciate her. Vietnam and the Orient helped me grow up. But Beauvais has hung in with celibacy despite all that he's suffered. First he's accused of being a queer, then he's said to be giving scandal with a woman! I sneak around and no one asks me to leave. He lives honestly and he's destroyed. I'm not blaming you, Bishop. You're as trapped as anyone else. But we've got to open up or we're going to be talking to empty walls."

Sullivan looked crushed. He found it difficult to meet Santek's eyes. He had never imagined him living with a woman.

"What are your plans, Father?" He said it coldly.

"Angie left me, Bishop. *She* left me! I'm going to try to get her back. I still want to be a priest, I think I'm finally ready to be a good one, but I need Angie. Without her, I'm just another self-centered damn bachelor! But if Beauvais is thrown out, I go with him. If there's no place for him, there sure as hell is no place for me!"

Bishop Sullivan stared at Santek as if a favorite son had betrayed him. "I'm not free to make any decision I choose, Father. I'm bound by the same laws as you are." He thought of Santek in bed with a woman and banished the thought as quickly as it came. He had lived the celibate life to the letter. It was the only way he knew. "I will think about Beauvais, and I appreciate your priestly concern for him. I really can't approve of your . . . your woman. It's beyond my powers. But your . . . your honesty is moving."

"I understand where you're coming from, Bishop. I won't even ask you to close your eyes. But many priests and nuns are going to have intimate relationships." He chose not to use the word "sex," knowing what effect it would have. "The Church will force them to hide these relationships. But celibacy is not for everyone, Bishop. It just doesn't work for many of us. You and I know how many alcoholics there are in the priesthood. Just turning one's back on women isn't celibacy. It's isolation. We were never taught to be celibates."

Sullivan was finally exhausted. He stared out the window at the white and purple lilac bushes and the shapely mountain ash. He saw nothing. A fat robin announced the beginning of summer. "We'll talk again, Father," he said quietly. "I'm glad your wound is healing."

Then Santek was back in his Chevy and heading toward the highway to Farmington. He felt strangely relieved that he had

294

talked about Angie, as if a deeper wound had been healed. Somehow he was no longer able to lie. It was indeed a different world, a different Church, and a very different Santek. The only thing that was very much the same was his longing for Angie. He found himself praying that she would still love him.

Chapter 28

Gerry Beauvais had buried his mother at a Latin High Mass according to her request, even though his own heart was broken after his meeting with Bishop Sullivan. Her death was the final blow. After the obsequies and the gathering of the clan to drink away their sadness in a final toast to memories and childhood, Gerry wandered alone out into the backyard where it had all begun. Peggy, hiding nervously in the shadows, watched him make his way to the garage in the moonlight. She had kept out of his sight at the funeral and she hid from him now, fearing that in his shaken, depressed state he would order her from his life forever. He seemed to have no power over the decree of the bishop, which became under any circumstance the "will of God."

Her heart had ached for him at the funeral. He seemed so alone, cut off from everything that gave meaning to his life. His brother Louis clung to him for some respectability, but Louis had nothing to offer Gerry. No one did, not even Peggy. She wanted to reach out, to call to him, but she could not become his conscience. He had to make his own decision about the future.

She watched him wander in reverie about the yard and wondered if the bishop was not his domineering father all over again— and whether the battle he was afraid to fight as an adolescent had not returned in a strange new guise with Bishop Sullivan. Once and for all, he had to stand up and acknowledge his personal sovereignty. As he walked slowly toward the garage, she moved closer, stepping into shadows and behind bushes while he checked to see if the door was securely locked. He moved into the garage as if he had been drugged. When he emerged, she thought, she would approach him boldly, regardless of the consequences. She had to talk to him once more, to tell him that their life together could be honest and beautiful no matter what or where. She heard the engine start and wondered why he had not opened the garage door. She assumed he wanted to be by himself, away from the house and the family, to shed his private tears. Perhaps he had turned on the radio, but she could hear no music.

If he drove, she would follow him in her car. Perhaps he wanted to sip a drink somewhere in silent contemplation, or maybe he just needed the comfort of a moving car as he had in the past. She heard the engine continue to groan. The door remained closed.

Suddenly it dawned on her: Gerry was again attempting to take his own life! She rushed frantically to the door. It was securely bolted and did not budge. She pounded on it but there was no response. She thought of running to the house and rousing someone but at the same time feared an encounter with a half-drunk family member who would wonder at her presence in the middle of the night. She continued around the side of the garage, panting hysterically, looking for a window to break. She found a side door. It was locked. She pushed on it fiercely. It could not end this way. It was her life as well as his.

She threw all of her weight against the door and the simple hook began to give. She could already smell the exhaust fumes and pushed more violently. The door finally gave way, and she fell against the front of the car. She got up quickly and rushed to the driver's seat. Beauvais was slumped down, his eyes closed, the radio playing. She pulled open the door and grabbed him by the shoulder as a rush of air from the side door entered the garage. She screamed at him but he was unconscious.

"My God, Gerry, not this! We can do something!" Once again she saw the figure of the small, wounded boy, now dying. "You've got me, you're not alone! We can make it together. The cloud will go away; it did before! We can't run from life. The bishop doesn't know everything, he's as confused as you are!"

He did not respond. She dragged him from the car. His face was rosy and flushed, his lips were red, but he was still breathing, or at least she imagined he was. Yet his body was a dead weight. Peggy was terrified. She managed to open the main garage door and pull him out into the yard onto the grass. He did not move. The three-quarter moon filled the yard with an eerie light which was no longer beautiful because of the pallor of death it cast over everything. Even the once-friendly crickets sounded ominous. A nighthawk screamed and startled her.

"We're going to fight!" she screamed. She shook him fiercely. "The Church needs us. One frightened bishop is not going to get rid of us. You've got to fight, you've got to want to live! I can't do it for you any more. You've got to help me!"

She pushed on his chest, and he fell over on his side and began throwing up and gasping for air.

"I can't take it any more. I just can't, Peggy," Gerry said. His voice was rasping and barely audible. "My head is splitting. My God, my head!"

"Breathe, damn it, breathe, we've come too far to quit," she said, as she pushed at his chest.

"The dark cloud came back. I can't go through it again. I just can't."

"You can and you will, but you've got to want to, Gerry! I can't live with you knowing that every time I turn my back in some crisis you are going to give up. You've got to get mad! The bishop calls you a 'queer' and you humbly bow your head! Then he kicks you out of the cathedral and takes away your music and you accept it as God's will. You're not some medieval monk, you're Gerry Beauvais, a brilliant, dedicated, gifted priest! Now the bishop says you're sleeping with me. You fight him and lose! He wins and you die! No way! It's not going to happen!" Peggy was exhausted. The sweat poured from her body as she hovered over him like a warrior.

"I don't want to die, I just can't take the pain," he answered.

"You've got me! We've almost won!"

If Bishop Sullivan doesn't want us, she thought, there are plenty of places that do. We can go to Appalachia and work among the poor. We can start our own church. We can do anything we want, but he's got to believe that Farmington isn't the world and Bishop Sullivan isn't God. He should have fought this fight years ago. No wonder he's depressed. His anger is strangling him. He's been insulted, put down, humiliated, judged, and attacked and he doesn't strike back.

She continued consoling him and pressing on his chest. "Giving up isn't real Christianity! That's cowardice! If we don't fight, the Church will fall apart! Everyone walks away, or runs away, and a few out-of-touch old men tell us what is the will of God. We'll make it," she said softly. "Together!"

"Where can we go?" He rubbed his head. The pain was excruciating.

"Right now we'll get you something for that headache. Then we can go right back to Farmington. If he wants us out, let him throw us out."

She lifted him cautiously to his feet. He was still dizzy and almost fell. She walked him slowly around the yard until he regained his balance. The flush began to leave his face as the carbon monoxide was dispelled from his blood.

"My car is parked out in front. Santek's coming on Saturday, so it's time for us to leave."

"You won't tell him what happened . . . ?"

"There's no need to tell him anything except that we're going to do battle. Together!" She embraced and kissed him warmly. "My God, I thought you were gone!" She let her tears come. "You can't do this to me or to yourself. Why don't you go in and get your bag. If you're not out in five minutes, I'm coming in after you." She smiled broadly, then dropped down on the grass, exhausted.

Ten minutes later they were on the road to Farmington. He took three aspirin and his headache began to subside.

"I still feel dizzy," he said. "My God, I almost died."

"Not a chance," said Peggy. "We've got a whole life to live. You just can't roll over and play dead any more. The priesthood isn't the only life. There are a thousand ways for us to go!"

"You're something."

"I've been trying to tell you that."

Back in Farmington, Beauvais and Peggy talked Friday night until after two, resolving nothing.

"Sullivan's mind is made up. I'll have to leave the priesthood."

"Do you want to leave?"

"You know I don't, but I don't see any alternative."

"Then why don't you fight? At some point, you have to fight! You're the one who told me that Vatican Two gave currency to the personal conscience! The bishop can't control you."

Beauvais got angry. "But he doesn't have to talk to us. He still runs the institution, and the institution can fire me."

"We'll make him talk to us! The same way you should have made your father talk to you. You've got to break the chain."

"You sound like my psychiatrist. All right, let's try. I've already been condemned. It can't get any worse. The people are hiding behind the bishop with secret letters. Nothing's in the open. They don't confront me. They went to the bishop like grade-school kids. Damn it, we'll fight!" He smiled softly. "I never thought it would come to this. I feel like I'm a man again. My God, the Church took that away from me."

"I think you let them take it away. It just won't happen any more. We were all victims of authority and guilt and fear. I thought I had to stay in a marriage that included a beating every two or three days. We're all the same. Nobody challenges anyone. The nuns are little girls, the priests little boys, and the people are like sheep. When it gets too bad, they all abandon the Church and break their hearts. Most ex-priests and nuns will be working in the welfare office or selling shoes or marrying badly. All the training and good-will lost, just because no one fights! We talk about the Church belonging to the people, and it's a joke. It belongs to the pope and the bishops. We kiss their rings and grin like children. You're the one who's been telling me that it has to change. Well, let's change it!"

"Maybe we can't."

"And maybe we can."

Then they were silent, lost in Beethoven and their own thoughts until they fell asleep, cuddled on the floor. It was dawn when they awoke. Peggy kissed him and went into the kitchen to make coffee. Beauvais walked out on the front porch and watched the sun rise in full splendor. For the first time in his life, he felt ready to meet the Eve of Pentecost. And ready to fight. It was also the first morning in weeks he had not felt the least fear of depression lurking around the corner. He was finally alive!

Chapter 29

It was after noon on Saturday when Santek arrived in full dress uniform. He embraced first Beauvais and then Peggy.

"I'm really sorry I couldn't make the funeral. I'm on my way to reassignment in Chanute, and there were a dozen things to do. I said Mass for your mother Friday morning."

Beauvais nodded appreciation. Then the talk turned to Bishop Sullivan, and Santek told them about his visit.

"It sounds like he hasn't made up his mind," said Peggy eagerly. "We planned to see him."

"I'm not sure I'd do anything," said Santek. "Let him make the next move."

"But I've been ordered out."

"Hell, he's not going to shoot you down. Put yourself in his place. Maybe he won't do anything."

"I don't want to live with the uncertainty and wondering who it is in the parish that's making a report."

Santek shook his head. "Why make a federal case out of it? I think the bishop will be some time making up his mind."

Beauvais was not convinced. There was a long silence.

Finally Santek broke it. "I'd like to get hold of Angie."

"I promised her I wouldn't give you her number."

"I figured that. Why don't you call her and ask her if she'll talk to me? Or maybe we could meet tomorrow for a picnic."

Beauvais made the phone call after dinner, before the evening confessions. A beaming Angie was just leaving the house to have dinner with Dave Phillips, who had brought roses and perfume.

Pregnant or not, she had made up her mind to enjoy his warm, caressing love without protest. She felt aroused just thinking about how long it had been since she let go and how much his gentle sensual ways attracted her. Besides, he was beautiful to look at.

"Ted is here and wants to talk," Beauvais said quietly.

Angie was suddenly completely flustered. "I . . . I can't talk now. I . . . I have a date. How . . . how is he?"

"He looks great. Older, more mature, but still the same Ted."

"I don't know what to say. I—"

"Can you meet us at Grand Haven State Park tomorrow afternoon? We'll be there around two thirty."

Angie hesitated. "I don't know if I want . . . I think I have plans. . . . Well, I'll try to be there at two thirty. I can't say for sure."

She paused again, then hung up the phone.

Beauvais conveyed the message as gently as he could.

"Didn't she want to talk?" Ted asked.

"She was on her way out the door."

"Did she say where she was going?"

Beauvais shook his head. Santek looked frightened.

"Maybe it's all over. I'm not sure I could handle that. She's probably dating." The thought of Angie with another man crushed him. "I know I can't handle that. God damn everything!"

Peggy tried to soften the blow. "I don't think she can get over you so easily."

Santek, unlike his usual practice, retired early. "What time are the Masses?" he asked sadly on his way to bed.

"Eight and ten. Why don't you sleep in? There's not too big a crowd at eight, but ten is packed and we have a choir."

"I'll see you at the ten."

"I'll have coffee ready," Peggy said.

Santek slipped away.

"He looks really upset," said Beauvais. "It's been a long time since I've seen him like that."

"I don't blame him. It's been over six months since he's seen Angie. He doesn't know what to expect. She may well be involved with someone else. She's a beautiful woman, and men are going to pursue her."

"I hope she comes tomorrow, at least to see him. He seems different. More mature, somehow."

302

"I guess Vietnam has a way of doing that. How did Angie sound?"

"She was going out on a date, but she was hard to figure on the phone. Maybe she was holding back tears, I couldn't tell. Or maybe the guy was right there next to her. I think she still loves Ted, but she's tired of following him around. He said she wants kids. Do you ever feel that way?"

"Sure, but I think we'll have family enough. Does our celibacy still make sense to you?"

"A whole lot of sense, but I don't know how I'll feel if I have to leave the priesthood. I wonder if another meeting with Sullivan would accomplish anything. Ted said he really listened."

Peggy slipped off her shoes, then Beauvais's. She began massaging his feet.

"God, I'm glad you're alive. We have so much to live for."

He nodded. "Tomorrow is the anniversary of my celibacy. Ted and I were ordained to the subdiaconate on Pentecost Sunday fifteen years ago. Somehow it always seems like a very special day."

"What are you going to preach about. Celibacy?"

They both laughed. "I'm not sure I would know what to say."

She leaned over and kissed him gently, then sat at the base of his chair, her arm draped over his knee.

Meanwhile Santek, in his shorts, lay on the bedspread, smoking a fourth cigarette. He could think of nothing but Angie, wondering how she had changed. He wished she were lying next to him. It seemed like forever since they had been together. He wondered if he could still be a priest without her, then wondered if there would be any kind of life without her. He feared there could be no other woman and he might become just another lonely chaplain, drinking away his free time and waiting for retirement. Nothing excited him except Angie. There was no place he wanted to go without her, no enthusiasm for Europe or the Caribbean, Hawaii, even Thailand. He wanted to share his life, to reveal his deepest thoughts, finally to let go, to have someone he could love and count on. He had changed profoundly. He was a different man. He only prayed that Angie would recognize it. For all he knew she might be in bed with another man at that very moment. He remembered her sounds of love, her explosive orgasms, recalled her odor and the shape and texture of her breasts.

303

"Damn it! I've got to stop thinking about her!"

He butted his cigarette and tried to sleep.

While Santek lay brooding in bed, Angie was toying with her dessert at the elegant La Table Française. It had been a quiet meal because she could not think of anything except Santek. She remembered the excitement of New Orleans, the very first time they had made love, his gentleness and patience and wild excitement. She remembered, too, Ted's futile attempts to get a job he liked and his new enthusiasm for the priesthood when they returned. She had almost forgotten Dave. He misunderstood her silence.

"Is your pregnancy depressing you? Or was it that phone call?"

"No, I can hardly wait to have the baby." She paused. "It was Ted who called. He wants me to see him tomorrow."

"Are you going to?"

"I'm not sure yet."

Dave grew suddenly angry. "You know damn well you're going to see him. I suppose I should be happy for you, but I'm not. I really wish he would get lost. I'm falling in love with you, but I can't fight some damn fantasy priest. Besides, this could just mean more confusion and lying and hiding out. You deserve more than that, Angie. You deserve it all! Are you looking forward to seeing him?"

"Yes," she said slowly, her eyes revealing everything. "But I really don't know what to expect. My pregnancy could terrify him. Or maybe what I felt is gone. I've grown up a lot. I wonder if he has." She saw Dave flinch. "I'm afraid I'm not much fun tonight. I'm sorry."

Dave looked away and signaled for the check. Angie reached out and touched his hand gently. "Maybe I'll come back crying on your doorstep."

"And maybe I'll be there," he said quietly.

"Are you angry with me?"

"I think I'm angry at Santek. Or jealous. Or whatever. I just wish you hated him for all he's done."

"He's a hard man to stay angry at. It hasn't been easy for him, either. There was a whole lot I didn't understand. I'll know when I see him. It won't take very long."

"That's what I'm afraid of."

The eight o'clock Mass in Farmington was sparsely attended during the late spring. Most of the farmers preferred to do their chores

304

first and then attend Mass and spend the rest of the day eating and relaxing. The early Mass was a convenience for the older parishioners.

Beauvais, beaming in the red gothic vestments, talked about spring as a symbol of Pentecost.

"God speaks to us in countless ways, in a variety of tongues— through our family and friends, through the birds and flowers and budding trees. He even speaks through our suffering. Only God can make sense of pain through the Spirit of Love he sends us today. If God doesn't speak it's probably because we don't find a quiet time to listen."

He looked around at the attentive faces and found himself wondering who had reported him to the bishop. Mary Thelen had raised twelve children, losing one in a car accident, two to cancer, and a son in Vietnam. Her husband had some variety of agoraphobia and had not been able to leave the house for years. She had reason to complain about a priest who had an attractive housekeeper, but he remembered bringing her husband Communion. Her eyes had sparkled their gratitude as she served Beauvais fresh cinnamon rolls and strong coffee. He had always been there when she needed him. So had Peggy. He doubted that Mary would have called the chancery office.

It could have been Helen Rademacher, an unmarried nurse, overweight and lonely and used by more than one man. He recalled her breakdown and the long talks he had with her in the hospital when she felt God had deserted her. She had given up, until Beauvais's patient counseling and encouragement had helped her to find her way again. She had known Peggy for years. Maybe she felt that she would have been a better housekeeper to attend to Beauvais's needs. She had even told him that she was available should anything happen to Peggy.

It was impossible to decide. He knew his people too well, and their love and appreciation seemed too apparent. Maybe no one had called the bishop. Maybe Sullivan had created the problem himself. It was hard to see the Church as a loving community when the bishop and the chancery were trapped in their legalistic traditions. Still, there was so much goodwill, so much dedication and love among so many. It was painful to belong to a Church that could not find a place for all its members. If Santek and Beauvais could not be priests, who could? He thought of their seminary days and early

305

priesthood, of Ted's work among the blacks and the poor, of his confusion over Angie and the pointless struggles with celibacy.

Beauvais gave his final blessing to his people. He loved them and found it impossible to believe that they could betray him—not for thirty pieces of silver, but out of resentment for the way they had been treated in an infallible, unyielding Church. He would not leave his post without a struggle.

When he returned to the rectory, Santek was already sipping coffee at the dining room table and perusing the sports pages of the Detroit *Free Press*.

"It looks like the Tigers are off to another great year," he said cynically. "Christ, why don't they spend some money?"

Beauvais grinned warmly. "Maybe I could become a baseball manager." It was a great feeling to have Santek there, with his anger and sense of humor restored. The thought of seeing Angie had given him new life.

Peggy walked in from the kitchen with more coffee and joined them at the table. She looked spectacular in a red linen Pentecost suit. Santek glanced up from the paper.

"Did you hear about the three couples who wanted to get back in the Church?"

Beauvais and Peggy were laughing already.

"Well, the bishop told them they had to abstain from sex for ninety days if they were to atone for their neglect. After the time was up, the first couple came to the chancery and announced that, despite a couple of wild temptations after an Elks picnic, they had remained celibate. The second couple said that they had all they could do to keep from screwing on the chancery porch, but they had made it. The bishop smiled and welcomed them back to the Church. The third couple came in a little late, looking sheepish. They admitted to the bishop that that very same day she had leaned over for a can of peaches and he had nailed her.

"'You'll have to leave,' the bishop said sadly.

"'Funny,' said the husband, 'they told us the same thing at the Safeway store.'"

Beauvais choked on his coffee and roared as he had in the seminary. Peggy could not stop laughing. It was like old times. Before Santek could start another story, Beauvais looked at his watch and took his coffee into his study, explaining that he had to get a few thoughts together.

"Maybe you should let Ted preach and demand an entertainment tax," Peggy called after him. She looked at Santek. "Nervous?"

"Christ, yes! I just wish it were two thirty."

"It won't be long. I'll be praying for you."

The Church was already crowded when Peggy and Major Santek found a pew in the middle of the congregation. There was a hum of fans and the smell of starch and Ivory soap. He glanced around at the ruddy faces and thick tanned hands of the men who sat up straight and devout, waiting for the Mass to begin. The women, glancing at errant children with stony stares, looked still and motherly in their assorted hats and plain hairstyles. To Santek it seemed a church of twenty years ago, with lines of children and silent communication with God.

The congregation roared to their feet when Beauvais appeared in his splendid red vestments to celebrate Pentecost and the more than adequate choir burst into "Come Holy Ghost, creator blest, and in our hearts take up thy rest." The word "ghost," now obsolete, seemed refreshing in a Church that had altered an ancient, comfortable language. Santek, of all people, still missed the Latin. He was aware that his air force uniform attracted a variety of stares. There were not many air force majors who had attended St. Mary's of Farmington. Peggy was lost in her tattered missal, obviously a battered survivor from childhood and hopelessly out of date. The rustle of the newer leaflets and the muffled response in English to the prayers seemed self-conscious and somehow strange in this seventy-five-year-old parish where people were baptized and buried, married and confirmed in warm and familiar surroundings. A new family was rare, and when someone moved out everyone in the parish was aware of it. It was a strange experience for Ted to be part of a Catholic congregation again. He felt restless and estranged and could understand why Catholic people were fond of a priest like Beauvais who did not dawdle his way through the Mass.

Gerry looked like a priest, the strong shoulders and thinning hair, the deep-set dark eyes and gentle mien, the powerful voice and perfect inflection. The people rose for the Gospel, heard the apostles communicate in a variety of languages and saw the fiery tongues resting over their heads. Beauvais kissed the page and turned to address his people. He made a few announcements about parish activities, then someone turned off the fans and he stood silently for a few brief moments, assessing his congregation. He smiled as he saw Peggy, wearing her red pillbox hat, shoulder to shoulder with his dearest male friend, looking very much like the soldier he could never be. Beauvais started off slowly, choosing his words carefully.

"Pentecost is really the birthday of the Church, the descent of the Holy Spirit upon the apostles and the people to establish contact with God. It was the fulfillment of Christ's promise that he would not leave his friends as 'orphans' and a guarantee that every Christian would have a unique opportunity for contact with a personal, loving God through the Spirit, who would be a private counselor to all of us, because God does not relate as the IRS or traffic court."

There were broad smiles everywhere.

"No one relates to God in the same way. Everyone has a personal Spirit guiding him or her to understand what God wants done in our daily life. It was the Spirit who led you to your family, the same Spirit who led me to the priesthood, and the very same Spirit who has spoken to the Church to change and grow to keep up with the needs of men and women and children today. 'The Spirit breathes where he will.'

"A few days ago, in fact on the very day my mother died—and I do appreciate the many prayers and Mass cards and expressions of sympathy I received—on that very day, I had a conversation with the bishop of our diocese."

Peggy looked as if she might faint and Santek turned pale. Beauvais continued, almost jubilantly.

"The bishop said that he had heard complaints from our parish that my relationship with Peggy Santini was a source of scandal to some of you."

Every sniffle and cough suddenly stopped. There had never been such a silence in St. Mary's Church. Peggy felt her face burn and her hands sweat. Her heart beat as if it were pounding its way out of her chest. Santek found it difficult to look at Beauvais and gently touched Peggy's hand. A bead of sweat appeared above his lips. Beauvais continued as if some final bond had been broken. He was all but smiling, and his voice was full and softly resonant.

"The bishop said I was to give up my priesthood if Peggy Santini and I were to continue our relationship."

He paused for several seconds. They seemed like a minute.

"You are well aware that Peggy cared for me during my entire illness. It took great courage and love. You see, it was not my back that gave out but my mind and emotions. I sank into a deep depression and did not want to live. I actually wanted to end my life. It was she who fought with me to face the greatest struggle of my life. Otherwise I wouldn't be here today. I grew to love her more than I thought possible, and that made it difficult for me because my priesthood, and Peggy's own religious faith, forbade the intimacy that men and women who are in love long to share. But our religious faith did not protect us from our feelings. The priesthood is no protection from human desires, and my sexuality is no different from yours."

The church grew even more hushed, and several parishioners blushed at the word "sexuality" and wondered about the children present. Beauvais continued.

"And yet we decided, even as our love continued to grow, to remain celibate. So one night at midnight before Mary's altar in this Church we renewed our promise to God to dedicate ourselves in celibacy to the service of the people of this parish. It was our gift to you.

"We would not know the physical intimacy of marriage, and you would be our only family. Even though celibacy is confusing, and certainly not for everyone, we believed timidly that our Holy Spirit was asking this of us. Both of us are happy in our life of religious service and our commitment to each other. I would like to remain here as your priest, but I will not live my life without Peggy. After considerable prayer and reflection, I thought I would share with you our struggle and let your Holy Spirit speak to you as well.

"I believe that the Church is somehow dying because it cannot accept new ways. I sincerely believe that there would be many more priests and nuns if we accepted marriage as a possibility for them and created new kinds of religious service. Sometimes we forget that the apostles were married, that priests today in the Eastern Catholic Church are married, and that celibacy was a monastic way of life that somehow became imposed on all priests. It could be changed with one stroke of the papal pen. I think that unless it is changed, the Church will increasingly be deprived of adequate leadership— male and female."

Santek's color was beginning to return and he could now look at Beauvais. Peggy felt a deep personal relief and betrayed on her face the tremendous pride she felt in Beauvais's honesty and courage.

"St. Mary's parish is our personal religious home, and the Spirit of Pentecost will speak here too if we permit. If you do not want Peggy and me to remain here, that is up to you and our bishop. We want to stay, but we do not want to live with rumors and suspicions within our own family. I am not certain the bishop will permit us to remain, but I would like him to know, and to know myself, how *you* feel. Your opinion is the voice of the Spirit in our midst. If you trust us and want us to remain here, we want to hear about it. Or even if you want us to leave. It is up to you. Let the Spirit speak!"

Beauvais stood facing the congregation, his hands clasped on his chest, his eyes smiling and without fear. There was a prolonged silence. Beauvais did not move. Peggy looked down at her purse and Santek sat erect, staring straight ahead. Gradually there was some mumbling in the congregation and Marlowe Gintzler, a vice-principal at the public high school, stood up. She had been divorced for twenty years, was nearing sixty, and had raised her three children by herself. Her face was pinched, narrow, and angular under a large straw bonnet, and her thin hands trembled. The whole parish knew that she had wanted to marry again eight or nine years before and had been turned down by the chancery office. She had done considerable drinking in the ensuing years and had taken a month-long pledge from Beauvais more than once. As she cleared her throat, he expected the worst.

"I suppose I have every reason to be bitter about anyone receiving liberties in the Church. You all know about me. Sometimes I think my own life has been ruined by laws that never seemed human, let alone Christian. But that's another story. Father Beauvais has been a good and devoted priest. I understand his need and admire his courage. I find it hard to unlearn all that I have been taught, but I wonder if the bishop has had enough practical experience to know how life is really lived in the trenches."

She was out of breath. It was remarkable boldness in a traditional congregation of largely Germanic people who loved their *gemütlichkeit* but found it hard to express their feelings. Personal privacy was an unwritten code etched in granite.

There was a prolonged tense silence after Marlowe spoke. The building seemed ready to explode. A baby cried briefly, until a calloused thumb inserted gently as a pacifier quieted him. Santek felt the urge to say something as all of his own frustration gathered in his throat. After a long minute or two of silence without Beauvais's moving a muscle, Jack Zerfas, the head usher, a thin sinewy man of fifty with dark curly hair and a sun-wrinkled face, walked from the back of the church to the middle aisle and stood next to his seated wife and children. His voice had a pleasant rasp and the low-German inflection.

"Father, I want you to stay. So does my whole family. We've heard the rumors and gossip, and in all honesty even we've talked about Peggy Santini living in the rectory and working so close to you. In my heart I don't think any parish could have better leadership or more loving. Maybe together you two can continue to help us become the kind of people Christ wanted us to be. My Spirit says, 'Stick around, Father!'"

It was just enough of a rousing speech to relieve the impossible pressure that had built up in the pews. There was an awkward moment of silence, then a burst of applause never heard in St. Mary's Church before. The applause grew stronger until everyone in church, including Santek and Peggy, were clapping their hands. The younger children, unaware of exactly what was happening, were delighted with the most exciting moment they had ever known in church. The applause continued for five minutes. Santek timed it.

When the clapping finally quieted, Dick Schaeffer, president of the men's club, stood up, smiling widely. Another farmer with ruddy face and bushy brown hair, he spoke in a booming voice that demanded attention.

"I move we send a delegation to the bishop from the men's club and altar society. Perhaps we can stay after Mass and hold a meeting over coffee and strudel. All in favor say Aye."

An unbelievable roar went up from the congregation, and Bart Stovall, the choir director, started singing "Come, Holy Ghost." The whole congregation stood and bellowed the hymn as never before. Peggy was crying. Santek had his arm around her, and Beauvais stood smiling and singing in the pulpit. Then he returned to the altar and finished the Pentecostal Mass. Never in his whole life had he so felt the presence of God.

After the Mass, several parishioners embraced Peggy warmly in the vestibule, and Marlowe Gintzler gave her a warm kiss. When Beauvais had unvested and completed his prayers of thanksgiving, he walked into the parish hall to another burst of applause. Someone brought him coffee; someone else handed him a piece of strudel. He sat down with Peggy and Santek. It seemed that the whole congregation had remained for the celebration. It was like a family reunion, and a visitor who happened in would have thought the parish had gone as mad as Pentecost.

Meanwhile, the delegation was formed. Four men and two women were selected by the parishioners to visit the bishop early in the week if he was available. Marlowe Gintzler was one of the delegates.

"I haven't been so happy since you tight-assed Teutons voted us a decent teachers' retirement program," she said.

They all roared and Jack Zerfas sent his oldest boy out for beer before the crowd broke up. It was that kind of a day, and only with great reluctance did Beauvais beg off from an all-day celebration.

Santek, thrilled by the response of the parishioners, had briefly forgotten about Angie. By the time he returned with Beauvais and Peggy to the rectory, it was already time to leave. They quickly changed their clothes, Peggy filled a cooler and picnic basket, and they were off to Lake Michigan, still bursting with excitement.

"I've never seen anything like it," said Santek. "Next time warn me, you clown."

Peggy just kept repeating, "I can't believe it."

And Beauvais could not stop smiling. "If we would only let the people back in the Church."

"I wonder if the bishop will hear them," asked Peggy.

"He'll hear them," said Santek. "He damn well better or he's going to lose a lot of people. Including me!"

Chapter 30

They arrived at Grand Haven almost on time. The Lake Michigan state park with its pure white dunes was already crowded with families celebrating the first warm weekend of the year. Santek spotted a table near the entrance to the park from where they could be certain of seeing Angie's arrival. They unloaded their basket. Peggy started making ham and roast pork sandwiches, and Beauvais opened two Stroh's beers and a bottle of Chablis. Ted was a nervous wreck, and glancing at the entrance to the park every ten seconds. It was after three o'clock when Angie appeared, just as Santek had finally convinced himself that she wasn't coming.

"Life goes on," he had said, but the ache around his heart and the pressure in his cheeks told him he was lying.

At first he didn't recognize her. Her hair was cut short, her face was fuller than when he last saw her, and she was dressed uncharacteristically in jeans and a loose light-brown shirt. He moved toward her cautiously with a colorful bouquet of tulips held like a football and was within ten feet before it dawned on him that she was pregnant. Peggy had noticed immediately and exclaimed to Beauvais, but Santek had already moved out to meet her. He stood there speechless, awkwardly holding the tulips. All his well-prepared words froze on his tongue. Finally he shyly handed her the tulips and took her beach bag and a bottle of his favorite Chateauneuf du Pape, still standing and gazing lovingly into her eyes. He could not say anything but her name. When at last he nervously reached out to hold her, she fell into his arms and began to cry for joy. He held her for several minutes, whispering her name and telling her over and over again how much he loved her, how he had missed her. She could not say anything except his name and kissed his fingers as if they were the most precious gift in the world. Then he grinned his widest grin through moist eyes.

"Well, I suppose we should think about giving our little bastard a name!"

Their combined laughter broke the tension and they moved toward the picnic table. Peggy rushed out to embrace her, crying as joyously as Angie.

"Why didn't you tell me? Oh, Angie, you look wonderful!"

Beauvais stood by, stroking her hair, almost overwhelmed by the unending excitement of the day. Santek could only hold her hand, while Beauvais filled four wineglasses and raised his ceremoniously as the others lifted theirs.

"To celibacy!" he said. Again they all dissolved in laughter and began hugging each other in succession and drinking the chilled wine. Peggy passed out sandwiches but nobody could eat. Beauvais poured more wine, but Angie and Santek just stared at each other and couldn't say a word.

Gradually, with time and wine, Ted began to recover and loudly toasted his new baby to everyone in sight until half of the park was aware that he would soon be a father. From then on it was the same old Santek.

"Did you hear that Hugh Hefner and Pope Paul died the same day? Well, Hefner went to heaven and the pope went to hell through some mix-up of files. Finally they got it straightened out and they passed in open elevators about halfway between heaven and hell, the pope saying his rosary and Hefner nursing a scotch and leafing through a final copy of *Playboy* magazine.

"'I'm glad they got things worked out,' Hefner said with a warm smile.

"'You're glad!' said the pope. 'I've been waiting all my life to see the Blessed Virgin Mary.'

"Hefner looked sheepishly up over the centerfold, took a large swallow of scotch, and said, 'Sorry about that. You missed by about fifteen minutes.'"

Santek was back. And so was Angie. To stay.

The night before the parish delegation was to meet with the bishop, Santek and Angie knelt before the same altar where Beauvais and Peggy had taken their vows of celibacy. Angie wore a white tulle dress designed by "Peggy of Paris" and carried a bouquet of white lilacs picked by Santek and Beauvais from the parish yard. The altar was adorned with the familiar candelabra and with flaming tulips and purple irises from the rectory garden. Santek was again in dress uniform, and Peggy stood by as a rapt attendant. The ceremony was the traditional Catholic one requested by Santek and Angie.

They took each other in the presence of God and their dearest friends "for better or worse, for richer or poorer, in sickness and in health, until death do us part." Finally, Angie had her ring and her husband, and in two more months she would have their baby. The ceremony was concluded at midnight and Beauvais insisted on preparing the "wedding breakfast" with kielbasa and eggs for the groom, lamb chops and eggs for the bride, and champagne for everyone. He also recited the toast.

"To the only Polish joke I love and his beautiful bride."

Santek lifted his glass and could not be restrained. "I haven't been the greatest priest, but I'll be one hell of a father!"

"And husband," warned Angie.

Peggy threw cooked rice and it was official. It was almost four in the morning when Santek took his wife to bed. He told her how beautiful she was and how much he had missed her, until she fell asleep in his arms. His last words before she went to sleep were total Santek. He rubbed her belly tenderly and said, "If it's a girl, I hope to hell this isn't bigamy."

Then he quietly thanked his God and pledged the best priesthood in the world.

"They're gonna think Your Boy's back on earth."

And he fell asleep.

It was almost noon the next day when they awakened. Angie borrowed a robe of Peggy's and the "newlyweds" joined the others for blueberry muffins, coffee, and more champagne. Beauvais kept watching the driveway, waiting for word from the parish delegation. It was almost one thirty when Jack Zerfas drove up and joined the group at the dining room table. Beauvais introduced him to Santek and Angie, and Jack seemed not at all curious about their relationship. It didn't seem to matter.

"I can't believe the meeting," said Jack. "The bishop listened to everything we had to say. In fact, he insisted that each of us talk and explain to him our feelings about the matter. It was almost like he wasn't sure of himself. It gave me a feeling I've never had as a Catholic."

"Did he make a decision?" asked Beauvais.

"Not a final one, but he saw no reason to change anything. He said something about the 'appearance of evil,' and Marlowe said that people had always misinterpreted the lives of priests and nuns. 'Some don't really believe that celibacy is possible or sensible for anyone. We can't be concerned with narrow minds.'

"She told him she had been celibate for years, 'not by choice but by circumstances,' and she knew that people had gossiped about her. If she had a woman friend, they wondered, and if a male friend, they were sure. She was dynamite! The bishop just said he would like to take things one step at a time. If there were complaints from people, he said he would deal with them, but meanwhile he saw no need to lose another priest over vague gossip."

"I can't thank you enough, Jack," said Beauvais.

"Don't thank me, Father. You started the ball rolling. I really think we have the beginning of a parish."

Two hours after the meeting, Bishop Michael Sullivan still sat reflectively in his office with Monsignor Kelley and his young secretary, Father Kincaid.

"Maybe we need to be challenged. We could have destroyed Beauvais and Mrs. Santini."

"I doubt that Rome would be as understanding, your excellency," said Kelley crisply.

"I'm not sure that's important. Perhaps Rome does not understand the American Church. We make overtures to the Protestants and Orthodox, even the Communists, and we ignore our own." He laughed. "When I was growing up, it always seemed that the neighbor kids were better understood than we were." He looked reflective, almost sad. "Beauvais has suffered a great deal. I wonder how he has managed to stand it."

Kincaid nodded sympathetically.

"You were only respecting the code, Bishop. There was no malice in your actions," said Monsignor Kelley.

"I appreciate your opinion, Monsignor, but I think it's time we stop hiding behind the Code of Canon Law. Sometimes I think I have been a very docile and frightened bishop. I have not stopped thinking about Beauvais since I last talked to him. And Santek's words had a marked effect. These are strong men who have 'borne the heat of the day.' I haven't listened very well. There must be something wrong when good, dedicated men and women walk away. We can't continue to judge their morality and quote canon law. It may well be obsolete. We've consulted Rome too often. It's time we consulted ourselves and the people and took responsibility for our own diocese."

Father Kincaid nodded hasty approval. So did Monsignor Kelley.

Santek and Angie left for Chanute the following day to begin life again. It was a warm farewell of friends who promised each other monthly contact. During a coffee break at a truck stop outside of Chicago, Angie and Santek planned the logistics of her return from Peoria to Champaign-Urbana, and then she looked at him.

"Do you ever wish that we were celibate like Peggy and Beauvais?"

He laughed briefly, then his eyes grew intense and reflective. He lit a cigarette and drew on it deeply.

"I'm not a celibate. I never was."

"Did you ever wish you weren't a priest?"

"Never," he said firmly. "I doubt you'd ever have fallen in love with me if I weren't a priest." He looked pensive. "Now it's almost like I'm starting over. I learned a lot in Vietnam and Thailand. I learned that God has a thousand faces and none is enough by itself."

"The baby will make a difference," she said confidently.

"Hell, yes, I'm aware of that. It may be the end of my priesthood, I don't know. But I want the baby as much as you do. Maybe more. I can hardly wait!" He paused. "I'm not going to hide like we did. No matter what!"

"They may make you leave the priesthood," Angie warned.

"Not without one hell of a fight. But if that's the way it has to be, so be it. Gerry's sermon really got to me. I'm tired of hiding and lying and ignoring your needs. You've been one hell of a good wife, and I'm not going to lose you. And I can be one hell of a priest if they let me!"

"I love you," she said, taking his hand and kissing his anointed fingers.

He grinned. "You ex-nuns are all alike!"

Beauvais received a letter from Bishop Sullivan a week after the meeting. It did not really give any final resolution, but Beauvais and

Peggy were delighted. In keeping with his new policy, Beauvais read it from the pulpit.

"Reverend and dear Father:
"This letter serves as a follow-up to our meeting of May 25, 1968. It is our judgment that the pastoral work you have undertaken at Saint Mary's of Farmington has been well done. It is our hope that you will continue the divine labors with the same spirit of dedication you have exemplified in the past.

"In the future, we would like to maintain closer contact with you in your work, and it is our desire that you continue to provide the kind of spiritual leadership that the people of God are so much in need of. If there is reason to change our mind in the future, we will engage in further dialogue with you at that time.

"Sincerely yours in Christ,

"Michael R. Sullivan,
Bishop of Lansing"

Beauvais knew that the final sentence was an expression of Sullivan's reasonable fear of a Roman reprisal. Like any corporate executive whose destiny was not in his own hands, Sullivan had to protect himself. Beauvais did not begrudge him that. On the contrary, he admired his courage.

"I knew we would win," said Peggy.

Beauvais smiled at her exuberance. "For now, at least. Maybe the Church can change. I'm still not certain. I think Father Kincaid helped a whole lot. But I admire the bishop for his effort to understand. With his background and training, that decision took a lot of humility and courage." He laughed. "And I still doubt very much that our celibacy is as difficult as raising kids."

Late one night in June, they lay together on the floor in front of the glowing fireplace that warmed a rainy evening. The sound of raindrops beating against the weathered old frame house mingled with the melodies of Chopin.

"It was a great day," said Peggy. "Covering the hospital and the old folks' homes. And buying groceries for Mrs. Goretsky. I've never felt so good in my life. And to know that I can share everything with you at night."

"I had a good day too. I worked it out so Bill Wexler can keep his farm. Ed Devaney at the bank offered him interest only for a year. By that time Bill will be back on his feet."

"I used to think it would be difficult not to have a child," said Peggy softly. "Now I know that we've got a bigger family than we can take care of. My whole life is beginning to make sense. Everybody needs so much love and attention."

"Don't forget me!" He laughed, then grew serious as she kissed him. "I'm going to make a point of visiting every family in the parish starting next week. I think we should go in the evening and stay around long enough to get them talking. All I've ever really done before is pop in on people. I think it's flattering and pleases them, but I don't think we get to know them. I had no idea Joe Wheeler was an alcoholic or that Dick Schaeffer's daughter had left her husband and was living with her parents."

"It's so exciting to love what we do. I was so bored by the work at the creamery." She paused and looked worried. "Do you think Ted and Angie will get in trouble?"

"It's hard to say. I think they're ready to face what they have to. I don't think Rome would tolerate it for an instant. Or us, for that matter. The Church may not be ready for any of us, but I think they are finally beginning to be frightened by the alarming leakage." He looked at her and laughed. "The four of us may end up on a street corner somewhere ringing our bells at Christmas."

"Well, we're all family now," said Peggy softly. "It feels good. I guess I don't have to know about the future."

They lay side by side silently watching the gentle flames, not unlike Pentecostal tongues of fire, and whispering their night prayers together. The music stopped and there was only the steady, rhythmic beat of the rain, against a strong roof that had heard a thousand voices of lonely men and women searching for love, against patient wood frame windows that had seen a thousand faces, young and old, longing for some fulfillment. All the pieces of life, disparate and broken, soft and hard, had merged to create a fragile and special human dream. Even the contradiction of celibacy, mysterious and strangely archaic, had slowly found its place as Gerry and Peggy—even as Santek and Angie—struggled like everyone else to give some transcendent meaning to their life upon earth.

As long as men and women inhabit the earth, Gerry mused, they will explore and ponder, try and fail, learn and unlearn whatever there is to know. Some will bow before history and authority and live according to their own light, or with an abiding fear that narrows dreams and abbreviates lives. Others will be open to any possibility, to any path, no matter how overgrown with brush or dark and shaded. They will make their way, often painfully, with an attending hope that there's a God who directs their lives along narrow roads and detours, successes and near disasters, as they move ever closer to the light. The only failure, Gerry thought, was not to have tried, not to have created a dream of one's own making, not to have followed the relentless urgings of one's own Spirit. Not to have loved.

So much had changed in the course of time's sculpting—kings and tyrants, heroes and despots, the brave and cowardly had all moved on. And still no one had unraveled the mysteries of time and life and death. Gerry now knew that every answer reveals another question, every certainty is only certain to those who make it so. For the many, life is lived as it has always been lived, and any straying from a known path is a deviation. For the few, life is revealed in the living, and change is but the reflection of what one dares to see. And, seeing it, to act.

Celibacy or marriage, abstinence or sexual fulfillment are neither the question nor the answer. Love is. And love is the free choice of the Spirit of man and God—or it is nothing at all.

Epilogue: 1980

Bishop Michael Sullivan of Lansing sat in his darkened study in white clerical shirt sleeves and chatted quietly with Monsignor Kelley, still his chancellor in October 1980, and the now Monsignor Kincaid, in his late thirties and still the bishop's secretary. A bout with lung cancer had reduced Sullivan to a thin replica of the ebullient Irishman who had come to Michigan from Philadelphia so many years before. His once-powerful baritone was now a soft rasp and the once-ruddy cheeks now revealed the sallowness of radiation and death. His illness had transformed him into a gentle and reflective man of prayer. He hardly seemed the powerful hierarch who had attacked Gerry Beauvais and challenged Ted Santek.

"I'd like to have a solemn memorial Mass for Father Beauvais in the cathedral," the bishop said.

"I don't think Peggy would permit it," said Kincaid. "She's a strong woman and has little love for the Church." Kincaid paused as if he were treading on sensitive ground. "Whatever really happened, Bishop? I thought they were doing a great job at Farmington."

Sullivan's voice grew suddenly strong. "They were! There wasn't another parish in the diocese that was as alive and exciting. They were there three years and—"

"Almost four," Kelley said.

The bishop nodded and continued. "I got a call from the Apostolic Delegate and he gave me no choice. Beauvais and Peggy were to leave without announcement or ceremony. '*Roma locuta, causa*

321

finita.' I asked Ed Olivier to take over, and the people were out-raged. They sent a delegation to me but I was afraid to do anything. Half the parishioners left the Church."

"Where did Beauvais and Peggy go?" Kincaid asked.

"I think they went to Texas for a time to be with Santek, but he had two little boys and his wife was pregnant with their third. Gerry then apparently moved to California, near Fullerton, I believe. He had an older brother there. Peggy worked in a Catholic parish in Anaheim until they discovered Gerry was a priest. Then she worked as a waitress and, I think, an insurance salesman. Gerry kind of fell apart for a while; then he tried a variety of jobs. No Catholic parish wanted him, so he worked as choir director at an Episcopal church. His former pastor, Monsignor O'Brien, visited him out there before his own heart attack and told me he worked briefly in a music store and a library, gave voice lessons, even sold shoes. Then he had an-other major breakdown while working as a janitor in a public school. He just couldn't get over the priesthood, according to O'Brien. Farmington was in his blood, and he was never the same after he and Peggy left. He was in and out of hospitals till he died at home. It appears he took his own life."

"My God!" said Kincaid. "What a tragedy!"

Sullivan's face flushed. "The tragedy, Bill, is that he was a damn good priest, and she was as devout as he was. Now I put an alcoholic in St. James's, a total recluse to assist at Sacred Heart, an Indian missionary at St. John's who writes begging letters to everyone in the country, and I have four parishes without resident pastors. I've closed twenty grade schools, eight high schools—"

"Nine," said Kelley. "Benton Harbor closed this year."

Sullivan nodded. There was some of the old power in his voice. "And the pope comes to Chicago to be mobbed and cheered and to lecture the bishops. We haven't learned a damn thing in a dozen years! My old seminary recently was sold to the Moonies. I thought the whole American Church would be incensed, but no one even stirred beyond a few editorials in the *National Catholic Reporter*. Now the hallowed halls are sending little Moonies out to convert the world to some new madness, and nobody really cares.

"We've closed convents, monasteries are practically empty, and we make use of every kind of priest available. The pope attacks homosexuals while I ordain them. We still base our whole moral code around sex in an ancient, eradicable, celibate obsession. And a

322

Gerry Beauvais sells shoes and waxes floors, then takes his own life because he loves a woman and can't get the priesthood out of his heart. And Peggy devotes her life to God and her priest until there is nothing left. My God!"

The room was suddenly deathly silent. Sullivan motioned to Kincaid to fill his glass and instinctively lit a forbidden cigarette. He coughed hoarsely for almost a full minute, then angrily crushed the cigarette in the ashtray.

"I still feel as guilty about Beauvais as if I were his executioner."

Kelley shook his head. "There was nothing you could do, Bishop."

"Like hell! I could have made him choir director of the cathedral. I could have told him I believed in him and Peggy. I could have arranged work in another diocese. Bill Boyle would have taken him in Arizona, or Dave Bell in Florida."

He began coughing again and sipped his drink. Unconsciously he lit another cigarette but extinguished it before he put it to his lips.

"The thought of Beauvais just tears me apart and I want to blame the pope, as though he's the magician who can make everything right. We're the ones who could make it right if we had the guts of a Beauvais or a Santek!"

Kelley looked down at his breviary on his lap. "I was no friend to Beauvais. I wish I had it to do all over again. I truly cared about him, I even admired his courage, but I just wasn't able to tell him. I criticized him, reported him, insulted him. I doubt my own conscience will ever be clear."

Sullivan looked at him compassionately. "None of us knew any better, Kel. You did what you were trained to do. So did I. So does the pope. We just never learn anything until we have to. I keep remembering the time Santek came to the house and pleaded Beauvais's case. He looked at me with those honest blue eyes and said, 'When you have a Beauvais, Bishop, you can't afford to lose him.' He was so right."

Sullivan paused, then continued painfully.

"It was Santek who called me about Gerry's death. No editorializing. He just told me, without a trace of bitterness. I'm grateful for his kindness. I doubt that I deserve it. He was flying out with his wife to conduct the funeral at Peggy's request."

"Where is Santek now?" asked Kincaid.

Sullivan looked away and Kelley stared at the wall. There was a long moment of silence.

"That's another story," said the bishop. "He lost his commission through the Chaplain General's office when Angie was seven months pregnant with their third child. Courtesy of another Vatican directive.

"They came back to Detroit hoping to have the baby there, and his mother refused to speak to them or even see the kids. She must have been dying inside. Actually he was denounced from the pulpit of the family parish after he did an interview with the Detroit *Free Press*. It was one of the most beautiful interviews I ever read. Totally honest. I remember feeling ashamed, thinking that Santek loved the priesthood more than I did.

"Then they moved to California and got married in the Church. He started some kind of a nonprofit institute and retreat center out there for people in transition. I sent him a damn good letter of recommendation. Not that he needed it." Sullivan grinned. "Nothing could stop him."

"An institute for priests and nuns?" asked Kelley.

"Hell, no, for anyone who needs help. You know Santek. The world is his parish. I'm sure he works with some priests, but also with young men from Vietnam, divorced Catholics—Jews, for that matter—anyone who is looking to find direction and a new way of life. He sent me one of his brochures. It sounds wonderful. I think he's somewhere near Los Angeles. One of my classmates out there said he's doing great work with young couples, too. I guess he gets some funds from the community and the rest from foundations and private donations. I sent him a thousand bucks myself," the bishop admitted sheepishly.

"He wrote a typical letter back. He said he loved his new priesthood and only wished he could be working for me. He talked about his three sons and a visit from his mother. He ended by saying he'd see me when his oldest was 'playing quarterback for Notre Dame.' Still the same charming Polack he always was. God, I miss him!"

The room had darkened as day progressed into night. No one bothered to turn on a light or make a move to freshen drinks. Bishop Sullivan seemed even more sallow and shriveled than before. Kelley closed his eyes as if there were no more words that made sense. Kincaid shifted restlessly in his chair. Finally, after several minutes, he stood up. He spoke softly, and the bishop leaned forward in his chair. Kelley opened his eyes.

"I'll be leaving tomorrow. My dispensation came through yesterday. I'll . . . I'll miss both of you. I'll keep in touch."

The bishop seemed to sag in the brown leather chair that devoured his emaciated frame. "Will you write to us from San Francisco?"

"As soon as Anne and I get settled, Bishop."

"Is your job set?" Kelley asked solicitously.

"Yes, Monsignor. I'll be working at a wholesale meat packing plant. A friend of my father's set it up. And Anne will finish her degree at Berkeley."

"Do you need money?" the bishop asked.

Kincaid flushed. "No, thank you, Bishop, we're okay."

"You could do me a favor."

"Anything, Bishop."

"Check on Peggy, if you can. I'll get her address from Santek and send it to you. And if she needs anything, if she would accept it from me, please let me know. Tell her I would like to write her."

"I will, Bishop."

"And call if you need help." The bishop's eyes were filled with tears. So were Kelley's.

Kincaid moved toward the bishop. Painfully the bishop stood up and embraced him. Then Kincaid knelt for his blessing.

"If you ever want to come back . . . for a visit . . ." He was too choked up to speak.

Kelley moved over and shook Kincaid's hand warmly. "You'll be missed. You and your damn detective stories . . ." He tried to laugh.

Finally Kincaid was gone and the room was almost dark. The two prelates sat down again reflectively in their chairs and were absorbed in their private thoughts for several minutes.

"Where will it all lead?" asked Kelley softly, his head still bowed.

"I don't really have enough time left to find out. It was a great Church once. I know it can be again. I still love her with all my heart. The wrinkles and scars don't seem to matter. Maybe it will all lead to some great spiritual renewal long after the pope and I are dead." He paused. "But I guess Beauvais's death was a kind of final blow for me."

He looked directly at Kelley and spoke with difficulty.

"Santek told me something else in that phone call, Kel."

Kelley looked up slowly.

"He said Beauvais and Peggy were celibate to the end. Still hoping to come back to Farmington. It was only after the pope's visit to Chicago that he took his life."

"My God!" said Kelley. "Oh, my God!" By now the room was totally dark and the dying bishop and his aging chancellor could think of nothing else to say. That mattered.